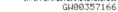

Also by Marita Conlon-McKenna

THE MAGDALEN
PROMISED LAND

and published by Bantam Books

Please return to nina's Library

Aug 2016

MIRACLE WOMAN

Marita Conlon-McKenna

BANTAM BOOKS

LONDON · NEW YORK · TORONTO · SYDNEY · AUCKLAND

MIRACLE WOMAN
A BANTAM BOOK : 0 553 81369 2

First publication in Great Britain

PRINTING HISTORY
Bantam edition published 2002

1 3 5 7 9 10 8 6 4 2

Set in 11/13pt Sabon by
Kestrel Data, Exeter, Devon.

Bantam Books are published by Transworld Publishers,
61–63 Uxbridge Road, London W5 5SA,
a division of The Random House Group Ltd,
in Australia by Random House Australia (Pty) Ltd,
20 Alfred Street, Milsons Point, Sydney, NSW 2061, Australia,
in New Zealand by Random House New Zealand Ltd,
18 Poland Road, Glenfield, Auckland 10, New Zealand
and in South Africa by Random House (Pty) Ltd,
Endulini, 5a Jubilee Road, Parktown 2193, South Africa.

Printed and bound in Great Britain by
Cox & Wyman Ltd, Reading, Berkshire.

Chapter One

The dog days of summer were upon them, New England sweltering in the late August heat as Martha, crab like, darted in and out of the shade of Easton's canopies and store-front porches, the air shimmying above the baked ground as she attended to the messages scrawled on a notepad in the bottom of her purse. Unhelpful, her daughter Mary Rose dawdled along behind her. Today was Martha's mother's birthday and already she was frazzled at the thought of ten of them sitting down to dinner, a meal she had offered to cook. Frances Kelly would sit at the the top of the table, resenting the thought of being another year older and admitting her true age, the rest of them trying to jolly her along. It didn't bear thinking about.

She needed lemons, and icing sugar and fresh cream, not to bake a cake, as one had already been ordered from Jesseps bakery, but to give the appearance of having baked one. She sighed to herself, remembering the dry cleaning to collect and the wine and bottle of Irish whiskey needed from the liquor store on the corner. The street was busy and the grocery store bustling with Saturday shoppers.

Finding the small purple ticket, Martha collected Mike's fawn-coloured summer jacket and taupe chinos, along with a linen shirt of her own which thankfully no longer bore the red wine stain from the barbecue at Kathleen and Jim's, the previous weekend.

Mary Rose and herself deposited the clothes in the back of her old Volvo and set off again. Ignoring the tempting smell of fresh brewed espresso and cappuccino and melt-in-your-mouth fudge browns that greeted entrants to the best home bakery store in miles, Martha joined the queue at the counter to collect the cake. Jenny Jessep tilted it towards her for approval before ensuring that the walnut frosted cake sat snug in its gaily coloured pink box. Martha added a dozen donuts and an Italian tomato bread to her purchases. She passed her daughter the box along with the keys of the car.

'Put it carefully on the back seat, honey. Mind you don't squash it!'

Mary Rose sighed.

'I want to listen to something on the radio, Mom, so I guess I'll just wait in the car.'

Martha licked a line of perspiration off her top lip, annoyed that her daughter couldn't even be bothered to help with the rest of the groceries.

She grabbed a small shopping cart as she entered the Easton Market and flew along the familiar aisles, mindful of the things she needed. She crossed off the list. Usually she hated people who made lists but knew in her heart there was nothing worse than setting to cook a meal for a large group and discovering that you had forgotten something. She added a peanut Hershey bar at the checkout as a reward for her endeavours.

Driving in the glaring sunlight Sarah Millen pushed the hair back off her face and adjusted her sunglasses; she was tired and could feel the familiar tension and start of a splitting headache as she passed along Commonwealth Avenue. Rachel her three-and-a-half-year-old had already managed to pour her cup of orange juice all over the floor of the car and was probably sticky as hell and Kevin the baby had scarcely stopped crying since she had put him in the car seat. The poor kid had been awake half the night teething and his gums were swollen and painful. He needed some more of that teething gel that numbed the pain and one of those plastic teething things you stick in the freezer to cool.

She was mad as hell with her husband Ryan. It was meant to be equal partners with regards to caring for the kids, what with both of them working full time, but somehow it always ended up with her getting up in the night missing her sleep, not him. She was the one busy finalizing designs for the architect's office where she worked, which were due on the partner's desk on Monday and it meant her having to work most of the weekend. Yet, after lunch when she'd asked him to run to the drugstore and get what she needed for Kevin he told her he was already late for his tee-off time for golf and that she'd have to just go fetch it herself. Fetch it herself sounded nothing but she had hoped to crawl back into bed for the afternoon when the baby slept and now she had had to shower and dress, drag Rachel away from the cartoons and battle with a sleepy Kevin to get him strapped into that darned car seat.

Torturing her kids was not her idea of fun, and in the sweltering heat she turned the air conditioning on full blast, hoping to cool herself and the kids right down. The shops were busy and she needed to park right up close to the drugstore so she could get in quick and out and home as soon as possible. In the distance she spotted a student in a small red Chrysler pull out of a space. Pushing her foot on the accelerator, Sarah surged forward, turning the wheel sharply. The power steering of the Jeep made it extra easy to pull in.

Timmy pedalled as fast as he could, his skinny legs pumping the heavy pedals of his brother's old bike as he tried to keep up with the rest of them.

Sweat clung to his head and behind his knees with the effort but his mom had told him to stay with Ralph and the other boys that afternoon. Hanging out with his big brother and his gang of friends was special, and made him feel way older.

Blinking, Martha McGill exited the store, the automatic door heralding her return to the sweltering heat and sunlight. In the distance she could see her daughter, singing along to the car radio. Just as she stepped off the kerb a bunch of boys flew past her on shiny bicycles, a smaller boy bringing up the end, cycling past Mary Rose, trying to catch up on them.

A second! An instant! Martha couldn't believe it!

A black Jeep came out of nowhere and swung right across. The boy and his bike crashed against the enormous front grille and bumper, disappeared under the crushing weight of the car, heavy metal, tyres, plastic all screaming together in that frozen time when she realized the child was mangled somewhere underneath. There was a baby in front in a car seat and a toddler strapped safely in the back. The driver, distracted, couldn't have seen him, the flash of movement beside her vehicle unnoticed as she touched the accelerator, the trusty mountain bike folding under the huge wheels, the boy tumbling on to the ground, the thud and noise as the heavy vehicle moved over him, the aghast driver instantly slamming on the brakes.

Martha stood transfixed as people rushed by her. The driver's face blanched snow white at the realization of the small boy lying on the tarmac of the car park, underneath the weight of her car. The security guard pushed past her as a crowd gathered around the injured boy.

'He's bad! Real bad!'

'The kid's not breathing!'

'I think the boy's dead.'

Martha kept a firm grip on the recycled brown paper bag she was carrying. It couldn't be! It just couldn't be that on a bright summer's day she would witness the end of a life. That her child would see another child die. It just couldn't be!

She pushed through the crowd. Why, the boy was only about nine or so, just a kid, his bones and the bike frame mangled together, the spokes of the bike wheel sticking through the bones of his leg. The security guard knelt beside him, his head bent down watching his chest. A young girl and an elderly man were already trying to help, searching frantically for a pulse, any sign of life.

'Don't move him!' ordered the guard. 'And don't move the Jeep. It could make things worse.' The name Hal was written in large green embroidery on the badge on his shirt. 'I've already called for an ambulance,' he said.

Martha edged closer. Something about the boy was familiar. Dark hair, small for his age. Baggy navy shorts, a white Nike T-shirt, torn and tyre tracked and steeped in blood, his eyes closed, one side of his face almost embedded with dirt and gravel. It was the Lucas boy, the youngest. Timmy! That was his name. Why, he'd gone to the same pre-school as Alice, her youngest. The family lived down around the corner at the bottom of their street, she knew his mother.

'Let me through. Let me through!' she insisted. 'I know the boy! He's a neighbour's child.'

Shoving and pushing, the crowd of onlookers was swelling. Curious, they were moving forward, ready to witness the tragedy of a small boy's death.

Panic filled her voice as she knelt down beside him: the security guard was making a sign to her that the boy was already gone. The young girl kneeling beside her on the roasting tar admitted there was no pulse.

'Timmy, don't go! Don't leave us!' Martha ordered, touching the abnormally still figure crushed under the enormous wheels. 'Can't you try getting him to breathe again!' she demanded angrily of the elderly grey-haired man crouched beside her. 'You've *got* to try. Please!'

Hal was reluctant to move the boy but they all agreed they had to try something. The retired nursing home administrator took charge as in a haphazard way they took turns and began life support, trying to force air into his lungs, his chest moving up and down like a balloon as they inflated it.

'Timmy! Please, Timmy, you've got to try and breathe!'

The old gentleman, defeated, shook his head and gave up. Martha touched the boy's under-developed arms and stroked the good side of his face, the small dribble of freckles along his nose, aching to remember which part the small boy had played in the kindergarten Nativity play. She pictured him jumping through the water sprinkler with all the rest of the neighbourhood kids out on their front lawn, or hiding behind his big brothers when he came trick-or-treating. Pedalling furiously on his bike, playing snowballs, a myriad images of a childhood shared with her own children flashed before her eyes. Timmy couldn't die – he just couldn't! His mother should be here with him. He would listen to his mother's voice.

Running her hands along the small chest and ribs she felt the pain his body had endured: unbearable. She gasped with it. It was too much for a child. She wanted to lift the pain from him, ease it, she wasn't prepared to let him die, not here like this: she wasn't going to let him go.

'Timmy, you just got to stay with me,' she ordered in that voice that all parents reserve for their children. 'I know you can hear me,' she insisted. 'You *cannot* go! I won't let you go. Your mommy and your daddy and your brothers need you! Do you hear me, Timmy, you have to stay right here. You have to stay.'

The pain was intolerable; as she laid her hands on him she could sense it. The searing sharp agony, the intense pressure on his organs.

'Here, lady! Give us some space!'

The paramedics had arrived and were anxious to move the public out of their way. Martha refused to budge from Timmy's side as they matter-of-factly checked him.

'It's too late,' one of them said softly, looking over at the driver.

A murmur went around the crowd. Martha was conscious of Mary Rose's pale scared face, and of the driver of the car breaking down, hysterical, only a few feet away.

'I didn't see him! As God is my judge, I didn't see him! I had the air on to cool the car down for the kids.'

'We'll transfer him to Children's Hospital, but there's nothing more we can do,' declared the chief paramedic, a forty-year-old family man who tried to disguise his dismay at the death of a child.

Fury filled Martha as she realized they had already given up on Timmy and were just going through the motions for the sake of the shocked huddle of people standing around. God couldn't do this, shouldn't do this. Silently she prayed. *God, let him live. Come on, Timmy, hang on in there! Fight! Don't give up. Come on, Timmy, live! You've got to fight and not give up.*

There seemed no response.

'Please, lady, I have to ask you to move out of the way, we got to try and move him from under these wheels.'

She couldn't let go of him, there was such pain in his heart and chest and stomach, inescapable pain, Martha could feel it as her hands rested on him, she wanted to take the pain away from him, draw it out, release the fear of taking a breath or moving that was killing him, making him want to run away and hide from it and leave his small broken body behind.

'I'm here, Timmy,' she said slowly. 'The pain is going, I can feel it going, leaving you. You must be able to feel it too!'

The heat was burning through the palms of her hands, running up the bones and veins of her arms as she reached that hiding place; her own breath caught in her throat with the impact.

'Lady, I told you already. We've got to move him,' insisted the senior paramedic as he gestured for a few of the men to step forward and help raise the heavy vehicle. Hal was organizing them as the ambulance team tried to lift Timmy on to the gurney.

Martha kept her hands on him.

'You his mom?'

She shook her head.

'I'm a neighbour, that's all. His name's Timmy. Timmy Lucas. He lives down on Sycamore, just off Mill Street. I know him, know the family.'

She held her breath as the front end of the

Jeep was lifted, the grimacing faces of the lifters testament to the enormous weight of metal and rubber that had crushed the boy. There was such pain in his heart and chest! It was unbearable.

She had to untangle it, ease it. The energy was passing between them, pulsing from her to the child, like jump-starting a flat battery; she could feel the shudder of response, the faint flicker of life. There it was! A breath, so slight you would barely notice it, a breath!

'Timmy!' It was Timmy. The real Timmy, she could feel him. 'He's breathing.'

'Oxygen, get the mask on him quick!' ordered the driver, pushing her aside as he slipped it over the boy's nose and mouth. 'He's back.'

A low gasp went up from the swelling crowd of onlookers, and Martha noticed Hal, the security officer, wipe tears from his eyes.

'You want to ride with him to the hospital?' offered the attendant.

'Is he going to be all right?'

'He's got a lot of injuries . . . who can say. It looks pretty bad.'

Martha scanned the crowd, looking for Mary Rose. She noticed the older boys who'd been with him standing silent, holding their bikes at the back.

'I think that's his brother.' She motioned to a tall gangly fourteen-year-old standing just a few feet away, misery and guilt etched all over his skinny face. Ralph Lucas clambered into the back of the ambulance at the paramedic's request and hunched worriedly over Timmy.

'You next of kin?' asked the driver.

Martha shook her head. She wasn't family, and besides she wanted to go fetch his mother quickly and bring her to the hospital. That's what Timmy needed most, to see his mom and hear her voice. Tearful and shocked, Mary Rose stood in the sunlight waiting for her. Martha hugged her daughter close.

The crowd did not move: silent, as if waiting for something else to happen. One or two people patted her on the back.

'Hey, lady, you saved that boy!'

'Only for you he was a goner!'

'I ain't never seen anything like it, never.'

Two cops were taking a statement from the driver and some witnesses. Martha gave them her name and number. She looked over, pitying the traumatized driver with her two small kids, her hands still shaking. One of the girls from the store was bringing her out a glass of water as Hal began to take charge and clear that part of the front lot. The ambulance turned and headed out of the slip road and the shoppers returned to their tasks, while the young mother sat stunned in the front seat of her Jeep as her baby roared and a police officer made notes.

She and Mary Rose were both still upset when they got into the car, but Martha was filled with a deep sense of gratitude and immense relief that the boy had survived.

'Mom! If it wasn't for you that kid would have died.'

'Hush, Mary Rose, don't say such a thing.'

'But I was there, I saw how you touched him. We all thought he was dead and then you just laid your hands on him and he began to breathe again.'

Martha didn't know what to say. It was the strangest thing. She remembered touching Timmy, wanting to take the pain away from him and praying to God not to do this, not to rob this child of his life, and feeling the immense heat and power come into her hands and the knowledge that somehow or other she was able to help lift some of the pain from him.

'I don't know, Mary Rose.'

'Mom, I saw it! You just put your hands on him and I don't know what happened but you saved him. Everyone around saw it.'

'I prayed, Mary Rose.'

'Prayed?'

'That's all I did. I prayed and asked God to help and I don't know but I could feel my hands get hot, tingly, the strangest feeling, like there was electricity or something in them, and I was just sure and certain that Timmy was meant to live.'

This seemed to silence her daughter as they drove, both lost in thoughts of the boy and crazy explanations of what had happened. Turning into the bottom of Sycamore Street, Martha pulled up outside the Lucas house, noting the neatly mowed lawn and the tub of creeping roses in the porch and wondering what she should say to his mother. She jumped out of the car and quickly ran up towards the front porch.

'She ain't there,' the old man from next door informed her, busy tying up a cascade of magenta petunias that tumbled from a basket on his front step. 'Had to go to the hospital in a hurry as one of her boys got hurt.'

Martha turned around, relieved at being spared the onerous duty of being the bearer of such bad news.

'Shall I give her a message?'

'No thanks, it's fine.'

Pulling into her own driveway minutes later, she felt sapped of energy, depleted. She couldn't take this heat and promised herself the luxury of a cool shower before the evening, as she and Mary Rose carried in the things from the car.

Chapter Two

The McGills and the Kellys gathered around the table that night and Martha's mind was still haunted by the thought of the injured child as she crushed garlic and juiced lemons, automatically going through the motions as she prepared the chicken dish.

Mike and the children had made a great fuss of her seventy-two-year-old mother when she arrived. Frances Kelly passed her overnight bag to Patrick, their eldest, to carry up to the guest room. Her brother Jack and his wife Annie and their eight- and five-year-old boys were making themselves comfortable as they first presented their grandmother with her birthday gifts.

'You shouldn't have! You just shouldn't have gone and spent money on gifts! You all know I've got everything I need already,' she protested.

Annie's eyes met Martha's. Both of them knew how hard it was to buy for the ageing Irish matriarch, who was now unwrapping the fine knitted lamb's-wool cardigan in a delicate heather colour that would show off her eyes and skin tone perfectly, and a bottle of lavender perfume.

Frances sprayed a mist of it across the room.

'It's beautiful, Annie. You know I don't hold with those fancy expensive French perfumes at all. The simple fragrances of nature are much better.'

Martha could see Annie blush almost as if her mother-in-law had been at the counter of Neiman Marcus when she had chosen the inexpensive bottle over the classic French Nina Ricci one. Frances Kelly still had her wicked way with words.

Alice was hopping up and down with excitement and Martha watched as she clambered on to her grandmother's lap with their gifts. The specially wrapped and matched paper with its Celtic motif was torn and tossed unnoticed to the wooden floor.

'I'll help you to open them, Granny,' offered their eight-year-old daughter with her green eyes and winning ways.

Martha had bought a new Anglepoise reading lamp for her mother.

'It'll go beside your bed, Granny, and help your tired old eyes,' said Alice.

Martha bit her lip trying not to laugh as Jack winked at her.

Then there was the new housecoat in a soft pink, which would be snug and warm in the winter, and a hell of a lot better than the tattered tartan one her mother had worn for about ten years.

'And I suppose this is if I have to go to the hospital or suchlike. Between you all I'm gathering up a fine collection of night attire, a fine one!'

Lastly was a book of *Irish Country Dwellings*, which Martha had managed to unearth in a small bookstore the last time she'd been to Cambridge. Her mother turned it over appreciatively, glancing at the photo spreads.

'Look here, Alice, there's an old farmhouse like the one where I lived with my mammy and daddy before we came to live in Boston.'

Frances Kelly slowly flipped through the book filled with images of stone cottages and whitewashed farmhouses, and simple dwellings with thatched roofs, and slates and tiles. There were kitchen gardens, straggling floral borders, henhouses and gateposts and warm pine dressers. All a reminder of her girlhood, spent watching out those tiny squared windowpanes, wanting to see the world.

'Thank you, Martha love, and all of you for such a thoughtful present.'

Martha busied herself in the warmth of the kitchen as Mike served drinks. Uncomplainingly he'd run out and gotten the remainder of what they needed. Now Jack and he were busy discussing the Boston Wolfhounds' coming rugby season. Checking that all was ready, Martha smoothed down her pale blue Liz Claiborne soft denim skirt and co-ordinating round-necked shirt, before getting them all sitting down around the old cherrywood table talking. Lemon chicken and baby roast potatoes, a big dish of mixed salad and minted peas – even the kids were happy with the meal.

The temperature had dropped outside and she'd been tempted to move the party to the wooden table and chairs out back, but knew instinctively her mother wouldn't hear of it. Barbecues and insects were all very fine for Fourth of July, Labor Day and beachside gatherings but not for her mother's birthday. Frances Kelly, if she was to sit and enjoy a birthday meal, wanted to sip her chilled wine from Waterford Crystal, and fold an Irish linen napkin on her lap and feel the weight of traditional Newbridge cutlery between her fingers. 'Small things, but a part of who we are,' she'd insist.

Martha could remember a few glasses with a mishmash of patterns that had been called 'the crystal', when she was a girl, as well as a table-cloth and a few off-white almost beige starched napkins which her mother produced at Thanks-giving, Christmas, Easter and other festive days, but otherwise she had no idea where her mother got her notions from. Fiercely proud of their heritage, Martha and her brothers had been raised to celebrate their Irish roots, not in a shamrock and shillelagh way, but in the quiet knowledge of who they were and the people they had come from. Her mother had been more delighted by the news that her new son-in-law Mike McGill had some Irish in him than that he was an honours graduate from Boston College.

'Go and get your granny's birthday cake,' Martha said to the children.

Alice and Mary Rose were up in a flash. That was one thing that kids never outgrew – putting the candles on the cake and carrying it in. She hoped they wouldn't overdo the candles.

'Mom, you look great! Annie and I were just saying you'd never guess you were seventy-two – never!'

Only her eldest brother Jack could get away with it. Her sister-in-law cast her a despairing glance.

The candlelight highlighted her mother's good complexion and softly tinted fair hair which made her look years younger than she actually was. Frances Kelly had always taken a pride in her appearance. Mike passed her mother a measure of Bushmills whiskey – only the best – adding water from a small crystal jug.

'Easy, Mike, easy! There's no point in drowning a good drop of whiskey.'

Martha laughed aloud. Her husband should know by now that his mother-in-law's glass of whiskey was sacred. One glass only, except on very special occasions.

'Brian and that Lisa one sent me flowers. They were delivered this morning.'

'That's nice,' murmured Martha, who had sympathy for her brother and his new wife. No matter what he said or did, Brian could not appease his mother, who still believed marriage was for life and divorce was a sin. She had virtually ignored his partner of two years and had refused to attend his re-marriage in California. They lived in San Jose in California.

'And I didn't even get a card from Sean,' sighed her mother.

'They must be having a good time then,' joked Jack. Her brother Sean and his wife Carrie had gone to Maine with their children for a well-earned break. Her mother was put out at not having been invited to join them for a weekend, even.

'Mom, you know he'll be in touch the minute they get back!'

'Aye, I suppose so.'

'You know so.'

Her nephews Liam and Tommy and the girls all arrived with the cake almost aflame with candles. Every bit of frosting was covered. Patrick, their fifteen-year-old son, who considered himself beyond such childish things was commandeered to photograph the family occasion.

Her mother's vague annoyance was overruled by her love of her grandchildren. She made a great to-do of huffing and puffing and trying to blow each and every candle out, little Liam giddy with the excitement of trying to help her.

Martha had just finished slicing the cake and passing it around the table when the doorbell went. Mike automatically rose to answer it.

When he ushered Paul Lucas into the room, Martha rushed over to greet young Timmy's father. 'How is he?' she asked, keeping her arm around the dark-haired middle-aged man who looked exhausted.

'They think he's going to make it. But he's on one of those breathing machines and from what they can tell he's got a broken pelvis and they had to remove his spleen. He's got cracked ribs, a tear in his lung and some internal bleeding.'

'Oh my God!'

'His right leg's busted real bad too but at least he's come through it.'

'Oh thank heaven,' moaned Martha, relief flooding over her.

'Sue stayed with him. I'm on my way home from the hospital to check on the boys and to get some fresh clothes so we can stay the night. I felt I just had to drop in and let you know how my son is and thank you for helping to save his life.'

Martha demurred, embarrassed. Her mother and the rest of the family gazed at her with curiosity.

'I was there, that's all, and only tried to help.'

'You did more than that, much more. My older boy Ralph told me how they all thought he was dead but that you held Timmy and laid your hands on him, and all but brought him back to life.'

'Paul . . . it wasn't quite like that. I just couldn't bear to see him in pain.'

'Ralph said he never saw anything like it. Never. He said even the paramedics thought my Timmy was gone, and if you hadn't been there and healed him he would be gone!'

'I was only doing what anyone would have done, honest.'

'I don't believe there is anyone else that could have saved my son, Martha, only you!'

Martha felt hugely embarrassed.

'Anyways I wanted to thank you,' Paul Lucas insisted sincerely. 'We will never forget it, Martha, never.'

She escorted her neighbour to the front door, promising to visit Timmy and sending every good wish to his wife Sue. Watching as he crossed the street and climbed into his car to drive to the hospital, she was grateful that her own children were safe under their own roof.

'Well!' said Annie on her return. 'What in heavens was all that about, Martha?'

'His boy Timmy got knocked down today, outside the Easton Market store.'

'Aw, the poor kid!'

'Mom and I were there,' interjected Mary Rose, 'and it was just awful. He was on his bike and got crushed by this big Jeep! He was right underneath it and it seemed like he was dead. Mom was amazing, she went straight over and helped him.'

'And what's this about you healing him, Martha?' enquired her mother, concern in her voice.

'Mom, I just did what I could. I wasn't going to watch a boy not much bigger than Alice die before my eyes.'

'God, the poor kid! It must have been awful.'

'He was in a terrible, terrible state, crushed, lying there. We couldn't move him. His life just slipping away, with all these gruesome strangers standing around watching and doing nothing. I *had* to help him.'

'What did you do, Martha love?' asked her mother.

'All I did was to touch him, just like I'd touch any of the kids here if they were hurt or injured and try to ease the pain, rub it away. I kept talking to him too, while we waited for help. Just laying my hands on him I could feel his fear and pain, and I wanted to lift that from him. If that's what you call healing then I guess that's what I did! I wasn't prepared to give up on him and have him die. I knew he was still alive. And somehow I could reach him. It was as if we were connected, linked, if that's the right word.'

'Didn't you feel any different?' enquired Annie earnestly.

'This kind of energy surge seemed to flow through me and I felt real scared because I realized how bad he was and that he was slipping fast.'

'They all said he was dead,' interrupted Mary Rose again. 'Then when the ambulance came and they were trying to lift and move him Mom said he was breathing and they put the oxygen mask on him.'

'Like in the Bible,' murmured Annie.

'Come on, Annie. It was just one of those weird things like you read about in the papers, where some man gets the strength to lift a ten-ton weight off his trapped wife or a mother runs through a fire to get her child and doesn't even feel the burn. A bolt of energy or light, an adrenalin rush – I don't know! I was in a crisis and my body or intuition or whatever responded to it.'

'Did you pray, Martha pet?' asked Frances.

'Believe me I prayed! I prayed to God, to whatever power controls this universe. I prayed for that little boy, cos I was not prepared to give up and watch him die.'

'Thank God, then,' murmured her mother, squeezing her hand. 'Thank God that you were there.'

'Maybe you have a healing gift or something, Martha, maybe.'

Martha shook her head vehemently. Annie was into all this new age stuff, healing and crystals, of which Martha knew very little. She didn't believe in any of that kind of thing anyways.

Martha yawned. She felt tired. Maybe a cup of

strong coffee would perk her up. A drooping hostess was no good to anyone. She was glad the boy was all right, relieved that his life had been spared and that Susan and Paul Lucas still had their son.

'You OK, Martha?'

Mike came over and bent down, his breath, like her own, smelling of garlic.

'Fine.'

'Hands up who's for coffee!' she offered.

'C'mon, I'll give you a hand.'

In the kitchen, she stacked some of the dirty dishes and set the kettle to boil. She got down the rich roast Colombian coffee that was kept for special occasions: no decaf tonight. She watched as her forty-two-year-old husband set out the cups and saucers on the tray, adding the cream jug and sugar. His fair hair was starting to recede ever so slightly but golf and trips to the local gym had ensured that he stayed in shape, his body still well muscled and lean. Still as handsome and even more attractive than when she'd met him eighteen years before.

She filled the coffee pot and carried it back to their waiting guests. The kids had repaired to the den where they were likely already involved in some computer game battle of skill; their laughs and shouts filled the air.

'Here you go, Mom,' she said, pouring the coffee into a white china cup. She was glad to sit down by her mother and relax. Mike and Jack, at the far side of the table, were now talking about golf.

'That was a lovely meal,' said Annie. 'It was good of you to invite us over.'

'Family should be together, gather round the table,' said Frances, 'though you can't help thinking about the ones that are missing.'

Martha smiled, unsure if her mother was referring to her missing siblings or her father who had passed away over twenty-two years ago.

'Anyways, you had a lovely birthday party, Frances!' cajoled Annie.

Martha knew that her mother held a grudging respect for the neat, blond-haired young woman who had managed to tie down her wild son Jack and turn him into a good husband and doting father.

'That I did, that I did!'

Frances regaled them with stories of her best friends, Bee and Louisa. It had crossed Martha's mind to invite them over too but she had felt it would be tempting Mike's patience too much to expect him to sit and listen over dinner to her mother and her friends' stories for hours on end.

'Bee had a perm at the salon, but they did it wrong and now her hair's coming out in clumps.'

'Poor Bee,' murmured Martha.

'Well, she's got herself a lawyer and he's going to sue them for a fortune, millions of dollars likely. That hair falling out could be the making of Bee!'

Martha and Annie smiled at each other, knowing well that Frances Kelly was about to launch into more stories about her women friends. Martha slipped off her shoes and curled up on the couch, only half listening to her mother. She was thinking about the day's events, glad that in some small way she had helped the Lucas boy survive the accident.

Chapter Three

The drive along Penton Avenue and Columbus Drive was busy as mothers like herself ferried their offspring to the local schools, open finally after the long summer break. Martha dropped Patrick and Mary Rose first at St John's before driving back in the other direction with Alice, who attended Bishop Delaney Junior School. Alice was fussing about the hardness of her new shoes after weeks of slopping around in sandals and was worried in case she was not in class with her best friends.

'You've just got to wait and see,' she told her.

It was unlike her youngest to worry so Martha decided to accompany her to the school yard and give her a bit of moral support. The two of them joined the growing throng of parents and children outside the school.

'Be positive and optimistic and your child will sense it.' That's what all the good parenting books told you to do. Martha did her best to appear relaxed, aware of her daughter's small hand clenched in her own as they walked towards the main entrance, both of them searching for the familiar face of any of Alice's schoolfriends. She nodded as Abe Harrison and Kate Nils, both teachers she knew, passed by, trying to look cheerful at the start of another term. It was hard on everyone getting back into the routine of school.

Crowds of children pressed past them: new bags, new shoes, new haircuts.

'Mom, there's Becky!'

Martha smiled, recognizing her daughter's play-mate who had just returned from vacation. The two girls raced toward each other, as she and Evie Hayes watched on.

'How you doing, Martha?'

'Fine, Evie. Fine. You look great! Tell me, how did the house on Eagle Lake work out?'

Her friend seemed totally relaxed and refreshed, her skin a golden honey colour, her short brown hair sun-tinted a shade lighter.

'We had the best time ever. The house was right on the shore and the kids just swam and fished and sailed from sunrise to sunset while Frank and I lazed and unwound. You and Mike would adore it. I honestly think it was one of our best vacations ever.'

The two girls' heads were together, whispering as two more friends arrived over. Martha was relieved that Alice had company as the yard bell

37

sounded and the children began to organize themselves into some semblance of a file to line up at the school entrance.

Alice wrapped her arms around her and hugged her tight, Martha breathing in the sweet scent of her daughter's apple shampoo as they said goodbye.

'See you later, Mom!'

The parents stood clustered together as their offspring entered the school building, one or two dabbing at their eyes or running to look in the windows. Martha almost dreaded the still and quiet of home that awaited her. As she stood chatting with Evie, a few of the other mothers joined them.

'I heard about the Lucas boy,' Kim Hamilton interrupted.

'I know, it was such a terrible accident!'

'No, I mean about you. How you saved his life – healed him.'

Martha took a deep breath. She was real fond of Kim, with her sparky sense of humour and good nature, but her friend did have a tendency to get things wrong. 'Kim, I just happened to be there, and did what any of you would do, that's all,' she said.

'That's *all*? Not the way I heard it! I heard you all but brought that poor boy back to life! That in front of everyone you laid your hands on him, and somehow he started to breathe again.'

She could see a flabbergasted Evie staring at

38

her, and the others intently watching for her reaction.

'Hey, come on. Don't be crazy, I just helped him. You know, he was in a lot of pain, and shock, stuck under that Jeep.'

How could anyone imagine that she had such a power? It was just her adrenalin and sheer necessity that had made her keep trying to save the Lucas boy.

Kim raised her eyebrows. Evie looked puzzled and Martha could sense everyone else's curiosity.

'How's he doing anyway?' interrupted Berry Wilder, who had four boys of her own.

'His mother Susan's still up at the hospital and he's had a lot of surgery and is in pretty poor shape.'

'It's just awful for her. I don't know what I'd do if something like that happened to any of my boys, some lunatic driving over them.'

'I don't think it was her fault,' argued Martha. 'Timmy just came out of nowhere.'

'Still, she should have been more careful!' insisted Kim forcefully.

The school yard began to empty, and Martha and Evie walked companionably to the roadside. It was an unspoken agreement to stay home the first morning of school and not to go gallivanting, in case the school principal phoned. Mindful of this, Martha arranged to meet Evie later in the week for coffee.

*   *   *

39

Dishes and laundry and mess were all there waiting to greet her as she stepped through the door of 552 Mill Street. Putting on an old Paul Simon CD to cheer herself up, she set to her household chores, trying not to notice the silence of a house absent of children. An image of each of them sitting at a desk and learning comforted her. She made a long phone call to her mother and read four chapters of a novel that had been languishing behind the range of cookery books in the kitchen. A dark and depressing story of family secrets that she was really in no mood for, so she put it aside yet again. She resisted the urge to click on the remote control, knowing that if she did she would waste an hour or two watching some stupid soap or mindless TV game show. The day dragged on as she counted the time until she was to collect Alice and hear all her news.

Sunlight splattered the pavement as Alice Kathleen McGill skipped through the school gates, smiling gap-toothed, triumph written across her face. Martha was pleased at such happiness as she rushed to greet her.

'Becky and Gary and Lisa are all in my class!'

The very air was electric with currents of expectancy, seconds later balancing out and calming as parents and children were reunited.

As she bent down to hug Alice, Martha was aware of heads turned in her direction, of being the subject of whispers and gossip and nudges.

'You heard, Martha healed the Lucas boy!'

'Fifty people saw it! She just laid her hand on him and got him breathing again.'

'Martha McGill, you know the woman that drives the silver Volvo, is some kind of healer, saved the Lucas boy's life.'

Embarrassed and not wanting to get into conversation with anyone, Martha grabbed Alice's new dolphin schoolbag and began to walk quickly toward her car.

'Mrs McGill, Mrs McGill! Please wait up!'

Martha turned. A woman with a son of about eight and a small boy sitting in a stroller was coming towards her.

'I'm sorry to disturb you. My name's Ellen Glass. My son Karl is in the third grade with Susan Lucas's boy and this here is Mark. I heard what you did for Timmy the other day. Susan says it's a miracle he survived, and that likely he would have died excepting for you.'

Martha felt awkward and unsure of what to say.

'Well, I don't mean to interrupt, I know you must be busy, but I wonder if you could look at my son, help him?'

Martha hadn't a clue what the skinny woman with her hair tied up in a streeling ponytail was talking about, or what she was expecting.

'Listen, Mrs Glass, there's been some kind of a mistake. I don't know what you heard about the other day but whatever you heard, it's wrong. It's a mistake. I'm not able to cure or heal people, really I'm not!'

'My boy needs help, Mrs McGill, honest he does. He's got asthma real bad and I'd try anything, anybody, if I thought it would help him.'

Martha let out an exasperated breath. What did this woman want from her?

'I'm not a doctor or nurse,' she told her.

'I know that. He's been to them all! Paediatricians! The hospital and all sorts of doctors. They keep on trying him with different medicines and sprays and inhalers, but he just keeps wheezing. Sometimes he wheezes so bad I get scared. I have to get up in the middle of the night and use a nebulizer just so that he can get enough breath to sleep.'

'I'm sorry I can't help you,' Martha insisted. 'I truly can't.'

'I get scared! Please, Mrs McGill, Martha, please try it, just lay your hands on him.'

Martha laughed, hysterical almost, hoping that no-one could overhear this crazy lady who'd pushed the stroller almost across her. Alice's eyes were huge, questioning, confused. How could anyone possibly think that she might be able to heal their child? The mother must be unbalanced to believe such a rumour – or plain desperate! The small boy in the buggy looked up at her. His face was pale, with a sheen of grey blue under his eyes. He should have been running around roughhousing at home instead of sitting there, looking tired and resigned.

'Honest, you should bring him to a clinic or the hospital, Mrs Glass.'

'What harm will it do? Please, just touch him.'

Martha could see the anxiety in the other woman's face, and the small boy looking up at her, worried.

She bend down towards him; his eyes were clinging to hers, watching her. He had a Disney T-shirt on and a pair of elastic-waisted denim shorts. Martha touched him without thinking, stroking his cheek with the side of her finger and cupping his face. 'You are such a cute boy, Mark. Such a good boy,' she said.

His brother Karl and Alice watched as the child listened to her.

Even now she could feel it, the sense of fear, of worry, far too much for a small boy. Running her hands along the base of his neck and across his chest-bone she felt it: the slightness of breath, the irritation of his lungs that made him cough and wake and wheeze. The palms of her hands and fingertips were warm already as she spread them against his skin, conscious of the heat that seemed to be flushing through her own flesh and bones. What was happening? Perhaps it was some weird kinetic connection. Was it the same as the last time? She wasn't sure. The mother was watching her, her face filled with hope.

Martha was touching Mark, feeling his every

breath, but it didn't seem to be working. His perplexed child's eyes stared up at her. Martha was unsure what to do next. The children, curious as to what was meant to be going on, stood transfixed beside them. Martha was about to give up. She felt like some kind of sideshow fraud pretending to do something she couldn't.

'Please! He's been so sick for so long.'

Martha studied him. No little boy deserved to have such poor health, not to be able to run about and take a proper breath of good air. Silently she prayed to that greater power, to God above, to help this child and make him stronger. She felt the heat travel through her and move inside him to soothe and coat and protect those raspy lungs from infection, and irritation and allergy. She knew that Mark could sense it too. A few minutes later she stopped.

'Is that it?' demanded his mother.

'I guess so.' Martha shrugged; this hadn't been her idea, for sure. 'I touched him like you asked, Mrs Glass, but I don't expect it will make any difference to Mark and what's wrong with him. What he needs is the care of a good paediatrician or allergy specialist – not someone like me.'

She could see the other woman's disappointment and managed to detach herself and Alice from her, with the excuse that she was already running late and had to collect her other children from school.

*   *   *

That night, curled up in bed against Mike's back, a position she much enjoyed, Martha ran her hands along the familiar map of her husband's ribcage and stomach.

'Mmmm,' he sighed.

'Mike – listen, how do my hands feel?'

'They feel good . . . real good.'

'No, Mike, honest, tell me, do they feel different?'

'Is this some kind of a trick question, Martha?'

'Do they feel warm, I mean hot when I touch you?'

Mike McGill laughed aloud.

'Of course you're warm, you've been snuggling up to me for the last quarter-hour.'

'Mike, be serious! I was just wondering if there *is* anything different . . . different about me?'

Mike rolled around to face her, his arm pulling her closer; and he reassured her that despite sixteen years of marriage little had changed and she was still the woman he wanted. Trying to push away the crazy thoughts that plagued her, Martha relaxed and concentrated on Mike and their lovemaking.

Chapter Four

Lara Chadwick scrolled down through the article she had written on the opening of Boston's newest art gallery overlooking the Charles river, all steel and glass and urban chic. She had double-checked the names of the artists exhibiting and also the patrons, Boston's finest, the socialites whose names and faces constantly graced their newspaper's columns. Some of them had made a point of getting to know her and one had actually approached her the minute she stepped into a room, expecting her to produce her notepad and take down some copy about the latest happening in their crowded lives.

Last week she had gone to see her nephew in his college play and had been waylaid by that same stupid socialite who assumed she was writing it up for the paper, almost as if she was not entitled to a night out on her own.

She had sat fuming for the first few minutes of the show but then had gotten over it and relaxed and laughed at the college humour which thankfully never changed as she watched her nephew Ben, looking most unappealing in a parody of transvestism in her sister Nell's turquoise satin suit which she hadn't seen for years. She had to wipe the tears from her eyes as she hooted and hollered with Nell and the rest of the audience. Ben was one of those tall athletic types who would not in a million years pass as a female no matter how much slap was layered onto his chiselled features. He was in his final year of chemical engineering and by all acounts was an honours student.

He had a bright and brilliant career ahead of him, judging by her sister and brother-in-law's genuine pride and pleasure in their only son.

Lara herself had studied English and politics, taking a Master's in English literature about three years after she qualified. Then the world had seemed full of hope and opportunity and she had dreamt of a job in publishing or of writing herself.

Her publishing job had entailed posting on multiple fan letters to one of the queen bitches of American literature and booking hotel rooms for her and her partner on endless book tours. Her own simple manuscript never seemed to get beyond the great total of thirty pages. In the end she had binned it, reckoning that if she the author couldn't entice herself to write it the likelihood of a reader enjoying it was zero. A friend of a friend had called someone who had eventually offered her the job as a junior with Boston's top newspaper, and filled with high hopes she had joined the fledgeling ranks of journalism.

Any hope of working on the political pages had been quickly dashed and she had been assigned to the wedding and funeral section for a start-off. Checking the daily obituaries was hardly the stuff the Pulitzer was made of, but she had swallowed her pride and done her best to prevent howlers making it into the paper. Dealing with top names in Boston society meant she had got picked to help out on the social column, which appeared once a week. In between, she had taken to hanging out around the news desk midweek hoping that with any luck she would be thrown a story or two to check out or follow up.

She did a final word count on her article before she sent it up and left a message for the photographer to have the photos ready for that evening's editorial. She was just slipping on her linen jacket when her boss, Ritchie Allen, called her over.

'You going home, Lara?'

'Yeah, just for a short while. My cat got neutered two days ago and I want to check she's OK. I should be back in an hour or so.'

'You live out Easton direction, don't you?'

'Yeah, why?'

'Picked up a call about some kid getting badly injured at the local grocery store. Witness was talking something about a Good Samaritan coming to help. Listen, would you check it out before you come back. It might just do for the local section or one of those human interest spots.'

Lara sighed. She'd hoped to spend about an hour mollycoddling Pom her cat, and now had to waste time ambulance-chasing. It wasn't fair! Nothing ever happened in Easton. Ritchie knew it and she knew it but the good people expected their name to appear in the local news for some reason or other.

'All right,' she agreed. 'But it might take a while to track down.'

Ritchie had already lost interest and was busy emailing a colleague as Lara grabbed her keys and headed out the office door.

Pom was feeling very sorry for herself. Lara had to admit she felt guilty about putting her pet through such a procedure, but the thought of her apartment being overrun with kittens, and a recent near-escape with the tomcat down the hall, had strengthened her resolve about the need for the operation.

'You poor old baby,' she crooned, lifting the sad-looking ginger cat up onto her lap and talking to her. Pom was not only her companion and room-mate, but made living in this bachelor girl apartment just about bearable. The cat glared reproachfully up at her as Lara petted the silky fur gently, not wanting to hurt the animal. She re-filled her milk bowl and opened a foil pack of the most expensive cat food on offer in her local store, forking it out onto the cat's dish.

'Here you go, Pom. Just eat a little bit for Mommy, that's a good girl.'

The cat had dozed off again when Lara crept out of her apartment.

She often shopped in Easton and ate regularly in the Bistro restaurant and Flanagan's, the well-known oyster and fish restaurant on the outskirts of town.

The main grocery store was Gerald's and she assumed it was the one Ritchie had mentioned as she turned her Toyota sports car into the parking lot. Parking was at a premium in Easton and she was glad to have found a spot. Grabbing her purse, she decided to have a look around. She noticed a lanky boy with greasy hair collecting the shopping carts. He had absolutely no idea what she was talking about and Lara wondered if she'd deliberately been sent on a wild-goose chase.

She wandered inside the store, hoping to spot a manager or someone she could ask. It was quiet, and judging by the two bored-looking teenagers on the registers probably the crossover period between night and day staff. She asked the one with the name-tag Jeanette and the triple studs in her right ear if she'd heard of the accident a few days before.

'Someone said something about a kid, I think,'

she shrugged vaguely, 'but ya know I wasn't really listening.'

Lara tried to smile nice and friendly, hoping there was somebody left from the day staff who actually gave a toss about what went on in their place of work. Then she spotted an older man. He was standing over near the exit and had pulled a navy shirt on, but she could see he was wearing the store security uniform underneath it. Racing through the frozen goods aisle she managed to catch his attention.

'Excuse me, sir!' she interrupted. 'I was wondering if you could tell me anything about the accident here involving a child on Saturday?'

He looked up. The pale blue eyes which lurked under a clump of rough grey eyebrows were immediately suspicious.

'You from the insurance company or something?' he replied.

'No! No, sir. Nothing like that at all,' she assured him. 'I'm a journalist on the *Boston Herald* and, well, I actually live in the neighbourhood and I was wondering what exactly happened.'

He stared at her for a moment or two, until she produced her ID.

'Can't be too careful!' he murmured as she put it back in her black leather purse. He relaxed a bit and she followed him towards the door.

'Just one of those things, a crowd of kids on bikes. You know what boys that age are like.

Racing and chasing all over the place, use the lot here for stunt riding sometimes. The parents can't keep watch on them every hour of the day. The lady pulled in too quick, wasn't watching I guess. Had one of those big fancy Jeeps, high off the ground. She couldn't have seen him. I heard the brakes and the crash. She rolled right over him and his bike.'

'The kid?'

'About nine or ten I guess. Well, he was hurt real bad. I did everything I could to help. The store gives us all a course on first aid. I done mine about six years ago when I came here first, but he was in bad shape. Myself and a few folk tried to help, but he was real bad, trouble breathing. Looked like he was dying, then this lady who was helping just kind of laid her hands on him. I don't know exactly what she done but she brung him back. Even the paramedics thought he was dead, but the lady she kept saying he was going to live. It was the strangest thing I ever seen in all my born years. She saved his life, gave it back to him.'

'Where's the boy now?' Lara asked.

'Ambulance took him to Children's Hospital. My boss Mr Williams phoned to check on him. Doesn't do a store no good for someone to die in the lot, you know. Hospital said he was critical but stable.'

'The boy's name, did you get it?'

'She knew him . . . Lewis, no – Lucas, that's it! Timmy Lucas, that was the boy's name.'

'What about the woman? Do you know her name?'

The security guard shrugged.

'I've seen her in here a few times but I don't rightly know her name or where she lives, but it must be somewhere local.'

Lara thanked him warmly for his help. Something about him reminded her of her late grandfather and she wondered what he had worked at before he had taken on the security job to bolster up his retirement pension.

At least she had some information to go on. She went back outside to place a call to the directory service for the hospital number.

The hospital staff would give her no information about the boy: it was hospital policy unless you were next of kin. Thanking them, she rang off and decided to drive back into town. The hospital was *en route* to the office and she'd have a try at getting a bit more out of them.

The staff on the door assumed she was a late visitor as, gazing straight ahead, she marched right past them. She had spotted the sign for the fourth floor. Trying to look like a parent, she slipped into the lift and pressed the silver-ringed button. The doors opening right in front of the nurses' station slightly spooked her, but forcing herself to be calm she walked slowly over to the plump nurse sitting near the phone.

'Excuse me, I'm looking for Timmy Lucas. How's he doing?' she asked.

The nurse covered the mouthpiece with her chubby fingers and looked up.

'You a member of the family or something?'

She smiled and nodded. Not agreeing or denying, just inclining her head in a way that could be seen as a positive.

The nurse hesitated for a second. Lara looked her straight in the eye as the woman pointed down the hallway.

'He's in room 14, but I think he's still very drowsy. Sue's gone to the day room for a nap but if you run you might just catch her.'

'Thanks a bunch,' Lara said gratefully.

Passing the door she could see the sleeping shape of the boy hooked up to a monitor and drip and God knows what else.

The day room was right down the far end of the corridor and she pushed the door gently. An elderly man, concentrating on the sports section of the newspaper, had his back to her. Over in the corner she spotted a dark-haired woman rubbing her face with her fingers. She looked as if she had hardly slept the previous night. There were circles of grey under her eyes and her mascara had smudged under her lower lid.

Lara pretended to be busy and sidled over to the small counter where a pot of coffee was still hot. She got out a mug for herself and turned around as though absent-minded.

'Anyone else for coffee?'

The old man studiously ignored her, the woman nodded gratefully.

'Milk and sugar?'

'Yeah, please, I could do with the energy boost.'

Lara carried the two mugs over and sat down near enough to the boy's mother. She looked wrecked.

'That's good, thanks,' she murmured softly. 'You got a kid on the floor too?'

Lara's eyes widened and she thought rapidly.

'No, I don't. My cousin's on the fifth floor but the coffee machine's broken there.'

The other woman thought nothing of it.

'Have you got a child here?' Lara asked.

'Yep, a boy, Timmy. Got knocked down in Easton on Saturday. The car ran right over him.'

'Oh, I'm sorry, how's he doing?'

'Not too good. They had to remove his spleen, bleeding everywhere, lacerations to his liver, a punctured lung, broken pelvis and fractured thigh and ankle bone,' she said, then shuddered. 'Doctors thought at first he wouldn't make it and had him on one of those life support machines, but thank God he stabilized earlier today.'

'I'm glad,' said Lara. 'What about the driver?' she asked.

'By all accounts she's fine! My kid's half dead, but there's not a scratch on her. Said she didn't see Timmy at all, that he just cycled out of nowhere.'

Lara nodded sympathetically.

'My other boy Ralph was with him, he said that Timmy almost died out there, would have died too only that this woman – she's actually a neighbour of mine – apparently she just would not give up on him. The ambulance men, the nurse, the paramedics and my older boy all thought Timmy was dead, but Martha, that's her name, just kept on trying to help him, laying her hands on him, talking to him real slow, telling him he had to live, and then out of the blue he suddenly began to breathe again!' Her voice broke with raw emotion. 'I owe my son's life to her. Whatever she did, it was some kind of miracle, I guess!'

Lara smiled easily, trying to hide the growing excitement she felt.

'And you say she's a neighbour of yours?'

'I don't know her that well but the McGills live on Mill Street just two streets away. Timmy's in school with one of their kids.'

'Wow, this lady just came out of nowhere and touched your son and . . .'

'I know, it's like some kind of miracle. My husband Paul and I can scarcely believe it ourselves, but lots of people saw it. She must have some kind of rare healing gift.'

Lara could tell Sue Lucas was being totally sincere. She didn't strike her as the kind of woman given to sensationalism or exaggeration; in fact if anything she was probably too honest and truthful. She was simply dressed, wearing well-pressed denim jeans and a white T-shirt, her dark hair pulled back in a neat ponytail and her face without makeup except for a trace of mascara which accentuated her dark brown eyes.

The door of the family room opened and a sandy-haired nurse popped her head around the corner.

'Mrs Lucas, I just came down to get you,' she said. 'Mr Franklin, the orthopaedic surgeon, is up with your son at present and he'd like to talk to you.'

Sue Lucas jumped up immediately and Lara caught her purse as it tumbled to the floor. The boy's mother's face had drained of colour and she swallowed hard.

'Lots of luck,' offered Lara.

'And lots of luck with your cousin.'

Sue Lucas was gone from the room before the flush of embarrassment tinted Lara's face. She hated deceiving people and lying to them, but it seemed to be a prerequisite of her career. She needed to develop a thick skin if she wanted to make her mark in journalism and track down good stories. With this one there was obviously the interest in the Lucas boy but there was more to it than that.

Lara checked back in with the office over an hour later, running through the proofs of the famous and would-be famous at the art opening. She confirmed two of the photos to be used in the

57

gallery piece, as there was always hell to pay if names got mixed up, before starting to work up a few lines on her computer about the Lucas boy. The local police department had confirmed the accident with her and had said there would probably be a charge against the driver who had hit the child.

She read it back, following a spell-check, and knew that somehow she had managed to make the awful minutes that had almost robbed Sue Lucas of her child into something boring. She cursed and decided to hold it over and look at it again in the morning. She pored over her notes again. Funny, the security guard and the mother had both mentioned the woman, the neighbour, the Good Samaritan who had helped with the child. Even Sergeant Kostick had said how lucky the boy was.

Lara's instincts told her to sit tight, that in twenty-four hours with a little bit of research back in Easton about the McGill woman she might have more worthwhile copy to show her editor. Grabbing her purse and keys and switching off her computer, she waved goodbye to the night staff as she set off home, thoughts of a truculent feline high in her mind.

Chapter Five

Martha and Evie watched as a passer-by stared in the window of Evie's embroidery store, both of them waiting for the shop bell to jangle and announce the arrival of a customer. Martha was almost glad when the woman decided to move on and not disturb them.

She had fetched two large cappuccinos to go from the donut store across the street, and licking the frothy top off her own one she lowered herself into one of Evie's hand-decorated chairs.

'God, it's so hard to get back into work after having such a great break! That's the worst of vacations, you get to almost dread coming home.'

Martha smiled. Herself and Mike never managed to ever get more than about seven or eight days away as Mike always pleaded having too much work to do and acted as if the other software engineers up at CPI couldn't be trusted to keep things running smoothly without him.

Evie rooted about in her bulging leather purse

and drew out a wad of freshly developed photos. She passed them over to Martha to peruse, explaining the ins and outs of their holiday in Maine, and the picnics and expeditions they'd enjoyed. Martha admired them but was glad to have her closest friend back home.

They sat in companionable silence drinking their coffees and gazing around the small store. Martha had to admit that opening an embroidery store off the corner of Centre and Lime Street hadn't really seemed a good idea when Evie had first mentioned it to her. Evie had been bursting with excitement at the idea of taking over the old hat and glove shop and opening a store dedicated to embroidery, the fiddly craft that she enjoyed so much. Martha had thought she was mad, guessing there were probably only a handful of people in the Easton area with a similar interest to Evie's. Luckily her friend's enthusiasm and innate good sense had prevailed and Golden Threads, named after a line in the poem by the famous Irish poet W. B. Yeats that they had all learned in school, had come into being. New England must be full of needlewomen, judging by the amount of custom that Evie had already built up.

'Martha, look at this amazing sampler I discovered in an old secondhand store.'

'It's fine work, Evie. Whoever made it must have spent days and nights working on it, to get that intricate stitching right.'

'Just look at those colours – all hand-dyed. I

know they've faded but can you imagine it re-worked?'

'Will you sell it?'

Evie vehemently shook her head. 'Never. This is too good a piece of work!'

Martha agreed.

'It'll hang on the wall.'

Martha smiled to herself. All Evie's favourite samplers and precious pieces that she collected ended up on the display wall, there to be admired and commented on and even copied, but most certainly not for sale.

'So I've told you my news, now what about yours?'

Martha laughed. Evie and herself had known each other ever since kindergarten, two little Catholic convent girls who had grown up only two streets from each other and had been close friends all their lives. College and marriage had separated them for a while but Mike's move to work in software development and information systems at CPI in Cambridge had found them back living only five miles from each other and ready to pick up their friendship again.

'Mike's fine, the kids are fine and Alice is sure glad to have Becky back in class with her again this year.'

Evie laughed. 'Did we ever think that we'd end up old married ladies with kids going to the same school?'

'Never!'

'Anyways, Mar, what's going on with you? What's this I hear about you being a healer and saving some kid's life?'

'I helped Timmy Lucas, that's all. And it's so kind of weird because one or two people have come up to me and asked me to lay my hands on their kids, as if I could do something to heal them.'

She could feel Evie's hazel eyes watching her, reading her as she'd always been able to.

'And can you?'

'Can I?'

'Yeah, can you heal them?'

'I don't know, Evie, honest to God I just don't know. I definitely felt something that day when I touched Timmy. It was like an energy or strength going through me. I don't know where it came from. I only know that I really wanted to try and help him, to stop his pain and suffering, I just wanted it to end.'

'And what did you do?'

'I didn't think, I just touched him, that's all! I put my hands on him and maybe prayed a bit.'

Evie sighed.

'You were always a great one for the prayer and believing in things.'

'So were you.'

'Yeah, but the nuns loved you better!'

'Ah, shut up, Evie!'

'I was too ordinary, they thought you were a far better prospect for joining the order.'

'Go away out of that!'

'It's the truth, Martha, you were far more spiritual than the rest of us. Still are.'

Martha laughed, thinking of herself in a nun's habit and Mike and the kids' reaction.

The other woman patted her arm. 'Go on, and what about the others?' she asked.

'I just put my hands on them too.'

'Did you feel anything?'

Martha considered.

'I wasn't sure but I got that same feeling as I did the time before. Not as strong, but well, something. I don't know if the children sensed it too.'

Evie was engrossed in what she was telling her, excited almost.

'And what happened to those kids?'

'I don't know! Honest I don't. One had asthma, real bad. I told his mom she should bring him to the paediatrician. One had warts, you know the icky kind kids get all over their fingers, can't get rid of them so his mother says.'

'And you touched *him*?'

'What was I supposed to do – refuse to touch him or hold his hand like the other kids do?'

'And anyone else?'

'A girl with tonsil problems – and you know Jeanie Sheldon, she works up at that beauty parlour? She made me put my hand on her throat as she wants to give up smoking.'

'Whew!' Evie exhaled. 'That is a lot.'

63

'How do you think I feel, Evie? How the hell do you think I feel?'

'Obviously they must think that you're some kind of medicine woman or healer.'

'I know,' she sighed. 'I know.'

'And are you?'

Martha sat quite still, concentrating on the glass drawers filled with the wondrous coloured tints of embroidery thread spread out beside her.

'I am not . . . I don't know!'

'What happened to the rest of them?'

'Mark's mother said he's doing fine, and Jeanie Sheldon phoned to tell me she hasn't even as much as lit a match in the past three days.'

'And the warts?'

'Who knows about warts!'

Evie laughed, tossing her short brown hair. 'Martha, maybe you really can heal!' she said.

'Don't be joking. It's not funny, honest to God it's not!'

'I'm not. Maybe you have a genuine gift for healing.'

'I don't think so.'

'Why not? Look at all those crazy people you see on the TV who set themselves up as healers. Do you believe they can heal people?'

'I don't know, Evie.'

'Well then, why shouldn't someone genuinely good and caring like you be chosen? You are such a good person and, well, good people can do good things.'

Martha couldn't understand what her friend was trying to say.

'I do believe that. Maybe the powers that be have decided that this is for you, that you in your own way can now help people,' Evie explained.

'Don't be so stupid.'

'No, listen! You are a good person, probably the best I know. You listen to people, talk to them. You've been helping other people for years, but not so much that you yourself might have noticed it . . . Maybe this touching and healing is just, well, another step up from that, another dimension.'

To say Martha was surprised that her old friend would even consider the remote possibility that she could alter anyone's physical state by touching them was just ludicrous. Evie usually had more sense. The coffee was cold and Martha didn't want to intrude on any more of Evie's work time.

'What you doing next Tuesday?' enquired Evie.

'I'm meant to be working in the Highlands sanctuary, why?'

'There's a house auction over Newton direction and I thought the two of us might drive over and have a look. The old lady who lived there is meant to have a fine collection of early American craft work, quilting, samplers, who knows.'

'Sounds interesting. Maybe I can change days with one of the other volunteers?'

'Yeah, I thought we could go over way ahead of the auction and have a look at the items and then grab a bite of lunch.'

'That sounds good.'

'All going well, we'll be home in time for the kids.'

Martha liked the sound of it, the two of them having a few hours together. So much had been going on in the past few days, she knew that Evie was the only one likely to understand the quandary she was in. Nothing like this had ever happened to her before and she hadn't a clue what to do – whether to go along and try to help people or just ignore it and hope that they would get fed up and leave her alone. She needed to talk to someone. The sanctuary would understand and she'd swap days with one of the other volunteers. A day out with Evie would be great.

The shop bell clanged and a large-breasted woman in a crochet waistcoat and pale blue denim skirt entered. Evie greeted her warmly, and introduced her.

'Martha, this is one of my favourite customers, Connie Jackson. She teaches a craft class over at the women's centre in Concord.'

Martha shook hands politely, noticing the long list being produced from the woman's purse and the scraps of fabric she was stretching out onto the counter.

Evie and the customer would be bound to spend the next half-hour at least considering various loops of embroidery thread and an age discussing colours and going through which size needle was the best.

'Listen, I'll leave the two of you,' she said.

Evie nodded.

'I'll see you next Tuesday then.'

There was a large black car parked on the street outside her driveway. Martha recognized the driver immediately as soon as she stepped out.

Sarah Millen looked wretched and Martha could see she was still distressed about the accident, and unsure how she would react towards her. The woman was on her own and must have organized someone to mind the kids for her.

'I hope you don't think I'm intruding, but I had to come by and see you and thank you for what you did helping with that poor boy I knocked down. If he had died I don't think I could have lived with myself!' she admitted, her voice breaking.

Martha could see how upset she still was.

'Listen, would you like to come inside, Mrs . . .'

'It's Sarah, please call me Sarah.'

'Can I get you a glass of water or a soda?' Marth offered.

'Water would be just fine, thanks.'

She left the woman sitting in her living room and a minute later watched her gulp down the iced water as if her life depended on it.

'Are you OK?'

67

Sarah Millen just shook her blond head silently.

Martha was filled with pity for her but unsure what to do.

'I could have killed him! I can't sleep or eat with thinking of him, of his mother and father. I try to work and I keep seeing that Saturday, that Godawful day! I can't get it out of my mind.'

Martha blinked, hesitating, wondering what this stranger expected of her. The younger woman sounded frantic, hopeless, and her eyes were welling with tears.

'My husband says it's all my own fault. I know that – I'm not trying to blame anyone, I should have been concentrating more. I told that to the police sergeant, that I totally admit it's my fault. That I hit that little boy!'

She was becoming even more distraught and upset.

'I already made a statement,' Martha admitted.

'I'm not here about that. God, I'm not! I need you to help me. I saw what you did for the boy, the way you touched him. I think I'm going crazy, I have these bad dreams and I can't eat, and trying to take care of the kids is . . .'

'Do you want me to help you?' Martha offered softly.

Sarah nodded, a shuddering breath gripping her.

Martha closed her eyes and as she reached forward and laid her hands on the woman's shoulders she felt the tension and stress and fear within her so strong that she could almost imagine it running up her own veins.

'Sarah, I need you to take slow soft breaths and feel the warmth and energy flow from my fingers into your muscles, I need to lift some of that awful heaviness from you, let it sift and run away like sand,' she began, the healing energy flowing through her as she began to work.

Chapter Six

Lara's enquiries bore fruit: she managed to locate the Lucas and McGill households, which were situated close to each other in Easton's quiet suburban neighbourhood. Well-maintained one- and two-storey homes clustered together under the shade of broad-leafed sycamore trees. The lawns were parched, summer blooms struggling to raise their heads in the intense heat; even the few kids still outdoors were wilting. Generations of middle-class Irish Catholic families had been raised in this neighbourhood and attended the large parish church and school only minutes away. Two small boys lazily cycled on the quiet streets and she guessed that on summer evenings the air was filled with the scent of charcoal and hickory smoke. Sensible family cars were parked outside decent homes.

Her few lines on the accident had already appeared in the paper but something had attracted her back to investigate the story further,

her sense of intuition telling her that she might stumble onto something far more interesting.

An older boy had answered the Lucas door. Defensively he'd told her that both his parents were at the hospital as his brother was having a big operation.

Minutes later she turned into Mill Street and parked outside the McGills' home. Sitting for a few minutes, she tried to construct a reasonable introduction to this stranger she was so interested in meeting. It was swelteringly hot and already she could feel her cotton T-shirt sticking to her under-arms. She wished that she had put her ice stick of cologne in her purse.

Steeling herself and armed with her notepad and mini recorder she walked up the driveway, unsure of the welcome she'd receive. Huge over-blown roses tumbled from a lattice fence and creepers twisted and turned through the thorny stems, the scent of jasmine fragrant in the humid air. A pair of child's sneakers lay abandoned on the front step, and she stepped over a half-dressed Barbie doll which looked rather dishevelled and in need of a bath. She ran her fingers through her short dark hair as she rang the doorbell and waited.

'Mom! Mom! There's somebody at the door for you. She wants to talk to you,' announced Alice, who had scarpered to answer it before Martha even got a chance.

How many times had she warned the kids not to answer the front door unless they knew who it was? Alice especially. Maybe their youngest would listen to Mike, and follow some of his guidelines. She'd get him to have a little chat with their eight-year-old when he came home from work. Looking through the glass panel, Martha immediately realized that she didn't recognize the beautiful dark-haired young woman with her flashing eyes and wide smile. She noticed the sporty red car outside. Single girl with a bit of money, she surmised, no mother of three would fit into that piece of machinery with her brood. Curious, she pulled the door open.

'Yes?'

'Hello, Mrs McGill, my name is Lara Chadwick, I'm a reporter on the *Boston Herald*.'

Martha didn't know what to say.

'I'm writing a piece for the paper on the accident you witnessed down at the market on Saturday.'

'Oh yes. Is Timmy OK?' she asked, suddenly alarmed.

'As far as I know he is. I spoke to his mother the other day and I believe he's undergoing surgery today.'

'Oh thank God! He's such a nice kid, I couldn't bear it if anything happened to him.'

'Would it be OK if I stepped inside?'

'Sorry, what am I thinking of? It's far too hot to be standing in the sun, come on in and cool down.'

Martha – wearing a pair of pale denim shorts, a sea blue T-shirt and her old strappy brown leather sandals, her hair frizzing and piled up with a hairgrip of her daughter's – led the immaculately groomed visitor inside.

The living room with its cream walls was pleasantly cool, large and filled with wide comfy navy couches. A state of the art sound system and TV and video sat on the low shelves along one wall. A huge glass jug with an array of tall delphiniums had been placed on the fire hearth. They reminded Lara of her parents' garden. Side tables and shelves were cluttered with an array of family photos in a mixture of frames, Waterford glass, polished silver and dark pine. The journalist's gaze briefly scanned the photos of the woman's husband and children.

'Sit down, Miss . . .'

'Chadwick. Lara Chadwick.'

'How can I help you?' Martha was very unsure about talking to a journalist and worried about what sort of questions she might be asked. 'Is it about the driver?' Martha was reluctant to discuss Sarah and the accident.

'No, not particularly,' Lara admitted. 'But please, could you just tell me in your own words about the accident?'

Martha sat for a minute trying to recollect the details. It had all happened so fast and she had been distracted trying to get organized for her mother's party. Taking a breath, she slowly recounted what she had seen and what she had done. She was slightly put off by the small tape recorder that the journalist placed on the coffee table and though she tried not to dwell on it was over-aware of her words and thought she probably came across as being slightly nervous and jumpy.

'I interviewed the store security guard and Mrs Lucas. Both of them mentioned to me about your laying of hands on the boy and how somehow your action seemed to have saved him,' offered Lara.

'No, no!' Martha protested. 'It was just that I was there, that's all.'

'A Good Samaritan.'

'I was hardly going to walk on by and let a small child die,' Martha replied edgily. 'Maybe Timmy heard my voice or felt my hands touching him. He just needed to hang on till help came and I just happened to be there. All the while I had my hands on him it felt almost like there was a narrow connection between us, but that was enough to keep him here on this good earth.'

'Are you a religious person?'

'I was born and raised Catholic and go to church every Sunday, if that's what you mean.'

Lara didn't reply.

Martha could feel a stirring sense of annoyance. What exactly did this journalist want from her? What angle was she trying to exploit or use for her purpose? She just couldn't figure it out.

'You are a good person, by all accounts.'

Martha felt embarrassed. The street was full of good people – the world was, for that matter – what in heaven's name was this journalist woman trying to get at?

'The people I spoke to all said that you had healed Timmy Lucas, that you had saved his life when you laid your hands on him.'

Martha sat stock still.

'Are you a trained healer of some sort?' Lara persisted, pushing for some sort of a response.

Martha just shook her head. She didn't understand it herself so how could she possibly rationalize what was happening?

'There are many witnesses who say the same thing,' murmured Lara, staring intently at her. 'That you healed the boy.'

These accusations: Martha did not know what to do to refute them. 'I don't know what to say,' she admitted honestly. 'I just happened to be there when Timmy needed me.'

'Thankfully,' said Lara softly. 'And Martha, have you ever helped or healed anyone else?'

'Just one or two kids down at the school, I . . .' Martha replied without thinking, suddenly remembering the tape recorder and immediately regretting her own stupid honesty.

The journalist wrote something on her pad. The two women's eyes met, the information hanging between them.

'Look, I'm really glad that Timmy's improving

and recovering but there's no story here,' insisted Martha. 'I simply did what any other parent coming along would try to do. I helped an injured child – nothing more.'

'People said it was a miracle!' interjected Lara. 'That's what they actually called it.'

'Listen, Miss Chadwick, I'm just a stay-home mom with three kids, who helps at the school, helps at the animal shelter and gets to do all the things moms get to do. It's no big deal! I'm ordinary. Just plain old ordinary!'

Lara stood up and switched off the recorder. She didn't intend antagonizing Martha McGill, not at all, but she knew in her heart that she had stumbled onto something and that even if the woman across from her was unaware of it, the gift she had was one she would not be able to keep secret much longer.

'If you'll excuse me, Miss Chadwick, I have to go pick up my mother.' Martha didn't have to leave for another half-hour but she wanted this young woman out of her home.

Lara, sensing her change in attitude, regretted the way she had approached things. Picking up her keys, she tried to make amends.

'Martha, thank you for speaking to me, and letting me into your beautiful home. I'm sorry for disturbing you and holding you up.'

She stretched her hand out to shake the other woman's hand. The farewell handshake was brief but even in that few seconds Lara could feel it, the heat and energy that radiated from Martha.

Relieved, Martha stood watching her go, inwardly cringing at her own sheer stupidity.

'Martha!' Lara called back as she went down the front path. 'Ordinary? I don't think you're ordinary at all!'

Furious with herself afterwards, Martha replayed the interview in her head, admonishing herself for being foolish enough to have let the journalist across the threshold of her home. God knows what that girl would write! She picked up the phone and punched in Mike's number: her husband would be angry but at least she could talk to him about it.

'Mom,' interrupted Alice. 'Can Katie and Rachel and I have a drink? We're real thirsty.'

The three of them looked hot all right, they'd been playing some makeup pony and jumps game in the back yard and needed some time out in the shade.

Disappointed to find that Mike was away from his desk, Martha left a message on his voicemail.

'Alice honey, I've got a jug of almost ice cold orange in the fridge, how's that sound?'

The girls did a joyous canter, Rachel O'Malley tossing her long red hair over her shoulder and almost neighing. Martha laughed aloud. She was just being foolish worrying about something that might not even happen.

Chapter Seven

The *Boston Herald* carried the story about three days later. Martha hid her head in her hands, disbelieving the words on the page. How could any respectable, responsible newspaper print such things!

Mike read it over and over, as if by looking at it long enough somehow or other he could manage to change the content of Lara Chadwick's article. 'Those bastards!' he complained, smashing his hand against the kitchen counter.

Mary Rose gave Martha a scared, embarrassed look and she only thanked heaven that Alice was in the other room engrossed in *Songs from the Little Mermaid* on the TV.

'New England Miracles'. That's what she'd called it.

'At least it's not on the front page,' argued her husband, clenching his jaw and mouth with tension.

'Mike!'

A threatened airline strike at Logan, a profit warning from one of the huge over-hyped new technology companies and the fining of a local actress for drink driving had mercifully saved her from that.

Martha sat on the kitchen chair feeling numb and miserable, her family around her. Patrick bent down and wrapped his arms around her.

'It'll be all right, Mom, no-one really reads the newspapers and if they do no-one believes them!'

'D'ya think?'

'Yeah, Mom, definite!'

'For sure,' Mike added, coming and sitting beside her.

'The only thing is, Mom,' added Mary Rose, 'is that you *did* do it! I saw you heal him. Everyone else saw you too, so it's not like that journalist woman made it up or anything.'

Martha gazed at her daughter's serious face, the slightly lopsided full lips, the pale fair skin, the intelligent, brown-green eyes that were scrupulously honest and fair. Mary Rose had never been able to lie and had a forthrightness about her that some considered difficult and that often got her into trouble both at school and with her friends.

'Most of what she actually said in the paper is true.'

Faced with such honesty, Martha had to agree, but it just was so weird to read words written about yourself and try to be rational about what was printed. She was only getting used to the healing gift herself and certainly hadn't reckoned on anything like this happening.

Alice ran in. 'Granny's on the phone, Mom,' she said.

Mike cast her a knowing look, warning her not to say too much to her mother who could spread news quicker than anyone.

'Hi, Martha love, how you doing?'

'Fine, Mom, fine,' she lied.

'Did you see today's paper yet?'

She was tempted to play dumb and ask which one but could hear the concern in her mother's voice.

'I saw it, Mom, I saw it already.'

'How did that journalist woman ever find out those things? That's what I'd like to know.'

Martha let out a deep breath.

'She came here to the house, Mom.'

'What! You let her into your home!'

'I know, but I didn't realize what she was writing, honest I didn't.'

'You didn't think to ask?'

'No, I didn't.'

There was silence at the other end, which was a pretty rare occurrence when her mother was on the telephone line.

'Anyways, I'm right proud of you, darling,' admitted her mother a few moments later. 'Ever since you were a little girl you always wanted to help people. Your daddy and I were sure you'd end up a nun or a nurse.'

Despite herself Martha laughed.

'Maybe you always had the healing power and we didn't notice,' pondered her mother. 'Sure, do you remember the time poor Brian got his hand caught in the door of your daddy's car? He set up such a ruckus with the pain and you were the only one could get him to quiet down and he let you hold his poor hand under the cold water and you kept on rubbing his arm and wrist until the pain went away. He had the worst bruising I ever saw, his fingers nearly turned black, but funnily enough, he hardly complained of the pain at all afterwards.'

'Mom,' said Martha, genuinely surprised that her mother could remember such a childhood event.

'I do remember, Martha,' declared her mother, as if reading her mind.

'Listen, Bee wants to say a word for a minute.'

Beatrice Patterson was her mother's best friend and confidante, the two of them having become close companions on moving into the Belmont Retirement Home. Somehow or other Bee had almost managed to replace Joe Kelly in her mother's eyes. Two elderly women, enjoying the years they now shared together.

'Hello, Martha,' she now interrupted in her distinctive husky voice. 'Frances is all of a fluster here, but I'm just wishing you all the best and I'm so glad that the Lord has blessed you with this gift, for in this cruel world there is much good work to be done.'

'Thank you, Bee.'

Martha appreciated the other woman's sincerity and she found that talking to her mother's best friend had released something within her. Martha realized that being scared was plain stupid for in reality she had been granted a blessing, the gift of healing people, and she must learn to overcome her reluctance and embarrassment and *use* this gift.

'You OK, Martha?' Her mother came back on the line.

'I'm fine, Mom, just fine.'

'Don't you mind what those papers say, honey, or journalists write about you! Martha, do what you have to do helping people. Just you remember that if you hadn't been there the other day that poor Lucas woman would likely have buried her son, and nothing is worse than the loss of a child – nothing!'

'I know, I realize that.'

'Good!'

Frances Kelly rang off, and no sooner had Martha put down the phone than her sister-in-law and her brother came on the line. Jack was calm and nonplussed by what he'd read, but Annie was in a right state.

'Martha, I can't believe it! They are actually saying that you are able to work miracles. God Almighty, it's so crazy! Jack's baby sister – I can't believe it. That boy you told us about – *and* the kids in the school yard.'

'Listen, Annie, hold on, this thing is being blown up out of all proportion. You know what the papers are like, the things they write.'

'It isn't true, then?'

'No, it is true about Timmy, but it's not like what they say.' She tried to explain, knowing full well that Annie was so excited she wasn't even properly listening to her.

'Imagine, I'm related to someone like that. Martha, it's just so amazing.'

'You don't believe it, then?'

'Martha, come on, you are a truly good person, even Jack says you're a saint the way you're always doing things for people – looking after Frances, helping out with the kids and the family. You're always there when people need you. I guess if I were to pick someone to help and heal people, I'd pick you.'

Martha was silent. Annie's sincerity and trust and faith in her had both moved and surprised her. She had not expected it and was genuinely touched by her sister-in-law's honesty.

'Thank you, Annie,' she said simply.

The phone continued all day: family and friends curious, offering support and trying to glean more information from her.

By afternoon the tone of the calls had changed: strangers' voices, urgent, pleading, asking her to see their child, heal their wife, help with a dying parent. Martha sat cradling the receiver listening to their torrent of words, hesitant, unsure of the help or comfort she could give them but none the less arranging to see those who needed her and trying to find words for those whose spirit was wounded and broken and in need of healing.

Mike returned from work that evening, his eyes blazing with temper as he walked by the scattering of cars parked all along Mill Street: cars of those who had parked in the hope of seeing Martha, or touching her.

'We'll sue that paper for what they've done!' he shouted, getting himself a cold beer from the fridge. 'We have a life, a family. This is a total invasion of our privacy! Who the hell do these people think they are, coming along and parking in our street, disturbing our neighbours?'

'I'm sorry, Mike, I'm sorry. I never meant any of this to happen. Honest I didn't.'

'I know you didn't. I know that. Listen, with any luck in a few days all this gossip and rumour will have died down.'

'They're all just scared and worried,' said Martha, peering through the window. 'See the man and woman in the green car there?'

'Yeah.'

'They want me to go visit with them and see if I can help their son. He has motor neurone disease and has only recently moved back in with them.'

'Christ!'

'I know. They want me to fly to Washington

with them in two days' time and lay my hands on him.'

'Jesus, I don't believe you!'

'It's true, Mike. I told them I couldn't go with them but they're just prepared to keep a vigil out there in the hope I'll change my mind.'

'Jesus, those poor people.'

'I know. I never could have imagined all the desperate things people have to endure. If I can help even one person in any small way I've got to try.'

Mike came close and wrapped her safe in his arms, his lips kissing her forehead and nuzzling her hair. 'Aren't you scared of all this?' he said.

'Course I'm scared, Mike, I never expected anything like this to happen, but something changed the other day. I don't understand the why or how of it, but maybe I am meant to help people, and to help them heal themselves. Laying my hands on Timmy I could definitely feel the healing power go through me. It's so hard to explain, but I can't walk away now and pretend none of this is happening because it is. And I guess you and I might have to get used to it.'

He held her so tight she could feel his heart beating through the cotton of his shirt. It was as if he was trying to hold onto her and protect her from something that neither of them could yet imagine.

Chapter Eight

Beth Armstrong watched anxiously from the corridor of Boston's Children's Hospital. Sue Lucas had been most definite that the woman who'd helped at the accident, the healer, was coming to visit her son today. Timmy Lucas had finally been moved, from the intensive care floor to the surgical one, his condition now considered stable. Fortune had smiled on her: she had got talking to his mother in the ladies' rest room and discovered that the McGill woman was actually coming to see him. It was an opportunity too good to miss – she might actually be able to tell her about Cass. If she could work a miracle for one child maybe she could do it for another!

Martha was overjoyed to see Timmy again, so relieved that the child she'd almost believed dead was lying there, a metal cage over his bed protecting his leg which was in some kind of weird cast with metal bars and screws protruding from it, but otherwise far better than she had imagined. He looked pale and lost in the hospital bed, his black hair standing on end, his cheeks grazed and one eye still covered in a blackberry-coloured bruise. If he had any memory of the accident he made absolutely no mention of it and Martha decided to ignore the subject herself, as it wasn't fair on the boy.

'I asked your mom about dropping by, Timmy, and she said it was OK.'

He just nodded.

'I wasn't quite sure what to bring you so I asked Patrick my son, and he was the one picked out this robot game.'

She could tell he was real pleased with it by the way he let his hand slide over it. 'Do you like games?' she asked.

He nodded again and she knew that as soon as he was able he would be making use of the games console fitted under the hospital TV set.

'You feeling all right?' she asked gently.

'Much better, thank you, Mrs McGill.'

'That's good.'

He still looked tired, she thought as she reached out for his arm, but the feeling was nothing like before. His body was trying to heal itself, renew and recover from deep trauma. It would take time but she sensed he was going to be fine.

She sat by his bed and made small talk about all the kids in the road, telling him that young Johnny Rynhart had already placed a pumpkin out on his front step, although Hallowe'en was miles away yet.

'I think the sun will cook that pumpkin it's so hot outside!' joked Martha.

'Rynharts are always first with everything,' he said solemnly. 'They always like to get a march on the rest of the neighbours. November 1 his dad starts getting ready for Christmas.'

Timmy yawned, Martha chatting away as his eyes became heavy and finally closed. His body was still in shock and needed much sleep and rest to recover.

She rode the elevator down to the ground floor and decided to stop off at the hospital cafeteria for a cup of tea before driving home. It was between meal times and was fairly quiet and Martha picked a spot overlooking the small paved courtyard.

'Excuse me, Mrs McGill. I hope you don't mind me interrupting you?'

Martha paused, cradling the hot tea in its polystyrene cup and wondering why she had bothered to purchase something she knew she would scarcely enjoy as the stranger slid into the seat opposite.

'I'm Beth Armstrong,' the other woman introduced herself. The name meant nothing to Martha.

'I got talking to Sue Lucas the other day. She told me what you did for her son. My daughter is a patient in this hospital too, right up on the third floor.'

Martha held her breath. She was waiting for it. She could guess what was coming, see it in the other woman's eyes: the flicker of hope, the silent plea for help.

'I'm sorry,' Martha sighed. 'Sue shouldn't have said anything to you.'

'Please, Mrs McGill, my daughter is very ill. If anyone needs your help, Cass does. She's spent more than half her life in and out of this hospital and she's just ten years old. Do you have any idea what that is like, what it does to a family?'

'No,' said Martha quietly. 'I can't begin to imagine.'

The other woman ignored her and began to fill her in with the medical details of her daughter's condition, her face livid with rage at what had happened to her child.

'We found out when she was about three months old. She wasn't like other babies, not thriving. Sometimes when I was feeding her, her little lips used to turn blue. We took her to the paediatrician and fortunately he sent us here. Children's Hospital is the finest hospital for kids in the country. Multiple congenital heart defects, they told us, and they operated on her, then another surgery the following year and the one after. Cass has had that much surgery, you should see her chest – it's like a stitch and sew pattern kit. They've been talking about a transplant, so now we're waiting for a heart. The surgeons here have already done more than a hundred successful transplants.'

Beth Armstrong's hands were shaking and, without thinking, Martha reached to console her.

'Cass is getting weaker and weaker by the day. She can't walk or run any more and some days it seems like she hasn't even the breath to talk no more. We don't know how much longer she can last out.'

'I'm sorry. Truly sorry,' murmured Martha.

'Please – will you see her?'

Beth Armstrong looked stressed, adrenalin and fear raging through her gaunt frame. She looked as if she needed a few decent nights' sleep to rid herself of the dark grey circles under her eyes and wire-sprung nervousness. Martha was at a total loss as to what to say or what to do in the face of such overwhelming fury and pain.

'You could help her. I just know you could! The doctors are saying that there is nothing much else they can do. Please, Mrs McGill. You are a mother too. Please just come and see my child.'

Martha wiped her hands with the paper napkin. The other users of the cafeteria, sensing the distress of her table partner, were turning around, curious.

'Just a few minutes of your time. That's all I'm asking!'

'You're mistaken, Beth. I'm nothing special. I can't do anything to help someone like Cass, honest I just can't.'

She could tell Beth didn't believe her and was choosing to ignore unwanted information.

'Come upstairs and see her!' pleaded Beth Armstrong.

Lifting her jacket, purse and newspaper, and against her better judgement, Martha rode the elevator upstairs with the child's mother.

'What room is she in?' she asked.

'Number 325.'

Upstairs a mural of Peter Pan flying over a pirate ship decorated one wall of the corridor of Boston's Children's Hospital.

Beth pushed in the door of her child's room. A blond girl with a pretty face turned, curious about the new visitor.

'Cass, this is an old friend of mine, Martha. We just bumped into each other down in the coffee shop, and she wanted to drop by and say hi and see what a beautiful daughter I got.'

Cass raised herself higher in the bed, letting go of the book she'd been desultorily glancing at.

'Hello,' she said shyly.

'Hello, Cass.' Martha introduced herself.

'How you doing, Cass?' her mother asked anxiously. 'Did you eat the nice lunch the nurse brought you?'

Cass stuck out her tongue.

Martha couldn't help but notice how frail and undersized the child was.

'Maybe there'll be something nicer to eat later on!' Beth encouraged her.

Cass sighed. Food and how it tasted or looked didn't mean a thing to her any more.

'Martha, please sit down!' said Beth, and pulled another chair up beside the narrow hospital bed. Martha was perusing the handmade cards that adorned the windowsill and locker top.

'They're neat!' she said.

'The kids in my fourth-grade class did them. Mrs Marshall my teacher makes them all do stuff like that every time I'm in the hospital.'

'But they're really beautiful,' smiled Martha, noticing that the drawings and colourings of kids running and jumping and skipping and cycling were the ones that Cass kept closest to her bed, while the ones with pictures of stick-thin figures lying in giant beds looking pretty miserable were banished to the further corners of the small room.

'Your mom tells me that you are not doing too good.'

Cass studied a puzzle book abandoned on her bed.

'Cass, I think that Martha might be able to help you to feel a bit better.'

Cass looked disbelieving, suspicious even.

'You a doctor or something?' she asked.

Martha laughed. 'Something, I guess.'

The child was puzzled and looked towards her mother for reassurance.

'This lady, my friend, she sometimes helps people who are sick, honest she does!'

Martha tried to quench her annoyance with the

parent, for already Beth had said far too much and compromised her position with the child.

'I'm just a friend, Cass.'

'Can you touch her, Martha, lay your hands on her?'

Martha tried to make a silent plea to the mother to at least give herself and this sick child some time and space to weigh each other up and decide on things. 'Your mom tells me that you got problems with your heart, Cass,' she said.

A scared look filled Cass's eyes.

'The doctors said I need to get a new one, they can't fix this broken one no more,' she told Martha matter-of-factly, her gaze travelling in the direction of her mother, looking for a response. Martha was trying to appear relaxed in the face of such knowledge. This child already had enough to cope with.

'Cass, honey, will you let Martha put her hands on you and try and help to make you better?' suggested Beth, her face contorted with concern.

'You can do that?' quizzed the child.

'She can! She helped a boy on the floor below and lots more people besides.'

Cass looked doubtful, almost afraid. 'Does it hurt?' she asked.

Martha shook her head.

'I don't think so. My hands may get warm, hot even, but that's all.'

'What do you do, how does it work?'

'I'm not sure,' she declared honestly, 'but it

seems that sometimes when I touch people and lay my hands on them it helps.'

The small girl looked sceptical as if Martha was some kind of hospital worker about to play a trick on her. Subconsciously she began to push back against the pillow and retreat from her.

'I won't hurt you, Cass, I promise.'

This was foolish and stupid, Martha thought to herself as Beth leant forward and began to un-button her daughter's pretty pastel pyjama top.

'What do you want her to do?' she whispered.

'Just relax, that's all.'

Martha rubbed the tips of her fingers and palms together to warm them as the child's skinny scarred chest was revealed, leads with sticky circular pads attached to it from the monitor hooked up beside the bed. Martha sighed. Cass was staring right at her, her elfin chin pitched forward. Martha held her hand first. She was like a small wounded bird. The energy level was low, even lower than she had expected. Running her hands up along her arm she could sense the battle to move blood and oxygen through her system. She stroked Cass as she would a small baby, feeling the ribs and the telltale erratic flutter and pattern of her dysfunctioning heart, willing it to steady and fall into a more defined logical gentle rhythm than the staggered one she was picking up. She moved her hands slowly, gently, hoping some of the warmth and effort would pass through into Cass. It was like running up and down a maze of circuit paths, hoping that one or two were free and clear to work, trying to hide her dismay at what she was picking up and realizing the precariousness of Cass's grip on life. Silently she prayed for strength and energy for this child. Cass's eyes followed her own, understanding as Martha finished.

'Well?' Beth's skinny face was full of expectation.

Martha took a deep breath, trying to compose herself.

'Thank you, Martha. Thank you so much.' The mother's voice was choked with appreciation and hope.

Martha had no idea how much or little she had done.

'Well, Cass, how do you feel?' urged Beth.

The small girl was busy re-buttoning her pyjamas, concentrating. 'I could feel it! As if something was moving inside me, I don't understand it,' she said.

Martha laughed nervously.

'To tell the truth, Cass, neither do I! But when I'm laying my hands on I ask the good earth and sky and the Holy Spirit to help heal the person who needs it. I guess I'm just a sort of go-between, that's all.'

'Didn't you feel anything more, Cass? Anything?' insisted her mother.

Cass stared right over at her.

'It felt real nice.'

Beth Armstrong looked triumphant.

Martha stood up to go, wanting desperately to be out of the room and extricate herself from this impossible position. 'Listen, Beth, I have to go and pick up my youngest,' she told her.

'Thank you so much for coming up to see Cass, it's much appreciated, Martha, and I hope it didn't delay you too much.'

'Martha!' said the small voice. 'Martha, will you come visit me again?'

She sighed. It had been inevitable. The child needed help, needed support. The path of her illness was such that it would be too much for her to deal with on her own.

'Yes, I'll come again, Cass. I promise.'

Chapter Nine

Martha watched proudly as Alice and Becky hopped, light-footed as two fairies, to the music of the lilting reel, Alice's long fair hair bouncing on her shoulders. The crowd of eight-, nine- and ten-year-old girls weaving in and out, learning the complicated steps of the traditional dance, were giggling and laughing, bumping into each other as they swirled around the room.

It was her turn to collect the girls from Flannery's Irish dance class, which was held in the old Lutheran school hall on Tuesdays. Thanking Mrs Flannery, she gathered up their bags and shoes. She dropped Becky off and had a few quick words with Evie before returning home.

She could scarcely believe the apparition that greeted her when she turned into Mill Street, for there were at least twenty cars parked in close proximity to their driveway. At first she wondered if one of her neighbours was throwing a party or having some kind of meeting, but seeing no sign of any such occasion she realized that the occupants sitting inside the silver and grey and blue vehicles were all waiting for her. Car doors slammed and three or four people began to approach her as soon as they recognized her.

Martha grabbed Alice by the hand, as she quickly pulled her key out of her purse and let herself into the house. Patrick was sitting at the kitchen counter and she was surprised by the look of relief in his face.

'Where the hell were you, Mom?'

'It's all right, Patrick, I'm here now,' she comforted him, wrapping her arms loosely around his broad shoulders. It was unlike her fifteen-year-old son to make any enquiry as to her whereabouts and she guessed that he'd been anxiously waiting for her return.

'I just picked the girls up from dance class, Patrick, that's all! Why, what's been going on here?'

He jerked his head in the direction of the window.

'They've been sitting there all afternoon, Mom, just waiting for you to get back. A few of them came and rang on the doorbell and I told them I didn't know when you'd get home but I guess they didn't believe me. One or two even phoned. They wouldn't go away, no matter what I said. Those fucking freaks have just been waiting in their cars for you!'

'Patrick!' she scolded. Her son might be inches

taller than her already, and like most of his generation tried to act like a cool dude, but inside he was still only a kid. Scared by the crowd outside – and who could blame him? Blast that stupid journalist and her piece in the paper. Evie had said she thought the local radio channel had also mentioned it. What right had that journalist to go stirring things and giving people false hopes?

Mike was right: she should have said nothing instead of trying to be honest and helpful and giving her time. Now, here she had a load of strangers believing that she could help them. The doorbell rang almost immediately and it wasn't fair to ask Patrick to fend them off any longer.

'I'll get it, pet, don't you worry.

'I'm sorry but I can't help you,' she apologized politely to the crowd outside the door.

Martha tried to put them right and tell them the truth, but the waiting people had no interest in listening to her protestations and denials. All every single one of them wanted was a minute of her time.

'Ma'am, a minute!'

'Just one minute so's you can hear me out!' argued the sixty-four-year-old retired surveyor who lived over in Dedham, crippled with arthritis in his spine, begging for a relief from pain that pills and prescription drugs could no longer contain.

Unembarrassed, he'd pulled up his check shirt

on her front step, begging Martha to lay her hands on his back. Too shocked to refuse, Martha had done what he requested, feeling immediately the heat and energy run from her fingers into the almost honeycomb sensation of the man's vertebrae. A shy young girl with severe acne had followed on. Faced with the despair and depression caused by the raised pustules on her pretty face, Martha had asked her to come inside and ended up, after almost a half-hour conversation, sending her healing both inside and out. Then there was a businessman with failing hearing who had a fear of being deaf like his father. Martha felt the burning heat scorch from her hands into the auditory canal, removing anything that blocked the vibration of sound and its interpretation.

'Pppleeasse, Mmrs McGgill, pppleease!'

The nineteen-year-old Boston College student's severe stammer was exacerbated by his nervousness at meeting her. Martha, reading the plea for help in his eyes, sensed that her laying on of hands was not going to do much to ease the tension and self-doubt that overwhelmed his young life. He needed to learn to accept himself as he was if he was to have any hope of getting over his problem. Most of all he needed someone to talk to and when she laid her hands on his lips and throat Martha found herself agreeing to see him again. Her cousin Dermot had been plagued with a bad stammer for most of his life but Martha could honestly say that it had not stopped him achieving all that he had set out to do. He had always wanted to be an oceanographer and had got through college and exams, and now lived in Australia, where at the last count himself and his wife Neeley had five kids. They still kept in touch by phone and email.

'Look, Matthew, I'll see you again,' she promised.

Rheumatism, chronic fatigue, dizzy spells, back problems, nerve trouble . . . Martha breathed a sigh of relief when eventually the last person went and she had the small study at the front of the house back to herself. Why in heaven's name had she ever agreed to let one of them across her doorstep, let alone tried to help? If she didn't believe that she could help she should have just got rid of them by threatening to call the traffic police and having them towed away instead of wasting her time and giving some credence to their belief.

Mike was already home and he and the kids were sitting having dinner when she finally got to join them.

'I'm sorry for the delay, gang.'

'We got some chicken and wedges from the freezer,' Mary Rose said. 'There's some for you left in the oven.'

Patrick was busy eating but she knew from the way he avoided her eyes that he had given his version of events already to his father. Mike was hopeless at disguising anger or bad humour and the kids had picked it up and were eating as quickly as they could.

'Mom, were they all sick people who came to our house?' enquired Alice.

'Yes, they were, honey. They hoped that Mommy could make them feel a bit better.'

'And did you?'

'I'm not sure, Alice, maybe.'

She could see Mike's jawline tense and she knew he was having a real hard time believing or accepting anything to do with her ability to heal people. Patrick finished first and refused dessert saying he had to work on an assignment for school. Mary Rose darted her a sympathetic look as she placed some plates in the dishwasher. Only Alice held out for a bowl of raspberry and vanilla ice-cream as Martha ate her own meal.

Afterwards, sitting at the table, Martha braced herself for the expected tirade from her husband, knowing full well that his annoyance could no longer be hidden.

'What the hell, Martha! What the fuck? I come home from one hell of a day, and I mean one *hell* of a day with Bob and that new guy Roland breathing down my neck, and find a load of wackos in my home! Patrick was scared out of his wits this afternoon, and as for the girls I don't know what they must think about their mother getting involved with these kind of people!'

'Mike, I know it's scary. I didn't ask or invite any of them. You know that!'

'I know it's not your fault, Martha, but well, you'd better do something about it. It's not fair on the kids or the neighbours.'

Martha said nothing.

So much for Mike's telling her that this would all blow over and be forgotten about in a few days. Listening to those people today and laying her hands on them had in a strange way convinced her that somehow her work as a healer had only begun.

Chapter Ten

On Wednesday morning Martha was glad to escape the phone calls and visitors and drive up to Highlands Animal Shelter, where she'd worked as a volunteer for almost three years. Things had gotten crazy since that journalist's article and she'd been approached by four magazines, who wanted to do a feature on her. The local radio station had invited her in to the studio to do an interview but she'd refused, and she'd been asked to appear in an open forum discussion on *The Morning Show* about faith healing, which she had absolutely no intention of doing. Coming up here to walk the dogs and care for the animals seemed a lot more appealing.

The small animal rescue centre was situated off Highway 128 on a piece of run-down land at the side of an old gas station. It wasn't an ideal setting but the volunteers all did their best to find homes for the animals. For those that had lost all trust in humans and would never be likely to fit into living with one of that species again, they provided as good a care as they hoped a distressed animal needed.

Martha usually worked from 8.30 to two o'clock and would do another morning if they were low on volunteers, covering for others during holidays and flu epidemics and the like. She loved walking into Highlands and hearing the excited bark of the dogs who recognized the volunteer staff, their tails wagging furiously as she went and said hello to them all. The phone lines were always busy and she could never get over how many unwanted and uncared-for animals existed. Neighbours, annoyed shopkeepers, security guards all phoned in with problems, which they hoped the shelter could help them with. Old people who had to go into hospital or into long-time care, who'd nobody to take their pets and could not possibly afford the cost of expensive kennelling, regularly called. Their dogs and cats, often elderly too, had a look of resignation and betrayal when they were brought in which no amount of volunteer care could remove. Martha tried to console those noble companions of man as best she could.

The hours she spent in the shelter went all too quickly. She enjoyed not only tending to the animals but also meeting the eclectic mix of people who were volunteers. Women like Joanna Little who had raised large families and were still willing to give of themselves again, Hank

Caulfield, a retired army man who had a way with large dogs and worked two full days there. He also had a keen interest in reptiles and was an expert in their care. Mim Brewster, a former heroin addict who had been sentenced to community work eight years ago and still kept coming back to help, never blinking an eyelid at the distressed and diseased animals that she helped to clean and brush and groom every Wednesday. Teachers, plumbers, a librarian, college students – all of them gave of themselves without looking for payment.

Now the dogs went crazy when they saw her, sensing that because she was still wearing her jacket she might take them out. The dogs always needed exercise, though sometimes a little holding and petting could help them feel just a little bit loved.

Mim indicated the ones that she was going to groom, and Martha took down three leashes. She clipped one onto the collar of a boisterous golden retriever that had been found wandering up at the parking lot at the drive-in Dunkin Donuts near the shopping mall. Its owners obviously decided that it was a good place to abandon the animal, who was probably eating them out of house and home and couldn't be accommodated in a small environment. He jumped up on her nearly knocking her over, his paws pushing against her chest. Martha gave him a huge welcoming hug in return.

'Take it easy, Donut. Take it easy. That's a good boy!'

A few cages down she clipped a leash onto a jaunty black and white mongrel who'd been with them for about five months. He yapped excitedly, running round in circles so she could hardly catch him as she tried to fasten the leash securely. Last but not least she took Dollar, an overweight black Labrador who could do with the exercise. Donna Brady, a retired beautician, decided to join her, and hooked up four more dogs to join the walk. Martha had a great respect for the middle-aged woman who had successfully battled with cancer over the past three years yet was willing to give her time and energy to the shelter. She was a stalwart fundraiser and organized suppers, breakfasts and Christmas parties to ensure the shelter could remain open.

Walking across the back fields, which stretched along behind the highway, with Donna, Martha felt totally relaxed, both of them laughing at the antics of the animals and their different personalities. Donna already had three dogs of her own, two of them from the shelter, but still volunteered. She had the most generous spirit and Martha found her a pleasure to be with. Donut pulled ahead, anxious to run and race around, Minty, a Jack Russell cross, trying to keep up with him. They came to a spot the volunteers called the Gallops, which was unofficially fenced off and was the only place they could safely let the dogs off for a run around. Donna's beagle pair were in an ecstasy of doggy joy as they romped together.

Donna and Martha kept a close eye on them all.

'I've been reading about you,' Donna said.

Martha gazed directly ahead, watching Dollar who had found a patch of sunlight and sat down in it.

'Is it true?'

'I suppose, but you know what those papers and magazines are like, Donna, they just write what suits them.'

'Healing is a wonderful gift, Martha, a wonderful gift. I'm pleased for you. Humanity can do with all the help it can get, believe me. There are a lot of sick people out there who could use a bit of healing, and I don't just mean the likes of myself. What about the sons of bitches that tortured those two?'

Martha remembered how the beagles had been when they came in. They were missing pieces of skin, had been shaved all over and had claws pulled. They had whimpered and cried for a week, the noise disturbing the rest of the animals. The vet had wanted to put them down, but Donna and Janet Rimaldi, the head of the shelter, had pleaded on the dogs' behalf, and had got a stay of a week to see if they improved. Watching them now Martha knew that Donna's instinct and perseverance had been well rewarded.

'They're fine dogs now,' Donna said proudly. 'Janet thinks a family out in Newton might take them. They love beagles apparently and lost their one two weeks ago.'

'Ah, that'd be great, especially if they get to stay together!'

'It's the least they deserve.'

Calling the dogs, they began the half-hour walk back, chatting easily about their families and the latest pets that had arrived and the condition they were in.

Martha managed a quick cup of coffee before she went on the phone line, knowing well she would hardly get time to draw breath once she sat down, her notepad and pen at the ready to write down names, addresses and contacts. A cat who'd a litter of kittens in a packing case behind a liquor store and seemed to be in a distressed condition; a white rabbit found on the landing of a building on Store Street and refusing to budge.

'He sounds like he's in shock, ma'am.'

'Do you think you could lift him in a blanket and drive him over to us? I have no-one available right now to collect him, but if you could get him to us it would be much appreciated. No, there's no charge.'

She scribbled down the details as more and more calls came in.

'Martha, that you?'

Smiling, Martha recognized the voice on the line immediately. It was Frank Graham. 'Hello, Frank, how are you? How are things going?'

Every Wednesday the old man called from the public phone at the Emmanuel Residence for the aged and infirm to enquire about his pet.

'How's Dollar?'

'I took him for a long walk this morning, Frank, and he's doing fine.'

'Does he still miss me?'

'You know he does, Frank, but he's not pining. Labradors are loyal.'

'Has that Mrs Rimaldi said any more about getting him a home?'

'We have tried, Frank, but Dollar's an old dog and set in his ways. He's not suitable for a young family or anyone out at work all day.'

She could sense the relief in his voice.

'So I guess he'll just have to stay put for the moment then.'

'Yes, we expect so.'

'Did he get the biscuits I sent?'

Martha tried to suppress a smile. Every week without fail a package was delivered by Fedex to the shelter containing sweet digestive biscuits, the type the Labrador loved. 'We got them, but you know we're trying to cut him back a bit, Frank,' she told him.

'I know, I know. It's just that they were always his favourites.'

'You could come and see him if you'd like.' She could picture the old man standing at the phone thinking of his best friend.

'No, I don't think that's a good idea.'

There was silence for a minute and she wondered if she had lost the call.

'That would be too upsetting for us both. It's best to leave it as it is, Martha.'

She told him about Dollar lying stretched out in the sun, giving Frank time to compose himself.

'You have my number here?'

'Yes,' she assured him.

'Should anything happen.'

'We know, Frank.'

'I'll phone again next week. Thanks a lot, Martha, thanks a whole lot.'

She had barely finished his call when a woman phoned looking for a mature tabby that had escaped from a ground-floor apartment about two blocks away. She was pleased to tell the distressed owner that a cat matching the description and wearing a pink diamanté collar had been brought in, none the worse for wear, by a concerned patrol officer the evening before.

'Thank God.'

Martha transferred to another line.

'Hello, is that the Highlands Animal Shelter?'

Martha responded to the male caller.

'I want to talk to the woman, the healer that works there, the miracle lady. Is she there?' he asked.

Martha almost dropped the phone. Quickly she glanced around. Janet was on another line in her office, arguing with some animal feed supplier by the sound of it, and Donna was sitting with a cat in her lap trying to put eye drops in its eyes.

'I'm sorry, this is an animal shelter. How can I help you?'

'I want to speak to her. Is she there?'

'Is there a problem with an animal, sir?'

'I want to speak to that woman, it's urgent! Put me on to her!'

Martha didn't know what to say. The man was screaming down the line at her. She held the phone away from her. How could she pass the call on to one of the others? They were already busy enough. And how did the caller know about her volunteering at the shelter? She had no choice but to deal with him.

'This is Martha,' she said resignedly. 'What is the matter, sir?'

A torrent of misery followed as the man, called Pete, told her of years of addiction to alcohol and prescription drugs which had ended with him trying to take his own life only a month before. Appalled, she closed her eyes thinking of his disturbed spirit and the torment he endured. Now he was threatening to do the same again. He had failed his wife and five-year-old son and had abandoned his promise to attend an addiction clinic daily, as he felt it was doing him no good.

'I have no options left, Martha, there is no cure to this, no end to it all.'

Desperately she tried to reason with him, asking about what would happen to his son and wife if he did what he planned and trying to persuade him to attend the clinic one more time.

'That's no good!' he screamed, demanding instant answers, instant results.

She closed her eyes. Imagining him, she tried to get a sense of placing her hands along his chest, above his ribcage, near his heart and soul.

'I am going to send you healing, Pete, but I need you to sit down quietly and to be silent and still so I can think of you, try to help you,' she pleaded.

She could sense the heat and energy running through her already, as perspiration began to gather on her forehead and hairline.

'I'm sending you healing, Pete. Can you sense it?'

There was silence and for a minute she imagined the worst. The lines were going crazy. Ten calls were waiting. Janet looked over at her, puzzled as to why she was not dealing with them.

'I can feel it,' he said finally.

'Will you promise me you will go to the clinic today?' she begged, 'and tell them how bad you are feeling?'

'I suppose,' was all Pete said.

Martha imagined the worst as he suddenly hung up. She had no control over what he might or might not do and no way of warning his family or doctor.

'You OK, Martha?' Donna asked, concerned. 'Was that some crazy on the line?'

Martha nodded. She felt sick to her stomach

thinking of him and the state he was in. Janet Rimaldi stared over at her and Martha made a show of looking busy. The next caller had found an injured squirrel in her yard and wanted directions to Highlands.

Chapter Eleven

Martha's mind was in turmoil. Nothing could have prepared her for the demands now being made on her, and the expectation of utter strangers that she could help them. More stories had appeared in the newspaper. Lara Chadwick had tracked down two people who both claimed to have been healed by her: the student with a stammer she remembered, but for the life of her she couldn't recall the child with a broken wrist that she was supposed to have helped.

How could anyone believe that she – Martha Anne McGill from Easton, Massachusetts – had been blessed with the gift of healing! She was just an ordinary woman, nothing special, so why had this happened to her?

A quiet person by nature, she was uncomfortable with so much attention and the invasion of her privacy. There were people constantly outside her home or driving up and down her street; already her neighbours were complaining. It had got so bad that now even in traffic she became suspicious of cars stopping beside her. The intrusion of these strangers on her family life was unbearable and at times she even worried for her children's safety. Mike blamed her for it all, she knew that. If he had his way she would never have volunteered to help the Lucas boy and would have simply stood on the pavement with the rest of the onlookers. A thought she could not begin to countenance! Would it have made a difference? That she would never know.

What she did know now was that she found it impossible to turn away those that came to her for help, who were in need of healing.

'You're far too soft, Martha!' joked Evie. 'That's your problem.'

Her best friend was right. She was prepared to spend time and listen to people, and in the simple act of laying on hands experienced a power and energy for which there was no rational explanation. It was all so complicated! She stretched her fingers and hands, studying them, feeling her palms and wrists and pulse points, searching for an answer.

She phoned Rianna Lindgard's surgery. The receptionist told her there was a six-week waiting list excepting emergencies.

'I'm a friend of hers,' insisted Martha.

Moments later the girl managed to slot her in for a cancellation appointment the following day.

Martha left the car at the station and took the T to town. Boston was a nightmare, with roads up everywhere as the planners tried to sort out the tangled mess of city traffic by building new roads, tunnels and bridges. It had been christened 'The Big Dig' and seemed to be going on for ever.

It was raining lightly as she made her way towards Huntingdon Avenue, where Rianna's surgery was situated. Two other people were already in the waiting room but the receptionist ushered her in ahead of them.

'Well, Martha, what brings you to this neck of the woods?' asked Rianna. 'I thought you went to Gibson Daly out near where you live.'

'We do,' she sighed, settling herself into the ultra-modern black dental chair, which even contained a TV screen. 'It's just that I want your opinion on something, Rianna, and I hoped you might be able to help me.'

'Tooth trouble!' smiled Rianna.

Funny, she looked different in her white coat with her dark hair pinned up off her face, a little older.

'No, that's not it.'

'Oh, gums bad?'

'No, Rianna. I should have probably phoned you, but I want to ask you a favour. Will you have a look at my hand?'

'Your hand! Are you mad? What do you want me to look at that for, have you hurt it?'

'No, Rianna, but I want to get it X-rayed. Both of them.'

'You should be going to a doctor, Martha, that's certainly not my field.'

'Please, Rianna. The doctor's going to think I'm crazy if I go ask him and I'd have to get an appointment for the hospital.'

Rianna considered for a minute, then leaning forward she took Martha's right hand in hers.

'The magic hand,' she murmured, turning it back and forwards, feeling the fingers and knuckles and wrist and palm. 'Seems totally normal to me, Martha, but I'm not really set up for anatomy. Still, I'm sure we can get a photo of these beauties if we try.'

'I just feel such a freak, Rianna, and I need to know is there some strange kind of reason why I have this power.'

'You're not going to go blowing all my expensive fancy equipment on me now, are you!'

'I hope not.'

Rianna and herself had met in the hospital after giving birth to their firstborn sons more than fifteen years ago. Patrick and Alex had been born within hours of each other, which seemed to create some kind of bond between them. The kids and moms always sent cards and presents to each other and kept in touch over the years. Even when she and Mike had moved to California, Rianna would make incredible long-distance calls to tell her the most trivial things. After they had moved back East Martha was only glad that she was there to offer her love and support when Andrew Lingard was involved in a tragic skiing accident in the Blue Hills and broke his neck. Three months later Rianna and young Alex lost the most important person in their life. She was filled with admiration for Rianna, who had gone back to dental school to continue her studies and ended up taking over her husband's practice.

Rianna asked her to spread her fingers against the solid base of the instrument table as she manoeuvred the X-ray camera into position.

'OK, keep still a sec.'

She repeated the procedure with her left hand.

'Right, we have to wait a few minutes. Do you want me to give you a nice polish while we wait?'

'Sure!'

'Why not!'

Martha's teeth were white and sparkling when Rianna told her that her hands were perfectly normal. 'There is slight evidence of a break years ago on your middle finger, that's all.'

'Basketball when I was about sixteen.'

'Well, there you go then, but otherwise horribly normal and no need to call out the *X Files* brigade.'

She felt relieved as she thanked Rianna and arranged to invite her and Alex over for Sunday lunch in about a fortnight's time.

'Tell Mike and the kids I said hi,' added Rianna, as she left her office.

Somewhat reassured Martha went out into the street. She had some time to kill before she went home and the evening rush hour started, and decided to do a bit of shopping in the stores up around Copley Square.

Rianna Lindgard stretched her aching legs and feet. She had just finished an exhausting root canal job on a very tetchy businessman who was booked to fly to Tokyo first thing in the morning. She was as polite and kind as could be but longed to be home with Alex, eating spaghetti carbonara and drinking a chilled Martini. Lucy her assistant had gone already as there was no point in her missing her train to Braintree.

She checked everything was unplugged and turned off, and that her equipment was sterilized for tomorrow. Noticing Martha's X-rays over on her desk, she thought she'd leave them for Lucy to file in the morning. Lifting them up, her eye was drawn to a whitish circle of light that seemed to have developed around the edge of the hands and finger bones. Was it a fault in her machine? It hadn't been there earlier on, she was sure of that. Curious, she placed them safely away in her own drawer. Maybe Martha really had the power she believed in.

Chapter Twelve

Mike McGill pulled on the freshly ironed white shirt, tucking it into his fine silk black trousers. At forty-two he reckoned himself to be still in good shape, playing golf whenever he got a chance and using the company gym at least thrice a week to keep fit. The Institute had a firm belief that those who maintained a healthy body had a higher energy and concentration level during the long working day and testing had proved it boosted intelligence and performance.

He had finished work an hour early and had driven home, giving himself time to shower and relax before he and Martha had to dress for dinner at Bob and Gina Forrester's. To be invited to a sit-down dinner at the home of the Institute's president was a major step up the career ladder as far as he was concerned. Until now, Martha and he had attended the crowded cocktail party thrown every summer by his boss in a marquee erected on the lawn of the large colonial-style home to cater for the Institute's large number of staff. Tonight was different.

Bob had told him they were having a few close friends over and that Daniel Kendrick from Powerhouse, the giant technology company in San Jose, would also be attending. Mike, adjusting the fastener on his bow tie, could scarcely believe that in an hour or so he would actually be sitting across the table from what the *Wall Street Journal* had called one of America's most intelligent and richest men.

Martha had gone to the beauty shop and had her hair and nails done. Her light brown hair was highlighted and worn simple and straight as she was wearing a classic pale blue dress which Mike could tell had cost a fortune; the colour accentuated her pale skin and blue-green eyes.

'You look great, honey!' he declared, pulling her into his arms.

'You don't look too bad yourself,' she teased, admiring him as he pulled on the black dinner jacket. 'James Bond, eat your heart out!'

Martha touched his face gently. Mike responded by bending down and touching his lips to hers, her mouth opening to his, her arms pulling him closer. They were still like a pair of horny kids, Mike thought, as he gently disentangled himself from his wife's embrace. Bob Forrester was a stickler for punctuality at their weekly progress meetings and he certainly had no intention of arriving late to their dinner party.

The kids had all been fed earlier and had promised to be on their best behaviour. Martha dabbed perfume on her wrists and neck before grabbing her midnight-blue wrap off the bed. Mike checked he had his cell phone and wallet. Patrick whistled his approval as they stood at the bottom of the stairs. The girls told Martha how beautiful she looked.

'Mom, you look neat. That dress is just perfect,' complimented Mary Rose.

'And you smell like the garden at night time,' added Alice.

'That is such a sweet thing to say, Alice. Thank you.'

'Dad, you are real handsome too,' laughed their youngest daughter.

Mike glanced outside, seeing the cab that he had ordered draw up in front of the house. 'Come on, Martha! Time to go. You lot be good and don't stay up too late.'

Martha picked up the gift-wrapped, small embroidered cushion that Evie had helped her to select as a token for the hostess who probably had everything. The intricate rose had been picked out in the palest shades of damask and pearly pink by a seamstress in the last century.

Mike was nervous during the drive to the Forresters' home off Maple Street. The landmark house stood on about ten acres and was ringed by high shrubs and trees, which managed to hide all but a glimpse of the white gabled windows that overlooked the garden and tennis court. When Martha squeezed his hand he could sense his wife's reassurance that it would be a fine night, spent in good company. The driveway was lit up and Mike let out a whoop of disbelief at the brand new English Rolls-Royce parked out front.

'That must be Kendrick's. He collects cars.'

Paying the driver, Mike helped Martha from the cab. The front door was opening before he had time to ring the bell.

'Welcome, Mike! Welcome,' offered Bob Forrester, his dapper figure rushing out to greet them.

Mike introduced him to Martha, knowing full well that even though they had been guests at Rockhall before, Bob would not be likely to remember his wife's name. Martha, smiling graciously, let herself be kissed on both cheeks by his boss as if they were old friends, his brown eyes flicking over her evening attire.

'Come in, come in, the both of you!'

They were ushered into an Italian tiled marble hallway and a young woman appeared to take Martha's wrap. Gina Forrester came over to welcome them, fussing over them and telling them how divine they both looked. Martha politely admired the figure-hugging black sheath dress that their hostess was wearing, which showed off her perfectly toned and tanned body.

'Come inside and have a glass of bubbly. I do so

want tonight to be one of those nights where everything sparkles.'

Mike reddened with pleasure whereas Martha suddenly felt dowdy as Gina guided them inside where three other couples were clustered around a magnificent fireplace sipping glasses of chilled champagne. They chattered and laughed in low tones and Martha noticed that curious glances were bestowed on them as Gina Forrester introduced them to the rest of the party.

'Everyone – this is Mike McGill and his lovely wife Martha. Mike is one of those computer geniuses that works over in the Institute with Bob.'

Embarrassed, Martha smiled and tried to appear relaxed.

'Martha and Mike, this is Ted and Megan Harris. Ted is involved in the new digital TV station that's been set up and Megan is a media buyer for a whole host of clients, including the Institute.'

As Mike shook hands with them, Martha was taking in the tall good-looking man with greying hair cut close to his head, and a grey moustache and warm brown eyes. His wife, as thin as could be, wore wine palazzo pants and a sleeveless silk top, her almost jet black hair pulled back from her face to highlight her amazing bone structure which reminded Martha of the actress Audrey Hepburn.

'And meet Kaye and John Stillman. John is the

chief partner in Stillman Peterson's, the architects' firm downtown.'

The narrow-shouldered fair-haired man who was only a little taller than herself seemed a bit put out at the interruption of his conversation, but magnanimously smiled and appeared charming. His wife, bored, turned to resume her conversation with a stunning redhead who was balanced on the arm of a large cream armchair.

Martha sipped at her glass of champagne slowly, letting herself get used to the taste. She had got a little drunk once before on champagne when she and Mike had made a visit to Napa. What with the heat and a few glasses of cool champagne she had found herself giddy and giggling after a wonderful meal, Mike having to put her to bed early, ruining the romantic night they'd planned in the beautiful wine château they were staying in. Her husband threw her a warning glance and Martha almost laughed aloud as her hand was caught in a strong grip.

'Nice to meet you, Martha.'

Daniel Kendrick was twice the size of the other men in the room, his tall broad figure almost bursting out of his tailored dinner jacket. Through a tuft of greying hair his balding head shone in the glow of candlelight. He was certainly not a good-looking man but there was a kindness and interest in the hazel eyes that made her feel a little less nervous.

'How you doing, Martha?'

'Fine, thank you, Mr Kendrick.'

'It's Dan,' he reminded her as he shook hands with Mike. Her husband's eyes shone and Martha realized that he was in his element talking IT development with someone on the inside track.

'Encryption is the way to go,' he added excitedly. 'There's a kid in Trinity College in Dublin and the work she's doing on maths and numbers and solutions . . .'

'A kid!' murmured the redhead, who hadn't even bothered to introduce herself. 'What the hell do kids these days know about anything!'

'Actually, Natalie, some kids know a lot. This particular kid signed on with Kendrick Development about five days ago,' Dan told them delightedly. 'Jerry Dargats, my number two, flew over to Ireland to meet her and negotiate a contract. She will finish out her two semesters in college and then come out to work with us in San Jose, or on the campus project here in Boston. We were lucky to find her: apparently she has been offered places in Oxford and Cambridge and Stanford.'

'Seeing that creative pool of talent and genius come together must sure be exciting,' suggested Mike. 'The Institute are always looking for graduates with those kind of qualities, but they're rare enough.'

'Sure are, but this young lady will get to meet the best brains in the industry and be involved in a new programme we're running in conjunction with NASA. Powerhouse needs people like that.'

'Geniuses!' joked Bob Forrester.

Martha wondered if the conversation was going to centre on high tech industry stuff all night. Mike looked animated: he was at home with such discussions whereas Martha was way out of her depth. Turning sideways, her eyes met Kaye Stillman, who seemed equally at a loss as the waiter moved around refilling their glasses.

Minutes later Gina Forrester led her guests into dinner, to the large cherrywood table laid with modern Danish crystal and Irish linen and sparkling silver tableware. Martha was surprised to find herself seated between Ted Harris and Daniel Kendrick. Mike was across from her with that Natalie woman and Megan. Gina Forrester had tried to ensure that the balance of her guests would encourage some lively conversation. Bob Forrester led them in grace, the mighty humbled by those simple words spoken before they dined.

Gina urged them all: 'Eat! Enjoy!'

An array of exquisite seafood laid out in a fan shape, shrimp and salmon and crab, adorned the white tableware and Martha realized just how hungry she was. She had been so busy racing around getting her hair done and visiting Alan Ronell, a middle-aged engineer whose wife had persuaded her to try to relieve some of the extreme pain and discomfort he was experiencing following major knee surgery, that she had actually forgotten to eat lunch.

Across from her John Stillman was explaining a new project he'd just begun, and she turned to make small talk with Ted, who talked enthusiastically about the advent of digital, the changes it would reward the ordinary viewer with and the huge profits those companies involved in new ways of broadcasting would enjoy. Martha tried to keep up with the conversation and add something to it as the main course of rack of lamb was served.

'And what do you do, Martha?' Ted asked good-naturedly.

'I'm a homemaker.'

Martha noticed that old familiar reaction that usually occurred when a woman told the person sitting beside her that she was content to spend the most part of her day minding her kids and running a home.

'How nice.'

'I used to work with the County Education Board, in the remedial, special ed. department.' She was annoyed with herself for even bothering to try and explain. 'But with Mike's work we had to move to San Jose a few years back and what with settling in and getting the kids sorted we both felt it was easier for me to stay home and be with the family. We have three great kids.'

She could see the flicker of interest in Ted's eyes

dissipate and a mask of so-called interest slip down over his features.

'That's neat, real neat, Martha. Megan would love to be home with our daughter, but the demands of her business are such that we have a live-in girl. Well, Cora's not really a girl, she's about thirty-five and from Carlisle, Pennsylvania originally. Never married and devoted to our Caroline and runs the house as smooth as pie. I don't know what we'd do without her.'

'That's neat you found such a good person.'

'Nothing wrong with staying home minding kids,' interjected Dan Kendrick. 'My mother raised seven of us on a shoestring. She was some woman!'

Martha smiled at him. He was a nice man but she had no intention of the dinner conversation turning to the choices she had made. She toyed with the food on her plate; the tossed vegetables were cooked to perfection and were a perfect choice with the mint sauce and lamb that was being served. Mike was enjoying himself immensely and she thanked heaven they'd had the foresight not to drive as her husband drank another glass of red wine.

Gina Forrester stared down at her.

'Why, Martha dear, you are too modest! You are a very talented young woman with a God-given gift.'

Ted looked over at her curiously and even Natalie and Megan stopped their conversation.

Martha looked up across the table: all eyes were focused on her and she blazed with embarrassment.

'Martha is a healer. A very fine healer, by all accounts.'

'Oh my God, are you that woman that saved the little boy's life and got him back from the dead?'

'She is, she is!' insisted Gina Forrester.

Conversation had ceased and Martha could see the glance of wariness that crossed her husband's face.

'I just try to help people, that's all,' she said simply.

Bob Forrester beamed at her from the top of the table and she suddenly felt like a dancing bear who was expected to perform for its supper as the other guests stared at her expectantly. Did they want her to grab the crystal water jug and change it to wine before their very eyes?

It amazed her that people's opinion of her could change so radically at any mention of the healing. Some like the Stillmans were clearly sceptical, while others were both curious and fascinated. All through the rest of the meal as the array of tortes and berries and crème concoctions were savoured, the other dinner guests reached over to talk, some even tried to touch her. Unembarrassed, sitting beside her, Dan Kendrick suddenly rolled up his sleeve, showing her a hard fleshy swelling just under the skin on his elbow, which was giving him problems with playing sports.

'I've had X-rays and anti-inflammatories and steroids and God knows what, it's giving me hell but I guess I've just got to put up with it like Gus Stephens my ortho says!'

Martha stared at his muscled and freckled arm. Touching it automatically, she cupped her fingers around the elbow. Half joking and half serious, she laid her hands on the joint itself and could see his eyes widen as heat spread through it. The lump felt solid and deep, its tentacles weaving through the surrounding muscle and tissue. It felt bruised, something dirty that did not belong in the body of a strong and healthy man. The others watched them as she worked, trying to draw it out and away. Gina gave a little clap when she'd finished as Dan let down the shirt-sleeve, and re-buttoned his cuff. The lump was still there but Martha hoped that she had eased the pain a little.

Coffee and liqueurs were served in the drawing room, Martha enjoying the glass of Bailey's Irish liqueur that Bob insisted she have. Its creamy warmth spread through her. It had been a delicious meal and she could see the relief in Gina's face that it had been such a success. The caterers would most definitely be used again. The men stood around the fireplace cupping glasses of brandy and whisky and talking mostly sport and business, while the women pulled their chairs close to each other and chatted easily about their own concerns. The soft firelight made them all seem more relaxed and at ease with each other and Martha was prepared for the onslaught of questions about her new calling.

Natalie with her admission of irritable gut, Kaye whispering of the cystitis that had plagued her since she was about nineteen years old and Gina patting the couch beside her and asking her all sorts of questions about healing and how it worked. Martha admitted she hadn't a clue but that the power just seemed to come naturally to her.

Doe eyed, Megan Harris stared at her, telling her of the terrible migraines that stalked her.

'Have you seen someone about them?' enquired Martha rather naively.

'Of course I have,' retorted Megan. 'The two top neurologists in Boston, though little good they've done.'

'Slowing down and taking some time out sometimes helps with migraine,' Martha suggested, seeing immediately that this was not the answer Megan Harris wished to hear.

'Do a bit of your healing!' urged Natalie Leonard, who turned out to be one of Gina's friends who had only recently divorced. 'Go on and have a go with one of us! Poor Megan having to lie in a darkened room. Surely your healing could do something to help her?'

Martha was dismayed. She couldn't produce a cure out of thin air, if that's what they wanted.

'Couldn't you help her, Martha?' asked Gina softly.

'It doesn't always work like that,' she tried to explain. 'I can't tell what the outcome will be, as it's something from outside that works through me. I'm just the conductor of this energy or power that makes the healing happen.'

Gina seemed disappointed.

'Someone talking conductors and power over here!' interrupted Bob, taking in the look of despondency that had flitted across his wife's face. 'Kendrick's your man for that!'

Martha was relieved when Mike and the others pulled in the chairs and joined them. Dan, glass of whiskey in hand, regaled them with tales of his tough Chicago Catholic childhood and boyhood money-making schemes.

Driving home in the cab at about 1.30 a.m. Martha listened to Mike's boasting about the discussions he'd enjoyed with Kendrick and his boss. She stared out the window, already regretting the alcohol that had loosened her own inhibitions and made her behave like some side-show freak. Mike had surprised her with his view that the only reason they had been invited to the head of the Institute's dinner party was in order that Gina Forrester and her cronies could meet Martha.

'Mike! Don't say such things,' she retorted, not having the heart to admit she had already come to that conclusion herself.

Chapter Thirteen

Gina Forrester had called about four days later. Martha was in the middle of cooking a huge dish of bolognese sauce, half of which she intended freezing, when Patrick passed her the phone.

Wiping her hands on the apron, she mentally thanked heaven that she had already sent a 'thank you' card for the lovely evening.

'Hi, Martha, it's Gina, Gina Forrester, Bob's wife.'

'Oh, hi, Gina, thanks so much for the wonderful dinner last week. Mike and I had a really great time.'

'Oh, I'm glad you enjoyed it. Bob and I love having company. This big old house of ours it's just made for parties!'

'You have some lovely friends,' added Martha.

'Actually, Martha, that's part of the reason I'm phoning you. I hope I didn't embarrass you too much. I shouldn't have put you in a spot like that, with everyone trying to get you to lay your hands on them. I couldn't help myself, it just slipped out about you being a healer, and well you know what people are like! I hope that you're not too vexed with me.'

'It's all right, Gina, don't worry about it.'

She could sense Gina's reluctance to finish their conversation and turned off the pan on the stove, to give the other woman her full attention.

'Did you like the cushion?' she enquired gently.

'Why, that was one of the most thoughtful gifts I've received in a long time. You know, I have a thing for roses. My mother used to grow them. The colours that we had in our garden when we were young, every variety of rose – hybrid, tea, rambling, every kind, and I can still remember the scent of them.'

'I'm glad you like it. One of my friends has an embroidery store up near the station and it's a real treasure trove for finding special things.'

'Well, thank you for choosing it for me.'

She could sense the hesitation in Gina's voice.

'Martha, I don't suppose you'd be free to meet up for lunch or to come over to the house some day later this week? There's something I'd like to discuss with you.' There it was, what she'd been expecting: the true reason for the call.

She waited, but realized that Gina Forrester was not about to divulge the nature of her problems over the phone.

'Yeah, that would be great, Gina. I'll come over to you. What day would suit?'

'What about Thursday?'

'Morning?'

'Are you free then?'

'Yes, and I'll be over to you about eleven.'

'See you then, Martha, and thanks a lot, I sure do appreciate it.'

Martha cradled the receiver in her hand long after Gina had rung off. Was she stupid to let herself get involved with Bob Forrester's wife? She wasn't much of a one for secrets but hiding the fact that she was meeting his boss's wife was bound to cause bad feeling between them, something she sure didn't want to experience any more of.

She pulled on a pale mauve button-thru cardigan with mid-length sleeves and a pair of clean cream pedal-pushers, applying a light coating of mascara to her sun-bleached eyelashes and a slick of raspberry-coloured lipstick, before setting off to meet Gina Forrester. Listening to her favourite Van Morrison CD, she drove to Newton, passing Boston College and the surrounding leafy suburbs. She pressed the button on the security panel on the gate, realizing just what a magnificent home Rockhall truly was as she swung into the driveway and parked in front of a rather ancient cherry tree.

Gina came out to greet her, dressed in tailored pale cream trousers and a co-ordinating shirt. Martha was glad that she had made a bit of effort about her own appearance. They passed quickly through the hall and Gina led her into the kitchen, which was fitted with a vast array of cabinets and an enormous hutch in a hand-painted off-white beech wood. A state of the art cooker stood in one section and a cosy wood-burning stove in another. Expensive glass and china vied with old-fashioned ceramic ducks and hens.

'This is my favourite room in the house,' admitted Gina, gesturing for Martha to sit at the table as she set about making a pot of coffee. 'Martha, I'm sorry for dragging you all the way out here, I know how busy you must be with three kids, but I – truth to tell I don't know where to start.'

Martha smiled lightly, knowing it was important for Gina herself to be able to voice what was troubling her.

'I know you are going to think that it's really sad, someone like me having the nerve to ask you what I'm going to ask, but I promise I won't be annoyed or put out if you just say no, honest I won't.'

'Gina, how can I say no, when I don't know what you want me to do!'

Colour flooded Gina's face.

'I want to have a baby. There, I said it!'

Martha couldn't hide her surprise.

'A baby!'

'Yes, Martha. I know I might not look it but I was forty-four last June. Bob and I have been married nine years. He has two boys by his first wife. They're all grown up now, the eldest has a little girl called Roma, she's a real sweetheart. Bob and I are nuts about that child.'

'It's nice to have grandchildren . . . satisfying.'

'That's just it, Martha. Seeing Roma makes me want to have a child of our own. Bob says it doesn't matter, but it does. The boys only see their father a few times a year, and I know that breaks his heart and little Roma is being raised in London. Robbie Junior has a big job over there with Merrill Lynch.'

'Have you tried?'

'Oh God we've tried, believe me we've tried. You name it and either Bob or I have done it: fertility clinics, insemination, test tube, hormone treatment, nothing works! It's been humiliating for both of us. And in the end it made no difference. I'm just some barren woman that fills her days doing things that are at the end of the day totally unimportant.'

'Gina, don't say such things. Look at all the good you do helping people with your fund-raising, and charity benefits. Mike's always telling me what a Trojan worker you are for so many causes.'

'Oh, that's just money, and Bob is such a generous man that everybody wants his wife on their committees.'

Martha heard the bitterness in her admission, and was doubtful about what to say. 'What about adoption?' she suggested, thinking of the wonderful home and life they could provide for some child.

'No,' insisted Gina firmly. 'We want a child of our own.'

Martha was shocked. She couldn't just produce a child for the Forresters no matter how much they wanted one.

'Martha, do you think you *could* possibly help? I'll understand if you say no and think I'm just a vain, self-centred woman looking to satisfy some whim, but believe me, having a child of our own is the most important thing in both our lives at the moment. It's all either of us wants.'

Martha was uncomfortable and embarrassed by the fact that she had been made privy to such intimate details.

'Will you try to help me, do one of your healing sessions on me?' Gina asked gently.

'I'm not sure if I can be of any help, honest I'm not. My healing ability might not work for something like this, I . . .'

'Please, Martha.'

'Are you going to tell Bob?'

'Maybe later, but for the moment no, I don't want to get his hopes up.'

Martha considered. It was ludicrous to believe that laying her hands on Gina could accomplish what doctors and fertility clinics and drugs had failed to do but she could see the hunger and need for a child of her own in the other woman's eyes. She herself had always assumed her own fertility and remembered the joy and naturalness of discovering after about only three months of marriage that she was pregnant. Mike had swooped her up in his arms and kissed and hugged her as if she had achieved some complicated and amazing feat.

'I can't promise anything,' she admitted, 'but . . .'

'Please, Martha, it would mean so much to me, to both of us. Dan told me what you did last week for his arm. I know this is something totally different and that I shouldn't expect or hope for anything but surely it can't do any harm.'

Gina Forrester was if anything persuasive and to tell the truth Martha could only imagine how hard it must be for a woman not to have children. Money and privilege were nothing in comparison to motherhood.

'Of course I'll try, Gina, though I'm not sure that I can really do anything more than your doctors – but if it's what you want . . .'

'Oh, thank you, Martha. Thank you!'

Gina's eyes were shining, triumphant as she embraced Martha.

'Where do you do it?' she asked. 'Is it like a massage, do you want me to lie down on the bed or couch or something like that? I'll show you upstairs to my room.'

'It's all right, Gina, that won't be necessary. All I need is for you to maybe lie down somewhere.

What about the couch over there in the sunroom?'

A magnificent rattan recliner couch, covered in luxurious pale mauve and cream cushions lay between an enormous terracotta pot and a co-ordinating low table. Martha followed Gina over and sat down near her, trying to talk to her and discover what her expectations of the healing truly were.

'Martha, all I want is a baby, a child of our own!'

Martha drew back, realizing that this middle-aged woman was literally hoping for some sort of miraculous conception, for Martha to wave her arms around, say a few words of hocus-pocus and create a child, pure bloody magic! Did she actually really believe that Martha could do that! She almost giggled aloud.

'Gina, I can't give you a child, make you pregnant, if that's what you are after!'

'No, Martha, I didn't expect . . .' she protested.

'It's better I'm honest with you,' Martha said. 'But I will try to discover the reasons why you haven't yet conceived, try to ease them if that is at all possible. Now show me the area where you've had your medical problems and hopefully I'll pick up something from there.'

'Do you think I'm just far too old and meno-pausal?'

'Ssshh now! My hands might feel kind of warm when I touch you.'

Gina lay down, with a look of concentration on

her face, as the palms of Martha's hands touched the firm taut skin and stomach muscles that were tanned a perfect honey gold. On the outside her body looked young and perfect but Martha felt the unease almost at once. On one side there was so little sense of female energy. It was as if everything had stopped there and fresh tissue had hardened and died away.

'I had an ovarian cyst when I was about seventeen,' Gina confided, 'and when it burst the pain was so bad I'd thought I'd die but my mother drove me to the hospital and demanded they got me the best doctor in town, an old guy called Sheldon. He told me I might have problems in the future but I guess when you're young you don't like to think about those things and manage to push them to the back of your mind, hoping they're so far back that eventually the problem will have disappeared.'

'Problems tend not to go away.'

'Tell me about it. We've spent a fortune, and I mean a fortune trying to . . .' Gina's voice wavered, her eyes filling up.

'Hush, Gina, just let me work,' advised Martha, stretching her hands into circles and moving them around and around and around, circles of warm pulsing energy, flooding the area. She watched as Gina closed her eyes, her lips moving soundlessly.

Martha moved her hands to the other side, feeling a normal rhythmic pulse, and smoothed her fingers along the other woman's ribs and chest. There was tightness around her throat, a suppression of thoughts and anxiety, something which was pretty unexpected in someone so articulate and outgoing. She tried to ease it, to draw out that pain. She smoothed Gina's forehead and, concentrating on her head, tried to create balance, feeling Gina's energy almost bounce off her own.

'That's it!' she whispered softly.

'That's it?'

'Yes.'

Gina seemed puzzled.

'Didn't you feel anything?' Martha asked.

'I could feel the warmth of your hands, and this strange pulling inside me as if things were unravelling and unwinding, like you were untying knots and tangles and stretching me all at the same time.'

Martha smiled. It was a good description of what she had experienced during the healing too. 'Did you pray?' she asked.

'When I closed my eyes I could feel that warmth, and for some reason my mother came into my thoughts and I asked her to help me,' Gina said.

'Do you pray to her often?'

Gina looked embarrassed.

'I'm not a religious woman, Martha, I don't hold with churchgoing and bible thumping, but my mother was a saint, a truly good person. She never said a bad word or hurt anyone during her

144

lifetime. That woman lived the Bible every day of her life.'

Martha helped Gina sit up.

'Take it easy for the rest of the day. People often feel sort of tired and sleepy after a healing. It's just that your body needs to rest.'

'I was going to have a game of tennis but I guess I'll phone and cancel it.'

'That'd be wise.'

'Is that it?'

Martha shrugged. 'I'm afraid so, Gina, that's all it is.' She could see a look of disappointment flash across the other woman's features.

'Would you like to stay for lunch? I could fix us up a nice chicken salad or a little pasta.'

'Thanks but no, I really have to go. I need to get to the market and get some food before my lot get in from school. Patrick's eating me out of house and home at the moment. He's on some sort of high protein diet and I promised I'd try out this braised beef and garlic recipe for dinner.'

'I'd say you are a great mom, Martha, your kids are very lucky.'

Gina stood up and they began to walk back out to the hallway.

'You have such a beautiful home, Gina,' Martha said.

'A home!' She took a sharp intake of breath. 'Where you and your children live, Martha, that is a home. I live in a beautiful, beautiful house, but it's not a home, not really.'

There was such a poignancy in Gina Forrester's words that Martha was tempted to abandon her plans and turn on her heel and march back into that gleaming perfect kitchen and sit herself right down at the table, eat the chicken salad and just talk to the woman, but one look at her tilted face and fixed smile was enough to determine Martha to admire her pride.

Chapter Fourteen

As the early morning sun slanted in the windows, Martha stretched lazily out across Mike's side of the bed, watching her husband perform his daily routine of showering, shaving and dressing. Martha told him of her plans to visit Cass Armstrong again.

'Have you actually gone mad!' he remonstrated with her, almost nicking himself with the razor blade. 'Getting involved with such a seriously ill child is plain crazy.'

'But I promised her, and I want to keep my promise.'

'You're getting yourself deeply involved with a child and her parents, and God knows what they'll expect of you.'

'If you just saw her, Mike, you'd understand. She's sick and scared and her mother's just stressed out with it all. Maybe I can really do something to help her,' she said softly, not wanting the kids to hear them yelling at each other so early in the morning.

'Jesus, Martha! I worry about you! You are actually beginning to believe the things they're writing and saying about you.'

Martha stared at him in disbelief, realizing that he had absolutely no faith in her abilities.

'That's not fair!'

'Of course it's fair!' he argued. 'You're my wife and the mother of my children, not some bloody religious do-gooder saint. You have our kids to look after, isn't that enough for you without wanting to become some kind of Mother Teresa ministering to the sick?'

'Don't you believe that I can heal?'

He turned away from her, pretending to put on his shoes and search for his jacket.

'Mike!' she demanded.

'Listen, Mar, I don't know. Call me a doubting Thomas, whatever, like that guy in the Bible. For me the jury is still out. I'm a simple guy and I ain't sure of what's going on. Why God would choose my wife over some holy nun or something beats me! I don't understand it and I'm not going to bullshit and lie to you about it.'

Martha drew in a deep breath. If there was one thing sure and certain about Mike McGill it was his honesty. It was a part of his attraction and she supposed one of his most valued traits, though at times like this it hurt like hell to be on the receiving end. 'Thanks a bunch for your support,' she replied, raising herself up on the pillows. 'I don't understand anything you do in CPI, and yet it's never been a problem for me. I listen to you talk on and on about work and the office and systems and chips and protocols, and support you as much as I can. Yet when I ask you for a little bit of support it's just not there.'

He hesitated for a second.

'I'm not getting into an argument with you, Martha, I'm already running late and this is not the time or the place. I've given you my opinion,' he added as he walked out the door. Martha almost howled with frustration as she jumped into the shower, relieved that she had not told him about her meeting with Gina.

Evie seemed equally cautious about the idea of the visit. For once Martha's best friend was somewhat in agreement with her husband.

'Maybe you might be getting yourself in too deep. I know your intentions are good, but that little girl has been sick most of her life. You might get too emotionally involved,' Evie told her.

Martha gave it some consideration but in the end ignored both of them. Deciding to follow her own instincts, she drove up Longwood Avenue towards Boston's landmark Children's Hospital later that day.

Visiting Cass Armstrong again, she was almost relieved that her mother Beth wasn't there. The child was dozing, eyes closed, when Martha peeped in the door of her hospital room. Perhaps she *was* interfering and getting far more involved than she should, but one look at the ten-year-old's unnatural pallor and the gurgle of the oxygen mask hooked up beside her bed was more than enough for Martha to sense the child's distinct need for help. Cass's eyes fluttered and flicked open, aware of the arrival of a visitor.

'I can go if you're too tired, Cass. I was just popping in to say hi.'

Cass shook her head, tossing the mask from side to side and gesturing for her to pull up a chair and sit down close by the bed. Martha did.

'How you doing?' she asked.

Cass shrugged her shoulders.

'You are obviously not feeling any better.'

The young girl shook her head. Martha could tell she was forcing herself not to cry. She had that same expression on her face that Alice often got when she was trying to be brave about something and not let Patrick and Mary Rose know how upset she really was. Without thinking, Martha took hold of her hand and squeezed it. The two of them were silent.

Still and quiet, Martha could sense the sheer misery and hopelessness that the young girl felt. The loneliness of the hospital room and the sheer immensity of her illness were stifling her.

Cass lifted up the mask a second. 'I had to go on this two nights back. Dr Hopkins says I need it until they get me a heart,' she told Martha.

'You must be anxious waiting like this,' suggested Martha gently.

Cass nodded, her deep brown eyes serious.

'I hate it! I don't want some other kid to die just so that I can have their heart. Honest I don't!' she protested. 'I don't want their stupid heart. Even if I have the operation, it mightn't work. I might reject it. All kinds of things could happen.'

'Cass, someone else's dying has absolutely nothing to do with you, get that straight! You needing the transplant isn't going to make something bad happen to someone else. Believe me.'

'That's what Mom and Dr Hopkins say,' she admitted.

Wordlessly Martha slipped the mask back over the girl's face. 'I'll just sit with you awhile, Cass, if that's all right.'

They sat quietly, Martha watching the light rhythm of Cass's breath and heartbeat, sensing how truly fragile the girl really was and how much strength was needed for her to be fit for surgery. Anything she could do to help she would do gladly. She couldn't imagine how distraught she would be if one of her own children had suffered this fate. Cass was watching her too, equally curious.

'My mom says that you can heal people, that you got a gift of healing and making people better. Is that really true?' Her voice was filled with doubt and disbelief, which Martha had no intention of destroying with some inane promise.

'Some people say so. But to tell the truth, Cass, I just don't know. I'd like to help people if I can, but that doesn't always mean I can make them better.'

'Do you think that I'm going to get better?'

'I'm sure Dr Hopkins and all the doctors and nurses here are doing their best to help, Cass. It's probably just a matter of waiting and . . .'

'I've been waiting it seems most of my life,' whispered Cass. 'I'm fed up of waiting and being in hospital.'

'I know it can't be much fun stuck here instead of back home with your friends and family.'

'My dad doesn't like hospitals. He says they make him feel sick. One time he fainted when he came to visit me after one of my operations. He tried to pretend he slipped on the floor but I knew that he'd fainted. Mom doesn't mind, she says she's used to them, like me.'

Martha tried to disguise her dismay at what the Armstrong family must have endured over a number of years; she doubted herself and Mike would have been so strong. Cass wriggled around in the bed. She looked uncomfortable and out of place in the pristine starkness of the hospital room. Despite the attempts to disguise it with balloons and posters and get-well cards, she was still a small scared little girl in a place she did not want to be.

'Would you like me to read to you?'

'Yep.'

A pile of glossy pre-teen magazines lay strewn on the bottom of the bed, covered with pictures of the latest film and pop idols. Concerts, films, discos! Martha wondered if Cass would ever enjoy the things that teenage girls cherished.

Under the pile, Martha discovered a copy of Frank L. Baum's *Wizard of Oz*. She remembered reading and re-reading it for Patrick and Mary Rose and Alice. Her own children had been entranced by the story of Dorothy and her quest to find the Great Wizard. Removing the bookmark, she took up where Cass had obviously left off and the child's eyes relaxed as she listened to the familiar words. Right up close together, Martha kept reading as Cass leaned towards her. Laying her hands along the child's shoulder and arms Martha was shocked by the overwhelmingly intense emotions Cass was feeling. She could feel the immediate weakness and irregularity of her heart but could also feel the child's bewilderment and sadness. Cass needed to cut loose from all that and have some kind of a normal kid's life, even if it wasn't going to be for ever.

'What would you truly like, Cass, if I could click my heels and give you a wish?'

'I'd like a new heart so I could go back home, to Mom and Dad and Billy and Jay and my dog Samson,' she murmured softly, turning over on her side, her face pressed against the pillow.

Martha, not trusting herself to speak, just kept on reading.

*   *   *

Beth Armstrong had phoned her at home later that night, breathless and excited.

'Martha, thank you so much for coming by the hospital to visit Cass today. I'm sure it helped. I'm just sure it did.'

Martha bit her lip.

'I went out to get some fresh air and pick up some things for Cass in the store so I'm really sorry that we missed each other, but I do appreciate you seeing her.'

'I'd promised.'

'Anyways I know I shouldn't say it but Dr Hopkins is very hopeful of getting an organ soon. Cass is top of the list. Top of the list, that's what they keep saying.'

Martha could hear the fear and hope in Beth's voice, the expectation that her only daughter would be returned to normal life again.

'That's great, Beth. Really great!'

'Why, Martha, she could be having her operation any day now, tomorrow even. That soon, imagine!'

Beth was doing her best to appear upbeat and positive and ignore the risks of such an operation, and Martha hadn't the heart to worry her.

Getting off the phone about five minutes later Martha said a silent prayer for the child and her mother.

Chapter Fifteen

Dan Kendrick took a practice swing with his new titanium putter, the plastic ball rolling perfectly across his office floor and towards the bright yellow hole. Perfect! He tried it again, this time stepping back further. His elbow felt good; the stiffness and throbbing tight pain he'd experienced before had almost disappeared. He moved his arm backwards and forwards gingerly, noticing that the swelling had certainly gone down. Sitting in his high-backed black leather chair he punched in the number of the private clinic he attended. The secretary put his call through to Dr Phil Turner.

'I tell you, Phil, my arm and elbow it's way better!' he insisted. 'Even the size of the swelling has gone down.'

'That's because you're resting it!' was the reply.

'Look, Phil, you know how important playing in the Valley tournament is to me. Surely if the swelling has gone down and the joint is a bit looser I might get out.'

'Dan, both your specialist and I have recommended you to rest it and that's the advice I still stand by.'

Dan Kendrick could barely disguise his annoyance.

'I'm telling you it's improved.'

Phil Turner was used to dealing with people like Kendrick, with more money than sense, who bent the rules, paid for good advice and more often than not refused to follow it, but he knew he had to be polite and seem to give the correct answer.

'Perhaps you should come by the office and get it X-rayed and have somebody here check it over,' he suggested.

'I have a business breakfast at eight and will swing by here after but I should be with you by ten thirty.'

'That's fine by me! So I'll see you myself then.'

The girl with the Aussie accent and the friendly attitude took the X-rays and sent him in to Phil straight away. The physician examined his arm, moving it gently; the Aussie talked to him on the phone a few minutes later.

'Well, there definitely has been a slight improvement, Dan, but I wouldn't be happy to let you take on any exercise till Gus himself sees it and gives the go-ahead.'

'Gus is in Hawaii, for Christ sakes!'

'He gets back in a few days and you're already scheduled for a biopsy of the lump, but my secretary will set up an appointment with him for the minute he gets back. That's all I can do.'

Disgruntled, Dan Kendrick left the expensive San Jose medical centre and drove back to Powerhouse's corporate headquarters, the flagship building with its curving glass and stone, shimmering in the bright sunlight.

Phil Turner looked at the X-rays again. There most definitely had been an improvement and a noticeable decline in the size of the suspicious tissue which had suggested some form of tumour. He'd speak to Gus the minute he got back from Maui: perhaps there had been a mistake in the original X-ray and the scheduled biopsy surgery might not now be necessary.

The Silicon Valley Golf Classic was one of the most important social-cum-business events in a very busy calendar: the head honchos from every rival technology and computer company in the state played golf at Pebble Beach – a group of good old buddies – with a dinner and raffle afterwards. Powerhouse had already booked five places at $400 a head for the golf alone, and Ken Franklin, his head of electronics, had been told that he was playing instead of his boss. Dan Kendrick picked up the phone, checking Franklin's number. He and his lovely wife were more than welcome to join them at the $1,000 meal in the clubhouse afterwards but Ken's golfing ability was no longer needed now.

Under a clear blue Californian sky, in perfect light, the Nasdaq's favourite sons gathered along the lawns and courtyard of the Pebble Beach golf club. The greens were immaculate, the flags barely stirring in the slight breeze, and the scent of honeysuckle and jasmine filled the air as Dan Kendrick checked in. His caddy, Will, was standing over by the pergola checking his bag.

'Hey, Dan! Heard you weren't playing – that you were off injured,' said Arnold David of Delan Digital.

'Rumours of my demise have been much exaggerated,' quipped Dan, pulling his lucky plaid baseball cap over his balding head.

The PAs and PR people ran backwards and forwards offering drinks, checking itineraries, making sure sponsorships of prizes were clearly visible. Dan Kendrick ignored them and trusted that Brigid Lamanns, his own Girl Friday, was attending to everything and that all he and the Powerhouse boys had to do was play golf.

Two over on the first, par on the second, disaster on the third.

Pebble Beach might be the most beautiful baby on the West Coast but she sure was no pushover golf-wise, Dan Kendrick thought as he watched his ball land neatly on the fairway. His team-mates were Ritchie Stevens, his CEO, a rock solid player, nothing fancy or foolish; Lewis Jansen his thirty-four-year-old knowall head of sales and marketing; and his new research and development designer Gary Wiseman. It was the younger two with their showing off that concerned him. Gary Wiseman had come first in his year in Stanford and had done five years with NASA and Dan and Arnold David had gone to a chequebook duel over him. Brigid's inspired choice of a gift of a Harley 1500T was a clincher, as the guy had a thing about motorbikes and worried about getting caught in some kind of nerd trap. Looking at him with his wispy fair hair down to his shoulders and all-black golf attire, Dan couldn't help but worry that he'd bought himself a fucking freak. The fact that his father was a golf pro down in San Diego had only been discovered long afterwards; and the fact that Gary Wiseman's other obsessive interest beside computers and bikes was golf, and that he played off four. Certainly a company asset!

Dan watched him drive: Gary's wiry frame almost corkscrewed itself around as the ball climbed higher and higher into the air, the beauty landing right on the green.

His own arm was holding out well, with only the slightest jarring sensation as he drove. Whatever that woman healer Martha had done after dinner, in Gina and Bob Forrester's a few weeks back, it had certainly done the trick.

Three to get on the green and a birdie putt! He certainly couldn't complain.

Will passed him a bottle of spring water, and drinking it he took time to look around and appreciate his surroundings. The course itself was a rich man's dream, an oasis in the desert of work and money and deals and concepts – green hills and trees and water features, bordering on the rolling Pacific Ocean. Paradise, a far cry from the working-class neighbourhood in Chicago where he grew up. His father had laboured in the auto shop on the corner of South Street till the cancer got him, leaving Dan's mother Lorretta to raise all seven of them on a minuscule pension and her part-time job as a classroom assistant. Times nearly as tough as that guy McCourt wrote about in that sad book of his! Danny Kendrick was only a know-nothing fat boy then, who could strip a car engine faster than anyone and, what's more, put it back together in double quick time, and who could run sets of multiple numbers in his head and keep a track of them all. Danny Kendrick who could put food on the table and still have a few dollars tucked away for himself. Paradise, my arse!

Ritchie was keeping score and felt they were playing well, but Dan warned them not to become complacent so near to home. Lewis Jansen, the suave Santa Cruz boy, ran his eye over the score-card and flexing his shoulder muscles promised a good finale. Dan was nervous again about the young bloods as they drove onto the fifteenth. Ritchie and he watched in amazement as the other two proceeded to burn up the course, Lewis's dark eyes flashing as he scored an eagle. Their youth and bold confidence amazed their elders. Dan was pleased to hit a par and a one under on the eighteenth.

Refreshments were served in a flower-bedecked pergola. Dan put his arm around his team, commending them all on a game well played, as the rest of the teams came in. Iced beers, chilled champagne and cool sodas were served by the club's waiters as the men congratulated themselves on the day's outing. Tom Ryland of New World was checking the scores and putting them up on the board.

'Hey, Dan, look at that!' called Lewis. 'We're well up there, and there's only two teams left.'

'Guys!' yelled Wiseman. 'We won!'

Dan put down his glass of Napa's best and walked over to check with Tom. It had been more than five years since Powerhouse had won, and the last two years they'd missed making it into the final three.

Jeez, the freak was right, there it was up in black and white. 'Winning Team: Powerhouse. Captain: Daniel Kendrick'!

He jumped so high with delight he almost knocked Wiseman over. As Tom and David, Bruce Carling and Bill Fortune, all came over to shake his hand, Dan basked in the glory of it all and introduced the rest of the team. Wiseman like a little kid was on a cell phone to his father with the news.

Out of nowhere Brigid suddenly appeared with the trademark 'Powerhouse' baseball caps. Dan gave her his sweat-soaked plaid one to mind with her life as he pulled on the other, just as the press journalists appeared across the courtyard.

'Mr Kendrick! Mr Kendrick! How does it feel to be a winner?'

'How does it feel to beat all your competitors for the industry prize?'

He smiled magnanimously. 'We all have our good days.'

'And what is the secret of your team's success?' asked the business journalist from *Corporate Magazine*.

'We have a good team. We all work well together both on the field and in the office, and young Wiseman here was an unexpected find, you might say.' He laughed, catching Arnold David's eye.

'We heard that you weren't meant to play today, that your doctors had advised against it,' joked Nick Mandleberg. 'Though you look fine to me.'

'I had a problem with my arm and elbow there a few weeks back. The doctors and experts told me I was out of golf for a while but I was lucky when I was visiting Boston to meet by chance a wonderful healer called Martha McGill with a rare gift of healing and she put me right, got me back in the swing as they say.'

'So you made a miraculous recovery?'

'I suppose you could say that!'

Brigid nodded at him as Tom Ryland announced the presentation of the prizes. Dan Kendrick donated the $10,000 worth of high tech computer equipment they'd won to the local charity, St Vincent's, which aided needy families and ran back to work and necessary skills courses for those who were less fortunate. His peers cheered loudly as he ordered champagne for everyone.

Lara Chadwick scanned the San Francisco paper. There it was in print – another reference to the McGill woman. It had to be her! She'd phone Nick Mandleberg, the journalist who'd covered the golf tournament, determined to ask him more about it.

Mike McGill groaned, reading the latest edition of *Corporate Magazine*. There was a full-length interview with Daniel Kendrick, his photo on the front of the magazine beaming in a pale blue Lacoste shirt after winning the Silicon Valley's annual industry golf prize. Martha's name and where she came from were mentioned about half-way through the piece.

Martha ran to get the door: she could see the black delivery van parked outside.

'M'am, please sign for this,' requested the driver.

Martha obliged. Lifting the heavy cardboard box inside, she grabbed the kitchen scissors to open it, discovering a half-dozen bottles of the best champagne wrapped in protective sheets of bubble plastic. She opened the accompanying card, wondering who it could possibly be from, smiling to herself as she read:

Martha – I couldn't help but notice that you have a taste for Napa's best! Hope you enjoy the champagne and thank you a hundred times over for saving my golf swing with your wondrous healing gift. Every good wish – Daniel Kendrick.

Chapter Sixteen

This time reports of her healing did make the front page, the local newspapers dubbing her 'The Miracle Woman'. Martha reeled with absolute fury as Lara Chadwick's article highlighted her meeting with Dan Kendrick and implied that he had given her some vast payment in return for a healing; it also mentioned a few of the people who had visited her home and whom she had successfully worked on.

'What am I going to do?' she wailed to Mike. 'Why can't she leave me alone! The people who come to me deserve their privacy: they've had enough bad things happen to them without seeing their names and faces plastered over the newspaper.'

'I agree with you, honey, but I guess she's just a journalist looking for a story or an angle.'

Two more newspapers phoned requesting interviews or a comment. While at first reluctant, Martha agreed with Mike that she would take their numbers and decide later about phoning them back.

Bobbie Meyer from Channel WBZ4 phoned again and asked her to do a spot on her weekend morning radio show, *Faith and Hope*.

'I promise it won't be too daunting,' encouraged the highly respected journalist. 'Just you and I having a little talk on a Sunday morning. You will have ample time to explain about your healing, clarify any misconceptions and I guarantee there will be total confidentiality with regard to those you have treated.'

After much discussion with Mike and the kids, she decided to brave the airways and try and clear up the rumours. Bobbie Meyers welcomed her to one of the East Coast's favourite radio stations, and Martha was shaking like a leaf the minute she stepped into the studio. Her mouth dried up with nerves as Bobbie's researcher kindly offered to fetch her a glass of water.

She had absolutely no memory of the interview afterwards, only that Evie had said she was a natural. Reading between the lines she guessed she had said far too much. The switchboard had been deluged with people phoning wanting to talk to her and looking for help with various complaints and illnesses. Martha tried to talk rationally and calmly to them, suggesting if possible they visit their local MD or nurse practitioner.

'I think we'll have to get you back for a phone-in,' smiled Bobbie, 'as there's been such a huge response.'

Evie and Kim had both called over to congratulate her, and she was grateful for the support of friends who just accepted her for who she was and weren't being swept along in this torrent of change around her.

'How is Mike taking it?' Kim asked.

'So-so. Mike is sceptical.'

'Your husband is a born sceptic, Martha, he questions everything and believes nothing,' jeered Evie. 'I suppose it's his science training.'

'I'm worried about the kids, though. Patrick isn't saying much, so God knows what he's thinking. Alice is too young to really understand and Mary Rose is mad as hell that I'm not able to give her my undivided attention. She's like Mike – she hates all that strangers at the door stuff.'

'Poor you,' smiled Kim.

'Hopefully this will all die down and then I'll get back to normal.'

'Normal,' sighed Evie ruefully. 'I don't think you realize the impact your healing is having. The chances of things returning to normal are very slim.'

'Don't say that,' Martha begged. 'Just don't say that!'

Her sister-in-law Annie arrived just before they left, a whole pile of books under her arm.

'I think you should read some of these,' she suggested, dumping them on the coffee table.

Surveying them, Martha asked, 'Annie, what did you do? Rob a library?'

'Oh no. Some are my own or I borrowed them. I think they'll help explain to you something of what you are doing, Martha. Reading about auras, and the chakras, and balancing out the mind and the body, is all so interesting.'

Annie was one of the most generous-spirited people she knew. Thanking her, Martha wondered when she was ever going to get the time to read even a quarter of the books.

Two days later she took her usual drive up to the Highlands Animal Shelter. Donna pulled in just ahead of her and Martha could hear the dogs yelping madly at the sound of their voices as they opened the entrance door. Passing by the noticeboard to see what jobs she'd been put down to do, Martha couldn't find her name anywhere.

'Got a Persian in yesterday evening that is seriously matted, take two pairs of hands to sort her out, and try to groom her,' mentioned Donna.

'Hey, my name's not up there.' Martha was puzzled.

'Must be! Look, there's me and you must be somewhere down . . .'

Both women looked up and down the list but there was absolutely no sign of Martha's name up on the monthly roster of phone, walk, cleaning out, etc. duties.

'Janet must have made a cock-up doing it,' joked Donna.

'I'd better go sort it out,' said Martha. 'I'll just pop into the office and I'll come back and give you a hand then, OK?'

'Sure.'

Janet Rimaldi put down what she was doing the minute Martha entered the small cluttered office with its bags of cereal mixer and bulging file cabinets.

'Janet, I think there's been some mistake . . .'

'Sit down please, Martha,' gestured the fifty-year-old with her greying perm and plain face devoid of any trace of makeup.

'My name's not on the list!'

'I know, I'm sorry.'

'What?'

'I couldn't put you down on the monthly roster, Martha. In the last few weeks there has been a constant stream of calls from people wanting to talk to you, looking for the healer woman. The staff and I are wasting a huge amount of time just answering them.'

'Listen, Janet, I don't have to do phones, I won't go on them at all, if that's what you want.'

'Martha, I don't think you understand. These last few days, so many are phoning that our main helpline is almost constantly jammed. That means we can't receive calls about animals that might need urgent rescuing or answer queries from anxious owners. The phone is our lifeline. You know that.'

'I'm sorry if I've caused any of this, but maybe I could just walk the dogs and . . .'

'Martha, you volunteering here is just not going to work any more. I'm sorry but I have no option but to take you off the volunteer roster for the moment. Honestly, I'm really sorry. When this hullabaloo dies down you are more than welcome to return, but for the moment I have to put the welfare of the animals first.'

Stunned, Martha went back outside. Donna had taken the Persian out of the wired cage and stood her on the table and was very gently trying to pull a wide-toothed comb through the mass of tangled pale grey fur.

'Hey, come on!'

'I've got to go home,' said Martha, lifting her jacket. 'I'm off the roster and the volunteer schedule, so I can't stay.'

'God, I'm sorry. But why?'

Upset, Martha explained the reason.

'Listen, we'll keep in touch,' said Donna.

'Promise?'

'Yeah, promise.'

'And you'll keep an eye on Dollar for me.'

'For sure.'

Driving back up along the highway she realized there was absolutely no point in being bitter or angry. Now her life was moving in a different direction, she must open her mind and heart to healing. Once she got home she would sit down and study some of those books. Annie had lent her and then everything else she could on the subject of healing, for it was high time she understood more about this gift she was supposed to have.

Chapter Seventeen

Mid-morning, Martha collected her mother from the Belmont Retirement Home. Frances Kelly wrapped a warm red scarf around her shoulders and neck, as already there was a slight chill in the air temperature. The trees on the entrance avenue were ablaze with fall colours, a grey squirrel zigzagging crazily in his hunt for provisions as the sprightly seventy-two-year-old locked the door of her apartment and walked out to the car.

Once a month Martha drove her mother to the small cemetery out beyond Westwood where her father was buried; the two of them would pay respects to the late Joseph Kelly and go for lunch afterwards. Martha valued that special mother–daughter relationship and knew that her mother still played an important role in her life. She couldn't understand why her mother always insisted on eating at one of the small restaurants nearby instead of letting Martha take her further afield to try out somewhere new and different.

'I'm a creature of habit, Martha, you know that, and I like to go and say hello to my poor Joe whenever I get the chance.'

Martha smiled. Somehow or other over the past twenty years her mother had managed to almost canonize her late father, bestowing a load of saintly qualities on him that he sure had never possessed during his lifetime. Her father had been big and loud and jocose to those who had frequented 'Kelly's Saloon', as he jokingly called the bar he and his partner had owned in south Boston. The anger and temper and frustration he'd felt at working nights and running a barely profitable bar had been saved for behind the closed doors of 151 Hillside where they'd grown up. His investments in real estate, which included the then due to be demolished bar, and a small family construction business had at one stage almost bankrupted them but prudent management had managed to keep the Kelly ship afloat. Martha still remembered the long hours her father endured, out on construction sites in all weathers during the day and working three or four nights a week fixing up the derelict bar, and then running it.

As a child she pictured him asleep in the big double featherbed with the woollen blankets pulled up around him, as she and her brothers got dressed and got ready for school. He was up and shouting at their mother, looking for his work clothes by the time they left. Cantankerous and bossy, that's how she mostly remembered him.

'Joe was a good man, rare enough these days, let me tell you,' said Frances.

Martha gripped the steering wheel, wondering what the definition of such qualities truly was.

'Your Mike is a good one too.'

Martha swallowed hard. Mike was nothing like her father, nothing like him. In fact that had been part of his appeal. She'd had enough of her father's erratic mood swings and blasting gusts of love for his wife and family followed closely by contempt and harshness. It was part and parcel, she supposed, of being the daughter of an alcoholic and never knowing what to expect.

Her mother with every year seemed to forget those bad old days and replace them with the good ones. Perhaps that's what the gift of age was: only the times that made one happy or brought joy were remembered, with the others pushed to the back of consciousness and disappearing from the drain of the mind like water down a plughole.

The New England countryside basked in low Autumn sunshine, the trees along the roadway wrapped in shades of red, orange and gold, the landscape a beckoning blaze of colour as they drove through it.

'Mom, isn't it awesome!' gasped Martha.

'I suppose all the leafers must be heading up our

way. I saw a busload of them yesterday with their cameras.'

'They're just trying to capture it, Mom, and it's so beautiful who can blame them.' Martha turned the heat up in the car as her mother always complained of the cold.

Frances commented with interest on the houses and stores they passed.

'Why'd they go and paint their door that colour? . . . She's got herself a good set of plants up on that porch. Protect them from the frost, that's what that garden guy on the TV always says . . . I don't know why anyone would hang such ugly drapes, there's no sense to it, Martha.'

It never ceased to amaze Martha the interest her mother took in strangers' lives, the curiosity it stirred up in her. Passing all these places gave her mother satisfaction; sitting in an armchair all day back at the Belmont complex watching soap operas on TV was certainly not something Frances Kelly was ready for yet.

'I see that house on the corner got a new birdhouse, that wasn't there last month.'

Martha caught a glimpse of the white and blue painted bird feeder that stood on the top of a slim pole in the corner of the front yard.

'Yes, Mom, I guess that's new.'

The cemetery at Westwood was about a half-mile out of the town and was as quiet and tranquil a place as anyone could be laid to rest. Her grandparents were buried there too, Mary and Joseph O'Malley, who'd emigrated from Galway in the 1930s. Her mother had brought flowers and now she bent down and placed them next to the stone where her husband's name was carved.

Martha stared at the stone, concentrating on the letters of her father's name.

'We'll say a few prayers,' her mother encouraged.

Martha, joining in, the words automatically tripping off her tongue, thought how she had grown up with prayer, a typical Catholic childhood dominated by Sunday mass, confession and communion. Prayers when her mother served the meal, prayers at bedtime, the rosary rattled around the fire on a Saturday evening, novenas for exams, for good health, and for those less fortunate than themselves. A while later she moved away to let Frances have the opportunity to speak to her father on her own.

'I'll wait back in the car, Mom, you take your time.'

The grey-haired waitress nodded in recognition as she showed them to a booth at the back of the restaurant. Both of them perused the menu, even though it never changed from month to month, or season to season.

'I'll have a burger and fries,' said Frances. 'Chicken salad and a baked potato,' Martha added.

As always, her mother talked about her father,

Martha sipping on a Diet Coke and just listening.

'Do you remember the summers, Martha?'

'Hot and sticky . . .'

'No! No, not those ones, I mean the summers back home in Cork.'

She remembered those all right. The few trips back to Ireland, her parents scrimping and scraping and putting money by for almost two or three years in order to pay for the fares and the expense of returning to the country they loved. Her father would visit Mossy Ryan's the tailor and buy a new coat and jacket and trousers, the boys would be dressed in their finest, and she and her mother would be treated to a trip to Filenes to array themselves in the latest style, as the Yanks, as her cousins called them, returned to visit all the relations back in Skibbereen.

'Do you remember it?' urged Frances. 'The excitement and the palaver of it – sure your father was in his element over there.'

She remembered her grand-uncle John and her father's older brother Tim and the farm snug in the rolling West Cork countryside and a myriad cousins who bore the same names as themselves and a similar appearance.

'Your father loved it there.'

Martha remembered being sick with excitement as the visit to Ireland drew nearer and nearer and her father making a big show of going on the dry and staying off alcohol for at least a month so he would look well and fit and not a bit like a bowsie, and the pledge being broken after only a few days of being back where he belonged. One year there had barely been the fare for her father to go and her mother had feigned illness so only the and Brian had flown to Shannon and taken the hire car down the country. The rest of them made do with the hose and the paddling pool and pink ice-creams and sitting up till midnight out in the open air with Frances and her women friends, smoking and playing cards and listening to Frank Sinatra.

'While the cat's away the mice can play,' was all her mother would say about that summer vacation in their own back yard.

'They were good times,' murmured her mother now. 'When you were all young and your father was still with us.'

Martha nodded and out of instinct squeezed her hand.

They made small talk with the waitress, and Martha watched as her mother drenched her meal in salt, scattering it partly on the Formica table top.

'Why don't they season food properly any more! All those people on them faddy diets and allergic to every morsel they put in their mouth. When I was a girl we just ate what we were given and were grateful for it. Food didn't make us sick then.'

Martha toyed with her pieces of chicken, hiding some of it under a furl of lettuce leaf.

'Kids and Mike OK?'

'Yep.'

'All doing OK?'

'Mike's caught up in this new biotech project for the company, designing some kind of information systems.'

Her mother's eyes looked blank. Martha couldn't blame her, for if she herself had so little understanding of the work that occupied her husband for most of his waking hours you could hardly expect a woman in her seventies with little interest in the information highway to be interested.

'Well, at least he likes what he does. In my time most men worked at jobs they hated. When I see Mike and your brothers it makes me realize how much things are changing.'

Frances Kelly speared three golden chips on to her fork asking, 'And what about you, pet? How are you doing?'

'I'm fine, Mom, honest.'

'All this talk of miracles. There was something more about you again in the papers.'

'Yeah, I know. Hopefully in time it will just blow over.'

'You can't blame them, Martha darling, people are only human and are bound to be interested in talk of miracles and the like.'

'I guess.'

'Are they still phoning and coming to the house? I don't know how you cope with it at all, I honestly don't.'

'Mike's going crazy about it.'

'Lord rest your father, but he would have been the very same.'

'He doesn't realize that I can't just pretend this whole Timmy thing hasn't happened. I can't turn my back on someone who asks for my help, I'm not like that! Mike doesn't seem to understand the need inside me to use this healing ability or whatever it is to help people.'

'You were always like that. Good-natured and kind, Martha love, even when you were a small girl. Do you remember that time Sean had that desperate fall from his bike and split open his lip and you carried him most of the way home?'

'For God's sake, Mom, I dropped him and he cut his knee and arm and I made things even worse!'

'But your intentions were good, you just wanted to help your brother.'

'He kept crying for you and wanting to get home, and then I went and dropped him on the pavement and he roared and roared.'

Frances Kelly laughed aloud. 'You were always such a Girl Scout!'

'Mom!' protested Martha.

'I just mean you were always in tune with others. Why, the nuns at St Teresa's were forever telling your father and myself that we were blessed to have such a daughter. You had faith. A great faith and goodness – I remember Sister

Alexandra thought you might even have a vocation and want to join the order.'

Martha giggled, remembering the religious phase she went through, with a statue of Our Lady on her dressing table and the hours she spent praying and trying to be holy and good and glide around the polished wooden floors at home like the way the nuns in the convent moved.

'It was just a phase, Mom, that's all!'

Frances Kelly raised her neatly pencilled grey eyebrows and the two of them burst into laughter.

'To tell the truth, both your father and I were doing novenas that you'd get a bit of sense and were mighty relieved when it did pass.'

'What about now?' Martha asked, hesitant. 'What do you make of what's going on now? Honest to God, Mom, what do you think?'

'I don't know what to make of it. I know that you're a good person and have always had a strong faith, and I suppose if the Lord wants to act through anyone, well, my daughter is as good as he'll find. The healing gift is a powerful one, mighty powerful. Perhaps it's in the family. Your great-grandmother had a way with her, and people used to come for miles looking for potions and cures. They didn't have fancy hospitals and pills and medicines in those days and I guess belief and faith came into it when a person got sick, for that was all they had! My mother told me she could close an open wound, staunch bleeding with just the touch of her hand, and the people in the district used to send out a pony and trap for her whenever there was an accident or injury. Even her mother before her was rumoured to be a great one for sick and injured cattle.'

'Mom, why in heaven's name didn't you mention any of this before?'

'To be honest, I just didn't think about it. It's all so long ago, before my time. When I travelled across the Atlantic with my parents, all that stuff seemed like a lot of old talk and superstition, something we were trying to put behind us.'

Martha ordered coffee for the two of them, trying to make sense of the connections between generations of women.

'Martha, I know you want to help people, heal them, whatever you call it, I'm not interfering but just be mindful of yourself, you have a husband and children, a family. I might be getting on a bit myself but I'm still your mother and I can't help worrying about you all.'

Martha understood her mother's genuine concern for her well-being and that of her family.

'Don't worry, Mom. This healing is something strange and kind of exciting. I can't explain it but it seems to create an energy within me that makes me feel good.'

'Energy or not, you just watch yourself – you're still my little girl and I can't help worrying about you,' declared Frances Kelly, standing up from the table.

The waitress, noticing their empty cups, came

over and offered them a refill. Afterwards Martha paid the bill while her mother visited the rest room.

On the way home they stopped off at a roadside stand piled high with orange pumpkins of every shape and size, dozens of them. Martha walked up and down, taking her time, picking out about five suitable for the kids to cut out and decorate. She added two pots of autumnal chrysanthemums to stand out on her front step, while her mother knowledgeably discussed pumpkin recipes with the chatty stall holder.

'I didn't know you knew all those pumpkin dishes!' Martha teased as they carried her purchases to the car.

'Ah, they're just out of my recipe books, sure you know I can't abide the smell or taste of those yokes!' laughed her mother, putting them in the trunk. The two of them automatically reached forward and hugged each other before setting off for home.

Chapter Eighteen

As word of her gift of healing spread, Martha felt as if she and her family were under siege, their home and family life no longer their own. Absolute strangers approached her in the street, prepared to share the most intimate details of their life with her and ask for healing. They came up to her in the stores, outside school, at the local swimming pool, where she was trying to teach Alice the backstroke. Polite, she listened and talked to them, often at pains to point out that their own medical practitioners were far better qualified to help than she was.

Their home was inundated with local and long-distance phone calls; the callers would break down at the sound of her voice, confiding recently disgnosed illnesses and long battles with disease, telling of children who might never grow to adulthood, heavy crosses these unknown soldiers carried. Aware of their fears and quest for hope and answers, Martha listened and spoke softly to them, making it clear that she could not possibly offer healing over the phone and recommending that perhaps they should talk to a counsellor in their area who might be able to help. Some were happy enough simply to have shared their problem, insisting that they had faith in her and believing they felt a little better already; others cursed her for wasting their time. Then there were the other calls, threatening and abusive, ranting and hurling insults, sly voices whispering, making her sick as these so called Bible-quoting, God-fearing Christians shouted and screamed abuse down the line at her and her family.

'Filthy slut!'

'Whore of the Devil!'

'Blasphemer!'

'Daughter of Satan! Sent to do his work!'

Furious, Mike had got on to the phone company and immediately demanded a new, unlisted number.

'You might want to give those stupid people the time of day but the kids and I certainly don't! This is our home,' he argued, 'and I'm not having Alice or the rest of the kids subjected to these calls. They don't need to listen to this kind of stuff.'

Martha, mightily relieved by her husband's protective action, gladly agreed that their new number was only to be distributed to close family and friends.

* * *

Then the letters came. At first a few stuffed in their blue-painted mailbox, bold handwriting, gentle curves, neat work-processed anonymous stationery, floral patterned and scented envelopes, vellum and rich parchment. But following the articles and interviews and word of mouth, more and more letters arrived, till Nolan their mailman was scarcely able to lift them and had to make special delivery arrangements.

'Wow, look at all the mail you got!' chorused her kids as they rushed to help her open them as if they were birthday cards. Martha had to stop them when she found Alice kneeling in the breakfast room weeping over a letter from a teenage boy telling her of his mother's terminal illness.

Mostly she attended to the mail when the rest of them were out of the house or at school. The writers opened their hearts to her as if they were best friends. She pored over the letters, touched by the words and photos, deeply moved by the courage and spirit of those lives affected by the tragedy of illness and pain. One young woman, Teresa, had been out of school for three years, suffering from chronic fatigue syndrome, and now almost bed-bound had begun to write poetry; Martha was amazed by the power of her verse. They were the sad letters, and often made her cry, but it was the letters from those devoid of hope, depressed and despondent, dependent on alcohol and drugs and whose very spirit was lost to them, that affected her most. She worried about those men, women and children, knowing they were the ones who needed help, who hungered for the spirit to raise them up and renew them. Some she wrote back to, others she called. Half afraid, she traced the photographic outline of some of their features and tried to transmit healing, asking the Holy Spirit to send them light in their darkness.

Many still came to the house in Mill Street in search of miracles, with immense faith and belief that she, a stranger, could somehow do what others had failed to do and heal them.

Patrick and Mary Rose and Alice were approached too. Martha was angry that her children were being dragged into something that was not their concern. One day Mary Rose broke down when an elderly man asked her to lay her hands on his stomach; the child sobbed hysterically for an hour when she got home.

'It's all right, pet, I don't think he meant anything bad by it, honest I don't,' Martha reassured her.

Mike exploded with anger when he got in from work and accused her of being totally irresponsible.

'Martha, I work darned hard in the Institute all day and I'll be damned if I come home to these lunatics and crackpots who seem to think they have some God-given right to intrude on our home and family. Let them fuck up their own lives if they want but tell them to keep out of mine!'

'Calm down!' she pleaded.

'You think you're some kind of bloody great earth mother that can heal the world, while the rest of us here at home can suffer! Well I'll tell you, I'm getting fed up of all these people in our lives. At the rate things are going if we want any privacy we'll have to sell this house and move somewhere else.'

'I don't want to move to another house!' bawled Alice, tears running down her face.

'Well, I'm not staying here to have my family threatened by a bunch of weirdos,' Mike said, storming out of the room.

'Don't mind Dad, Alice,' explained Martha, trying to console her youngest daughter. 'He doesn't mean it.'

Mike's temper and stubbornness had always got the better of him, his tendency to fly off the handle ensuring he never stayed long enough to argue a thing through and listen to anyone else's perspective. He'd been the exact same when they were dating.

'But Dad's right. He's just trying to protect you and the rest of us,' added Patrick, taking his father's side. Martha realized that perhaps she was out of touch with how her children and husband were feeling.

Not wanting any more arguments and feeling stressed as hell she decided to put on her trainers and jacket and go out and get a bit of fresh air, giving all of them time to cool down before she began to prepare dinner. Walking along the familiar neighbourhood paths she had to admit that the faults were as much hers as Mike's, and that neither of them were being exactly fair to the other. Something they would have to rectify if they wanted a happy marriage.

Chapter Nineteen

Martha studied the map of New England in her car, hoping that she had taken the correct exit off Route 84 to get her to West Hartford. She had driven almost a hundred and fifty miles to visit a thirty-two-year-old mother of three who had a large inoperable tumour on her spine. Thea Warrington had already undergone massive chemotherapy and radium treatment over the past few months but seemingly all to no avail. It was her husband Erik who had contacted Martha, deluging her with letters and phone calls and even a video of his family until she had finally agreed to come and see her.

Secretly, she'd been dreading the visit and expected dealing with the cancer victim to be harrowing. Instead she had met one of the most intensely peaceful and joyous African-American women she had ever been privileged to be introduced to.

Thea, despite the ravages of her illness, greeted

her with a warm smile which showed off her beautiful eyes and bone structure. Her grace and charm were endearing and it was clear she was adored by Erik and their three young sons. They had a striking modern home with tall glass windows about two miles out from the town centre surrounded by the most amazing landscaped gardens.

'I'm a landscaper,' said Thea proudly. 'Erik and I have our own business.'

Martha felt an immediate bond with her and although she had expected Thea's life force to be low and weak she was surprised by its balance and strength.

'The doctors tell Erik that I am going to die soon but, Martha, I don't feel it! I don't believe it! The Lord is good. He would want me to raise those three fine boys he sent me, live to watch them grow and get through school, I know that. The Lord is merciful, that I am sure of.'

Martha was amazed by Thea's faith and lack of anger, and by her incredible willpower. From the minute she laid her hands on her she could sense Thea's resolve to stay on this earth. She was grounded with a love of the soil and nature, which was probably due in some part to her calling as a gardener. The mass of the tumour was large and complex and Martha found she had to focus strongly on its congealed heavy structure as she sent healing to it, with Thea's own energy equally concentrated during the session. Her hand grew hot, vibrating as if filled with a pulsing energy as she tried to dry it out, draw off the fluid-saturated tissue and shrink it, pull it away from the cord and nerves it was damaging and negate its ability to spread.

'That sure feels good,' murmured Thea as she worked.

Passing her hands along the rest of Thea's body she could sense an incredible balance, and despite or maybe because of all her medical treatment there was very little spread and few hot spots she could detect.

At the end of the healing she joined Erik and Thea for lunch served in a bright wooden kitchen, with floor to ceiling windows which looked out over their acres of garden.

'It's stunning! I can't believe the range of planting and colours and shapes you've got,' she said admiringly as she took in a bed swathed in a variety of blues and mauves, flame-coloured grasses setting alight a dark corner. 'I've never seen anything like it.'

'I know it's our business, but it's a labour of love,' admitted Erik.

'Have you and your husband got a nice garden?' enquired Thea.

'I'm afraid I'm not much of a gardener,' lamented Martha, 'and I'm so busy it's been very neglected of late.'

'Gardens need time,' suggested Erik. 'They don't like being rushed and need a whole heap of coaxing. Every season brings its own work.'

'This place of ours is just coming into its own now, after five years' hard work. Now there's winter roses and heathers and pansies for colour, last flowerings likely before the first snow falls, but you should have seen it at the height of summer. Paradise – so pretty and the scents that came from that border I've created outside the window! Why, it's just glorious! Erik built it for me on a height so that I can still work on it from my wheelchair as I'm not prepared to give up the pleasures of weeding.'

Martha thought of her own overgrown back yard, where weeds rambled and propagated unchallenged.

'I hate weeding,' she laughed. 'I'm much too lazy.'

Thea was tired, drowsy after the session, and as Martha had a long drive back to Boston the two women eventually agreed to say goodbye.

'I'll have a nap when you're gone, Martha, that way I'll be awake when the boys get in from school.' Thea smiled, squeezing her hand. 'Erik and my boys are all that matter to me right now.'

Martha tried to hold back on the emotions she herself was experiencing as she kissed her forehead.

'You take care of yourself, Thea.'

'Will you pray for me?'

'Of course I will,' she agreed. 'And you keep

after the Lord for what you want. I think he listens to you.'

Erik Warrington had a selection of tall plants and small pots set out on the step near her car. He insisted she take them, and spread a sheet of plastic in the trunk before loading them into the back of the Volvo.

'Oh, thank you, Erik, that's so kind of you.'

'Some you can leave in the big pots till next spring, just keep them watered, and the rest, why you can plant them out right now.'

'I'm not much good with plants,' she warned him.

'These will grow,' he promised. 'Thea seeded and grew all of them from cuttings herself. Her green fingers seem to make everything grow.'

He stood in front of her, a strong stocky man, his face filled with concern for his wife. 'I don't want to lose her,' he blurted out, trying to control himself.

Martha touched his arm.

'I can't make any promises,' she said. 'You know I can't, but Thea is strong, and her body and mind and soul are joined in fighting this illness. She has faith and such a strong belief. I know what the doctors say, but sometimes they are wrong.'

'Sometimes there *are* miracles,' he insisted, staring at her. 'Sometimes!'

'God is good,' agreed Martha. 'And I pray he'll be good to her, to both of you.'

* * *

Back on the highway she couldn't get Thea out of her mind, asking herself why in heaven's name she was getting herself emotionally involved with someone else, when already so many were dependent on her. Yet thinking of Thea she knew that despite the poor prognosis of her illness Martha had felt during the healing a very definite sense of hope for the mother of three.

Her thoughts turned to her own family as she drove home and she realized the love of her husband and children were all that truly mattered to her.

Chapter Twenty

The Thanksgiving mass at St John's, their parish church, had been packed but she and Mike and the kids had managed to squeeze into a bench up near the front of the crowded Easton congregation. Martha had always found the ritual of the mass with its Old and New Testament readings and gospel, offertory prayers and communion, deeply satisfying. Not just from the spiritual point of view but also from a community one, as the traditional wooden church was mostly filled with their neighbours and people she knew. Glancing around at the heads bent in silent prayer, one could almost hazard a guess as to their needs and intentions. Patrick used to serve mass here along with other boys from his class but at the ripe old age of twelve had refused to do it any more.

Father Eugene Reagan, their ageing parish priest, stepped slowly up to the altar, but his voice and conviction were as strong as ever as he welcomed the parishioners and began the mass.

He preached a sermon on charity being its own reward. Patrick and Mary Rose both cast their eyes upwards, bored. At the offertory procession the small kids proudly carried up a range of gifts to the altar, including the large hamper which had been left at the door and would be distributed to needy families in the parish later.

Martha smiled to herself, watching Alice be very self-conscious and holy as she went up to communion with the rest of them. She tried to concentrate on her daughter and ignore the stares of recognition as they filed back down to their seat.

Afterwards they joined the large group outside on the step, chatting to each other. Evie and Frank with their kids Becky and Niall came over to join them. Father Eugene greeted the two men warmly and shook Evie's hand. Martha was totally ignored.

'Father Eugene, that was a lovely sermon,' she started to say, but before she could continue he interrupted her.

'Mrs McGill, I'm reading very sad things about you, very sad. You seem determined to get yourself involved in something you know nothing about, which is always a dangerous thing.'

'Dangerous!' She all but laughed.

'Yes, I believe so.'

Her cheeks reddened. How dare he! She felt like a small child being admonished and belittled in front of her husband, children and close friends, there on the steps of the church she had just worshipped in.

'Hey, Evie!' Embarrassed, Frank Hayes jangled his car keys. 'I think it's time we were going, if we want to get something to eat.'

Evie shot her a glance of commiseration. 'Martha, don't forget we've got supper at Kim's on Thursday. If you want I'll pick you up.'

'That'd be great.'

The priest was clearly annoyed with her and she was not about to let herself be bullied about what she could or could not do by some elderly man, priest or not!

'Do you wish to speak with me, Father?' she asked angrily.

'I do.' He stiffened.

Mike and the kids decided to make themselves scarce and to go sit in the car. Now that the mass crowd had cleared, Martha was nervous as to what the priest could want with her. As their church donation had been given on time and both she and Mike had helped out at church within the past few months, Martha knew exactly what he wanted to discuss.

'Yes, Father?' She tried to appear respectful to this man of God.

'Martha, I'm worried about you. These things I read in the newspapers and hear on the radio about you are upsetting, especially when we know that none of it is true. So why won't you come out and deny them and put an end to all this gossip and rumour and talk of miracles?'

'Don't you believe in miracles, Father?'

'Jesus and the holy saints performed miracles, not some Easton housewife with nothing better to do,' he said, acidly.

'Father Eugene!' She gasped, hurt by his tone. 'I have never claimed to perform miracles, never,' she insisted. 'All I do is try to help and heal those that need it.'

A vexed expression crossed his face.

'You make a mockery of your faith and this church. All this publicity and shenanigans is giving poor innocent people false hope.'

'Father Reagon, let me assure you my faith is strong, and although I may not have degrees in theology or Bible studies like you, I do believe that I am doing the Lord's work too. Now if you'll excuse me, my husband and children are waiting.'

Almost shaking, she walked back to the car, trying to control herself so that the kids didn't see how upset she had been by the patronizing words of a man who believed his was the only way to connect with the Holy Spirit.

Mad as hell by the time they reached Mike's parents' house, Martha realized she could not let the priest's words mar their family Thanksgiving celebration meal. It was the one day of the year when Pat McGill rolled out the red carpet and invited her son and daughter and their families to a huge meal. Aunt Dot and Uncle Harry, who'd no children, joined them.

The McGills had a beautiful home out near Beaver Brook, a white-painted colonial with a deck out back. The green lawn was perfectly mowed, the hedges clipped, shrubs and bushes pruned hard. The shame of it was that by the end of the week Patricia and Ed McGill would have packed and moved to the small bungalow they owned in Sarasota, Florida. The first snows and cold drove them south like the rest of the snowbirds to the sunshine state. At sixty-five years of age Patricia McGill had decided that she'd had more than enough of the cold, and would no longer contemplate another New England winter. Ed agreed and, packing up his golf clubs, looked forward to a daily round of golf followed by a leisurely swim under constant blue skies. The Thanksgiving meal was an annual farewell to their children and family until they returned after Easter.

'Martha! You OK?' asked Mike, squeezing her hand as the kids jumped out of the car and ran up the path and into Grandpa Ed's open arms, Alice squealing as her grandfather greeted her with a mighty bear hug.

'Sure, Mike, sure,' she replied, determined not to let the priest's words spoil the day.

Chapter Twenty-one

Gina Forrester threw up in the kitchen first, feeling weak and clammy as the wave of nausea washed over her. The second time she made it to the bathroom at least. Wetting a towel, she dabbed it against her skin as she leaned her head against the cool of the expensive Italian marble, in the vain hope that she would feel somehow better.

Bob hovered anxiously, trying not to invade her privacy but wanting to help. She reckoned she must have picked up one of those twenty-four-hour stomach bugs and decided it was better to go back to bed and take it easy for the rest of the day. She'd get Bob to phone and cancel their lunch reservations at the golf club. The thought of even reading a menu let alone ordering made her feel worse.

Four days later the possibility of it being a simple stomach flu seemed more remote and Gina had to admit to also feeling absolutely exhausted.

Bob wanted her to see their physician, have tests. Nervous, she told him of her suspicions.

'Then all the more reason to see the doctor,' he argued.

Gina shook her head. She could not face the possibility of sitting in one more doctor's office having yet another test done.

Grabbing her coat, she persuaded Bob to drive to the local drugstore, the two of them giggling like a pair of teenagers as they went up and down searching the aisles. Eventually they found the home pregnancy testing kit. So nervous her hands were shaking, Gina followed the instructions exactly the next day, sitting watching *Good Morning* on the corner of the bed as Bob went in the bathroom and checked the results.

'Yes!' he hollered.

Gina jumped up to run in and check, and recheck, the positive results clearly indicated by the line of blue in the test tube.

They were going to have a baby!

They were going to have a baby!

Overcome with emotion she began to cry.

Martha was thrilled to hear Gina Forrester's good news but was reluctant to claim any credit.

'I know this would never have happened but for you, Martha. I had all but given up hope of any chance of motherhood. You know Bob and I will always be so grateful for what you've done for us.'

'Gina! This is *your* baby, yours and Bob's, it has nothing to do with me.'

'You helped,' insisted Gina stubbornly. 'I know that!'

'Your body healed itself,' she suggested gently. 'That's all.'

That night when she told Mike about the Forresters' impending parenthood she could see a wary look fill her husband's eyes; he seemed unsure of how to react in front of her.

'Good for Bob, if that's what he wants. Another kid – even if he's almost old enough to be its grandfather.'

'Mike! They both want this baby very much.'

'They're just both a bit long in the tooth, that's all I'm saying.' He shrugged, hitting on the TV remote control.

Martha, although she had said little about her own involvement with Gina, was hurt by his kneejerk retort and his insensitivity to the others' feelings. She wondered as she tried to get to sleep how two people could live in the same house, raise a family, share the same bed and yet be such poles apart. She herself couldn't begin to fathom it.

Chapter Twenty-two

The flicker of candlelight in tiny ceramic pots all along the driveway lit up the darkness and greeted them with a warm welcoming glow as Martha and Evie rang the doorbell of Kim Hamilton's one-storey home.

Although she felt exhausted after spending most of the day visiting Cass and trying to heal a very depressed middle-aged man who'd only recently lost his job, Martha felt a night out with her friends would do her good, so after checking the schoolwork and Alice's reading, she dressed and got ready to go out. As she put on her pale blue top and a pair of soft blue pants with a fine cream crochet cardigan, Mike protested about her going out again. Pulling a bit of her hair up off her face and spraying herself with the reviving scent of Farouche she felt almost ready for anything.

'Kim's expecting me and I can't let her down,' she explained to Mike.

Her dish of garlic and tomato chicken had defrosted while she was out and she added some wholemeal Irish brown soda scones that she'd baked the day before, knowing they always went down well. Taking a bottle of wine, she kissed the girls goodnight and ran out to Frank Hayes's car. She and Evie would get a cab back later.

Kim lived about a ten-minute ride away in a bright ranch-style home in Brookline. She'd managed to hold onto the house as part of her divorce settlement and was pleased to still have her home even if she couldn't manage to hang onto her philandering rogue of a husband. Her two kids were spending the night with their dad so they had the place to themselves.

The house was ablaze with candles too, a log fire crackling in the grate.

'You bet there's candles,' laughed Kim. 'When the kids are here I daren't light one in case Nick tries to play with it but tonight he and his sister are at their dad's and we can have candles and wine and whatever.'

They set the food up in the kitchen, Martha peeking under the foil cover at Evie's speciality: beef jerky and cheesy potatoes. Mmm!

Jenny Erskine, who lived near Kim's, had picked out a few mellow CDs to put on the sound system and opened what she said was a really good bottle of chilled Californian wine.

Martha wasn't a great wine buff but when she took a drink from her glass she had to concur.

There, sipping her wine, she enjoyed the company of her old friends, her legs curled up under her on Kim's low squashy sofa in front of the log fire, everyone helping themselves to chips and dip as they chatted and caught up on each other's news while the food warmed up. Ruth Briggs, an old work friend whose son Shane was in school with Patrick, greeted her warmly, asking after Mike and the kids.

Kim fussed around them all: she looked different, younger, dressed in a wraparound turquoise skirt and a tight beaded top, which showed off her great figure. Her light brown hair hung loose around her face and her eyes were emphasized with a tracing of kohl. She looked content, happy even, the pain of her marriage break-up finally beginning to diminish. The old Kim Martha had gone to college with was reappearing.

Rianna Lindgard came straight from her busy late dental surgery. Grabbing a glass of reviving wine the minute she sat down, she squashed her tall frame in beside Martha. 'Sorry, Kim, but I missed the first T and had to wait for the next one,' she apologized, flashing them a perfect white smile. The rest of them instinctively covered their own mouths. She put them all to shame with her healthy lifestyle and as expected produced the most beautiful bowl of tossed salad and some unusual new Thai dish that smelled wonderful.

'So how you doing, Martha? How's my favourite healer?'

Martha simply grinned, both of them suddenly distracted by the arrival of Kathleen Ryan, laden with flowers for Kim, candy for her kids and an enormous heavy Le Creuset pot full of Prawns Provençal which she was in danger of tipping all over the living room rug in her attempts to hug and greet them all.

'Will someone get the woman a drink before she does some damage!' joked Evie, tapping the seat close by her. Kim relieved her of the dish and Jenny passed her a glass of wine. Kathleen flung off her jacket to reveal a low-cut top which showed off her cleavage and curves to their plump rounded best. She wore a pair of beige woollen pants, and her recently highlighted blond hair framed a broad face and candid blue eyes. She and Martha had been friends since childhood and Mike and Jim Ryan had worked for a while together.

'Well, everyone's here now!' Kim clapped her hands. 'And we'll be ready to eat in about thirty minutes or so.'

Sitting there on the couch, surrounded by her women friends, Martha realized this was exactly the kind of evening she needed. She felt relaxed and at ease and totally comfortable.

Politics, films, gossip, school boards, terrible teens – all got discussed as they sipped their wine and kicked off their shoes and listened and chatted, with Kim flitting in and out to the kitchen to check all was well as the food heated up.

'OK, OK, everyone! We're ready to eat, come and get it.'

They were like a bunch of kids ambling into the kitchen and grabbing the big plates; the fun of the pot luck supper was going around tasting and trying a bit of everything. Rianna's Thai dish had a weird name; none of them had ever heard of it before let alone tried it, but experimenting was all a part of the evening and if they liked it they'd beg the recipe off her. Jenny had a spicy Mexican bean plate and Ruth had made dessert, a huge glass dish of tiramisu. Kim herself had made a huge pot of creamy Italian risotto with shavings of cheese and mushrooms, which was delicious.

They sat around eating, Rianna after a few drinks telling them stories about some of her worst patients, which had them falling around the floor laughing.

Jenny told them how she had dealt with the problem of her boss pinching her ass in the real estate office where she worked. Borrowing her son's trick shock handshake toy, she had slipped it into the back pocket of her pants before she stepped into his office. OK, she got a bit of a shock to her bum, but it was nothing compared to his.

'Honest, I nearly wet myself between the shock and laughing, but it was well worth it. I don't think old Dave will be doing it again!'

They all reckoned she had most definitely cured him of his chauvinistic habit.

'How did you explain it being in your pocket?' laughed Evie.

'I just acted all innocent and told him I was picking up after my ten-year-old and must have just shoved it in my pocket before I left for work in the morning.'

Martha was too full with the risotto and prawns and cheesy potatoes to be tempted by dessert and helped Kim afterwards in the kitchen with setting out the coffee and cream and sugar.

'You look a little tired,' mentioned Kim.

'I feel it too,' she admitted, telling her friend about some of the demands being made on her.

'Jeez, Martha! I don't know how you cope with it.'

'You should see the letters I get, I *can't* just keep constantly saying no to them. On Saturday I'm going to visit a twenty-eight-year-old guy with early motor neurone disease in Rhode Island. His parents and girlfriend are devastated by the diagnosis.'

'God, Martha, are you sure this healing isn't all too much for you?' continued Kim.

'It is too much for her, only she's too darned pigheaded to admit it.' Evie had come into the kitchen, carrying a load of dirty plates.

'Evie, that's not fair!' protested Martha, who had to admit to herself that she was finding it harder and harder each day to cope with the constant demands being made on her. She was lucky that Mike had a good job because of late even the gas bill had gone through the roof with all the driving she was doing and, though she had good friends who would collect and take care of the kids if she was stuck, she had occasionally had to pay a baby-sitter.

'Come on, you can't be in the car every day travelling long distance to see people: you should organize it properly and let them come to you with their aches and pains and troubles.'

'Some are too sick to travel,' she reminded her friend.

'Martha, is there anything that I can do to help?' asked Kim.

There was her friend only getting her own life straightened out after a messy divorce and custody battle and offering to help her.

'No, thanks, it's fine,' she murmured gratefully.

'Hold on a minute,' suggested Evie. 'Kim's a flyer on the computer. Maybe she could help with printing out letters dealing with some of that vast correspondence you get.'

'I'll help with the letters if you want,' said Kim.

Martha was unsure – but having someone to help, even for a few hours a week, would take some of the pressure off her.

'Only if you're sure you want to.'

'Yeah, for sure, it'll probably make me forget about my own petty troubles.'

'Thanks, Kim, it's so good of you.'

Carrying the wooden tray back into the living

room with the coffee and mugs she guessed the others were already discussing her.

'To be able to lay your hands on someone and ease their pain or change the course of their illness is a pretty incredible gift,' said Rianna. 'Something the rest of us can only try and understand. It's just so awesome and weird that I guess we don't know what to say or do about it.'

'Come off it, guys,' begged Martha. 'I don't want anything to change between us, we've all known each other for so long. For God's sake, Evie and I went to school together and Kathleen and I were virtually in diapers together. It's bad enough I've been sacked from the Animal Shelter.'

'You *what*!' screamed Jenny.

'Yep, they said they would prefer if I stopped volunteering as too many people were phoning the centre trying to get me and that the phone lines were too busy and the other attendants found it distracting.'

'The small-minded shits!' Kathleen responded.

'Perhaps they were right, I dunno.'

'And Father Eugene had a go at you the other day after mass,' added Evie.

'Don't mind him,' laughed Kathleen, 'he's just jealous cos nobody's asking him to lay his hands on them!'

The candles were beginning to burn lower, their light casting shadows around the room as the night drew in and Martha opened her heart to her closest friends.

'Mike and the kids resent it, I guess they don't understand that I just can't walk on by and pretend none of this is happening to me, when it is.'

'Mike's probably just worried for you, honey, you know what he's like. He's one of those protective men.'

'I know that, Kathleen, I know that.'

'Maybe doing the healing at home isn't such a good idea,' suggested Ruth, her brown eyes serious.

'That's what I told her in the kitchen,' added Evie. 'She needs to find someplace out of the house, a separate space from the kids and family. Someplace those who need healing can come to her.'

Martha had to admit it sounded good and might ease some of the stress and tension caused by trying to work at home and having constant callers to their door. Looking around the room at their concerned faces, she could see her friends' belief in her and acceptance of this calling.

'Am I crazy, do you think?' she asked them.

'No!'

'No way!'

'You've been blessed by the spirit,' joked Rianna, 'which I guess beats drilling holes in teeth any day of the week!'

'Rianna,' warned Evie.

'I get to inflict pain on some of my patients while you manage to ease it. Martha, I envy you your gift for it's sure something I could do with.'

'You need any help, just call on me,' interrupted Ruth.

'That goes for me too,' insisted Rianna.

'I'm as free as a bird,' joked Kathleen, 'now that my kids have decided they've outgrown their poor old mom and want to be independent.'

That night they pledged their friendship and support for what she was doing and she knew she only had to lift the phone and any one of her female friends would be there for her.

Driving home in the cab at almost 12.30 a.m. with Evie, she expressed her gratitude.

'Evie, had you and Kim something to do with all this amazing show of support?'

Evie giggled, gazing out into the darkness.

'Kim wanted to have the supper party, and I suppose it just happened that everyone who came believes in you and your good work. That's all.'

In the darkness Martha felt the warm cloak of friendship and loyalty wrap itself around her.

Chapter Twenty-three

It was Kim who'd suggested making an appointment to see Catherine Morgan, the well-known Boston healer, and reluctantly Martha had to agree with her women friends that it might be a good thing to acquaint herself with someone who was a respected healer and ran her healing sessions in an organized fashion.

'I can't just turn up on this woman's doorstep and find out exactly what she does,' Martha protested.

'Of course you can,' they countermanded in unison.

'Martha, you've got to learn to use your gift properly, and be serious about it!' urged Ruth.

'Catherine Morgan is highly regarded and has been running her Center of Light for the past eight years. Going along to see her is not going to do any harm,' added Kim firmly.

So through a friend of a friend the appointment was made, and Martha found herself, two weeks later, sitting in the waiting room of a tall brown-stone house close to the Common. Nervous and uncertain what to expect, Martha lowered herself into the comfort of an over-large armchair near the window.

A selection of new age magazines were spread out on a huge gold-cushioned stool that acted as a table. Her eye was drawn to a beautiful piece of sculpture of the human body on a pedestal in front of the bow-shaped window, where natural light accentuated the curved features and skilled work of the artist.

The walls were painted a soothing pale green and there were comfortable cream-coloured couches with an array of scatter cushions. It was unlike any other waiting room she had ever been in before. Soft chanting music in an un-known language surrounded her, and Martha found herself relaxing, all trace of nervousness disappearing.

About fifteen minutes later she heard a voice out in the hallway and sat up as a tall grey-haired woman opened the door.

'I'm Catherine,' she said, introducing herself, 'and you must be Martha.'

They shook hands, Martha admiring the room.

'It's so soothing and calm here. You'd hardly believe we're in the middle of the city.'

'I feel it is good for my clients to be able to sit quietly and relax before we have a healing session otherwise we waste time while they're trying to get their breath back.'

Martha had to agree as they climbed a short flight of stairs and Catherine led her into a beautiful sunlit room which overlooked a narrow garden at the back of the house. 'This is my sacred space,' the healer told her.

One wall of the room was lined with bookshelves and Martha ran her eyes over the huge range of titles which seemed to cover every aspect of the human body and soul and mind, and included books on Indian mystics and shamans and healing.

'I see you are looking at my library,' said Catherine. 'There is much to study and learn about the human heart and soul.'

She sat down at a cream-painted desk, Martha noting her flawless skin and fine bone structure and lean angular frame. Catherine Morgan was dressed simply in a loose denim skirt and a simple cream linen blouse, her long hair swept up in a carved floral hairgrip. Reaching across she took out two sheets of paper, which she passed to Martha.

'Would you mind filling these in, please,' she said.

Martha took out her pen and wrote in details about her life, medical history, interests, aware that Catherine was studying her, the blue eyes almost looking through her. Martha took her time, amazed by the perception of the questions which asked not only about her physical well-being but also about her attitudes to life.

'They are rather probing, I'm afraid, but I do find a degree of honesty is needed when I am to perform a healing. You do want me to do a healing – or would you prefer to just have a chat?'

Martha could feel herself blushing, and couldn't believe the other woman's chuckles at her embarrassment.

'Please don't feel awkward, Martha dear. I am well aware who you are. News of your gift has already reached the circle.'

'The circle?'

'I mean those of us who have an interest in the special abilities, energies, of others.'

'I see,' murmured Martha, wondering if Catherine might ask her to leave or perceive her as a threat or rival.

'We are all friends here, my dear, pilgrims on the same long path, this journey through life. I have read of the great work you have already done and I'm enchanted to meet you. I truly mean that,' she said, stretching her long arm and hand out to clasp Martha's, her touch warm and sincere.

'Already I can feel the energy within you and see the strong colours of the aura that surrounds you and those that guide you.'

Martha hesitated.

'I think a little healing might be nice,' suggested the older woman, 'and then perhaps we can talk.'

Catherine asked her to stretch out on the long narrow bed in the middle of the room. Taking off her sweater, shoes and beige corduroy trousers, Martha wrapped herself in the thick white fluffy towel Catherine had passed her. She watched with interest as the woman took two scented candles and placed them in a ceramic jar close beside her. Pouring a trace of oil onto the curved lid, she lit the candles. At once the room was filled with the aroma of a strange essence, the scent assaulting her as it drifted through the air.

'Please, Catherine, would you mind putting out those candles! The smell affects me and makes me feel sick.'

'Oh, I'm sorry! Most people need the precious oils to help them to stimulate their senses, but with someone like you, why, your senses are already overdeveloped. Here, let me open the window and let some fresh air in.'

Martha nodded gratefully. The sharp sense of nausea and unease she had felt disappeared as fresh air filled the room. Catherine took her place at the bottom of the table by Martha's feet, catching them firmly in her hands. She could hear the healer's breathing change as she ran her hands along the bones of her toes, feet and ankles, pulling her legs towards her.

Martha closed her eyes as the woman walked around her laying her hands on her body, her breathing at times slow and deep, other times sharp and panting. Glancing sideways at one stage

Martha almost cried out as the figure around her seemed younger with long jet black hair plaited down her back, her skin tanned, a look of concentration in the strange face. Perturbed, she was reassured a moment later by the swish of Catherine's familiar denim as the woman worked around her. Laying her hands on the areas of her chakras, the healer worked. Sometimes Martha could feel the weight of her hand rest quiet and still above her womb, on her hip; at other times Catherine's fingers and wrists made a flurry of movements as if she was trying to draw something toward her. Martha felt warm and sleepy and was totally enjoying the experience. At the end the healer stood above her head and Martha felt as if the crown of her head had opened and light and energy were running from it, beams of it connecting herself and the healer.

Afterwards Catherine sat back in the swivel chair with its purple velvet cushion as Martha slowly sat up and stretched herself, like a drowsy child waking from slumber.

'Well, Martha, did you enjoy that?'

'Yes, it was so different, I felt like I was lying here connected with you, but in a strange way in a different place.' Truthfully she had enjoyed this new sensation, and the sense of release of energy and cleansing.

'You have a powerful gift with immense energy powering through you. The connections within you are strong and your ability to see through to the core of a person is unique. It has taken me thirty years of study and search and work to arrive where I am, where I can help those that need help and train those who have an interest in healing. You have found a quicker path, a short-cut. I sense the goodness within you, the reason you have been chosen.'

Embarrassed, Martha pulled her shoulder-length hair from her face, her mind racing and trying to take in what this woman was telling her.

'It is this goodness, this pureness,' insisted Catherine, 'that has drawn the spirit to work through you, to choose you to become a channel for this healing, this work of miracles as the newspapers like to call it.'

'Catherine, I'll be honest. I don't understand why any of this has happened to me, but I do know that I now find myself wanting to help and heal people, and when I lay my hands on them I can feel a strong energy flowing from me to them.'

'Where do you think this energy comes from?'

'Sometimes I pray when I touch them, it seems to help. Other times it's as if the power or energy comes out of the air or sky around me, or the earth itself.'

'The spirit is strong within you,' said Catherine, hugging her. 'And I am blessed to have met you.'

Martha began to lower herself off the table and reached for her clothes, the older woman watching her all the time.

'You have a slight stiffness on the right hip,

Martha, just watch it over the years, also you must be careful of your glands.'

'They always swell and get sore when I'm tired or run down,' she admitted. 'I had a really bad dose of glandular fever when I was a teenager.'

'Well then, you know to watch that. Listen to those warning signals and don't overtire yourself. People will demand much of you, but do not let them exhaust you or drain you.'

'I never feel tired after a healing.'

'That's because you are not using your own energy but there will come a time when the demands on you will be such that you'll have to protect yourself, must protect yourself.'

'Has that happened to you?'

'It happens to all healers, at times. We sometimes have to surround ourselves with light, create a buffer zone to protect ourselves from those that make huge demands on us. The self is important, Martha, you must remember that.'

Martha could see the woman was genuine, and had developed an immense wisdom over the years. She had read so much, studied so much. How could Martha even begin to think she would ever attain such knowledge and understanding of the healing gift!

At the end of the session Martha felt slightly awkward as she took out her purse to pay Catherine. The price had been clearly denoted in the waiting room, and as she passed over the $80, Catherine smiled warmly.

'Martha,' she scolded. 'The exchange of money is in return for exchange of service; that way neither of us feels that they have been taken advantage of. Do you understand?'

Martha nodded. It was what Kim and Evie and the rest of them had been saying to her about charging some sort of fee, but she still wasn't sure about it.

'Well, now I'm finished for the day,' smiled Catherine, putting away her folder and leading Martha back down to the hall. 'Would you like to join me in the kitchen for a cup of tea?'

'Thank you, Catherine, that is really thoughtful of you.'

She led Martha down to a simple Shaker-style kitchen which also overlooked the small back yard where a collection of wooden birdfeeders hung from the cherry and maple trees. Two or three small stone and ceramic sculptures stood enticingly along the back wall and path and Martha couldn't imagine a nicer spot in the city to sit out and read a book or relax in.

'It's my oasis,' admitted Catherine Morgan. 'My place to "chill", as my sculptor son calls it. My husband and I live about an hour out of the city, and I use here for work when I'm in town. My son Chris has his studio and living space upstairs.'

She made a pot of tea and produced homemade banana bread studded with walnuts. 'You should take it easy for the rest of the day,' she advised.

'People usually feel a bit tired and sleepy after a healing, so don't take on anything too exhausting today.'

'I don't plan to,' Martha admitted, yawning despite herself.

'I know I read a bit about you in the papers, Martha, but who knows what is truth or not when you read those things? Still, I would genuinely like to know how you discovered your own healing gift.'

As Martha told her about Timmy Lucas, Catherine listened, fascinated. 'Suffer little children,' she said softly. 'Funny but it is often a child that triggers this ability, this wondrous new sense! You called on the spirit to help you in a traumatic situation and he answered.'

She didn't seem at all surprised when Martha told her about the journalists and the letters and constant phone calls and people outside her home.

'I don't know what to do! What in heaven's name do they all expect from me?'

'What do they expect? You know what they expect, Martha. They expect magic, they want you to wave your hands and make their pain and cares and woes disappear. They want miracles, they want to be healed and for all their pain and suffering to be lifted from them and blow away like sand in the wind.'

'But I can't always help,' sighed Martha, cradling the warm mug in her hands. 'The healing doesn't seem to work that way.'

'I know,' agreed the older healer, 'but that won't stop folk from expecting and hoping. I can tell you that for nothing.'

'I guess I just wasn't expecting people to be so . . .'

'Needy!' smiled Catherine. 'That's the word you're searching for.'

'Has it always been like that for you?'

'Well,' Catherine confided, 'I suppose, like you, I had no intention of being a healer. I was working a summer job in the Fleur de Lis hair and beauty shop back in Frostburg, my hometown in Maryland, and seemed to spend most of my time sweeping the floor and painting people's nails – can't abide the darned stuff myself!' she joked, flashing her own bare cut and buffed nails. 'The rest of the time I was on the basins washing hair. Funny, just rubbing and scrubbing the customers' scalps and lathering in the shampoo and conditioners and treatments, I began to get a sense of their troubles and ills as I massaged their heads and touched them. I was majoring in art and music and that fall when I went back to college, I dropped the music and took up psychology instead. I guess that was the start of it and in some peculiar, roundabout way I've been studying people ever since.'

Martha was fascinated by the origins of Catherine's healing gift.

'The healing has created a great quest for knowledge about humanity itself, for there is nothing as complex as the human being, as I'm sure you've already discovered. I studied and researched for many years in New York and Baltimore and San Francisco, worked in some fine hospitals and research centres and met hundreds, no thousands, of people that in some way I tried to help and heal along the way. I'm not getting any younger and when my husband got offered a professorship here in Boston, I found myself setting up my stall here in this house. I guess I'd begun to realize that I was stretching myself too thin and decided the time was right to help others to develop their own healing gifts, and their knowledge of the subject. Those that need my help somehow or other still always manage to find their way to my door. My referrals are usually by word of mouth. I do not advertise.'

'I heard about you through a friend,' said Martha, 'and she was the one gave me your number.'

'I'm so glad she did and that we had the opportunity to meet and have our paths cross,' smiled Catherine. 'Any help or advice I can give, just ask! Honest, that's all you need to do.'

Martha could tell the other woman genuinely meant it and found herself telling the more experienced healer about Cass and her growing fear for the child's life.

'You are already involved with the child. She has bonded with you?'

'Yes,' sighed Martha. 'She trusts me, talks to me.'

'Then you cannot let her down,' confirmed Catherine. 'Perhaps there will be a miracle, perhaps not. We cannot save all those that come to us, Martha. Part of the healing gift is accepting that. Often we are lucky and can help relieve pain or suffering of the body or mind, but at times the true healing work is to help another living soul accept that their time on this earth is nearing its end, and lift the fear and anger from them. For a child and their parents it is even more complex. Cass and her family need you, so you will suffer too alongside them.'

Martha could see the sense in what Catherine said and realized that she had already chosen a difficult path by involving herself with the Armstrong family.

'If you should ever need to talk to me or get in touch, here are my private home and cell phone numbers,' offered Catherine, passing her a piece of paper. Martha couldn't believe the older woman's generosity in offering her good will and support and she hoped that in time the two of them could become friends.

'I travel quite a bit, lecturing and visiting Europe or the West Coast, for it's always good to meet others and share our experiences and learn from each other. But I do hope that you and I will keep in touch.'

'Of course,' she promised.

'Balance is all important, Martha, and is something you will learn in time, but for one with a gift like yours there will naturally be immense demand and pressure.'

'That is what I'm worried about.'

'You are young and strong and have your husband and family and friends around you. Surround yourself with those who will help and protect you and your gift.'

'I will.'

'Martha, you are a good person, but still you must be careful! You are vulnerable to those who demand and expect too much of you. Remember what I told you about protecting yourself.'

Martha nodded.

When they said their farewells in the hallway, Catherine Morgan embraced Martha warmly before she stepped back out onto the street. Her head was reeling with all she had discovered as she made her way to the nearest T station. Her mind was already filling with plans as she walked back towards the Common.

Chapter Twenty-four

The upstairs room above Golden Threads lay empty, a jumble of packing cases and junk scattered across the bare floorboards. Martha was amazed by her best friend's offer to let her use the room for her healing.

'It's so darned obvious, I don't know why I didn't think of it before,' said Evie Hayes, glancing around the spacious area which she'd barely used over the past two years except for storing old samplers, cushion covers, runners and unpopular patterns in the vague hope that they might in time become fashionable again, and a whole range of odds and ends that she hadn't got the heart to part with.

'The only way I could get the shop was by agreeing to rent the whole building,' she explained. 'All this extra space is a luxury and a total waste for a small shop owner like myself. It's a shame not to be using it, but I was reluctant to sublet as I was nervous about another tenant. It's not everyone I'd let it to, but if you're interested, Martha, the place is yours.'

'Are you sure, Evie?'

'Of course, I wouldn't offer otherwise.'

'It's ideal.'

'With the long windows, it's good and bright: you can see right across the street and it's close to everything. There's a small bathroom at the back and another bedroom or whatever beside it.'

'Hmm.' Martha walked all around the top floor trying to imagine it cleaned and painted and herself working there, running her healing centre from this simple setting. There was something nice about the building's orientation and the way the light hit it. She could see now why Evie had been excited about the ground floor and had snapped it up for her shop.

'Come on, Martha, what do you think? Isn't it just so right! This place would be perfect for you.'

Martha said nothing but concentrated on the atmosphere around her as she walked in and out and up and down. The original owner had lived above her hat store with her family and it still showed signs of having once been a family home. She liked it and every instinct told her to take it, but she felt she should involve Mike and her family in the decision. It was a big undertaking to start renting out a space of her own, and to agree to share the lease even if it was at Evie's generous rock-bottom price.

'I love it, Evie, and having you downstairs would be just great.'

'Think of the fun we'd have!' laughed Evie. 'We'd be bound to have the most eccentric clientele in the whole of Easton. Seamstresses in need of healing!'

The two of them rocked with laughter at the insane thought of it, and Martha couldn't imagine anyone better to share the building with than her old schoolfriend.

Mike and Patrick and Alice had come over on the Friday night after school and work to see it. She was disappointed that her older daughter didn't consider it important enough to miss going to the cinema with her friends, but supposed that at thirteen, like many of the girls of her age, adults and their concerns were of little interest. Evie had been good enough to give Martha a set of keys and told her to take as much time as she wanted to make her decision.

'It's kind of small, Mom, isn't it!' Patrick blurted out after a whirlwind run through the place.

'Patrick, have a good look, please. This is really important to me and I value your opinion.'

This time he walked around more slowly looking at everything, checking the light switches and the faucets in the sink and even the floorboards. Mike and Martha smiled at each other, both realizing that he was at times beginning to act like a grown-up and they needed to respect that about their son. Alice was in raptures, having found a whole cardboard box full of patterns of Evie's; she liked the one of a horse and its foal the best. A bundle of stretched tapestries, awaiting their frames, lay against the wall of the largest room and, curious, Alice hunkered down and sorted through them.

Mike had brought a measuring tape and a notebook with him and scribbled down details with his pencil. Martha watched him out of the corner of her eye and wondered how she had ever managed to marry such an organized and responsible man.

'Well, love, what do you think?'

Mike moved off into the other room, leaving her to trail along beside him.

'Mike, you didn't say anything!'

Sometimes her husband could be so infuriating. She could try and guess what he was thinking but with the male mind who could tell? Did he like the place or not? He was walking around as if he was some sort of professional building surveyor or architect she'd employed instead of being her husband and partner. All she wanted to know was his gut reaction to the place. She always trusted her own instincts and knew she certainly liked it, but wanted his opinion.

'Patrick, what do you think?'

Her son ambled over, his dark head bent forward as he peered through the window.

'I think it's sort of neat, Mom. If it weren't going to be for your office it wouldn't be half bad as an apartment. It's so near to everything, the T line, the café, the diner – just about everything. Yet it's not too noisy because of the one-way system and this side of the street being pedestrianized. If it were me, I definitely think you should go for it.'

Martha nodded, pleased.

'Alice?'

Tossing her long fair hair back off her shoulder, Alice turned and gave the question her undivided attention.

'I think it would be nice for you and Aunt Evie to work so close together. You are best friends for ever and it would be fun! Wouldn't it?'

'Yes, honey, I'm sure it'd be fun.'

'She'd be downstairs and you'd be upstairs!'

Mike sauntered over to join them.

'Well?'

'Well what, Martha? I can't understand why we're even here, looking into this. Why should you want to have a business or rooms or whatever?'

'Mike, we've been through all this!' Martha tried to keep the exasperation from her voice. 'I can do my healing from here,' she reminded him, 'which means that people will come here and not to our home. I thought that's what you wanted? They can make appointments to come for a healing session. It won't be rushed or disturbed and I can organize it properly, run it professionally . . .'

'Like a business,' he said sarcastically. 'You are not a businesswoman, Martha.'

'I never said I was,' she admitted. 'I'm just a healer and as you so kindly pointed out you are fed up with all the sick and weird people that seem to congregate around me, and around our home.'

'You know right well what I meant, don't go trying to twist my words and meanings, that's not fair! I work damned hard all day to keep our family, and I'll be damned if I have to sink a dime of my hard-earned cash into this place, the retreat for lost souls who want to see the blessed Martha!'

Martha recoiled in shock, resisting the urge to smack him across his smug face, remembering their children were in the room.

Patrick stared straight at them, unbelieving. 'You two!'

Instantly they both felt ashamed.

'Hey, Alice, how about we go across the street and see if we can get a malt?' he offered.

Martha flinched, seeing the look of wariness in her young daughter's eyes.

'You go with Patrick, honey, your dad and I are just trying to sort out a few things. It's not as bad as it seems, honest.'

Mike rooted round his trouser pockets for some loose change, passing it to Patrick as they left. She gazed through rather dirty glass watching her children cross the street safely and slip into the Easton Diner.

'Evie wants to let me have the place for almost nothing, so it'll cost you zip, but in time I hope to pay my way,' she said firmly. Her husband was surprised. 'You've made it more than clear you want the healing out of the house, not disturbing you or the children! Well, I happen to agree with you. This place might be the solution. I can work from here. A few hours a day only while Alice is at school. I'll see a limited amount of people and will be back home by the time they all get in.'

'Why can't things just stay the way they were always?' he said softly, his grey-blue eyes looking into hers. The laughter lines and creases there had now become wrinkles. How had she not noticed that before? She lay beside him night after night and woke up to his face beside hers on the pillow every morning. Was she that unobservant?

'I don't know, Mike. Why do kids grow up? Why do cute babies become crazy teenagers and when did we stop listening at night to see if they were still breathing? Everything changes, it has to, otherwise we'd be stuck back with diapers and bottles in our "Power to the People" T-shirts. Did you want me to walk by Timmy Lucas and leave him to die surrounded by strangers, for God's sake, he's the same age as our Alice.'

'No, I know you couldn't, wouldn't do that. It's just that I feel everything has changed.'

'How do you mean?' she said, standing in front of him. 'We still love each other, love our kids.

What has changed, Mike, I honestly wish you'd tell me!'

'This whole healing thing, I guess I'm afraid it's going to take you away from me and the kids. It's just not part of our plan.'

'Plan?'

'Yeah, our plan.'

Martha couldn't believe it! Mike was talking about something they usually talked about when they were snuggled on the couch, relaxed after a few cold beers or lying in bed after hot, heavy lovemaking.

'The plan that when the kids were old enough you would go back to college and do a Master's in psychology, write up papers on the areas that interested you, work a bit and take time out to develop your career,' he said stubbornly. 'That plan!'

Martha didn't know what to say. The realization that her husband basically wanted to map out her life for the next twenty years or so almost freaked her out. Everything Mike did was so organized and well thought out, he just couldn't seem to handle spontaneity and its repercussions.

'Mike, I hate to inform you but I think that plan has just gone out the window as something rather more important has happened in my life. Can you understand that?' she insisted. 'I have been given this blessing, this power to help and heal people. I didn't ask for it or look for it but

235

somehow or other I have been chosen to do this work.'

Mike looked embarrassed, his hands shifting into his trouser pockets, a gesture that had always given him away ever since they first dated. Whenever they'd had a row or argument and it came time to say sorry or make up, Mike found it so hard to admit he was wrong or climb down. He was still the same.

'Mike, I love you and all I'm asking is for you to give me a bit of support and to back me up. I know full well I'm not a businesswoman, you don't have to remind me of that, but I do know what I'm doing when I heal people. The feeling is so strong, so good that I feel energized and connected to them. I like talking to people, trying to understand them and find out what is going on in their lives. I think that also might be a big part of it, giving people time.'

'Ah Jeez, Mar! I'm such a selfish bastard!'

She smiled despite herself, a laugh escaping into the stillness between them.

'You don't have to agree with me!' he said defensively.

'Mike, I'm still me and nothing is going to change that,' she pledged, wrapping her arms around his neck.

By the time the kids got back Mike had worked out a few pricing details on a sheet of paper and made some suggestions.

'Are you sure you're happy about this?' he

pressed her. 'That you're not taking on too much?'

'Yeah, I'm fine about it. You were right, our family time together is precious and should be private. Renting here will solve the problem of people abusing our home situation and if they want or need a phone number or address to contact me, well, this will be it!'

'Is Evie OK about all this?'

'Mike, she was the one suggested it!'

'OK! OK! It's just that landlord and tenant is a different relationship than being friends, you realize that.'

'Yeah! And we're both fine about it.'

Any qualms Martha had about this new undertaking were resolved. She could hardly wait to get home and phone Evie with the good news.

Kathleen's older boy Joe and a friend had agreed to paint the place. They were trying to set up on their own as a decorating service and were touting for customers. Evie and Martha split the cost and were more than pleased with the resulting soft pecan-coloured walls and warm cream woollen drapes.

She took an old couch from their den and covered it with a navy throw and huge squashy cushions, with a rather modern elmwood desk and chair for herself. Framed photos from a gallery in Quincy Market of the sea, sky and earth seemed to sit well together and were a constant reminder of her healing mission.

Mike helped her to organize a new phone listing and in the smaller room they placed two simple chairs and an old coffee table of Evie's.

'Just in case someone is waiting,' she suggested.

To Martha it felt sort of scary having a place that was her own, like an office. She was used to the jumble of family life and tried to imagine herself arriving calmly at number 143 to try and deal with people who had a crisis in their life, and the responsibility it would involve.

Evie sensed her nervousness.

'Martha, do you not remember how bad I was when I was opening the shop, I was sure not a sinner would cross the threshold for months and that I'd be declared a bankrupt! Thank God it all worked out and now I couldn't imagine not having the store! You'll see, after a few weeks, coming here and walking up the stairs will just become part of your routine. You already have a notebook full of people only desperate to see you, so you won't be sitting twiddling your thumbs, I can guarantee that.'

Martha hugged her friend, wondering how she had been so lucky to have been put beside Evie O'Connor on her very first day of school. The two of them had been inseparable ever since and had shared the ups and downs in each other's lives. When Martha's father had died from a bleeding ulcer brought on from his constant abuse of alcohol, it was Evie who had listened to her rant and scream about how glad she was her father was dead and it was Evie who had eventually soaked a towel in cold water and placed it over her tear-sodden swollen eyes and held her till she fell asleep on the night before his funeral. You didn't forget a friend like that.

By the end of the week, everything was just the way she wanted it and the table she had ordered had arrived. Looking around her, Martha liked the clear simple lines she had created and hoped that nothing would distract her from her purpose – healing! Mike and the family all gave the place the seal of approval. Kim and Rianna had arrived with a huge bunch of white lillies and a magnificent dried floral arrangement of stretching dark wood branches, interesting violets and pale blue forget-me-nots.

'We came to wish you luck!' they chorused and gasped with admiration when they saw the result of all the hard work.

'Makes a big difference from all Evie's junk,' remarked Kim. 'This place really looks something now.'

Martha smiled, hoping she had managed to create a space that those in need of her help would feel soothed and relaxed in.

'It's just fine and dandy,' her mother declared, giving herself the great tour of inspection before sinking into the comfort of the couch. 'You did a wonderful job here, Martha pet, and I'm right proud of you.'

Martha smiled. Her mother was not generally given to fulsome praise. 'Thanks, Mom, I'm glad that you like it.'

'You know something? I always felt that you were a little bit different.'

'Different!'

'No, I just mean that you were going to do something different from the rest of the family!'

Different – this sure was different. Never had she imagined herself having such a calling.

On that first morning when she put her key in the lock and walked upstairs to her rooms her heart beat so fast that she could almost have convinced herself that she had a heart complaint. She resisted the urge to sneak down to Evie's and sit curled up in a chair gossiping, and settled herself at her desk drawing out the bundles of letters she had received that weekend. Kim had offered to help her file some of them and sort them out in terms of urgency, depending on the well-being of the writer or the person they were concerned about.

Martha sighed, reading of the sheer desperation of the family of a sufferer of terminal cancer of the oesophagus who had somehow or other heard of her and were willing to fly with the patient from Sacramento to Boston in the hope of seeing her. The condition of the almost fifty-year-old husband seemed far too serious for them to contemplate such a journey. Martha turned on the laptop and began to compose a letter to his distraught wife and sons telling them this and promising to pray for him.

Louisa Roberts was her first appointment and Martha greeted the sixty-year-old warmly. 'Well, Louisa, what do you think?'

'You have a beautiful home, Martha, but I think here is a special place for you to do your healing work.'

'How are you doing?'

'I'm doing great! That shoulder of mine hasn't given me one bit of bother since you laid your hands on it and now I was wondering if you could do the same for my knee.' Without prompting she rolled up the leg of her pale lilac polyester trousers and shoved the discoloured swollen kneecap towards Martha. 'It's giving me right torment at the moment and I can hardly go outside at all with the pain from it. The old steroids and tablets the doctor gave me don't seem to work so good no more.'

'Louisa, you must keep taking the tablets the doctor prescribed for you but if you want I will lay my hands on the knee and see if it can in any way help.'

There was utter trust in the older woman's eyes as Martha touched her and began the healing session. Louisa had such faith that the healing

241

would remove the swelling from her knee that Martha could feel the intense heat that seemed to be drawn into the ageing tissues and muscles and joint. Working together both of them felt the healing energy as they said a few words of simple prayer.

Afterwards Martha realized that healing filled her with a unique joy and sense of the spirit and a deep gratitude that she had been called to do this work.

Chapter Twenty-five

Beth Armstrong phoned that Wednesday, all excited and nervous, the words tumbling from her mouth, as she told Martha the good news.

'She's got a heart! Cass is getting a new heart!'

The transplant team from Children's Hospital had confirmed they'd found a perfect donor match for her daughter and Cass was already being prepared for surgery.

'I still can't believe it! Can you come by the hospital and see her?' Beth pleaded anxiously.

'Honest, Beth, I don't think that it's my place to interfere. Cass needs the doctors and nurses to look after her right now and get her through her surgery. You know she's in good hands. Why, I'd only be in their way.'

'What about healing?'

'Healing?'

'Yes, I was hoping that you could lay your hands on her at the start of the operation.'

'Beth, Cass has had healing, and now it's time to let the medical team do their work.'

'But it's bound to help, Martha, you being there, and my little girl needs all the help that she can get!'

'Beth, calm down. You've got to trust the surgeons,' she advised her gently. 'I'll pray for Cass, I promise, but it's not my place to be there, honest it's not.'

'So you're saying that you won't come when she needs you the most,' argued Beth Armstrong.

'No, I'm not saying that at all. I know how hard it must be for you all, I can imagine how I'd feel if one of my kids was facing such a big operation, but me being there isn't going to help. I'm sorry,' whispered Martha.

There was a stony silence on the other end of the line and Martha could almost sense the other woman's desperation and fearfulness.

'I'm sorry, Beth,' she repeated.

A few hours later Martha found herself kneeling in a bench in her parish church, enjoying the peace and stillness that a visit to St John's always brought her. She gazed up at the grey marble altar and the ornately carved cross; light slanting in through the stained glass windows above her sprinkled dashes of purple, pink, gold and blue along the wooden floor. A statue of Mary, the mother of Jesus, gazed down at her, opposite St Patrick, the patron saint of Ireland, in his green and gold bishop's robes. This place was an oasis of spirituality in a busy world, removed from the traffic and noise and constant music and sound that assaulted daily life. A place to come and offer silent prayer.

In quiet contemplation, Martha closed her eyes thinking of Cass, wishing her to be strong and for the Holy Spirit to watch over her. She found consolation and support within the walls of this simple church, felt her prayers were being listened to and that God was considering her requests. If that was faith, she supposed she was blessed with it. She had always felt close to the spirit, close to God and was unafraid to ask things of him, challenge him. Now she was asking for the child, words of prayer filling her mind in the silence.

She heard footsteps, and turning around spotted Father Eugene. She would have liked him to join her, to have told him about Cass, and for both of them to pray for her together. The priest, recognizing her, stopped for an instant, before turning his face away and collecting a book he'd left up near the lectern, disappearing inside the safety of the sacristy.

The day dragged on, Martha's thoughts constantly with Cass. She found herself barely able to concentrate all afternoon and was abrupt with Mary Rose when she collected her from piano lessons.

'You OK, Mom?' asked her teenage daughter perceptively.

She kept waiting for the phone to ring back home, and almost whacked Patrick when he tried to phone one of his football team-mates to discuss arrangements for the following Saturday's game.

'Get off the phone, Patrick, you know I'm waiting on news of someone.'

A look of bewilderment crossed his broad face and Martha knew her son had no comprehension of her involvement with people he considered just strangers.

Thoughts of the child haunted and disturbed her, in a strange irrational way that made her question her ability and the powerful call to healing. There was still no word by midnight and she paced the floor of her home wondering what she should do. Her repeated calls to the hospital had elicited zero information.

'For God's sake, will you relax and calm down,' Mike implored her.

'I can't,' she admitted. 'I just can't! I can't put her out of mind. You should see her, she's so sick.'

Her husband was a good and kind man; all right, maybe a little too wrapped up in his career and work, but he was a good father and had always been there for her and the kids.

'Mike, imagine if one of . . .'

'I'm not going to imagine, Martha. I don't want to do that, and if you have any sense you'll stop thinking of her too and concentrate on our kids. Patrick told me you almost bit his head off today when he tried to check if he was playing in Saturday's football team.'

'Oh Mike, I didn't mean it. Patrick knows that.'

She moved towards her husband, wanting to make things right between them, and was hurt when he turned away and began to read the newspaper, the conversation ended.

She couldn't sleep and stayed up late watching an old Hollywood musical on the TV. When she came upstairs, her husband rolled to one side of their bed, anger and confusion radiating from the hunched curve of his neck and spine as he turned away from her. Instead of undressing and lying warm beside him, Martha took a heavy sweater from her drawer and her purse. Beth hadn't bothered to phone and since there was no reply from her home phone number, it meant she was still likely to be at the hospital. Surely the operation was over by now.

Getting into her car and switching on the headlights, she pulled out onto the road and drove up on to the Mass Turnpike, her instinct leading her towards Children's Hospital. The road was quiet as it was after midnight and listening to David Gray, she tried to keep herself awake.

The night receptionist was reading the newspaper when Martha enquired about Cass, and he directed her to the nurses' station on the third floor. Martha, feeling a knot of anxiety in her stomach, had only just got out of the elevator when she spotted Beth Armstrong. She looked utterly worn out and wretched.

'How is she?' she asked, rushing over to Beth, noticing the red-rimmed eyes.

'She didn't have it, Martha! She didn't have the operation,' sobbed Beth, grabbing hold of her jacket and beginning to weep. 'That bastard! Dr Rourke, the anaesthetist, said she'd a slight chest infection and it was too risky to go ahead with the transplant. He cancelled the operation. Stopped her getting it!'

'What!'

'What harm would it have done? They could have pumped her up with antibiotics.'

'Oh, Beth, I don't believe it! I'm so sorry.'

Beth Armstrong was at breaking point.

'Tom took the boys home. My mother's staying the night and he'll come straight back.'

'Maybe they can operate on Cass tomorrow or the day after?'

'They sent it to Texas! A boy there about two years older than Cass, heart's a perfect match for him too.'

Beth began to shake from top to toe, Martha holding her in her arms. 'That's her chance gone! She's not going to get another chance like that again. Not ever. There's just not enough signed-up donors.'

'You don't know that! You can't say that for sure, Beth.'

'I do know that,' she said huskily. 'I fucking do.'

Martha held Beth in her arms. The other woman clung to her as if she was a life saver, letting tears of anger and disappointment fall. Tom Armstrong eventually took over from her on his return. Martha said goodnight to the both of them, and taking a quick peek at the sleeping child through the glass panel on her room door, decided it was time she was back in her own bed. The temperature was well below freezing and the snow ploughs were out on the streets as she left the car park.

Chapter Twenty-six

Cass went home on a freezing December morning, the staff from the cardiac floor of Children's Hospital hugging her warmly and wishing her well, before she disappeared into the elevator with her parents.

'You take care, honey!' Nurse Peterson called from the station as they all said their goodbyes.

Beth Armstrong stood at the entrance waiting for Tom to bring their Voyager to the front parking bay. There had been a fresh snowfall overnight and the weather forecasters were predicting a blizzard by the weekend. It was far too cold for Cass, coming from the constant maintained heat of the hospital to the chill vagaries of New England's winter. The child was only getting over her chest infection and was still weak.

A shiver of fear and panic ran through Beth at the thought of the cold piercing the armour of the fur-lined parka and heavy knitted hat and gloves and fleece-lined jog pants she'd made Cass put on.

She longed to turn the wheelchair around and race back up to the protection of the familiar hospital room, but one look at the animated expression in her daughter's eyes was enough to make her accept the agreed decision to return home. At least Cass was back up top of the transplant list and they had a pager that would let them know as soon as a suitable donor heart became available.

'Mom, there's Dad! I see the car!' Cass shouted. 'We're going home.'

Martha had driven up and down two streets searching for the Armstrongs' home. She should have brought a map with her: she was unfamiliar with this part of Boston, and in the snow everything seemed to look the same. There was no one about as it was much too cold for that and she peered through the windscreen looking for the street sign or turn for Thousand Oaks Drive. She admonished herself for her stupidity, as she must have driven by it at least twice. Beth and Tom Armstrong's house was in the middle of a row of similar two-storey bay-windowed wooden homes that clung together side by side. Some more dilapidated than others, theirs had been painted a pale blue that had faded with the weather. The porch was bedecked with coloured lights, and a small Christmas tree covered with angels and bells. A red-painted wooden Santa stood among the unswept leaves and weeds and rotting seed heads of the neglected flowerbed.

Martha rang the doorbell and waited for a response. In the distance she could hear a television and the echo of footsteps on a wooden floor as a boy of about twelve or thirteen came and let her in. He had the same hair colouring as his sister and a similar way of speaking.

'I'm Billy, Cass's older brother. You're welcome.'

His face was long and sensitive looking as if he had already been exposed to more sadness in his life than most boys his age.

'Dad!' he shouted. 'She's here.'

Tom Armstrong came out to welcome Martha with a small boy tugging and pulling at his jeans.

'Sorry to meet you like this, Martha,' he joked, 'but this young fellow here and I are having a bear wrestling match and I'm supposed to be a grizzly of the worst kind.' Curious, his five-year-old son desisted for a few minutes as he sneaked a look at her. He was a small plump version of his father and shook Martha's hand politely when introduced.

'Hello, Jay,' she smiled. 'Where's Cass?' she enquired, noting the serious look that filled Tom's face as he passed Jay over to his brother and led her upstairs.

'Beth had to go out for a while, so I'm minding the kids.'

As they walked up the staircase, Martha noted the enormous collection of family photos displayed on the walls. Cass was always a small white face in the middle of them.

'That's when we all went to Florida two years ago, before Cass got really sick,' Tom confided.

'How is she?'

'Tired, weak I guess, but to me she seems happier, more her old self now she's back home with the boys. She's been asking a lot for you.'

Martha touched his arm. Tom Armstrong was a kind, generous man who loved his daughter more than any words could express, and she was glad they were getting this time together.

'How's Beth?' she prodded gently.

'Well, you know Beth, always flapping and fussing about. She makes poor Doc Cantrell call every day to check Cass, instead of just leaving the poor kid be.'

'She's just concerned, that's all.'

Martha took a deep breath as she followed Tom into the child's room. It was decorated in pink with pale pink gingham curtains and a coverlet to match. Scatter cushions in various prints with stars and hearts and daisies were flung on the small chair beside the bed, and straight away Martha's eyes were drawn to the small pale figure lying against the pillows.

'Martha!' Cass called the minute she saw her. Both of them hugged each other tight. Martha had to mask the surprise she felt noticing how much paler and weaker the child looked at home in her normal surroundings. All her drips and drains and equipment were gone, leaving her looking small and very vulnerable.

'How you doing, Cass? Is it good to be home?'

'You don't have to ask that!' she joked. 'I'm sick of hospitals and doctors and nurses. I know they were all trying to be nice to me but another few weeks of that place and I'd have gone crazy. Honest, I would have.'

'There's no place like home, I guess. I remember when my son Patrick was about four he had his tonsils out. He must have been the most troublesome kid they'd ever had on the children's floor. He would not stay in bed for them and was running round the place creating mayhem though he was meant to rest quiet after his surgery. In the end Mike and I got a call begging us to come pick him up. The minute he crossed the door of home he relaxed and spent about two days crashed on the couch with his blanket over him. He was small but he knew well where he wanted to be.'

'That's all I wanted too, Martha, to be home here in my room, not stuck in some stupid hospital. If I'm going to die I want to die here at home.'

Martha heard the words that Cass spoke so matter-of-factly and tried not to show any reaction. She wasn't about to protest and pretend that such an event was not on the cards when in her heart she knew well how important it was for the child to begin to think of such things.

'You have a beautiful room, Cass. My girls would be dead jealous if they saw it.'

'My dad did it up last year when I was in the hospital. He painted it and sanded the floor and built those shelves for my books and stuff. He's real handy and he and my mom surprised me. He said it's a princess room, because I'm his princess.'

Martha had to look away and pretend she was studying a pile of games stacked in the corner, so as to avoid Cass picking up on the overwhelming emotions she was feeling. She had to get a grip on herself if she was going to be of any use to the child. 'And how can I help you? Are you in any pain or discomfort?' she asked.

'Just a little,' she admitted in a small voice. 'Sometimes when I breathe in it hurts me and I'm almost afraid to do it, and here on my side it's kind of sore.'

'Would you like me to try and ease it for you? To see if I can help any?'

'Please, Martha, yes please!'

Martha took off her jacket, as it was warm in the room. She rubbed her hands together and walked forward till she was standing over Cass. The child's attention was fully on her as Martha laid her hands on her. Cass's chest seemed cold, her heartbeat irregular, too fast, her lungs not inflating fully, her ribs aching and sore. Martha wanted to try and steady her, make the tissues in her lungs less irritated, soothe them so as the air could circulate more freely.

255

'Try and breathe slow and steadily, that's it! Good girl.'

She kept her hands on the rising chest, letting the heat from her hands flow into the child, praying all the time, asking for life and energy to be restored to her. When she was finished she squeezed her hand and Martha could detect a glisten of a tear in the child's eye.

'What is it, Cass?' she asked, concerned.

'It's nothing!'

Cass wiped her nose with the side of her fingers, and sniffed. Martha passed her a tissue from the Winnie the Pooh box on her bedside table. 'You OK?' she asked.

'Yeah!'

If Cass wasn't willing to talk about what upset or saddened her yet, that was fine by Martha. The young girl had a lot of things to sort out in her head. She might only be ten years old but she had an immense knowledge for one so young and probably had a good idea of the progression of her illness and was likely trying to figure out what the next stages might be.

'Would you like me to get your dad?' Martha asked her.

Cass shook her head vigorously. 'No!'

'OK. Do you want me to stay or go?'

'Stay, please.'

Martha sat back and said, 'Would you like me to read to you or play a game or just chat?'

Cass shrugged. Martha helped to make her

more comfortable, whooshing up her pillows and shaking her bedclothes.

'That any better?'

Cass smiled. 'A bit.'

She had those full Julia Roberts type lips and when she smiled it seemed to just light up her whole face, making her look almost pretty and well.

'Tell me about your family, about your kids,' Cass ordered.

Martha was a little taken aback but she guessed it was normal to be curious. Alice and Patrick had both asked her a few times about the girl that was sick in the hospital. Children were always searching for lines that connected them with one another. She described her son, seeing him from Cass's point of view, a boy who was strong and healthy and had never really known illness, a boy whose spirit and courage had not yet been tested.

'He's a good kid, Cass, an all-rounder as the teachers call him, but he's not sure where or what he's going to do when he gets older.'

'He's a bit like my older brother Billy. Billy always minded me when we were kids and wouldn't let anyone touch me.'

'Mary Rose is . . . well, she's just Mary Rose. She's just turned thirteen and is getting to be a teenager.'

'Is she pretty?'

Martha thought about it. Her daughter was more attractive than pretty, with her dark hair and dark eyes and fair Irish skin. She was like the proverbial duckling who would eventually turn into a swan. Another year and a half and her braces would be gone and the true shape of her figure would be more evident. Hopefully her daughter would grow more comfortable in her own skin and be happy for who she was. At the moment she seemed to be fighting and railing against everyone and everything and Martha could only stand by and watch powerless.

'I wish that I had a big sister.'

'Why?'

'It would be fun and neat doing things together, makeup and shopping and all that stuff. The boys just go yuk at anything girly.'

'You've got your mom.'

'I know, but a sister might be nice!'

'Sisters fight a lot. My girls sometimes kill each other, and argue over the most stupid things. If you heard them . . . it drives me crazy.'

'I think it would be nice for Mom to have another daughter for when I'm gone, then she mightn't be so lonely.'

There it was again, another reference to her dying. Martha just held her hand. Cass would talk if she wanted to, if she was ready.

Neither of them spoke for a minute, both staring at each other.

'I think I'm going to die soon, Martha. Mom and Dad are real upset about it but that's not going to change it.'

Martha just nodded. It was important for Cass to say what she wanted without insincere platitudes and protestations. If she felt her death was coming, she was probably right.

'They don't want to talk about it. They think if we don't talk about it then it won't happen. Mom cries at night, sometimes I can hear her, and Dad curses. I hear that too even if I'm not meant to listen to profanity!'

'They love you, Cass, that's all!'

'I know,' she said wearily.

Martha was filled with an immense sadness. She had not imagined that healing would bring such a sense of impending loss. In only a few short weeks she too had come to love the child and dreaded her leaving them.

'I'm scared, Martha, scared at leaving Mom and Dad and the boys and this house and all the people and things I know. I don't want to lie in a box in the ground, it might be dark and awful in there and I'll be so alone. I don't want to go there!'

Martha rushed forward to hold her.

'Hush, Cass! Hush! Don't think of such things!'

She held the young girl in her arms, wanting to protect and yet prepare her for what would happen. She was weak, her energy and life force seeping away. The miracle was that she had survived so long, had given her parents ten years of living within her presence. She was a child of goodness and light, a very special being. Martha rocked and consoled her, stroking her long fair hair and wiping the tears from her eyes. 'Don't be afraid, Cass. Don't be afraid,' she said.

'What will happen to me, Martha?'

Martha realized that she was being tested, asked questions that Tom and Beth would never be asked for fear of wounding and upsetting them. The child trusted her and she had to be as honest and truthful as possible.

'They say it's like falling asleep, you know the way you were when I came in, just drifting off as peaceful as that.'

'But what happens then?'

'Then . . .' Martha sighed. How could she even begin to answer that age-old question that people had been searching for an answer to for so many centuries. She knew full well that Beth Armstrong had made it clear that she did not have any religious beliefs.

'I was sixteen when my father died. He looked awful, as he'd been sick for a while. Lying on the hospital bed, I looked at that body and I guess I realized that although it looked a lot like my daddy, it wasn't him. It was just the shell, the husk that had held his spirit. My daddy was gone.'

'Gone?'

'Aye, Cass. Gone. Somewhere me and my mom and three brothers couldn't see him but, you know, for a long time afterwards we all felt he was still around us. We were raised Catholic so I guess my daddy must be in heaven, though I remember looking at the wind blowing through the trees, and the waves on the ocean and the clouds blowing through the sky that summer and feeling my daddy had become a part of it all, that in a way he'd never leave me.'

Cass was silent, considering, her thin cheek resting against Martha's arm.

Her breathing was becoming steadier, her heartbeat more regular and a few minutes later she moved gently back against the pillow. Martha hoped what she had said would be of some help, some consolation.

They heard footsteps coming up the stairs and Cass tried to sit up straight, pretend nothing was happening.

'Here you go, honey!' called Tom Armstrong, pushing in the bedroom door, carrying a tray with three cups of hot chocolate and a plate of nut cookies. 'Martha, would you like a mug of chocolate too?'

She nodded appreciatively, tempted by the warm aroma and Tom's relaxed manner. 'It's so good to have her home,' he said. 'You just can't imagine what it's like visiting that damned hospital day in, day out.'

'Dad!'

'Sorry, Cass, but you know I hate those places. I loathe them.'

'We know, Dad. We know.'

'Hospitals make people sicker, if you ask me,

they go in with one thing and come out with another.'

'Dad!' admonished his daughter again.

'OK, OK! The doctors and nurses there were real good to you but I admit it. Maybe it's just me, but those places give me the creeps.'

'Well then, you're lucky to have Cass home, Tom,' laughed Martha, trying to cool her chocolate.

Sitting there at Cass's bedside Martha was so glad to see the young girl at ease at least with her surroundings. Jay came in and climbed up on the bed, pushing in beside his sister, sneaking two cookies off the plate, Cass automatically picking up the crumbs he dropped on her quilt and eating them. Billy ambled up too, and sat on the end of the bed, his long legs and feet tucked in under him.

'I think I'd better get going,' said Martha, finishing off the end of her drink.

'Thank you for coming,' said Cass quietly, stretching her skinny arms around Martha's neck. 'You'll come back soon again?'

'Of course I will,' she promised.

Tom escorted her downstairs, his face serious.

'We really appreciate what you're doing for Cass, Martha. We really do,' he told her.

'Unfortunately there's not that much I can do, except perhaps help a bit with her pain and fear.'

His eyes met hers. 'So you think what the doctors said is true then?'

She nodded slowly, looking at the rag rug on the floor.

'She's afraid, Tom. Scared of what lies ahead.'

'Beth believes that Cass will get better once she gets that damned new heart!'

Martha sucked on her lip, not knowing what to say to him. A groan of despair escaped from his throat and Martha automatically put her arms around him. 'It's all right, Tom, it's all right,' she said, rubbing his shoulders, feeling the immense weight he carried.

He struggled to regain his composure; moments later, thanking her yet again, he walked her out to her car.

'You need to talk to Cass,' she suggested. 'Both of you.'

'We will,' he promised. 'We will.'

On the way home she called into her rooms. Kim was still there filing some letters. She got out the desk diary.

'Martha, you are almost full for the next seven –eight months, and I've got a waiting list the length of my arm. I've put people off by telling them I don't know your holiday schedule yet,' she said.

'Which is true.'

'Kathleen or I will have to phone them back.'

Martha turned the navy blue leather diary towards her, looking at the collection of names and addresses and phone numbers, many from out of state.

'God!'

'Listen, Mar, Evie and Ruth and the rest of us were talking. Maybe you could do one bigger session, hire out a large room or a hall and then get to do a healing on a whole group of people who need your help? Otherwise you're going to end up with an appointment calendar that will run into a year or two ahead.'

Martha hadn't thought of anything like that.

'Come off it, Kim, I'm not going to become like one of those big gospel healing missions that you see on the TV.'

'No! No, I didn't mean that. No-one is asking you to change yourself, least of all me. It's just that there are a lot of sick people out there and you can't get to meet or see that many of them over a twenty-four-hour period, even if you were to work at night. It's just not possible.'

Martha was silent.

'You only get to see a fraction of the people who really need your help, and maybe having one afternoon or evening session, you might accomplish more.'

'I work one on one with people, Kim,' insisted Martha, 'and I'm not sure if I could work with groups of people around. I . . . I don't know.'

'Listen, it's just an idea, that's all. But will you think about it?'

'I will,' she promised.

Chapter Twenty-seven

Gina and Bob Forrester had insisted on inviting Martha and Mike to a pre-Christmas dinner in one of Boston's most expensive restaurants. Bob hugged her like she was an old friend the minute she stepped into the entrance of Giselle's, Martha trying to smile and pretend she was used to eating in such places regularly as the French *maître d'* led them to their table. Mike was in strange form; he appeared over-polite and distant with the other couple as they were seated at the best table in the house. Fortunately both Bob and Gina were so wrapped up in the excitement of Gina's pregnancy that they scarcely noticed it.

'Well, Martha, the least we could do was buy you two the best dinner in the whole of Boston for what you've done for Gina, well, for the both of us!'

Martha blazed red, embarrassed by their host's effusiveness and insistence on her involvement in his wife's pregnancy, and she could see Mike was annoyed too. He was staring intently into his wine glass as if it were a crystal orb, not wanting to get drawn into any discussion about her healing prowess.

Gina looked absolutely beautiful. Pregnancy suited her and there was a new contentment in her eyes. 'I've already booked into the hospital and I'm having a scan in a few weeks' time to check everything is going all right,' she confided. 'They wanted me to have that test for foetal abnormalities but I told my doctor I already know this baby's fine.'

'Are you sure that's wise?' questioned Martha.

'I put my trust in the Lord and in you, Martha, that's good enough for me.'

Mike cast her a scathing look for a fraction of a second.

'And I told Gina, don't let that doctor go spoil it by telling you if we are having a boy or a girl,' joked Bob. 'Just let nature take its course and we'll find out when Junior makes his or her appearance.'

As they perused their menus Bob ordered the best champagne. The wine waiter filled all their glasses.

'Let me propose a toast to my wife Gina and a good friend – Martha!'

Martha was pleased to see such a happy father-to-be as she sipped the champagne. Noticing that Gina barely touched the alcohol, she got the waiter to fetch her a sparkling water instead. Relieved, she watched as Mike gradually relaxed, talking to Bob about the company and its future direction, and who would be the winners and losers long term in the technology sector.

'By the way, Dan was asking after you, Martha, last week when I was in San Jose.'

'Dan?'

'Dan Kendrick,' explained Mike.

'He's been singing your praises and said to say thanks to you again,' said Bob amiably.

Martha knew that Mike blamed the head of Powerhouse for some of the attention and publicity she'd received.

The food was delicious and Martha enjoyed getting to know Gina better and telling her about their own kids and the Irish family in which she had been raised.

'I envy you, Martha, my parents divorced when I was eight, and my mom remarried when I was ten and then again when I was sixteen,' admitted Gina. 'I must have been a right brat to those new husbands of hers and given my mom a real hard time.'

'What about your dad?'

'I saw him a few times over the first year or two after the divorce, and then we moved to New Jersey and he got a job as a project engineer in Nebraska. We wrote and phoned for a while and then I guess just lost touch.'

Martha couldn't imagine how one would lose touch with a parent or child no matter how good or bad they might be.

'I was just a kid then, and I guess I didn't know any better. Meeting Bob changed things, and I made contact with my dad again. He's in a retirement home now, and I'm not sure if he remembers that I'm his daughter any more, but darned sure I remember and know that he's my dad.'

'I'm glad you found him again,' said Martha.

'Along with my four stepbrothers, which was a bit of a surprise,' she giggled.

Gina was yawning by the time the waiter brought their coffees. 'I seem to get tired more easily,' she apologized. 'I guess with the baby I just can't keep up the pace of being a night owl any more.'

'That's OK. Martha used to be just the same when she was having our three,' smiled Mike, passing her the cream jug.

A half-hour later they had said their goodbyes.

'You take care of yourself, Gina, and try to put your feet up and rest over the holidays if you get the chance,' said Martha, thanking the Forresters warmly for the lovely night out. She was relieved that Mike had enjoyed it and had got on so well with Bob.

'They're a nice couple,' she said matter-of-factly as they rode home in the cab, the Christmas trees in the store windows sparkling like stars. Mike agreed. Laying her head on his shoulder she was glad that the awful row they'd had before going out about her interfering in his life, and overstepping the mark by trying to help his boss's wife, had blown over and that her husband had calmed down. Mike's lips tasted of mint chocolate as they began to kiss.

That season they spent a quiet Christmas at home. Frances Kelly and her friend Bee, as well as Martha's brothers Sean and Jack and their families, joined them for the usual slap-up Christmas dinner of roast turkey and boiled ham, followed by Christmas pudding and mince pies, all of their stomachs groaning with the excess food. Alice had lit the candle in the window to welcome the child Jesus, and the red felt stockings hung from the banisters in the hall, the scent from the pine Christmas tree Mike had put up filling the house. Evie and Martha had gone carol singing with a group from the church on Christmas Eve, ending up making creamy Irish coffees at midnight in the Hayes kitchen as Evie prepared the stuffing for the turkey.

After Christmas dinner Martha was so tired she'd fallen asleep on the couch watching an old Bing Crosby movie.

'Are you all right, Martha pet?' asked her mother, concerned.

'I'm grand, Mom. It's just been a busy day and I think Evie was a bit heavy handed with the whiskey in the coffees last night.'

'No harm in that,' murmured Frances, waiting for her son-in-law to refill her glass. Looking out at the deserted, snow-covered street Martha realized how relaxed she'd felt all day, despite the crowd and rushing around. There'd been no post, no phone calls except to her brother in California and to Mike's folks in Florida, and no unexpected callers looking for the Miracle Woman. Curling up in front of the fire with Mary Rose and Alice, she acknowledged how good that felt and the utter freedom of it.

Chapter Twenty-eight

Henry Madison put his hand in his trouser pocket, searching for the pen. Trying the top drawer and the cracked blue jug on the middle shelf of the dresser, eventually he found the good silver fountain pen he wanted. He got out the heavy quality writing paper and sat himself down at the kitchen table. Thankfully William was otherwise occupied watching *Star Wars*, his favourite movie.

It felt awkward composing a letter to a total stranger, something he really was not given to, but at this stage he had to resort to desperate measures. Every day he was becoming more and more incapacitated and immobile; the pain when he walked was excruciating and even standing for too long was making him grimace. The local clinic had made an appointment for him with a specialist who'd done all the tests and recommended a hip replacement, saying there had been a huge amount of degeneration of the joint. A few weeks in hospital, time afterwards convalescing and no heavy lifting or work for a few months, the surgeon had explained to him. Already Henry knew it would be impossible for him to go ahead with such a procedure. First off, who would mind William while he was in hospital and convalescing? His forty-five-year-old brother did not take well to strangers or to change. Then there was the whole question of not being able to lift or work for a long time afterwards. Who would there be to wash and dress him and take him for walks if he couldn't do it? The quandary was that if he didn't have the operation, in another year or two he might no longer be able to manage looking after his disabled brother anyways.

The responsibility lay heavy with him and Henry had consulted a few people about it. Regina Brown his social worker had assured him that she could pull a few strings and fix up a respite care bed for William somewhere close by and keep a good watch that he was doing OK. But Henry knew how upset William got whenever he attempted to leave him, crying and hollering like a toddler, and seeming totally bereft. Assurances and promises that he would come back were of no value as his brother had no concept of time or the future. It sure was a headache and he could see no way of resolving the dilemma. Celeste McGraw his neighbour, who sometimes watched William for him, had even offered to move into the apartment and mind him. It was a kind offer but one he would not be taking her up on, as even after a morning or evening minding him Celeste was exhausted. So how on earth would she last out for weeks!

Henry had no sister or other family he could turn to, and was not prepared to just go abandon his troublesome brother. There had to be another way.

He had been depressed about it, so depressed he had missed his meeting of the local historical society and the monthly poetry group. He was not in the mood for rhymes and words and research papers, with William totally unaware of the concerns he had about him.

Then by chance he had read the interview with the woman in Boston who was said to be able to heal, to perform miracles. Apparently many believed in her and said she was a truly good person. Henry, at first sceptical, reading it over and over again, wondered if this Martha McGill person might be able to help him. He had never been the type of man looking for charity or help but reading about the New England housewife and the numbers of people who had claimed to have been healed by her, he couldn't help but wonder if the Good Lord might see fit to help him, through this woman.

His own Presbyterian faith had always been strong and had sustained him through many difficult years. Growing up he supposed he had never really realized the burden his young brother had placed on their mother and father. He'd been busy at school and then later college and studying to become a teacher, something he had always wanted, the chance to grow and learn himself and the opportunity to open young minds. William had been in and out of special schools and day care facilities since about the age of five, his mother and father ignoring the advice to place him in a state-run institution that could deal with his needs. His mother was insistent she could cope and was not going to put her 'special child' away, no matter what the psychologists and psychiatrists recommended.

By twenty his brother was tall and big and a whole heap of trouble, needing constant watching. Henry would relieve some of the pressure on his ageing parents during school holidays, entertaining William, taking him for walks, devising activities that would help to keep him occupied, but he was always grateful when summer ended and he could return to the classroom. Marilyn and Joe Madison were left to manage on their own. They had died within four months of each other and Henry had taken leave from Rigby Junior High to look after his brother temporarily.

The weeks had stretched to months and by the end of the year he knew he would never be able to work a full-time job while his brother needed him. So he had stayed home, correcting exam papers, contributing articles on education and history to various journals, and privately tutoring local students who were weak. The opportunity to have a wife and home and family of his own somehow just passed him by. Sophia Ferrari, the pretty young science teacher he had developed a passion for, was put off for ever after a distressing dinner at their home when William had peed himself. He was not carping about his life, the pattern it had followed, the journeys to Rome and Venice and Paris never taken. His only concern was here and now and what would happen to his brother if he was not able to take care of him . . .

Chapter Twenty-nine

A multitude gathered in the old Tanner Radford school building waiting for the Healer, the Miracle Woman, Martha McGill to appear. Kim and Ruth and Kathleen had organized it all – the rental of the building, and the discreet notice in the paper – and had contacted all those on the crowded appointment waiting list, inviting them to come along to Martha's first open healing session.

Mike McGill drew in a deep breath on seeing the large number of people who had turned out on a cold wet Saturday afternoon in mid-February to see his wife. Nervously his eyes flicked to the exit door at the back of the hall.

Also nervous and full of misgivings, Martha could feel herself trembling, for she was not used to standing up in public in front of groups of people. Evie gave her arm a reassuring squeeze as she took in the huge crowd that had gathered for the healing session. There were far more present than any of them had expected. How could she possibly help so many people, talk to them, even connect with them! Martha's stomach churned with anxiety and dread; she had no idea what lay ahead.

As she walked up the hall through an open passageway between the metal chairs, every eye seemed to follow her, every head turn. Curious, needful, sick and hopeful, they stared at her. Martha's mouth was dry with anxiety, perspiration already clinging to her pale lilac shirt. Mary Rose, Evie and Martha had spent almost an hour back at home trying to figure out what was the right kind of thing to wear for a healing session without wanting to appear too clerical or flaky. A white suit, a long floor-length cream dress, a smart, figure-hugging black two-piece? Eventually they decided on a pale grey knitted suit that was both comfortable and classic. Mary Rose, hugging her, told her she looked just great.

'You OK, Martha?' asked Mike, concerned and sensing her shock at the numbers.

'Yeah, I guess.' Taking a deep breath, she tried to reassure him as much as herself, knowing full well his opposition to the afternoon and his reservations about holding such an event.

'They've all crawled out of the woodwork,' he muttered darkly, 'the poor divils!'

'Mike!' she chastised.

Evie marched on ahead of her. Kim, Ruth, Kathleen and Rianna, already sitting there in the front row, got up and hugged and warmly welcomed her, the crowd breaking into a spontaneous round of applause as if she was some sort of entertainer who was going to perform for them.

Evie stood on the raised dais and turned to face them all. She began to speak but a few people from the back called out that they couldn't hear her, as the microphone wasn't working. Martha and Evie's eyes locked apprehensively. How on earth had they got themselves in such a position? The janitor appeared from the side and produced an old-fashioned microphone. After a few minutes' fumbling, he got it to work, it crackled loudly before settling into the level necessary for Evie to speak.

Evie coughed, clearing her throat, and Martha recognized the familiar dogged 'I can do this!' expression set firmly on her face as she began to speak to the audience.

'Ladies and gentlemen, you are all very welcome to this hall today. I know that many of you have been writing and phoning and emailing Martha for the past few months, trying to reach her and hoping that she might be able to provide some healing for you and whatever situation you find yourself in. Today is a response to that need, and I can tell you that both Martha and I are amazed at the numbers here.

'Martha McGill is one of my oldest and dearest friends and I count myself lucky to have known her for so long and to witness this gift of healing that has been bestowed on her. Martha is a good person, she has always been that way and I know hand on heart that she will do her best to help each and every one of you!' Evie smiled, looking over at her. 'The format will be as follows. For those that need healing: each one of you come up, in turn, to meet Martha. There will be no singing or choirs, and Martha asks that you all try and keep as quiet as possible during this session of her laying on her hands, so that she can hear and talk to those she is working with. We hope that you will all have individual time with Martha and ask those who are finished to exit quietly by the side door on my right. Now I would like to introduce you to the woman herself – Martha McGill.'

A ripple of applause went through the room as Martha stepped forward. She could feel herself almost shaking at the huge expectancy of the crowd, but managed to steady herself as she greeted them.

'Friends! Thank you for coming along today. I don't know what will happen over the next few hours but all I can do is ask the Holy Spirit to guide all of us gathered here.' Glancing around the hall she felt the overwhelming wave of good will towards her, but was slightly taken aback to notice the journalist Lara Chadwick sitting only about six rows from the front.

She stepped back from the microphone as Evie called the first person. An elderly woman walked stiffly forwards, her joints obviously causing her pain and slowing her down as she approached the dais.

'Marjorie Buchanan from Lexington,' she introduced herself. 'My daughter Felice drove me here.'

Martha studied the resolute face of a woman who had lived through much joy and sorrow in her long life, and was now almost disabled by chronic rheumatoid disease. 'Sit down, Marjorie,' she offered, taking hold of her hand automatically, feeling the stiff swollen fingers and sensing the other woman's discomfiture at having to seek help from anyone.

'Can you do anything to help? I know I'm no spring chicken and I shouldn't expect much at my age, it's just that sometimes the pain gets so bad that I . . .'

'It's all right, Marjorie.'

Martha ran her hands over the older woman's shoulders and down the length of her arms, feeling the pain and discomfort there. She then placed a hand firmly on either knee and felt the jarring misplacement of inflamed and diseased joints, an intense heat flowing from her hands, soothing the inflammation and damping it down. Very gently she ran the palms of her hands down along each leg and foot in turn.

'Can you feel anything, Marjorie? The healing is passing through me to you.'

The grey-haired head nodded. 'I feel like a burning inside me, everything feels hot and different.'

'That's good,' murmured Martha, concentrating.

She took Marjorie's hands in her own, massaging the fingers and knuckles with her own hands, wanting the joints to ease and loosen. The older woman watched intently as Martha prayed.

When she'd finished, Marjorie slowly left the platform and the crowd watched in expectation as her daughter stepped forward to help her. If they had expected the seventy-five-year-old woman to bounce out of the hall like a twenty-two-year-old then Martha knew they must be disappointed, but she herself felt better, noticing that Marjorie was a little less stiff and took her daughter's hand easily.

A tall handsome young man was next and Martha tried not to flinch when Harry Broderick told her that he had been diagnosed with Aids two years previously and wasn't ready to die no matter what any doctors or hospitals said. She embraced him, feeling the pain deep within the realms of his soul, the pain of rejection and fear that was making him worse. Closing her eyes she laid her hands on his chest, right over his heart, sending the warmth and healing through his body and spirit, asking the Lord to mind this precious son and protect him from further hurt. A shudder went through him and Martha sensed some of the release that Harry was going through. 'You OK?' she asked as she held his hand and prayed, touched by his inner spirituality, which would help him much over the coming months.

Andrea Bennet blushed when she first stepped up. The overweight young woman from Cambridge was deeply embarrassed as she told the woman healer about the medical condition that made the hair on her head fall out yet forced her to have to shave her body; her ovaries were covered in small cysts that she felt had destroyed her chance of becoming a mother even though she and her husband George were anxious to start a family. 'I don't feel like a woman no more,' she whispered, her eyes welling with tears. 'I don't know how George can stand it.'

Martha's sympathy went out to the young wife and she placed her hands firmly over the area that was causing the problem, both of them praying for the spirit to help. When Andrea stood up to leave, Martha wished her and her partner well.

'You are a wonderful young woman, Andrea, and when the time is right you will be a wonderful mother too.'

Andrea's eyes stared into hers searching for the truth, and Martha was delighted to see the flicker of belief which now shone from them.

Kim led a small child and his nervous mother up to her next. The little boy was about six years old and the mother whispered to her that he was a bedwetter. Martha could see the look that shot between the child and his parent and the embarrassment of the small boy Taylor that his secret had been revealed to a stranger. 'I was wondering, ma'am, if you could do anything to help my boy with his problem.'

Martha thought of all the things she had done with her own three; Mary Rose had been the one who had the odd accident at night when she was small. Lifting them to the toilet, not giving them too much to drink before they went to bed. She supposed his mother had already tried most of these avenues.

'We got a mattress with an alarm and everything, but Taylor has already gone and wet himself by the time he wakes up. I honest to God don't know what to do!'

'He's not sick, though?'

'Oh no, ma'am. The doctors did all sorts of checks on him and say he's right as rain otherwise.'

'I see.' Martha smiled.

She patted the chair, trying to entice Taylor to come and sit by her. She could sense his wariness after all he'd been through already. 'I'm not going to hurt you, Taylor,' she promised.

Eventually he moved closer to her and Martha chatted to him about his favourite TV programme, trying to put him a little at ease. He was bright and intelligent and from being close to him and just holding him she could tell that when he slept he went into a heavy dream state. Just laying her hands on his straw-coloured hair Martha sensed that already he was beginning to feel different and alienated from his friends and classmates, humiliated by what was happening to him.

'His older brother John Junior won't sleep in the room with him no more and he's too shamed to go visit any of his friends. When we went down to Orlando last year, to visit Disney, why, I had to bring all sorts of plastic sheets and the like and Taylor didn't like it one bit, sure you didn't, son?'

The boy nodded, embarrassed, dreading the attention that was being focused on him.

'Mrs . . .'

'Farentino.'

'Mrs Farentino, I think it's best if I just talk to Taylor on my own a minute if that's all right with you.'

The mother's face was suffused with red under the glow of her tanning salon colour, but Martha could understand her worry for Taylor and what would happen to him in the future.

'That's OK, Taylor,' she smiled.

Martha, leaning forward, asked him about Orlando, and what he thought of the Magic Kingdom, a subject most kids had a lot to say on, whether they'd ever visited the place or not. As the young boy relaxed she placed her hands on his stomach. Energy surged through her as she thought of the child's shame and humiliation at not being able to achieve what his brother and sister and friends had done easily.

'You mustn't be scared, Taylor! When you

go to sleep you must not even think about what happens. Other people don't think about it or worry about it, believe me. They just close their eyes and sleep. Your bladder is a perfect piece of engineering and you are just going to have to trust it to work while you sleep. Do you feel that hot spot?'

'Yeah,' he replied, puzzled.

'I think that's what was causing your little problem, and we'll ask Mother Nature and the good earth to help you.'

When she lifted her hand from his T-shirt he still seemed puzzled. 'Is that it?' he asked.

'Yep, I'm afraid so,' she said, laughing and sending him back to his mother.

Kim and Ruth were signalling frantically that she had to move a bit faster, but Martha knew she had to take time to talk to people if she wanted to help them.

Hank Freeman pushed his way into the hall through the open back exit, he and his cameraman Don White getting seats at the end of a row. His corduroy jacket was soaked as it was still pissing rain outside and he'd had to park more than half a block away. He gestured to Don to keep the camera hidden: there was no point antagonizing the good folk sitting around them.

He cast his eye over the large assembled group, noting they were a hotchpotch of senior citizens, mothers with sick kids and the usual new age types that always believed in that kind of mystic stuff. He sighed. This healing gig was going to be a load of crap! A total waste of the afternoon. The only saving grace was the fact that he and Don were at least in out of the rain. They were supposed to have covered the huge organized protest at the cutting down of an ancient oak that shaded the children's playground over near Roxbury, where neighbourhood parents and kids had chained themselves to the tree while the chainsaws buzzed. It sure would have given them great footage for the evening news but for a last-minute stay of execution – the tree had gotten a reprieve from the parks department for another week! Left with no story for the evening news he'd chased over here, the address scribbled on a notepad by one of the station's researchers.

He watched the Martha woman up on the stage. She seemed to have spent an age with the small boy, whatever his problem was. Funny, she didn't seem like one of those usual gospel type faith healers and she had none of the glittery fire and brimstone showmanship of other healing ministers he'd seen on the TV. Although the audience were intent watching her, she seemed oblivious to them, concentrating on those she was working with. He noticed Lara Chadwick, sitting a few rows from the front. The two of them covering the same story – that's if there was a story. Sitting back into the hard wooden seat, he passed Don a square of peanut brittle, chewing on the syrupy sweetness as he waited.

So many of those who stepped forward had already done the rounds of doctors and hospitals and had no need for her to diagnose what was wrong with them; batteries of tests and X-rays and ultrasound scans had already done that. What they needed was to find a way to accept those diagnoses and in some way to heal themselves. She could lay her hands on them but they in turn needed to be able to receive that healing energy and have faith and let their body do the work. Migraine sufferers, diabetics – Martha was trying her utmost to connect with each and every one of them.

A fifty-year-old businessman with sky-high blood pressure, his wife worried out of her mind that he would die and leave her to raise their four children on her own. Hildi Jenkinson, a pensioner of seventy, too scared to agree to the bypass surgery she urgently needed, and yet in too much pain not to have it. Martha tried to soothe and calm her and remove the fear that was increasing her constant chest pain.

Martha prayed God to help her, to let his Holy Spirit fill her as she reached out to those in need of his healing. Laying on her hands she tried to ease the burden of constant pain suffered by many as they filed up to her. Not just the physical pain but the emotional and mental anguish of those who were lonesome and felt lost and totally alone in the world.

From the right side of the hall an emaciated eighteen-year-old had to be helped by both her parents, her skeletal figure drawing gasps from those around. Martha herself had to disguise her disquiet at the girl's appearance. She was obviously suffering from a severe eating disorder. Anorexic, she'd been in and out of clinics and psychiatric departments since she was fifteen and had all but destroyed her parents' life and marriage. She had only come to the session at their insistence, and appeared totally uninterested in both Martha and her surroundings. Her child's body hid a now adult mind. Her once pretty features were gaunt, her skin covered in a fine down of hairs, her eyes huge in her head as her parents, holding back their emotions, begged Martha to help her.

Taking hold of her hand, Martha told her truthfully, 'Melissa, I'm not sure that I can help you at all! The only healing that will help you now is for you to heal yourself. Your body has its own healing energy but you have tried to kill that. If you do not eat, it is no matter to me. Or in truth to anyone else. Your parents will grieve for you, that's natural, but they will live, and go on living without you.'

She could see the shock on the mother's face, how she wanted to protest.

'Time and nature have decreed you are a young

woman, so you must shed the skin of a child self and put on a new garment – that of a beautiful young woman. Melissa, do you believe me that this time has come?'

Melissa just blinked, staring at the floor, refusing to make any connection with her whatsoever.

Ignoring that, Martha laid her hands on her and silently prayed for the spirit to guide this lost child-woman, for food to nourish her body, and love and acceptance to nourish her heart.

At the end her sympathy went out – to the parents as they led their daughter away.

Evie brought her another jug of water, but Martha refused the sandwich she was offered. She felt no hunger and had no sense of time or place as she worked, the energy channelling through her to those who needed healing.

The crowd moved on gradually. Most were patient and calm. Those that complained or were peevish were soothed by Ruth and Kim, who did their utmost to make sure that Martha was not distracted.

A young man clad in black leather came up to meet her, using the support of a metal crutch. He had injured himself in a motorbike accident the previous year and still had problems with his ankle and foot on the right-hand side.

'My orthopaedic specialist says it might never come right again and that I should thank God that

I'm alive, it's just that I find it hard to accept,' he said, his voice breaking.

Martha took his hands in hers and could sense his strong faith and belief, before she leant down to touch his damaged foot.

Sean Peterson's eyes closed in concentration as she worked, his lips moving in silent prayer. Concerned, Martha walked around him. There was more, she could feel it, the pain around his chest so strong it was like a tight wire that bound him. She spread her hands along his breast bone, getting him to remove his jacket. There she could feel it – the pain almost knocked her off her feet as Sean stared into her eyes. Martha was overwhelmed with the torrent of grief that was choking the young man, who was held in a vice-like grip of suffering.

'Sean, I am lifting this pain from you. Taking it away! You have carried it for too long and your body needs to let go of it so you can begin to heal. Do you understand what I am saying?' He nodded dumbly, trying to control his emotions. Martha returned to his bad leg and foot, feeling the energy from her hands now race and criss-cross through a zigzag pathway of nerves and muscles. Sean felt it too. As he stood up to go, she noticed that he put his weight on his bad foot without thinking and could read the look of sheer astonishment on his face as he found he was able to walk normally.

'Mrs McGill, I can put my foot to the ground, I can put weight on it.'

He began to lean on it.

'Take it easy, Sean, don't damage it!' she warned.

'No, you don't understand, it feels like before, normal, like I can just stand on it.' To demonstrate he stood up straight, both arms stretched out, his crutch left against the chair he had been sitting on.

The crowd still remaining were riveted, focused on the young man standing hesitantly in front of them. A whisper rippled through them, and grew to a rumble of admiration as Sean turned to hug and thank Martha.

'I'm cured!' he shouted aloud.

'I'm glad that I've helped you to ease some of your pain,' Martha said modestly.

Huge applause erupted as the young man walked away. The crowd in a frenzy was shouting and clapping, thumping their feet, the old building filling with sounds of cheering as his mother ran up the aisle and embraced him, with tears rolling down her plump face. Martha was delighted for both of them.

From the corner of her eye she noticed as a tall long-haired man in his late twenties stood up and, using an expensive-looking camera, began to film Sean Peterson walking away.

Mike had spotted him too. He was down the hall in an instant and arguing with the stranger, asking him not to film and ordering him to leave the building. Martha watched appalled as he and his friend brushed past her husband and followed Sean to the exit, Mike chasing out the doorway after them.

Evie and Ruth signalled for her to continue and led forward an elderly woman who was with her son. Confused, the poor woman didn't seem to know where she was and after only a few minutes Martha realized that Edel Connolly, a former school principal from Bangor, Maine was suffering from Alzheimer's, a disease which had managed to destroy almost every piece of information and learning this well-educated soft-spoken woman had ever acquired. Her son had insisted on her coming to live with him and his family, leaving Edel with absolutely no sense of place and of where she belonged. Her heart went out to the both of them and after she had laid her hands on Edel she asked her son Greg to let her give him healing too.

The crowd was silent as afterwards Greg led his elderly and still obviously confused mother back down the hall, and Ruth led a pregnant young mother forward.

It was almost dark when they finished. The crowd finally dispersed as Mike and the rest of them began to tidy up and turn off the lights. The janitor, anxious to lock up the premises, set the alarm. Everyone was exhausted and Mike told them he had booked a table in the Italian restaurant on the next street. Martha was glad of his thoughtfulness. They were all concerned for her, imagining how drained and worn out she must be from giving so much of herself. Martha found it hard to explain to them that it wasn't her own energy she had used during the session, she was a channel for energy that seemed to come from another source; she was just the host. Still, she had to admit that every bone in her body ached and her muscles were sore from the constant bending down.

They ordered quickly, Martha opting for a Caesar salad and pasta in a carbonara sauce, Evie and Ruth ordering a big bowl of spaghetti bolognaise each, while Mike and Kim and Rianna, Kathleen and her husband Jim went for the pizza. All of them were glad of a reviving glass of the house Chianti.

'Martha, it was just amazing what you did there today. The response from those who got to meet you and have healing, I've never seen anything like it,' admitted Kim, who was whacked herself and longed for a soothing warm bath.

'All those people believing in you and having such faith,' Kathleen commented. 'I don't know how you handle it so well, I'd have a freakout!'

'And what about that guy in the leather jacket? God, did you see him! He was limping real bad when he came up to you and then after, he could put weight back on the foot and walk.'

'Hey, that was something! Did you know you were going to be able to do that?'

'Sean was in a lot of pain, I just helped to release some of it, that's all,' she insisted, twisting her long hair back up in a clip neatly.

'There was a news hound there with a camera,' said Mike seriously. 'I told them to stop filming but I think they got your friend Sean on tape. I saw them talking together outside afterward.'

'Shit,' said Evie. 'That's all we want!'

'Lara Chadwick was there too,' Kathleen added. 'She wanted you to do an interview with her, but Kim and I put her off and told her you'd be much too tired.'

'Thanks,' murmured Martha, as Mike refilled her glass.

Her husband was unusually quiet, talking to Jim at the far end of the table. Martha wondered what was bothering him. 'Mike – what did you think?' she asked.

Martha knew her husband well, and if there was one thing she could always be sure of as far as he was concerned it was his honesty.

'I have to admit everything went well today, better than I imagined. You girls had everything well organized and I guess I was surprised by how many people are out there, needing help.'

'We told you!' teased Kim.

'I'm just worried about that news guy and his pal with the fancy camera, that's all.'

'C'mon, Mike, forget it and enjoy your food,' urged Jim as the waiters carried over trays of piping hot pizza, layered with tomatoes and peppers and cheese and mushrooms. 'There's nothing you can do about it now. So enjoy!'

Martha glanced around the table, raising her glass to them all.

'Thank you! Thanks, everyone, for helping today. I don't know what I'd have done without you all. One thing I am sure of is that I am blessed to have such good friends.'

Martha barely tasted her pasta and salad as she thought back over the past few hours and all those who had come to her, confided in her, and asked for help; she hoped that she had not failed them.

As the others chatted and talked around her she was quiet, tired out, yawning by the time they came to say goodnight, and dozing in the leather back seat of their Lincoln sedan as Mike dropped Evie home first.

Chapter Thirty

Taylor Farentino turned around in the bed, feeling the sheet wrap around his middle. His soft Tigger toy fell to the floor as he waited for that familiar cold wet feel and the strong smell of his urine to assail him.

He turned around and glanced at the clock. It was almost seven and he waited for his mom and dad to come in and shout and give out. His hand slipped down to his pyjama bottom. It was dry! Maybe it had dried out in his sleep. He felt around him, then rolled out of the bed, pushing off his navy and yellow patterned planets and stars bedcover, letting his hand rest against his mattress cover. It was dry.

He blinked and ran across the landing, pushing into the unlocked bathroom behind his dad, who was busy shaving.

'Hey, Taylor!' he shouted.

Taylor made straight for the toilet and let the

yellow gold of his urine flow down into the white bowl.

The lady had told him he could do it! She'd told him, and somehow he'd believed her.

Hank Freeman worked at his desk in the newsroom at WBZ4. The footage was great, Don had got the crowds and the Peterson guy walking back down the aisle. OK, so they didn't have the actual moment of truth, but they had a bloody miracle on film.

Hank had wanted to run with the story on the Saturday nine o'clock spot but T.J., the show's editor, had insisted on him checking out this Sean Peterson and getting confirmation of the bike accident he'd been injured in, and some background in case the guy was a con artist or some sort of nut. Hank had spent all day Sunday in the clippings room and had come up with a few lines about the Tragic Bike couple story. Taking the address, he had phoned and organized an interview with Sean's mother. A born talker, she had told him all he needed to know. With the corroboration he needed the story would definitely run, T.J. saying the network might pick up on it too.

Chapter Thirty-one

IT'S A MIRACLE! and MIRACLE WOMAN
HEALS AGAIN!

Martha ignored the headlines as best she could,
Mike and the kids poring over the papers that
carried photos of the young motorcyclist Sean,
who claimed to have been healed by her.

The story was given huge coverage on the local
news channel. Hank Freeman had interviewed
both Sean and his mother and scooped with actual
footage of Saturday's session and the tragic fact
that Sean Peterson's girlfriend had died in the
motorbike accident. Poor Sean, thought Martha,
glad that she had been instrumental in freeing him
of his pain and his guilt.

All hell broke loose when she got to the store.
Evie told her that there had literally been
hundreds of callers trying to get in touch with her
and that she had caught some people taking
photos of her premises.

'I'm sorry,' Martha apologized.

'Hey, come on! It could be good for business!'

Trying to ignore the constant interruptions Martha did her best to focus on the morning's clients, Kim, much to her relief, arriving to answer the phone. 'I guessed it would be all hands on deck today,' she joked as she took over.

It was crazy and by lunchtime Kim and Kathleen had been approached by numerous organizations and halls both local and out of state from Providence to Springfield, New York to Philadelphia, asking could they book a healing session with the Miracle Woman? Both of them took down the details. Ruth had made a list of those journals and magazines who wanted to interview Martha or do a feature on her, curious to discover about her healing gift, and she had been invited on to morning TV for an interview. Evie advised her not to rush into anything and to take her time about making decisions: there was no need to go running around exhausting herself if she didn't want to.

'I counted the money left in envelopes in the donation box in the Tanner Radford hall,' Ruth informed her, 'and it more than covers the rent, so I suggest we put it in the bank account to go towards all your expenses.'

'Expenses?'

'Your rent here, the phone, gas.'

'Ruth, I told you I didn't want to start charging people. I don't want to be like those guys on the TV getting poor sick people to donate every spare dollar to me, or making them pledge their savings. I'm not doing this for the money.'

'I know that, but you know Mike is going to get pretty pissed if he has to start paying for all these things. It's not like you're charging anyone, believe me! Only those that can genuinely afford it will make a donation.'

Martha felt uncomfortable about the money situation but she knew that Evie had hardly taken any money from her, even though she was renting the whole building. It wasn't right to take unfair advantage of their friendship. She'd talk to Evie and to Mike about it.

Alice had a half-day from school on Wednesday and Martha promised to collect her, and then drive her to her friend's later. Back home she made a big fluffy omelette, which the two of them shared.

'You OK, honey?'

Alice just nodded, not saying much.

Martha watched as her youngest daughter sat on the carpet playing, a selection of plastic Barbie dolls and ponies and horses placed strategically around the furniture. 'I thought you were going to Jessica's house today, pet? What time do you want me to drop you over?' she asked.

Alice kept on playing with a skewbald jumping along the blue-lined carpet edging, her head down, concentrating. Her chin stuck out.

'You don't have to drop me, Mom.'

'Is Jessica's mom collecting you here then?'

Her eight-year-old daughter shook her head firmly, her red-gold hair catching the afternoon sunlight.

'I'm not going to Jessie's today, or any day,' she said matter-of-factly, her head and eyes glued to the floor again.

Martha stopped what she was doing, leaving the pile of washing she was sorting and folding down on the table.

'What is it? Did you two have a fight or something?'

Her daughter remained silent. Obstinately she bounced the soft brown and white animal higher.

'I'm not going over to her stupid house, that's all, Mom, no big deal.'

Martha sat down on the couch beside her, displacing a vivid pink sports car that her brother had sent Alice on her last birthday. 'Are you sure the plans have changed, Alice?' she asked.

Her daughter shook her head.

'Do you want to phone your friend and ask her to come over here? I'll collect her if you want. Maybe her mom is busy?'

Alice made no response, studiously avoiding answering her.

'Didn't you hear me, Alice?'

'I'm not phoning her mom! I'm not! Anyways she won't be let over here to play,' declared her daughter firmly.

'You don't know that!'

'I do, Mom, I do.'

'What is it, baby, what is it?' asked Martha, hunkering down beside her, knowing that Alice was trying to hide something from her. 'Just tell me what it is.'

Alice hesitated, glancing up at her as if watching for a reaction. 'Jessie's mom says that you're some sort of freak. A witch! And that Jessie ain't let play with me any more,' she said.

'Jessie's mom said *that*?'

'She isn't let come play with me any more. Jessie said she don't want to come to a witch's house anyways.'

Martha was appalled by the stricken look on her daughter's face, the hurt brought upon her for no reason. 'You don't believe that, Alice. That's crazy talk.'

Alice made no reply.

'Alice baby, you *know* that's crazy sort of talk,' Martha insisted. She supposed she shouldn't be surprised. From what she remembered of the child's mother from her last school meeting she was one of those parents who complained loudly and pointedly about everything.

Alice screwed up her small face, wrinkling her nose, trying not to cry, a sniffle escaping despite herself. Martha pulled her onto her lap.

'It's all right, Alice pet, I'm sorry about your friend, honest I am. Some people when they don't understand something they put a label on it, more often than not the wrong label,' she said angrily. 'You don't think I'm a witch, do you?'

Alice shook her tousled head emphatically. 'No! You're my mom.'

Martha held her daughter close, breathing in the smell of her skin and hair. That child smell she so loved was now almost gone, but Alice still needed protection and support like she did when she was an infant.

'What did you say to Jessie?'

'I told her you don't have a pointy hat or a broom and that you're not a witch, but that you can help sick people when you lay your hands on them and that the earth and spirit help you.'

Martha put her hand across her mouth.

'Sort of like magic, a Harry Potter thing!'

Martha burst out laughing, hugging Alice tight. 'Good girl!'

Mike was angry that night when he heard.

'Narrow-minded bigots,' he said angrily, flicking off the computer screen. 'How dare that woman say such things to her child. God knows what rumours she's spreading around about you.'

'Calm down, Mike. People won't believe such things. I know a lot of the parents in the school, do you honestly think they'd believe that of me?'

She was disquieted by her husband's non-committal shrug.

'Martha, at eight hearing people call your mother a fucking witch is no fun, believe me! It's not fair on Alice or Mary Rose or Patrick to be subjected to something like this.'

'They haven't been!'

'Come off it, Martha, Patrick was in a scrap last week.'

'He never said anything to me about it, Mike!' she protested.

'He's not going to do *that* – come and tell you the other kids are saying things about his mom? Wanting him to perform miracles in the school canteen, turn bread rolls into pizza!'

'God, I don't believe you!'

'Pete Golden told me about it,' said Mike, raising his eyes to meet hers. 'His boy's in the same year.'

'Mike, I can't believe it. What kind of people would let their kids say or do such things? Hurt a little kid like Alice who has done nothing, absolutely nothing to anyone.'

'Except be your daughter.'

'Oh, Mike, I didn't mean for any of this to happen, I never imagined people could be so mean.'

Mike swivelled his chair around to face her.

'Patrick gave as good as he got, but you know he's at a sensitive age. Last thing a boy his age wants is to be picked out as different from his friends. You know he just wants to be part of the pack.'

Martha nodded. Their son was not yet one of those tall hairy creatures who appeared every so often at their home, acne-marked skin and deep voiced, legs and arms stretched to some new proportion. Patrick was witty and funny and had much of his father's good looks and charm, yet they both knew his young confidence could be easily shattered.

'I'll talk to him tomorrow,' she promised. 'There's got to be something he can say or do to . . .'

'Will you stop kidding yourself!' Mike shouted. 'You know what's happening to you is having a huge impact on the lives of everyone in this house. We can't pretend it isn't.'

Martha had never expected her healing ministry to provoke such intolerance, and wouldn't stand for anyone hurting or wounding a member of her family. What good did it do to help others if Mike and the kids got hurt and damaged along the way?

'You go be a saint! Or Jesus come again! And do whatever you have to do but leave me and my kids out of it!' Mike shouted.

'Mike!' she called uselessly after him as he stormed out of the house, and left her standing in the kitchen wondering how much longer they could go on like this.

Chapter Thirty-two

The atmosphere at home remained tense and strained, with the kids picking up on what was going on between them. Martha was relieved at Mike's sugestion of a family outing that weekend.

'Come on, you guys!' he shouted. 'Get your boots and jackets and gloves! How do you fancy a hike in the woods and a trip to Concord?'

Perhaps what they really needed was to spend some quality time together relaxing and having fun.

'We're leaving in an hour,' he threatened. 'So be ready.'

'Yeah, Dad!' shouted Alice, jumping around the hall.

Martha remembered that same sense of giddy excitement when she was a kid on those rare occasions when the weekly routine of school and church on Sunday was broken and her father brought her and her brothers out for a drive somewhere in his old Lincoln estate. She could still remember the sense of anticipation and the pride of being part of a family who could enjoy such a luxury, as she waved to the rest of the kids playing or hanging around on the street as they drove by. Her mother would perch up front with her jet-black hair neatly washed and primped into perfect waves, her good dress on, and the heady scent of her perfume and lipstick filling the car, her hand resting lightly on her husband's thigh as the rest of them squabbled and pushed in the back.

Time and time again they would beg to know their destination, only to be told they were going on a mystery tour. They guessed wildly in the back: 'The Statue of Liberty', 'The Empire State Building,' 'Cork', 'Kerry', 'Blarney Castle . . .'

Her father would encourage them, excitement and talk fuelling those imagined journeys until they turned into the parking lot of Suffolk Downs, the local race track, or the driveway of one of his old friends. Their mother would disappear off with the rest of the women, and their father would press them with dollars and dimes and while the adults talked politics and business, the children were corralled together and glutted themselves on jugs of homemade lemonade and warm cookies or flasks of scalding tea and chunky ham or egg sandwiches. Her father was dressed in a good suit and shirt, his fair Irish skin covered for the most part from any glimpse of sunshine. His hair slicked back, his broad face shining, his voice commanded the attention of all those surrounding him.

Determined to leave her problems behind and enjoy the trip to the woods at Minute Man Park, Martha concentrated on filling the flasks with hot soup, packing up enough fresh crusty bread rolls, chocolate and cheese to feed an army, and making sure everyone had their heavy walking boots and weatherproof jackets as it was still cold out.

Mary Rose was in a huff and Martha prayed God she'd snap out of it before Mike let rip with some comment about premenstrual teenagers.

'The forecast is for it to stay dry so the park should be nice, and maybe we'll get the chance to visit Orchard House too,' suggested Martha.

'Is that the house where the Little Women lived?' questioned Alice. She was too young to have read the book yet but had watched the video over and over again.

'Yes it is! Well, it's where the lady who wrote the book lived and much of the story is based on herself and her family.'

'Dad, this is *so* unfair!' complained Patrick from the rear seat. 'I'm not spending my Saturday traipsing around old houses where some stupid women lived. It's pathetic!'

'Listen, Patrick, a bit of the Battle Trail will do us.'

Sighing, Martha remembered the times when

the kids were small and they'd just bundled them up in snowsuits and pushed strollers and Mike had strapped the youngest in the baby carrier and they'd gone exploring and walking for miles through the Massachusetts countryside. Nothing had fazed them then, or so it seemed. Grabbing a take-home pizza or wedging themselves in the booth of a small local diner and stuffing themselves with hot dogs and hamburgers, sharing their portions with the kids, had been part of their routine for years. She couldn't remember when it had changed or why but slowly things had become more rigid and set, with proper arrangements having to be made.

Today she was truly glad of Mike's initiative, and the fact that every so often he still did manage to surprise her.

The New England countryside was wrapped in winter, as if someone had emptied a packet of white frosting over everything, tinting each branch and tree, the ground dusted with a coat of snow. The trees were majestic in their bare simplicity, the evergreen pines stretching skyward and rustling in the wind.

They stopped off in Lexington, got out and strolled around the town, standing in silence at the monument to soldiers of the War of Independence. Mary Rose dived into one of those candle shops that were now a part of almost every New England main street and came back out bearing three heavily scented candles that filled the car with their strange perfumes. Patrick and Mike objected to the cranberry smell.

The Minute Man Park was quiet, with very few visitors, the air snappy as they pulled on their hats and gloves. Piling out, they found the free map provided and set themselves the target of a good two-mile hike. Mike and Patrick led the way, Martha and the girls following on behind. Martha was sure glad that she had decided to wear her fur-lined jacket and warm boots. The woods were silent and as they walked they could hear their own footsteps. Mike and Patrick chatted easily up ahead of them. Alice was all excited, making up stories about fantastic creatures that lived in the woods; Martha was hoping they might get to see some real animals, like deer in their natural habitat.

Martha looked across at her elder daughter. Mary Rose had her Walkman on, the rolling thump of rock music wiping out any chance of her hearing the birdsong and wind singing through the trees around her. Martha sighed, regretful at what she was missing.

'Come on you slowcoaches!' shouted Mike.

Martha was glad of the fresh air and exercise as she walked through woods of huge trees: ancient sycamores, maples and giant pines that towered over them. Bowled over by the sheer beauty of it, she produced her ancient Olympus Trip camera, wanting to take shots of the family.

'Mom! Honest, you're like one of those leafers,

with a camera around your neck trying to photograph everything,' complained Mary Rose.

'You hush up, and don't speak to your mother like that,' warned Mike.

'It'll be a sorry day when nature and beauty smacks me right in the eye and I fail to notice it,' replied Martha good-naturedly, having no intention of getting involved in an argument with her teenage daughter.

With the camera she framed them, trying to capture that incandescent quality of childhood, as Mike stood behind them, his arm around Patrick who now stood almost as tall as his father. Waiting for just the right moment, Martha managed to catch through the lens the sheer joy of Alice's dancing in the whiteness, kicking a pile of snow, her daughter's lopsided grin hers for ever.

They walked for two miles or so and eventually chose one of the smaller picnic sites with its wooden benches and tables. Having it all to themselves, the kids cheered as Martha tumbled the food out onto the wooden table.

The vegetable soup was still piping hot as she poured it into the plastic mugs, then unwrapped the bread, which they all used to dunk, Mike helping himself to another roll and the end of the soup. The kids filled up with slices of cheese, before attacking the chocolate.

'We'll have to walk this all off later,' she groaned.

Mike had spread the Battle of Independence

trail map out on the bench and he and Patrick were engrossed, their two heads bent close as they mapped out a route they wanted to try. The girls and Martha would follow the literature route and head back to Orchard House and would meet the others afterwards.

'You three going to be OK?' asked Mike.

'We'll be fine, don't you worry!' she insisted as she wrapped up the leftovers and began to walk back down towards the car.

The brown wooden house was set almost right on the roadway and boasted a simple but cheerful garden where the Alcott girls had played. Martha noted that Mary Rose had finally unplugged that dratted contraption from her ears and was actually listening as they walked to the back of the house, to the Reverend Alcott's old schoolhouse. Here the three of them joined the rest of the visitors to watch a video about the family. Then they crowded back into the small gift shop and ticket area before entering the front parlour of the old house, as the guide began the tour.

The interior had been unchanged for nigh on a century and a half since its most famous family had lived there, yet it had managed to stay homely and comfortable. Martha was intrigued by the intelligence and interests of its inhabitants and how they had filled those long days and lonely nights. Obviously neighbours and music and art and reading had been their comforts. Alice peeked and peered at everything and Martha could see her trying to take it all in, her mind assaulted by the history around her. Mary Rose was quiet but Martha knew her daughter well enough to know she was drinking in every word spoken about her heroine and was imagining herself living in such circumstances.

The kitchen too was unchanged and Martha stood still picturing those 'Little Women' running out the back door to the garden and coming in to hug 'Marmee'. Upstairs they saw where Amy's sketches had covered the walls of her bedroom studio and the place where Louisa May Alcott wrote. The wonderful grey-haired lady who was their guide was busy telling them about her early footsteps into journalism and the publisher who, not wanting to pay her a full fee for her family story, agreed instead to a small percentage royalty to be paid on each book sold. The room erupted into laughter and Martha's phone went off.

It seemed incongruous in such a hallowed place to have anything so modern and crass as a cell phone in your pocket, and Martha frantically tried to switch it off, noting that Cass Armstrong's mother had placed the call. Her mind was distracted as they continued through the rest of the rooms and came down the staircase.

Both girls had decided they wanted to purchase something from the gift shop, and were taking an age to find exactly what they wanted. Martha was anxious to step outside and return Beth's call, praying that Cass was doing all right and there had been no change in her condition.

She left them to it. Standing out in the fresh air, she phoned the Armstrongs' home.

'Oh Martha, thank God! Cass is real bad and she needs you to come over straight away!'

'Listen, Beth, I'm not at home. I'm up here in Concord with Mike and the kids, we're having a family day.'

'Please, Martha! You've got to come. She's in a lot of pain and is so scared. She needs you real bad. We need you.'

The other woman's voice dissolved into sobs and Martha stood there stricken at the thought of what was happening to that family.

'I'll come as soon as I can,' she promised.

The girls were annoyed when she went in and began to rush them. A large tour bus had pulled up outside and a crowd of middle-aged French tourists were stepping out of it and filing towards them. Martha was anxious to get back to Mike and Patrick.

'Come on, Mary Rose, choose something for heaven's sake, I'm in a hurry.'

'I thought we were collecting Dad and Patrick and going for dinner,' insisted Alice.

'Yes we are, pet, I mean getting your dad and brother, but we're going to have to skip the meal as I have to get back home.'

'Back home? Why, Mom, why?'

'Do you remember that girl I told you about, Alice, the girl that was real sick?'

Alice nodded, her eyes serious.

'Yep.'

'Well, I have to go see her, that's all.'

'Mom, can't she wait till tomorrow or later?'

'I don't think so, pet, I just don't think so.'

Mary Rose brushed past her, nearly knocking an elderly Frenchman over.

'*Je m'excuse!*' he mumbled, trying to step out of her way.

Her daughter marched purposefully out of the gateway and onto the roadside. 'This is crap, Mom,' she said. 'You just go and spend all your time with those other kids, the ones you really care for!'

'Hold on, Mary Rose, don't you dare say such a thing to me. That kid is sick, dying. Her parents are distraught. You cannot imagine for one minute of your cosseted, cared-for life what those people are going through. You have absolutely no idea! None!'

Two or three people were watching them, mother and daughter screaming at each other, Alice standing miserably between them.

'Get in the car, Alice.'

Martha fiddled with the alarm, grateful when the doors opened. Mary Rose was standing blinking and furious on the roadside.

'Get in!'

They drove in silence, Martha already regretting

her over-reaction. How could she expect the girls to understand the bond she felt with Cass, the almost spiritual link between herself and the sick child? Young and shielded from life's tragedies they were bound to be jealous of another child usurping her attention, and now disrupting their time together.

Mike and Patrick, to their credit, said very little when she explained the situation to them, although she could read the anger behind Mike's expression as he drove. She was glad that he did not display it in front of the others.

'Come on, you guys, it's not the end of the world. We'll drop your mom off and head up to that new Mexican restaurant near Harvard Square.'

There was mumbled agreement from the back and she shot a look of gratitude towards Mike, which he pointedly ignored. Looking out the window as trees raced by Martha steeled herself for the visit to the Armstrongs and seeing Cass.

Chapter Thirty-three

Martha tried not to think of the frantic tone of Beth's call as she drove immediately over to the Armstrongs' once they got back to Easton. Pulling up outside Cass's home, she took a deep breath, trying to pull herself together before going inside.

Tom's broad face was puffed and strained, like a punch drunk boxer clinging to the ropes, as he opened the door to her.

'The doctor says the end is near, that she can't go on much longer.' He swallowed hard, trying to mask his dismay as she followed him up the stairs. Billy and Jay stood at the bedroom door looking scared and miserable. On the landing Beth was arguing with Linda O'Hara, a tall blond young woman in nurse's pants and a white sweatshirt.

'God damn you! Phone for an ambulance and get my daughter to hospital immediately! They've got equipment there, they can revive her, stabilize her! They've done it before! It's her only chance!'

Martha could read the pity in the nurse's face as

she tried to talk to the distraught mother, reason with her. Out of the corner of her eye Martha could see Cass lying in the bed looking for all the world as if she was really tired and was falling asleep. Only as she stepped nearer did she notice the rapid movements of her narrow chest, like a small bird fighting for its life, the lungs sounding like they were heavy with two bags of water.

'Hi, Cass,' she said softly, hoping the young girl could hear her. She reached for the small pale hand and squeezed it, noticing that the bruising from all the intravenous drips she'd been on had only now begun to fade. The child moaned two or three times as if in pain. Martha softly stroked her skin.

'Cass, I think you can hear me. It's Martha. I'm here beside you. If you are in pain I will try to help you.'

She leant over, barely touching the child's skinny frame, letting her hands absorb the dulled pain and sending gentle healing waves through her fingers. She was conscious of waves of tightness, fear, confusion: these were the emotions the child was feeling in her last moments.

'Don't be scared, Cass,' she hushed. 'I'm right here beside you and the pain is going, going, going. Can you feel it leaving you?'

Cass seemed to try and murmur something.

'Don't be scared, Cass honey.'

Tears ran down Tom Armstrong's face as he reached for his daughter's other hand.

'Remember what I told you about my daddy
. . . well, Cass, I think soon you are going to leave
the shell of the old Cass behind. You are not
going to need this body much longer.'

A tear slid down the beautiful face.

'It's all right, Cass, don't be afraid.'

Beth Armstrong had stopped arguing. Sensing
the change in her daughter's condition, she rushed
back into the room.

'Please, please, Tom, I'll get the ambulance!' she
sobbed, trying to punch the number into the
phone.

Tom Armstrong never budged. He sat where he
was, staring at his only daughter. The crowded
bedroom was stuffy, a sickroom smell, so Martha
got up and walked across and opened the white
window. Fresh air wafted in, the sound of birdsong
and distant traffic filling the silence. Beth, now
silent, came over and lay on the bed beside her
child, pulling her gently into her arms. Martha
beckoned for the boys hiding at the doorway to
join them. Billy's eyes were raw and red with grief.

'Jay, sit up beside your sister,' she suggested.

He looked doubtful but Tom patted the spot up
beside the pillow, Billy climbing in near him,
careful not to disturb his sister or hurt her.

Beth was fighting to control her grief, her body
shaking with the effort. Martha stood behind her
and placed her hands on her pain-filled shoulders.

'Cass, everyone who loves you is here, pet, your
mommy and daddy and Billy and Jay and Nurse

O'Hara. You don't need to be afraid. It's a lovely clear blue bright day outside with a hint of breeze, can you feel it, the air, the wind? I have never seen a sky like it!

'Your daddy and mommy and brothers are all going to talk to you now, Cass, they know you can hear them.'

Martha stepped back from the bed, stepped back from the family. Cass's breathing was even more irregular now as she struggled for air. In her heart, Martha wished her God speed.

She went downstairs. In the small cluttered kitchen she watched the plants out back in Beth Armstrong's neglected yard dance as the wind tossed them, hearing the cry of grief almost twenty minutes later that racked the house as Beth realized her daughter was gone. Martha was glad in her own mind that Cass was finally free of all that she had suffered during her short life.

Tom Armstrong came downstairs, his face swollen and tortured with grief.

'It's over, finally over,' he said, breaking down. Martha wrapped him in her arms, wishing she could remove even a tiny portion of the pain and anger he was feeling. He sobbed and cried, Martha doing her best to comfort him.

'Tom, will I go upstairs to Beth?' she offered.

'No, Martha, no.' He shook his head vehemently. 'Beth just wants to be left alone with Cass.'

'Of course.'

Martha was concerned for the child's mother, knowing how absolutely tragic and awful it must be for her. Perhaps it was time for her to go. The doctor was on his way to certify Cass's death and the nurse had told her she was going to ask him to write up some kind of sedative for Beth.

Linda answered the door when the doctor came and showed him up to the child's room. Beth came downstairs a few minutes later. Martha moved forward to console her, offer her sympathy, but was totally rebuffed.

'Tom, what is that woman still doing in our house? Ask her to leave immediately!' she shouted hysterically.

'Please, Beth, I'm so sorry about Cass, truly I am.'

'Bitch, get out of my home. You are not wanted here. My daughter thought you were her friend. Some friend!'

'Beth,' pleaded Tom, trying to reason with her. 'Don't go blaming Martha.'

'I *am* blaming her! If that bitch had not come into our lives with her promises of healing and miracles Cass might still be alive.'

'Cass was sick, dying,' her husband reminded her. 'She was a very sick little girl.'

'If Cass was still in hospital she would still be alive, Tom!'

'She was dying, Beth,' he insisted.

'We might have had another month, a week or two – a few more days with her. Another hour with her, even.' Beth's voice broke down and Tom reached forward and grasped his wife, both of them locked in that inconsolable grief of a parent who has lost a child.

Heartbroken for them, Martha gathered her jacket and purse and slipped outside to her car. She turned the key in the ignition, glad of the instant response as the engine started. Who was she to interfere and tell parents what was the right thing to do? Perhaps Beth had been right: if Cass had stayed in the hospital, surrounded by machines and monitors she might still be alive. Tears slid down Martha's face as she drove and she was forced to pull off the road and stop in a lay-by as she gave way to the torrent of emotions she could no longer control.

Chapter Thirty-four

The house was still and quiet when she finally got back; the family, in their beds, already fast asleep. Bone weary, she climbed the stairs, too exhausted to eat or drink, only wanting to crawl into bed and sleep.

She couldn't get Cass out of her mind and a deep feeling of anger raged inside her at the loss of such a life, and that good people like the Armstrongs had been denied the joy of watching their daughter grow to be a young woman. What was the reason for it? Why had the Lord chosen Cass? There was no answer!

She – the healer! the chosen one! – had been asked to help and heal the child and get her well again. There had been no cure. No miracle. For in truth all she had been able to do was to relieve some of the child's pain and distress, perhaps provide some little support for her as she lay dying, but not nearly enough. Putting her head in her hands she gave in to the waves of despair she felt, self-doubt clouding her mind. She was stupid to have imagined that she could change anything!

Patrick was snoring softly when she looked in on him. His long frame almost off the bed, he'd managed to kick off his quilt. Martha pulled it back gently over him as she didn't want him to get cold. Mary Rose lay hunched up in her room, curled in the foetal position as she always was, as if she was trying to protect herself from someone or something that could wound her. Why her daughter was so argumentative and set in her ways was beyond her. She seemed to make everything difficult no matter how much reassurance Mike and she tried to give her. Alice, in the other room, slept soundly, her long wavy hair spread out along the pillow. Martha couldn't resist bending down to kiss her, and as she did so Alice stirred ever so slightly, a smile passing across her pretty face.

'It's all right, honey,' Martha reassured her. 'Mom's home.'

Mike had the bedroom door closed; she always left it open so she could hear the kids, whether they came in late or just called out in their sleep or needed her. He was fast asleep, his reading glasses perched on his nose, his side lamp still on. Wordlessly she removed the glasses, putting them safely back on the bedside locker, then lowered the latest John Grisham novel to the floor before slipping into their bathroom.

Switching off the bedside lamp, she climbed in beside him. Mike felt warm, and she did her best not to disturb him. Lying silent on the edge of their bed she gave thanks for her husband and children, and thought of Tom and Beth and the agony they must be enduring during these long, lonely hours.

Tears burned in her eyes and she did her best to control them, reaching in the dark for the tissues on the shelf near the bed. Gradually the warmth of the bed and the comfort of her husband's breathing lulled her into a sort of sleep.

Mike was gruff and annoyed with her in the morning as he shaved, showered and dressed.

'What in God's name time did you get home last night, Martha?'

'Late.'

'They don't like you spending so much time with other kids, they resent it.'

'Mike! She died.'

'Died!' Mike McGill swung around, half dressed, his cotton boxers and shirt on. 'Died?'

'Yeah,' she added wearily. 'Cass died. Did you know she was only two years and one month older than our Alice?'

'Jesus, I'm sorry. I didn't realize.'

'I sat in the car for a while after, I don't know how long.'

'You should have called me and I would have come and got you.'

His sympathy nearly destroyed her. Martha longed for him to climb back into bed and enfold her in his arms and make everything seem all right again. She watched as he turned his back to her and continued dressing.

'There's a department heads meeting this morning over this new encryption strategy we're testing and I have to be there. I'm late,' he explained, the scent of his splash cologne lingering in the bedroom even after he'd gone.

Slowly Martha got herself out of bed and into the white-tiled shower, the hot water sluicing down her as she lathered chestnut gel into her skin and tension-filled muscles, trying to revive and wake herself up.

Patrick and Mary Rose gave her the freeze treatment the minute she stepped in the kitchen, not even bothering to look up as she passed them fresh-squeezed orange juice and made toast. Deliberately she put the peanut butter jar out of reach to see if Mary Rose would ask her for it. Instead her daughter got up and walked around the table.

'Listen, I'm sorry about yesterday, about having to get home early and not being back for dinner, it couldn't be helped.'

Alice tried to keep her eyes concentrating on the bowl of Rice Krispies. Ignoring the traitorous glances of her siblings, she asked, 'How's that girl, Mom?'

For an instant Martha debated the merit of

keeping it from them but then decided it was better they knew the truth.

'Cass died yesterday evening, Alice. She was very sick and weak.'

'Jesus!' Patrick let the word slip out. 'Jesus! She died?'

Mary Rose's eyes met hers.

'You were there with her, Mom?'

Martha nodded.

'And still you couldn't save her?'

Martha didn't know what to say.

'No, Mary Rose, I couldn't. The healing doesn't work like that, not always.' She could see a look of disbelief flicker across her daughter's eyes but chose to ignore it.

Her children were standing beside her awkwardly, not knowing what to say when confronted by raw grief and pain.

'Come on you three, hurry up or you'll be late!' she urged, swallowing hard.

Patrick grabbed his bag and jacket and hugging her briefly pushed out the back door, Mary Rose following on behind him in a helter-skelter of scarves and bags and long untidy hair as they ran for the school bus.

Fifteen minutes later she and Alice set off. Looking in the mirror she could see the sombre expression on her youngest child's face.

'You OK, Alice?'

'Yes, Mom.'

'Sure?'

There was no usual 'for sure' back.

'What is it, honey? Is it about yesterday?'

Alice pushed her chin down. 'I'm just sad about that girl.'

'Cass, that was her name, Alice. It's all right to say it and it's all right to be sad about it cos I'm real sad too.'

When she stopped the car outside Bishop Delaney's, she pulled Alice onto her lap. 'Did I tell you that you are the best girl in the whole big wide world, Alice Kathleen McGill?'

Alice looked up, understanding in her eyes.

'Mom, you are the best mom in the whole big wide world too.'

Of all days that was the day she needed to hear it most. Profoundly grateful, Martha took Alice's hand in hers and walked as far as the school entrance.

Today she knew she couldn't face it: the faith and trust of those who expected her to heal and chase away the demons of pain and depression and channel energy into their bodies. She had no energy, nothing to offer them. Drained and defeated she could not face the upstairs room and those waiting for her. She called Evie at the store and asked her to cancel the first two appointments. The rest of the people she would try and contact herself.

'Are you sick, Martha?' asked Evie, concerned.

'Cass is dead,' she said simply, almost breaking down.

'Oh God, I'm sorry. I know how attached to that kid you'd got.'

'I knew she was going to die from almost the first instant I saw her, and that there was nothing anyone could do, Evie, only maybe help her prepare for it.'

'You saw that?'

'Felt it, I don't know.'

'Don't go blaming yourself, Martha, it isn't your fault.'

'Beth Armstrong thinks it is.'

'You know deep inside you helped that little girl, no matter what her mom says!'

'I pray so.'

'Now listen, don't worry about things here, I'll sort it out. You try and get some rest and I'll talk to you later, OK?'

Mid-morning, when she tried to place a call to the Armstrongs, young Billy answered the phone. She could sense his embarrassment when he told her that his mom was unable to take the call, and that his dad was off meeting the funeral director. Hurt, she sat there not knowing what to do, wondering what the funeral arrangements would be.

Chapter Thirty-five

The need to escape was strong and as Martha drove over Sagamore Bridge she felt that immediate rush of freedom that a trip to Cape Cod always brought. Off season, the journey from Boston on Route 3 had taken half the time it normally did during the summer.

Beth Armstrong had broken down, cursing Martha when she'd called to find out about Cass's funeral arrangements. Martha was deeply wounded by the fact that neither parent wanted her to attend. She couldn't abide the thought of sitting around pretending nothing was going on as the child she had grown close to was laid to rest. Desperately she wanted to clear her head and get out of Boston. She needed time to think, to consider all the changes in her life. Packing a small bag she decided she had to get away on her own for a few days, something she had never done before, leaving the kids and Mike to look after themselves.

'They'll not starve or pine away,' Evie had assured her.

Martha did her best to believe that, and left everything as organized as possible.

Mike had barely said anything when she told him of her feelings, explained her need to escape for a few days.

'If that's what you want, Martha,' was all he'd said, not even offering to come with her. 'A few days' rest will probably do you good and we can talk when you get back.'

Martha relished the thought of just getting in the car and driving as far as she could. Numb after Cass's death, she was tired and badly needed some time away. Since that very first time when she'd been called to heal, there had scarcely been time for her to unwind or think, or decide what was the right thing for her to do. She had acted on instinct and impulse, and where had it got her?

Perhaps Mike was right after all and she should walk away and turn her back on the gift. Too much of her life was being sacrificed for an ideal that she might never achieve.

From the minute she passed over the Canal, everything changed, the Cape's tempo dictating she slow down and relax as she drove along roads flanked by forests of evergreens, striking winter-stripped woodland and the haunting views of Nantucket Sound. Any of the large drive-in hotels and motels that were still open had vacancy signs up outside, and unbelievable discount occupancy rates in the hope of tempting the winter traveller like herself.

Deciding to drive to Hyannis, she pulled the car up along the harbour where the ferryboats for Martha's Vineyard and Nantucket set sail. The fishing boats had returned from their day's work and were being hosed and washed down, the seagulls screaming as the fishermen worked.

The chill air felt good and she pulled her windproof jacket on, gulping in the tangy sea breeze as she walked all along by the shore and Marina. The big hotel on the waterfront was still open and she thought she would see if they had a room. The receptionist, a plump young woman with a welcoming smile, was delighted to sell her one, and tried to hide her disappointment that it was only a single for two nights. Walking along the wooden decking she noticed the pool was shut for the season, and many of the rooms had their heavy curtains closed over. Opening her room she was pleasantly surprised by its comfort and magnificent view. It was tempting to just kick off her shoes and crawl into bed, but she decided to get something to eat before retiring. The quaint seafood restaurant on the corner was still serving till eight and overcoming her embarrassment about being on her own, she sat up at the counter and ordered the house special, which consisted of an assortment of tasty fish pieces, lobster, crab, calamari, served with a tangy sauce and baked potato with sour cream. A television in the corner was tuned to the news and she watched that as she ate. Mike would have loved this place, and she stifled the momentary pang of regret that he was not with her.

She was cosied up in bed by 9 p.m., her curtains drawn, the TV switched off, as she rolled up into a ball and wrapped herself in the heavy yellow and blue comforter. It felt good not to have to answer to anybody and to be able to switch off the light and lie in the darkness with the sound of the ocean outside her window as she fell into a deep and heavy sleep.

In the morning she momentarily forgot where she was, waiting for the sounds of the household to wake her up: Patrick in the bathroom, Mary Rose drying her hair, Mike putting on the local TV news for the traffic and weather report. Instead there was silence, broken only by the distant sound of a vacuum cleaner and the chugging engine of a boat. Turning over she ignored them, not waking again till 10.30.

How had she slept so long! She wasn't used to sleeping in and being lazy like this. She'd missed breakfast but after a quick shower got some coffee and a muffin down near the harbour.

Martha had stayed in Hyannis a few times when they were kids, in one of the cheap motels up near the roadway, her father making a big to-do about the vacation. They swam in the pool and spent hours on the beach playing football and chasing each other, their fair skin freckled and dry, scalps itchy with sand, wearing constantly wet swimsuits. One summer she had got burned on their first day on the Cape, red as a beet, refusing to believe that the sun could actually cause such damage, her shoulders and backs of her legs so painful and sore that she could barely walk for the rest of the two weeks. She'd had to lie in the darkened motel room for three precious days of the vacation, her mother covering her in cooling yoghurt and keeping her company, both of them miserable as her brothers and father went off fishing and swimming and enjoyed themselves.

Her father, an out and out Democrat, prided himself on going to the same part of the world as the Kennedy clan, those tanned and big-teethed rich kids regularly spotted in the distance going back and forwards in a legion of sloops and sailboats and power racers. He took enormous pride in the Irish emigrant Catholic family who eventually saw their son named President of the United States. 'Anything is possible in America!' he would say again and again to them all. He'd wept like a baby on hearing of the shooting of Jack Kennedy in Dallas, inconsolable at the loss of the man and the dream on that November day. Now a memorial park overlooked the beach and water. Martha stood there watching the seabirds wade giddily along the shore, boats bobbing on the distant blue swell; she remembered her father in his rolled-up shirt-sleeves and grey trousers and his grand belief in them all.

Two days later she drove on to Chatham, not bothering with lunch and buying herself a soda and a bread roll to eat on the beach. Resisting the temptation to linger in the myriad tourist gift shops and traditional inns, she parked and walked up along the Shore Road glad of her fleece-lined jacket and knitted hat as the sea breeze caught her. The old lighthouse looked out over the water and deserted golden sand. She sat in the rough grasses of the dunes and ate, watching the waves and listening to the roar of the ocean.

There, wrapped in the solitude, she asked herself how she had come to be in this place where so many people expected so much from her. She had tried to help one solitary child and now found herself deluged with those searching for hope, praying for cures and miracles and expecting her to intercede for them, lay her hands on them and cure their diseases, mend their broken limbs and heal their wounds, chase away the shadows that stalked them and soothe their damaged spirits. They expected too much of her, far too much. The healing power was deep within themselves, but many – no, most – of them had chosen to ignore it.

Cass was beyond healing, she'd known that the minute she'd set eyes on her, and yet she had been drawn to help the young girl accept the frailty of her human body and the strength of her spirit.

Could she have changed anything to do with Cass? She thought long and hard about it, realizing that approached by Beth Armstrong again, she would do the exact same thing, and become involved with the child. The parents were in a turmoil now, and she wished that she could help them assuage their grief as she knew it was one of the things that Cass had worried about: what would happen when she was gone. Sitting on the sand Martha had much to consider; the healing had propelled her to a prominence she was not sure she wanted, or enjoyed. Mike and the kids were her priority and yet as more and more people sought her help there was less time for her husband and children, something she had never intended to happen. How could she be all things to everyone? There was just one of her and at the moment she felt like a piece of elastic being pulled in all directions. But her energy levels were high and in the winter sunshine surrounded by sea, sky and earth she felt strangely renewed, the constant ebb and flow of the water giving her strength, the maze of puzzles in her brain unravelling and becoming clear strong lines which she knew she must follow. On the beach Martha truly felt at one with nature, and the spirit that ruled every facet of her life, her doubts and concerns soothed by the vast blue of the ocean. She had been granted the gift of healing and she must use it.

*   *   *

She drove up along the National Seashore to the very tip of the Cape to Provincetown, the place where the pilgrims first landed. Walking through its narrow streets and arty shops, she stopped to buy Alice a simple wooden whale mobile for her bedroom which she couldn't resist: hand carved and hand painted it balanced beautifully. She and Mike had taken the kids whale watching from here about three years ago when they had rented a beach house in Yarmouth for ten days. It was one of those rare and magical trips that each and every one of them remembered perfectly and still talked about.

It was getting dark by the time she checked into a narrow pastel-painted wooden house that bore the legend 'The Liberty Rose – Bed and Breakfast'. Her room was covered in swathes of floral chintz and had been decorated with loving care by someone obsessed with the colours pink and green; every little detail had been contemplated and co-ordinated, right down to the peppermints on her pillow in their shiny pink wrapping and a log fire set to light in the grate. Yawning with tiredness, she was more than happy to climb into bed and phone home. Patrick filled her in on what they were all doing as Mike and the girls were out. Disappointed, she sent them all her love and promised Patrick she'd be home real soon.

She rose early the next morning, checking out after a feast of crispy bacon and pancakes, syrup and coffee with cream that would probably clog every artery in her body.

The owner stared at her as she handed in her key.

'I know you,' she said emphatically. 'I definitely know you.'

Martha just smiled.

'Oh my! You're that woman who does that miracle healing that I read about and I saw you on TV, on WBZ4. I can't believe I had you staying here under my very roof last night!'

Martha just nodded.

'Are you working down here?' the woman asked inquisitively.

'No, I'm not, I just came down on a break.'

'Well, you're more than welcome and please come back and visit any time,' she said, as she swiped Martha's credit card details. 'Would you like to sign my visitors' book?' she asked, pulling a floral-patterned book from under the desk.

Martha, trying to think of something suitable to scribble in the side margin that would please her hostess, wrote 'A garden of delight!' Not very original but it seemed to please Kate Anne Brewster, the owner.

'Please come back again!' she laughed as Martha signed the payment slip and said goodbye.

Renewed by her few days of exile, thoughts of home now filled her mind. Martha knew it was high time she got back to her family and the fulfilment of her healing work.

Chapter Thirty-six

It felt good to be home. Martha was glad of the clutter and chaos of the house on Mill Street, as Mike and the kids welcomed her back. She still grieved for Cass but knew she had to concentrate on the living, her family and friends and those that needed her.

Mary Rose had tidied and cleaned their bedroom, vacuumed the den and scrubbed the shower tiles so clean that they looked almost brand new. Martha was gracious about her daughter's peace offering.

'I'm sorry, Mom. I guess I didn't think about how you were feeling and was just being jealous and stupid and stuff.'

'Mary Rose, you've absolutely nothing to be jealous about, you are my precious daughter and nothing and no-one can change that, do you hear me! You and Patrick and Alice are the closest human beings on the planet to me. I carried you under my heart, for God's sakes, and I'm not about to forget that. Ever since Timmy I guess it's been pretty crazy round here, and maybe I haven't been fair on you either. I'm sorry.'

Feeling revived and re-energized, connected to the world around her, Martha spoke with Kim and Kathleen of her plans to continue her work and devote more time to those she could genuinely help. She had written a long letter to Beth and Tom about their daughter and how much she loved them both.

That weekend Martha cooked a special dinner for Mike and herself, giving them the chance to unwind and eat on their own. The kids were fed earlier with pizza, Patrick and Mary Rose disappearing to the cinema and Alice dropped to a sleepover at Katie's house. They needed to talk, that's what Mike had said, and here in their own home there was less chance of being interrupted. Garlic shrimp, peppered fillet steak with baby potatoes and onion, and a chocolate rum pie, all her husband's favourites. She'd lit the fire and set the dining table, the candlelight dancing off the sparkling Waterford crystal glasses. Martha guessed, like Mary Rose, it was a form of peace offering.

Mike fetched the chilled wine from the fridge as she served the meal. The starters were good, the shrimp smothered in garlic and butter burning their mouths as they ate. They made small talk about the kids and school and work – which she guessed kept them off the thorny subject of themselves. Mike liked his meat rare and as they ate the beef fillet neither of them talked, just enjoying the cream and whiskey sauce. The dessert looked and tasted great; Martha was pleased when Mike took a second helping of the chocolate pie. The wine glasses drained, the bottle empty, Mike offered her a glass of Bailey's, fetching a whiskey for himself.

Relaxed she sank into the couch in front of the fire, pulling her feet up under her.

'Martha, we need to talk,' said Mike.

She sipped on the creamy liqueur. He was going to say all the usual things she already knew, about them not spending enough time together, needing to prioritize their marriage, stuff she was already fully aware of.

He seemed on edge.

'Martha, I don't know how to say it but I think we should take a break from each other.'

'A break?'

'Yes, I'll move out of the house. Maybe it'll help.'

Shocked, Martha didn't know what to say, but she could see that her husband was deadly serious.

'Move out!'

'Yeah, out of this house. I've had enough of this circus and I just want out of it. I'm just a normal guy, who wants a normal marriage. I don't want to be married to a saint!'

'What do you mean? What are you talking

341

about?' she demanded. 'You're married to *me*.'

'That's what I mean. All you think of is helping others, and I'm way down the bottom of that pile somewhere. And it makes me feel like a real shit most of the time. That's the truth of it.'

'Jesus, Mike, don't say that,' she begged. 'You know I would never, ever do anything to hurt you. I love you!'

'Love! You love too many people, Martha, that's your problem.'

'I love you,' she insisted. 'You are the only man I love and you know that.'

'Martha, I need to get out of this house. Out of this marriage. Away from what we're doing to each other. Maybe a break will help – I don't know!'

'Help? What the hell are you talking about?'

'I'm talking about us, Mar. To see if there still is an "us" under all the bullshit that's been going on!'

'Is there somebody else?' she demanded.

'No.' He shook his head. 'You know that!'

'Honest to God I don't know anything any more.'

Mike sat totally silent, letting her absorb what he was saying. He was never the one to rush into things or make rash decisions. That was more her domain. He had obviously thought long and hard about it and, Martha saw from his expression, had made up his mind.

'Mike, please don't do this to me and the kids. To our family.'

'I'm sorry, Martha, I have to.'

'Have to?'

'Everything has changed – you know it has. I don't think it will ever go back to the way it was before.'

'That's so unfair! When you got that job with Sun Systems, I stood by you! Everything changed then, but maybe you didn't notice cos you were working eighteen hours a day and only coming home to sleep, but I just got on with it and concentrated on keeping our family together.'

'That's what I've been trying to do.'

'But we are a family, Mike. I've supported what you are doing over all the years, and now all I'm asking is for you to be there for me,' she pleaded.

'I'm fed up with it, Martha. I want out. Our lives are not going to get better, the ripples from what you are doing are going to get wider and bigger and even more out of control.'

'We can control it.'

'It's gone beyond that. It's like a huge wave and I guess all I'm saying is I'm not willing to ride it any more. I've had enough.'

'Do you still love me?' she asked.

'Yeah, I guess.'

That's something at least, she consoled herself. 'Where will you go?' she asked.

'I can stay in the folks' house for a few weeks and then I'll sort something else out.' From the way he spoke Martha knew that his decision to move out had already been made and nothing she could say would stop it.

'When will we tell the kids?'

'I'll sleep in Alice's room tonight,' he offered, 'and I'll tell them in the morning when she gets back.'

Like a zombie Martha automatically cleared away the table and tidied the kitchen, throwing the rest of the chocolate rum pie in the bin. Mike sat on the couch on his own, staring into the flames of the dying fire.

Climbing into their double bed, pulling on her short silk Victoria's Secrets nightgown, his favourite, she waited half in hope that he would pull back the creamy white bedlinen and lie down beside her. Not used to sleeping alone at home she tossed and turned, conscious that the only man she had ever loved was sleeping two doors down the hall from her and no longer wanted to be a part of her life: a deep hurt, beyond healing.

Mike McGill packed up his suits and shirts and a few more pieces of clothing, folding everything carefully; then his shaving gear, his laptop and a few personal items, and carried them out to the car.

Martha watched, disbelieving that this was actually happening, and that Mike really was re-moving himself from her life.

'You don't need to take it all, Mike, just come

and go and get what you need – this is your home,' she pleaded.

He said nothing.

The kids had taken it badly, screaming at Mike – and at her! Demanding they make up and keep the family together. Not wanting them to break up.

'Listen, guys, this is not an overnight decision, there is a lot going on between your mom and I at the moment and I guess we have to sort it out.'

'Why can't you sort it out here, Daddy?' puzzled Alice.

Mike, stumped for an answer, eventually admitted, 'Because I don't want to. But I still love you all. I still love your mom! Me moving out isn't going to change that.' The usual platitudes! She could tell the kids didn't know whether to believe him or not!

'Nobody has done anything wrong, guys, nobody,' he assured them.

'Have you a girlfriend?' quizzed Mary Rose.

'There's nobody else involved. This is just between your mom and me.'

Martha sat on the kitchen stool listening to the hall door shut, and to Alice whimpering and crying like a wounded animal. For an hour, maybe two, she sat there listening to her own breath and heartbeat. Out of instinct, she'd phoned her mother, wanting to hear her voice.

Frances Kelly was equally upset when she heard

about Mike, the two of them going backwards and forwards over it again and again for more than an hour, Martha wondering what in God's name had made her choose her mother as the first person to tell!

'No, Mom, I promise there has been no mention of a divorce.'

'No, I don't believe he has a girlfriend.'

'Of course I love him! You know that.'

Mary Rose stood watching her on the phone, passing her some Kleenex. By dinnertime each of her brothers had called, berating Mike for not sticking by her and pledging their unswerving family support.

'What the fuck is Mike up to, Martha, putting a good marriage in jeopardy?' demanded Jack.

Martha was at a loss to explain it herself. Tense and tired, she longed to just go to bed and pretend none of this was happening, but for the kids' sake she couldn't do that. They were too young to understand the complexities of her relationship with Mike and the pressure it had been put under. It was hard enough on them to hear that their father would not be living at home for the moment, without her going to pieces too.

'Mommy, you must be really sad and lonesome too without Dad,' said Alice.

She just nodded, not trusting herself to reply.

As she sat in the kitchen with her head in her hands not even able to think without Mike, Alice pushed in close beside her and put her arms

346

around her. Patrick's CD player was blasting music from upstairs.

'I've a bit of a headache, pet, with the noise and everything, I just . . .'

'Poor Mommy!' soothed Alice, placing her hands on her head, across her temple.

'There, there, Mom.'

'What are you doing, Alice?'

'I'm trying to heal you, Mom, to take the pain in your head away.'

Martha sat stunned that her child would instinctively try to lift the pain from her, use her hands to relieve distress and hurt. She was afraid for her. 'Listen pet,' she said gently, holding Alice's hands in her own. 'Me being sad and upset over your dad moving out is awful, but I need to feel bad about it. Your dad is so special and important to me, and I'm really going to miss him. Miss him being home here with us, being around the whole time, you know that. We all will!'

Mary Rose and Patrick made dinner, all of them throwing concerned glances at each other, awkward as they ate the chicken tacos. Martha felt sick, and scared of living without Mike.

Evie came over late that night when the kids had gone to bed, hugging Martha as she bawled like a big baby. Her eyes and nose ran with snot and tears as her best friend tried to console her.

'It was so out of the blue,' she admitted. 'I just wasn't expecting it.'

Evie said nothing but only listened and commiserated and made her cups of tea and fried a whole plate of bacon and sausage and let her talk and rant and rave and fuck Mike McGill to kingdom come, till exhausted, Martha fell asleep on the couch, Evie holding her hand as she was scared of being alone.

Chapter Thirty-seven

Those were dark days. Mike's moving out of their home had left her devastated, in a no man's land so far removed from what she was used to that Martha felt disconnected, wounded; filled with so much self-doubt that at times she could barely leave the house. She felt raw and exposed. Mike had always been there to protect her. Now she was alone.

Kim, Ruth and Kathleen were as supportive as they could be, rallying around and trying to cheer her up, telling her how well she was doing – when she knew she wasn't. Kim reminded her of all the stages she herself had gone through before her divorce became final, the custody battles, the petty bickering, the hate and spite and jealousy and the nightmare of her alimony war. Martha prayed that she and Mike did not fall into that category. Kathleen fussed around her like a big mother hen, actually arriving with cakes and treats and ready-made meals as if Martha was about to stop eating and fade away, whereas Rianna, who knew about genuine loss, phoned her last thing at night and first thing in the morning, when she was lying in that big empty double bed: a comforting voice across the line talking with her and encouraging her to greet the new day. And of course there was Evie, her oldest friend, who never criticized or blamed and refused to take sides, and tried to encourage some sort of dialogue between herself and Mike.

The kids took it badly, Patrick wrapping himself in silence and not wanting to talk about it. Loyal to his father he didn't want to hear anything bad said against Mike and Martha agreed with that. She was not about to attack his father or try to make him choose between them! As far as she was concerned her kids had a mom and a dad and were entitled to love them both. Patrick at fifteen was acting the man of the house and insisting on taking over some of Mike's chores, trying to take care of her and the girls. Mary Rose on the other hand was angrier than she'd ever seen before, blaming Mike for walking out on them and Martha for somehow ruining their lives. Only Alice gave in to the true emotions she was feeling and admitted to being a small scared girl who missed her daddy.

Martha was determined, once over the initial shock, to behave decently. Neither of them had done anything wrong and they deserved respect. Mike was surprised when she invited him to come home one evening a week to share a family meal with her and the kids. She forced herself to be polite and rational and proud on those occasions, all for the sake of their kids, who needed to know that their parents did not hate or want to destroy each other.

Ruth was busy seeking out possible venues and dates for future healing sessions in a number of places. Martha had already agreed to do another in the Tanner Radford building, and a possible one in a school hall in New York.

'Can't we leave it for the moment, Ruth, until I see how things are with me and the kids? There is so much going on I just need to be there for them.'

'Martha, if we leave it too late there is not a chance in hell of us getting a booking of a good venue, and the top venues will hold a better crowd and have adequate seating and the extra facilities like the wheelchair access and ramps that we need.'

'I know, but I just feel that the kids might need me to be around and not off touring.'

Reluctantly Ruth agreed to hold off making any bookings for at least a month, so Martha could have time to consider what she truly wanted.

She preferred to work with the people who came to 'the upstairs room', where she had the time to talk and listen and get to know them individually, or to visit people like Thea with whom she had developed a relationship. Martha was the kind of person who couldn't help becoming emotionally involved and caring for all those that came in search of healing.

She still thought of Cass and prayed for her, and was upset when Sue Lucas told her that Beth and Tom Armstrong had sought legal advice about her so-called negative involvement with their child. Fortunately, it looked like it would go no further but Martha couldn't believe how Cass's parents had totally turned against her.

Chapter Thirty-eight

Henry Madison took the cab from South Station to the address written on the top of the envelope.

William was sitting quiet beside him; the taxi driver glanced at him in the mirror. His brother had got himself all upset on the escalator stair in Penn Station, frightened he was going to fall off with the crush of people all around him, Henry trying to keep a hold of the sleeve of his jacket. He'd dropped a bag of peanut M&Ms and had lurched forward to try to bend down and catch them, as they skittered and bounced all over and down the moving stairs.

Henry sternly told him to leave them and he'd buy him another packet when they got to Boston.

He'd liked the train. A kind gentleman gave up his window seat so they could ride together as by the time he walked slowly to the carriage only single seats remained. Celeste, his neighbour, had suggested flying, but Henry was nervous of taking

William on an airplane. He might not like or understand the notion of flight and get himself in one of his states; no, the train was a safer option.

He was tired and would have loved to close his eyes and just doze as the high-speed train hurtled between New York and Boston, but instead kept his attention on his brother who seemed fascinated by the constantly changing view.

He was nervous going to meet the healer woman in person after months of correspondence, but he'd come to look forward to those letters with their Massachusetts postmark. William looked tired and he squeezed his hand, passing him a small Hershey Cookies and Cream bar; the rest of the hidden candy he'd keep till later.

They drove through the city, with the Charles river in the distance. William closed his eyes when they entered a long tunnel, emerging in bumper to bumper heavy traffic, eventually leaving the city behind them to follow the busy highway, turning off at the exit signs for Easton. The cab came to a stop outside a white-painted colonial-style home on Mill Street, which was definitely the right address. Henry paid the driver first before getting William organized to step out, as he lifted their overnight bag.

He walked slowly up to the front porch and step, the car driver insisting on lifting the bag for him as he rang the house bell. He could feel his heart pound: what if the McGill woman wasn't in? What if she'd forgotten the day he was coming? Or had been called away to deal with something more urgent?

The door suddenly opened wide as Martha welcomed him and brought the two of them inside, Henry introducing William and explaining how he'd had to bring him as there was no-one reliable enough to sit with him.

'That's all right, Henry!' smiled the healer, shaking hands with his brother. 'I'm honoured to meet the two of you and glad you made the trip to see me.'

Henry smiled, glad to finally have the chance to meet the woman he had so much faith in. She was younger than he'd expected, prettier too and had piercing blue-green eyes that seemed to almost see through you.

'Let me make you a nice cup of tea or coffee. You must be exhausted after your long journey.'

'Coffee would be nice,' agreed Henry. 'William likes it too.'

Martha slipped out of the room leaving the two of them sitting there, William gazing around him, trying to make sense of these new surroundings which were very different from their own small living room at home.

'It's all right, William, honest it is,' Henry promised, trying to allay his fears and growing apprehension. 'I'm here with you and I'm not going to leave.'

Martha came back into the room. 'The coffee will be ready in a minute, my daughter will bring it in to us,' she told them.

Henry nervously made small talk about the journey, knowing the Martha woman was looking at William.

A teenager with long dark hair and a heavy fringe carried in the tray and set it down in front of them.

'Let me introduce my daughter, Mary Rose.'

When the girl smiled it lit up her whole face, which became extraordinarily pretty.

'This is Henry and his brother William. Henry and I have been keeping in touch with each other over the past few months.'

He could see the kid had no interest in either of them, writing them off because of their age.

'I brought some cookies and a few slices of that cherry cake that was in the tin.'

'Thanks, Mary Rose, that's great.'

Henry put the sugar and milk in William's cup, he didn't want him knocking the sugar all over the carpet, and put a cookie and a slice of cake on a plate for him. He had an enormous appetite and seemed to burn his food. He then turned his attention to Martha.

'Now tell me about your arthritis and what your surgeon says,' urged Martha gently.

Henry tried not to get himself upset when he thought of the choices ahead, his mobility becoming worse and worse and his use of painkillers growing. 'I don't know what to do,' he sighed. 'I just don't know what to do.'

When they had finished their coffee, Martha asked if he would lie down on the couch so she could lay her hands on him. However, Henry could sense that William, having cleared his plate, was getting anxious. 'Martha, do you mind if William watches TV or a video?' he asked. 'He gets bored real easy.'

'Oh, of course not. What kind of stuff does he like?'

'Fighting or tough stuff usually,' he laughed.

'Well, hold on then, I think Patrick's copy of *Gladiator* is here somewhere. I'll put it in the machine.'

'He likes to sit right up near the TV,' admitted Henry.

He watched as the young woman moved one of the heavy armchairs almost up in front of the screen.

'That better?'

William nodded, already excited by the first glimpse of the Roman general and his legion.

Henry breathed an inward sigh of relief that his brother was occupied and hopefully would not disturb them.

He lay down on the couch, his shoes on the floor, his cardigan and tweed jacket folded in a neat pile as Martha stood over him.

Her hands felt soft, gentle at first, almost like a child's lightly running across him, skimming over his frame. Henry tried to stay calm and relaxed as the healer worked.

He closed his eyes, feeling drowsy, aware òf pressure, of heat pervading his tissues and bones, warming them. He could feel the intense heat radiating from the weight of those hands, to his hips, his spine, his shoulders and neck. Even his own breathing seemed different as if the air was filling his lungs, every little corner of them, bathing them with oxygen. Images of childhood, times of happiness came into his mind unbidden and he felt removed from his surroundings but unsure of where he was exactly. He was aware of Martha moving around beside him, and gave his total trust to the woman who was using her healing powers to restore him. His worries and cares seemed to slip away.

'Henry! Henry!'

Martha was standing over him, gently touching his shoulder.

'It's time for you to sit up now, Henry. Take it slowly, there's no rush.'

Henry felt mortified. 'Was I asleep?' he asked.

Martha laughed a little.

'I'm so sorry, it's just I'm so tired I guess.'

'Listen, lots of people doze off, it's totally normal. I just let you have a bit of peace for a while longer.'

Embarrassed, Henry pulled on his chunky cardigan and began to slip his swollen feet into his soft beige leather comfort shoes as he searched for his wallet. 'Do you think I'm still going to need that surgery?' he asked.

'I'll be honest, Henry: the hip and knees are bad, just as your doctor says, but you are strong and I don't see any complications. Just give yourself some time. I've tried to lift some of the pain away for the moment, and that may help.'

'How much do I owe you, Martha?'

'There's no charge, honest there's not.'

'But I've taken up so much of your time,' he insisted.

'It's been a pleasure to meet you,' smiled the healer.

Martha glanced over at William.

'Would it be all right if I touched William?' she asked.

His brother was engrossed in the bloody spectacle at the Roman Games, jumping up and down in the chair, and barely looked up when Martha laid her hands on his shoulders. Henry watched as she lightly touched his head and neck, a shadow of concern flitting across her face. William looked up, puzzled by the attention, his eyes connecting with Martha.

Without a word she leant forward and kissed his forehead, as you would a small, brave boy. Henry was touched by the kind gesture.

They gathered up their things, Martha insisting they have a soda before they left and ordering them a cab.

'We're staying overnight at the Park Plaza

359

Hotel and getting the train back first thing in the morning. I promised William I'd take him to the Aquarium and maybe take a tour bus ride round the city.'

'That'd be neat,' murmured Martha, switching off the video player. William stood up immediately. Henry asked if she'd mind if they could both use the bathroom.

Henry hugged Martha close as they were leaving. He couldn't believe it but somehow he felt connected with this person who'd been almost a stranger.

'Now you promise me, Henry,' said Martha, taking a hold of his hand and squeezing it, 'that you're going to take good care of yourself and try not to do too much.'

Henry Madison was surprised by the realization that Martha McGill genuinely cared about him and William and their difficult situation.

Chapter Thirty-nine

Thea Warrington sat out back on the deck, by the small rock pool, a drawing pad on her lap. The weather was cool but she enjoyed the fresh air as she worked, imagining in her mind's eye a different landscape and the exact requirements of her client and his family. She always loved working on gardens for families, trying to ensure space for the adults to have quiet time, somewhere restful, with a seat or garden chair where they could unwind and forget their daily cares, and of course a family area, for entertaining, cooking and playing outdoors in the warm summer weather, and most important of all a hideaway spot for the children to run and imagine they were lost in a fairytale wood or cast away on a treasure island. There would be a sand pit and a swing and maybe a low stone bridge to cross from one world to another. She smiled, just thinking about it.

Her own boys were at school and Erik would collect them later. It was funny how the kids had just accepted the change in their routine once she and Erik had explained a bit about her illness to them. They now knew that it would either be their father or their home help Valerie who would collect them, as their mom could no longer drive. It was strange, thought Thea, that it was the little things that she missed doing the most – the boring school runs, helping at the Scouts' bake sale, taking the kids swimming, going to the market and complaining about the weight of her shopping kart and having to stand in line and check it all through. Now her groceries just seemed to magically appear as she could order all her requirements over the net, and her local store had a same day delivery service. The big things didn't seem all that important any more as she adjusted to a life governed by the cancer cells which remorselessly attacked her body. She refused to wave the white flag of defeat and listen to the doom and gloom prognosis of her illness given by her doctors. She was still a young woman with plenty to live for, and was not about to give in.

Like a good patient she had followed all the best of medical advice, tried the latest drug and radium therapies and when for the third time she had been told her cancer was back, agreed to go and see the hospice which her oncologist had suggested might be a good place for the final management of her illness, should she and Erik and the boys no longer be able to cope. The staff there had warmly welcomed her, giving her a guided tour. Thea had been impressed with the level of care and the holistic environment in which the patients enjoyed their final days. She had been fortunate enough to meet with its director and about two hours later, after explaining the reward and satisfaction she got from her landscaping work, she found herself being asked to design an informal garden for the younger patients and their visitors, a commission she had joyously accepted.

The work kept coming in and she even did it flat on her back in the bed, where Erik had erected a drawing board for her. The computer could do the rest: catalogue the plants, the stones and tiles and bricks, trees and shrubs that she wanted to use, provide a display for her clients to mull over. Creating and shaping the earth and ground around her seemed to take over Thea's thought processes and help her cope with the dark days as her illness took a hold. Her brain and mind were still virgin soil untouched by the creeping weed of her disease.

Erik was her rock and without him she did not know how she could have carried on. He was there for her and the boys, unflinching no matter how bad things got, constant in a tornado of utter change. Her husband refused to give up and accept the time span the doctors had allotted her; he was ready to wage battle against the might of an unseen enemy, somehow believing they could win! It was Erik who had heard about the woman from Massachusetts, the woman who was said to have the power to heal, like a saint in the Bible able to perform miracles. Thea had little belief in miracles but seeing the hope in her husband's eyes had agreed to his trying to contact her, pleading with him not to expect anything.

The miracle was that Martha McGill had actually responded, not to the letters and phone calls but to the five-minute home video that Erik had shot of the family, and that she had driven all the way up to West Hartford to see her.

Thea had been embarrassed at first at the thought of a stranger coming to her home; would she be a bible-thumping Jesus freak or a wacky new age spiritualist who would chant around her? Much to her surprise, Martha was neither and the two of them had got along just fine, Thea feeling unusually relaxed and open. A wife and mother like herself, Martha with her understanding eyes and easy manner seemed to have a rare understanding and empathy for what she was going through, and a line of complete trust had developed between them. The healer had made her lie down and then without even saying a word laid her hands right on her.

At once Thea had been aware of the enormous heat and energy that seemed to flow towards her as Martha began to lightly run her hands all over her body, concentrating on the areas that had been mentioned as trouble spots. She knew Martha had been startled when she touched the area where the aggressive tumour encased part of her spinal column, but unwaveringly she had continued, Thea giving herself up to the pleasant sensation of sunshine that enveloped her as Martha worked.

Afterwards, she couldn't explain it but she felt better – maybe it was a placebo effect, but whatever it was she was in less pain and seemed to have more energy. Erik kissed her and told her she even looked more beautiful.

'That Martha lady sure has a special effect, in that case!' she joked.

Martha came again and again, once a month and with every visit the advance of Thea's cancer just seemed to slow and halt. How Thea laughed when the doctors rechecked her X-rays and re-examined her, baffled, but admitting cautiously that perhaps she was in some form of temporary remission.

Thea didn't care what the reason was, all she knew was that the Good Lord was giving her more time to spend with her husband and boys, more days to sit in the sun and enjoy his greatness, and that somehow the healer, Martha, was connected with it . . .

Chapter Forty

Martha's time was taken up by her healing work. Many people were so sick, their conditions gone too far for her to be able to heal, that instead they needed the gift of acceptance. Wounds and injuries, twisted muscles and nerves, responded best to her touch, and like her forebears she seemed to be able to stop bleeding and encourage scars and tears and breaks to the body to renew and mend. Other diseases proved more difficult, the willpower and faith of the sufferer determining much.

She was surprised to get a call from *Soul and Spirit*, the network's popular daytime TV show which looked at new age therapies and ways to enjoy life as it explored the human mind, body and soul. The programme's producer asked Martha if she'd be prepared to take part as they would love to have her on the programme. At first reluctant to place herself in the public eye again, she agreed to do it only when the producer told her that Catherine Morgan the healer had already agreed to present five of the shows and had suggested inviting Martha on. Talking to Catherine later on that night at home, Martha hoped she'd made a wise decision.

'Martha, half Boston is talking about you already! This way the viewers will get the truth and find out about your work and your dedication to it and make up their own minds,' Catherine assured her.

The show was a great success, Martha at ease with Catherine as they discussed many aspects of healing and the aspirations of those who came to her. Catherine got her to talk about her childhood and the influences they shared. Long after they were off the air they continued the discussion when they had supper with a few of the crew in a restaurant near Catherine's home.

The days after the show saw a fresh wave of people in search of miracles and hope contacting her, from Texas to Utah, from Baltimore to Sacramento. Martha was unfortunately unable to meet even a tiny percentage of those who pleaded their case. Kim and Kathleen handled the huge amount of enquiries and diplomatically wrote and said no on her behalf.

Glenn Harris, a stockbroker and investment dealer, the darling of Boston's business press and financial community, was among them. Martha was amazed when she was approached directly by his personal assistant and asked if she would make an exception and meet Mr Harris for lunch. Politely she refused: wealth and prestige had absolutely no bearing as far as she was concerned and the man was welcome to join the huge waiting list if he wanted to.

She was busy in the upstairs room working on a small baby that suffered from terrible colicky pain when Glenn Harris in person came knocking on her door.

Excusing herself for a minute, she stepped outside, annoyed at the interruption. Politely she asked him to leave as she was busy.

'I'm sorry, Mr Harris,' she said, 'but I thought I'd made it very clear that I can't see you.'

'My, but you are a hard woman to track down,' he interrupted, standing in his immaculately tailored suit looking totally out of place.

'Please, Mr Harris, I am very busy with people who need my help,' she insisted. 'If you want to see me I'm afraid you will have to join the waiting list.'

She could sense his annoyance and his struggle to contain his anger. 'Is there any exception to this list?' he asked.

Obviously he was used to bribing his way to the top of every queue, just dangling his chequebook in order to be seen.

'The only exceptions are those that are extremely sick and in desperate need,' Martha added firmly.

'Then this definitely meets your criteria,' he said emphatically.

Martha looked directly at him. Silver haired and of average height, with a muscular build, which perhaps veered on being overweight, Glenn Harris looked otherwise fit and healthy. She waited for him to confide his problems to her.

A serious expression crossed his face.

'I'm not talking about myself, woman! It's about my son.' All his bluster and arrogance suddenly disappeared at the mention of his son's name. 'I need to talk to you about Joshua.'

Martha gestured for him to take a seat in the waiting area.

'I will be about another twenty minutes or so with the little fellow inside,' she said. 'Perhaps we could have a quick word then.'

Glenn Harris was still waiting for her. She sat across from him in the other chair. 'I don't know where to begin,' he apologized, obviously trying to control his feelings.

'Mr Harris, just tell me about your son, tell me about Joshua.'

'I guess Josh was the best kid any man could have!'

She passed him a glass of water as she could see how emotional he was.

'My wife Wendy and I adore him, and everything he has ever wanted or needed I have been lucky enough to be able to provide for him. That is . . . until recently. Two, maybe three years ago, when he went to college he got mixed up with a bad crowd, well, a wrong crowd! They started experimenting, messing with drugs. He had the money, and my son developed a very expensive habit and dropped out. It's been a nightmare ever since. His drugs, his uppers and downers, quack doctors, leeches of friends, hangers on, I refuse to pay one more red cent for the tools that are destroying my son.'

Martha sighed. The same old story – a kid gone off the rails and the parents expecting someone else to clear up the mess. 'What do you want me to do?' she asked.

'I want you to help me get my son back, work one of those famous miracles of yours and restore my son to me, cured of these addictions,' he said emphatically.

'With the best will in the world, Mr Harris, it needs to be your son sitting in this chair, not you.'

'I know that,' he said, leaning forward. 'God knows I know that, but to get him to come to you, I'm not sure. He's been in and out of every rehab and detox centre on the East Coast. There's always promises, programmes and . . .'

'Then?'

'Then – then he falls off the wagon.'

Automatically Martha reached for his hand, feeling the struggle within him.

'I love my son, Mrs McGill. Wendy and I had only the one child and I guess we poured all our love and energy into him. They say it's tough being an only child. Being the only child of a very wealthy man is even tougher.'

'Well, what do you want me to do, what are you expecting? I have no actual experience of dealing with drug addiction or addicts. Most of the people I see are in extreme pain and have severe and chronic illness. Any alleviation of their distress is an improvement; with someone like your son I'm not sure if I can help at all.'

Glenn Harris stayed motionless in the chair.

'You're all he's got right now, Mrs McGill! That's why I want you to see him.'

Almost as soon as the man had walked out the door, Martha regretted impulsively agreeing to meet him and his son later that week.

The lunch was supposed to be casual, a meeting of old friends, and although Glenn Harris had offered to send his driver to collect her Martha had insisted on making her way to the famous glass-fronted seafood restaurant right on the harbour.

It was packed at lunchtime with well-groomed young men and women in expensive designer black and cream. Martha was glad that she had chosen to wear a simple jacket and an above the knee black skirt and tights. She glanced around and as soon as she mentioned her host's name was shown to one of the best tables overlooking the waterfront.

Glenn immediately ordered a drink and Martha

asked for a sparkling mineral water; wine at lunch always made her fuzzy and relaxed, and she felt this was most definitely one of those occasions when she needed to keep her head. Glenn welcomed her warmly and she noticed people at one or two other tables glance over in their direction curiously.

The menu was extensive and she read through it deciding to opt for snapper, with shrimps to start. Glenn once he'd ordered began to fill her in with details about his son, who was due to meet him in about ten minutes' time.

'How are you going to explain me?' she asked, slightly amused.

'I'm going to pretend you're an old friend, and that we just bumped into each other and I insisted you join me for lunch.'

Martha was about to ask a hundred more questions when her eyes were drawn to the tall intense-looking young man talking to the waiter and then making his way to the table. He was the spit of his father, a younger, maybe less attractive version. Glenn Harris jumped out of his seat and threw his arms around his son, directing him to the chair beside him.

'Hey, Josh, you're on time!'

The boy nodded and sat down, staring over at Martha.

'Josh, let me introduce you to Martha McGill, she's an old friend. We haven't seen each other for years, and then we go and bump into each other up near the Hancock building. I hope you don't mind but I've invited her to have lunch with us.'

Josh Harris looked over at Martha, weighing her up: her face, her figure, her hair, her style. She could read the contempt in his eyes, as if he was used to his father introducing him to a series of different women.

She smiled and stretched out her hand to shake his, picking up on the nervous energy that exuded from him. He ordered quickly, barely interested in the food, and complained that they were sitting in a non-smoking area.

His father made it clear that he had no intention of moving table.

'How's your mom?' enquired Glenn.

She could see the dart of anger flicker in the young man's eyes.

'She's OK, I guess. She's planning a trip to Italy to visit the famous cities – Florence, Rome and Venice. She's got all the guidebooks out and well, you know her, she's planning her itinerary and all the palaces and churches and paintings to see that will tie in with her fine art course.'

'That should be interesting. I hope that she'll enjoy it.'

'She should, John is going with her.'

This time Martha could see the pain in Glenn's eyes. She should have remembered that the Harris divorce had filled the papers and the courts for days about four years ago, Wendy Harris citing her husband's appetite for affairs with a host of younger women as leading to the breakdown of their marriage. Martha felt she was involved in a weird tit-for-tat match like a tennis game where the players were throwing balls of resentment and misunderstanding between them and she was the umpire in the middle of it all.

Martha's eyes drifted off to the distance where a group of schoolchildren queued with their teacher to visit the aquarium. Her kids had loved it, and no doubt these young students would too.

'It's an amazing location,' murmured her host, looking out the window. 'One of my best investments was an old warehouse property over there to the left which got turned into a multimillion luxury hotel. Can't beat the waterfront, it's what people want.'

Bored, Joshua, was tearing up a fancy type of bread roll and spreading it thickly with golden butter.

'Josh!'

'I'm starving, Dad, I didn't get a chance to eat breakfast, so this will fill me till the food comes.'

'My son Patrick goes through a mound of bread and butter every day, he always seems to be hungry, no matter what I cook.' She laughed, trying to ease the situation.

'Tell me about your family, Martha,' smiled Glenn as if they were genuinely old friends, just catching up.

Cautiously she told him briefly about her three children.

Josh looked bored.

'Family is everything, I'm sure you agree!' Glenn said, running his hand along the edge of the table.

'What about you, Josh? What do you do?' Martha asked politely. The young man shifted in his seat uneasily, keeping his gaze on her face and ignoring his father.

'I used to work here in the city for Morgan Bank in the stockbroking section but now I'm involved in a start-up of my own, over in south Boston. It was an old mill and we hope to convert it into a few studio apartments, once we get the planning and the costs right.'

'Start small and grow big, that's what I always say,' smiled his father. 'That's what I tell all those hotshot Harvard kids and just hope they listen to me. You've got to walk before you can run!'

The chowder, calamari and shrimp were served. Martha squeezed the fresh lemon juice all over her large plate of delicious shrimp and the special house dip. Glenn tucked into his calamari with gusto and noticing two business colleagues at a distant table waved over to them. As soon as he had cleared his plate, he excused himself for a minute and went over to say hello.

'No matter where we go he knows somebody or they know him, it's always the same,' complained Josh.

Martha said nothing, she herself had studiously avoided meeting the eyes of one or two of the diners around, who she knew had probably recognized her, and hoped by doing so to convince them they had mistaken her identity.

'Do you work, Martha?' enquired the young man as he lifted the spoon of creamy chowder to his lips.

'I stayed home when my kids were small, but now they're getting older I guess I'm trying to develop new things for myself.'

'That's kind of like my mom. She's got her art.'

'I do a bit of healing,' she said softly.

'Is that how you met my dad?'

'Pardon?'

'Is that how you met Glenn? Did he come to you for a massage or something?'

'No!' she insisted. 'Not that kind of thing, I work with people who are sick or injured, or in need of help.'

'Well, that lets my dad out, he's as healthy as a horse unless you can cure an over-active dick!'

Embarrassment flooded Martha's cheeks. She was glad that Glenn was not sitting at the table at that moment for he'd probably have floored his son. She chose to ignore the remark and rinsed her fingers in the water bowl, drying them on her napkin. She wanted to make contact with this angry young man, ease the burning resentment within him, but had no idea how to take that first step which would earn his trust.

'It must have been hard on you when your parents separated?'

'It happens.' He shrugged. 'The all-American family is dead and buried in its grave.'

'You don't believe that,' she said, appalled.

'Ask the offspring,' he replied sarcastically. 'You still married?'

'Yes,' she replied hesitantly, unsure of herself. 'How is your mother?' she asked, changing the conversation.

'My mother is doing fine, better than when that bastard humiliated her leastways. Not that it's any of your business,' he added argumentatively.

Martha sighed to herself. Joshua had obviously been deeply hurt by the break-up of his parents' marriage, no matter how much they each claimed to love him.

'I know how tough it is on kids when their parents break up,' she said, sympathetically. 'My husband and I recently separated.'

Josh seemed bored.

'Your father's concerned for you,' she offered, finding herself unusually irritated by his attitude.

'What the fuck would *you* know about it, Mrs whatever your name is! He's put you up to this, it's another one of his frigging set-ups to try and manage the mess of my life!' Joshua shouted at her.

In the distance Glenn Harris spun around. Taking in the scene, he started to return to the table.

'No, Josh! It's not like that – honest it's not,' she argued. 'I'm just offering you some help if you need it. When I lay my hands on people sometimes it happens that I can lessen their pain, whatever that pain may be.'

He seemed withdrawn, but she could tell he was listening to her.

'It's up to you if you want to try the healing or not. There are no guarantees, no magic wands, just you and . . .'

'How you two doing?' interrupted Glenn. 'Sorry it took so long but I wanted to say hi to my good buddies over at the back. Ray Donnard and I used to run an investment portfolio together when we first left college.'

Their main courses were served and Martha busied herself enjoying the almost blackened, seasoned snapper with sweet potato and fresh green salad. Joshua toyed with his blue fin special, while his father finished off the large tuna steak.

'I've got to go,' Josh announced abruptly, pushing back his chair from the table. 'I've a meeting in about twenty minutes' time.'

'Hey, we're barely finished eating,' his father reminded him. 'And what about some pie and a cappuccino?'

'No, Dad, thanks, I'm full. I'm not used to eating such a big meal at lunch,' he excused himself.

'It was nice to meet you, Joshua,' smiled Martha. 'Remember what we were talking about, well, here's my number.' She took out one of the fancy new cards with her office number on that Ruth had insisted she get printed, and passed it up to him.

'Thanks,' was all he said before placing it in his jacket pocket.

Both of them watched him push his way frantically through the crowded restaurant, lighting up a cigarette the minute he stepped outside.

'Well, what did you think?' enquired Glenn as soon as their cappuccinos arrived. 'Did you have enough time to talk?'

'Enough time?'

'Why yeah, while I went over to talk to those two guys in the back.'

'Your friends.'

'Friends, why heck, Martha, I had no idea who those guys were! I just went up and introduced myself and told the tall guy that I was admiring his suit and asked him who is his tailor. I was just trying to give you two time to get to know each other a little, that's all.'

Martha couldn't believe how he constantly managed to manipulate situations to get what he wanted.

'We talked a bit, but I'm not sure that Josh is interested in my help, Mr Harris. There is nothing more to do but sit tight and wait. Josh himself must decide what he wants next.'

If Glenn Harris was disappointed in her, he

managed to mask it and on finishing the meal insisted she take a ride home with him. The limousine was parked only a few seconds away.

'You've already given my family a huge amount of your time, Martha, at least let me do this for you.'

He was a generous man and Martha graciously accepted his offer, the driver dropping him off at his office before taking her on to Easton.

Chapter Forty-one

On Martha's return visit, the Tanner Radford building was packed to capacity. Those queuing outside were told there was no possibility of a seat and advised to go home. Martha experienced a sudden burst of stage fright on seeing the crowd, and quaked at the long line of people, filing up to meet her, but the wave of good will that enveloped her as she stepped up on the podium helped to settle her nerves. Ruth had insisted on listing those who were severely ill or disabled and seating them in the front two rows, so that Martha could step down to them.

'We don't want any accidents, believe me!'

Overwhelmed by the immense faith people had in her healing skills, Martha knew full well it would be impossible for her to help everyone, but even if one or two were relieved of their pain it would be something.

She began by saying a quiet prayer, asking the Lord God and the Good Earth to help and guide her as Evie led an elderly man towards her. It always amazed Martha how many elderly people came to the healings, pushing their way forwards, demanding to be seen, clinging to life. She talked and prayed and laid on her hands until the sweat ran off her, repeating it all the following week in a small school hall in Bronxville, New York, where the hushed crowd of only a hundred people broke into a tumultuous cheer when a middle-aged woman began to weep and declare that the chronic back pain that had twisted her spine had lifted. In Manhattan some of the people had arrived in expensive cars and limousines to the racquet ball club hall they'd hired; Martha noticed it made no difference, as they were plagued with the same illnesses and fears as others.

Ten days after she got back Joshua Harris came to see her totally out of the blue. He'd phoned asking her to come to his apartment but she had insisted that he visit the upstairs room, Kim fixing an appointment for him. Casually dressed, his dark hair unwashed and unkempt, pale skinned and nervous, he'd lit up the minute he sat down opposite her. She was tempted to ask him to put out the offending cigarette, but realized he was only smoking it in order to distract himself.

'How are you doing, Josh?'

'Have you seen my father lately?' he asked, fixing her with his green eyes.

'No, actually I haven't.'

'OK,' he said, relaxing a little.

'How are you?' she repeated.

'I'm crap, I feel like crap. Every bit of me is sore, the pain is so bad that I can't eat or sleep or think. I'm screwed!'

'Have you taken anything?'

'I'm not using, if that's what you mean. If I was I wouldn't be going through this!'

'Maybe the clinic or the doctors you saw the last time might be able to help you better,' she suggested, feeling out of her depth.

'Screw them. You told me that *you* could help me. I got your fucking card and I came!'

'I'm sorry, Josh, I'm not sure that I can help.'

He looked up at her, the expression on his face lost, scared. Martha saw that he was in such a deeply agitated and unhappy state that there was no way she could turn her back on him or reject him further.

'It's OK, Josh, really it's OK. Your body has gone through huge turmoil and change and physical shock. It's probably totally out of balance and that might be why you are feeling so bad right now. The healing should help.'

'For sure!'

'For sure.' She smiled. 'Is it all right if I lay my hands on you and just get a sense of what is happening to you? My fingers and hands might feel rather warm but that's just a part of the healing process.'

She got the young man to stretch out on her

table, ordering him to kick off his trainers and heavy Abercrombie and Fitch hooded sweatshirt as she walked around him, getting a sense of what his energy level and life force were like. She stopped, confused. Both were scattered and weak. The brightness and spirit she usually associated with youth were absent and she felt the darkness and almost impenetrable depression that engulfed him. Every cell of his body had been affected and Martha had to control her expression in order to mask her dismay. He was healthy in that his heart pumped, perhaps a little faster than it should, his blood flowed, his lungs and kidneys and other organs worked yet he was deeply deeply wounded and carried an intense grief and pain, which he obviously had used drugs and alcohol to relieve. This internal wound was festering, poisoning every part of him as sure as if he had a septic cut. He'd been carrying this pain for a long long time and Martha felt that unless he released it his physical body would be overwhelmed.

Laying her hands over his heart she tried to send light into that darkness and to draw some of it away from Joshua.

A shudder went through him. As she worked, Martha realized how sensitive Glenn Harris's only son was.

'Where does it hurt the most?' she asked gently.

'All over, I told you!'

'I know but where is the pain really bad?'

'My shoulder and head, I guess.'

Concentrating on those two areas, Martha tried to unravel the tension and fear that had buried themselves deep within the walls of his muscles. Finishing off by placing her finger and hands over his head, she had to stifle her own gasp of pain. His mind was in utter turmoil, anger and self-hatred snaking through his thoughts. He had closed his eyes, no longer staring at her, which she found strangely disconcerting. She wanted him to feel a calming sense of peace and to open himself more to receiving the love which he so yearned for.

'You OK, Josh?' she asked afterward as she washed her hands.

He nodded, his head bent down as he retied the laces of his expensive trainers.

'I'd like you to come see me again. What about next week?'

He looked up and she could see a flicker, only a tiny flicker, of hope in his eyes. 'All right,' he agreed.

'Same time.'

Watching him walk out in the street and climb into the old beat-up Chrysler, Martha wondered how father and son could possibly be so different and have ended up causing so much pain to each other.

Chapter Forty-two

The journey from Newton to Providence had taken an age, an accident on the highway slowing things as Gina Forrester drove to the Rhode Island nursing home where her father now resided. She had brought him candy and some lightweight pyjamas and a smart short-sleeved polo shirt. For some strange reason she was anxious to see him.

He was sitting outside his bed in a comfortable support chair, and she kissed the top of his head as if he was a child. His lips and eyes smiled at her. There was no recognition, just a response to the kiss and the sight of the bags with her gifts.

'Here, Dad! You can open these.'

She watched as he pulled frantically at the wrapping paper and cellophane, tumbling the items onto his lap and the bed. The clothes ignored, he stripped a peanut butter cup of its wrapper and began to eat. She laughed: he'd always loved peanut butter ever since they were kids. Any time he'd ever minded them while her mom was out or away, his solution to feeding them had been a massive plate of peanut butter and jelly sandwiches.

She rambled on, talking to him, knowing he would not tell her anything of his daily routine and that it was up to her to fill the silence between them. She told him he was going to be a grandfather, and about her last visit to the obstetrician who'd told her everything was going well and that the baby was in the right position. She told him of the spare bedroom, beside their own, which was to be turned into a nursery. The colours and curtains and expensive wooden cot and changing table and wardrobe were already picked and paid for, but Gina was too superstitious to let Bob or the decorator touch the room till her child was born.

One of the nursing aides walked by and kindly offered her a cup of tea. Gina was glad of the refreshment as she sat there all afternoon with her father, fussing with his locker and checking if he needed anything, though she knew her half-brother Scott who lived close by would drop in once or twice a week to make sure the old man was all right.

When his evening meal was served at 4.45 p.m. she helped him to eat, knowing that not long after he would be prepared and changed for bed. She got ready to go, kissing him and promising to come back soon.

'Dad, I've got to go home now, Bob will be

waiting for me,' she said, stroking the side of his face, wondering if in a few minutes' time her father would remember anything about her or the baby.

Driving home she felt a little tired and disappointed; perhaps she'd hoped that her father would react more to her good news and be excited for her, something she knew in her heart he was no longer capable of. The traffic was heavy, only easing off as she got up onto the highway, listening to the news channel as she drove. A half-hour out of Boston she felt it, a warm trickle of water running down her legs as if she was peeing herself and soaking the seat of the car. Shit! she thought, scared. The baby wasn't due for another four weeks! And now her waters had broken. Undecided between pulling over into a lay-by and phoning for assistance or putting her foot on the pedal and driving to Mass General Hospital, she chose the latter. Praying under her breath, she tried not to think of the cramping pains in her stomach as she drove . . .

It was 5 a.m. when the phone went. Martha jumped up in bed and reached for the receiver, relieved to hear Bob Forrester's voice on the other end of the line.

'Martha, it's a girl! We have a baby girl!'

'Oh, that's great, Bob, I'm really pleased for you.' She yawned, still half asleep. 'How's Gina?'

'Oh, she's fine. She asked me to phone you cos

she's concerned. The baby's a little early and she's small. Real small! They put her in one of those incubator things and she's up in a special ward with all the other premature babies. Gina's real worried for her and she wondered if you'd come in as soon as you can and see her.'

Martha agreed straight away, knowing that neither Bob nor Gina were alarmist and wouldn't have asked unless they thought it necessary.

'Tell Gina I'll be there first thing this morning,' she promised, putting down the phone.

The baby was beautiful, her tiny head a cap of black hair with the face of a pixie. She lay still under the special lights and kicked her legs gently now and then.

'I couldn't bear it if anything happens to her.' Gina broke down. 'I couldn't take it, Martha!'

'Hush now, don't go upsetting yourself. You have a beautiful daughter who is already a born fighter.'

Martha studied the baby closely, watching the rise and fall of her chest, the rhythm of the pulse in her veins. She was fragile. Another few weeks would have made a big difference but at least here she had all the medical equipment she needed. Without thinking she reached across into the incubator, her fingertips touching the baby's little hands and fingers, one connecting to the other, warmth and strength flowing from the healer towards the sleeping infant.

Chapter Forty-three

Martha looked at her black leather-covered diary. She dreaded all the pencilled-in dates, the crowding out of her time, the hour by hour meetings and sessions and lack of freedom that such organization had brought. The kids were complaining about it too and the weekends were sacrosanct, only for her family.

Checking the date and time, she realized Joshua Harris was late. She'd seen Joshua several times over the past few weeks, and was convinced they were finally making progress. He looked stronger, healthier and had told her he was eating again. Diseases of the soul and spirit were a lot harder to heal and treat than the relatively simple ones of the body and she was much gladdened by his recovery.

She was concerned when Joshua failed to show up for his session. She sat waiting for him for over an hour and a half, imagining the worst, and when she finally got through on his phone was greeted by an indifferent apology about forgetting the time. She swallowed her annoyance and re-scheduled. Four days later Wendy Harris called her at home and confided that she was desperately worried about her son and asked her to see him immediately. Evie, Kim and Martha were due to go to the movies to a special showing of *Breakfast at Tiffany's* and then for a drink.

'Say no!' mouthed Mary Rose, listening to her conversation.

'I can't, I can't!'

Mary Rose got up and tossed the magazine she was reading on the floor, as Martha ended the call and took Wendy's home address, promising to be there within an hour.

'Mom, what about Evie and Kim? They're expecting you to go with them.'

'Listen, Mary Rose, it's no big deal. I'll phone them. I can catch it again another time. OK?'

Crossing the Mass Turnpike she drove for more than a mile and a half, taking the next exit and following directions for the turnoff to Wendy Harris's home. Pressing the silver button on the automatic gates she gained entry.

Joshua's mother was more beautiful and petite than she had imagined. Her white blond hair pulled up off her face, she wore a simple knitted sweater and denim jeans.

'Oh, thank you, thank you so much for coming and giving up your Saturday night, Martha. I hope you don't mind me calling you that but when Joshua talks about you he always uses your first name.'

'No, that's fine. How is he?'

His mother looked like she was going to cry.

'He moved back in with me about three weeks ago, he's always had his room here naturally, and it was just so good to have him back. Seeing you has helped him enormously and he was getting back to the old Josh, the one before . . .'

'And what happened?'

'I don't know, he went out last night to meet one of his friends at some nightclub. It was nearly breakfast time when he got back.'

'And?'

'And he had that look – the pupils dilated, that white tone to his skin, that stupid mellow expression on his face, I've seen it so many times before. I said it to him. He denied it of course!'

'Mrs Harris, surely you should be talking to one of Josh's counsellors or the clinic he was in,' suggested Martha, feeling well out of her league.

'He just wanted to see you, Martha, that's all.'

She followed Wendy Harris upstairs and knocked lightly on Josh's door before she entered.

He looked awful: skinny and pale, he was lying on the bed in a crumpled T-shirt and a pair of shorts, strung out, his eyes bleary.

'How you doing, Martha?'

She said nothing, torn between anger and disappointment in him.

'So Mohammed came to the mountain!' he joked, scratching his head and greasy hair.

'Josh – why?'

He laughed.

'I got high, and it's good, you know!'

'I can't help you when you're like this,' she insisted, staring at him. 'Why did you ask your mother to phone me?'

'I wanted you to touch me,' he said slowly. 'It's the only way to take the pain away, I need you to heal me.'

'Heal you? Joshua, I can't heal you, the only person that can heal you is you.'

'I can't do that,' he mumbled. 'I can't do that.'

'Yes you can, you know you can,' she cajoled.

He stayed silent, considering. Martha hoped that he would at least try again.

Wendy came into the room. 'His father wants him to go back into rehab again,' she said nervously, pressing her arms and looking out into the dark. 'They have a place for him.'

'What do you want to do, Josh?' enquired Martha.

He turned his face to the wall, his eyes welling with tears.

Martha moved forward to comfort him. Putting her arms around him she could sense his disappointment in himself and his need to regain some independent control of his life. Her hands picked up that he was bloody and torn and battle weary. She tried to lift the gripping pain from

393

him, only succeeding in creating a small chink of light in such darkness.

'I'll still be here, Josh,' she promised. 'We can take up where we were and I'll work with you for as long as it takes, but first you have to sort out your drug problem.'

'Josh baby, you need help!' pleaded his mother. 'Your father has it all set up, we just have to call him.'

'Joshua, listen to your mom and dad, they both love you and want what's best for you.'

Finally he agreed to be readmitted that night. Wendy phoned his father to arrange it. Glenn Harris was insistent that he would drive his son to the clinic in New Haven himself.

Chapter Forty-four

Kim and Ruth and Kathleen were all excited by the 'Miracle Tour'. They had persuaded Martha that it was the only way she could get to see so many people and promised her there would be no cheap showmanship or freak show element to her visits to specifically chosen venues across the country.

'There's enough money in the bank account to pay rental on the first few halls,' confirmed Ruth, who had taken over organizing the finances, 'and to cover transport and accommodation.'

Unsure about the increased expansion of her healing and realizing it was unfair to expect her friends to put in so much work without payment, Martha proposed they should all take some form of salary.

Evie and Rianna said they didn't need it but Kim and Ruth admitted that with the hours they were putting in, it was welcome. Martha left the arrangement of insurance, tax, and charity status to Ruth, who was the expert.

The 'Miracle Tour', as the press called it, hit the road that fall, starting off in her home area and travelling up first of all to New York and New Jersey. Martha met hundreds of people as word of her visit spread. She tried to limit the size of the crowds so that she would have time with the sick, the hurt and the lonesome who came to her for comfort. She told them of their own energy and how they must harness and use it as she struggled to remember their names and faces.

Kathleen and Ruth had volunteered to come with her to Chicago and California, but Evie was unable to leave her shop. Because of the distances involved, Kim and Ruth had decided to use an events organizer to book the halls and make arrangements for them and do some low-key publicity.

In Chicago, over a month later, it lashed rain, but even the downpour could not deter those who came along to meet her at the converted gospel hall. Every race, every creed, excited and hopeful, were there ready to believe in her and the miracles. They opened themselves to the healing energy and her exhortation that they should try and heal themselves. Some sang, some prayed out loud as Martha worked.

Back in her hotel room Martha felt so alone, wound up, her thoughts racing after the session, with no-one to talk to as the others had gone to bed. She missed the kids and resolved to phone them before she caught her early morning flight, glad that Mike had agreed to move back in and mind them for her for the few days.

California was different. She felt more relaxed as despite the three shows that were booked she was getting a chance to visit with her brother Brian and his wife Lisa, staying in their beautiful home in Mountainview, about an hour out of San Francisco.

They'd always been close as kids and when her older brother had pulled her into his arms asking, 'What's up, sis?' she could honestly have wept.

They'd sat over a bottle of red wine late into the night, Lisa discreetly slipping away to bed so brother and sister could talk. She told him about the collapse of her marriage to Mike, the fights and bitterness between them, and the mounting pressures that had been too great to resolve.

'Are you still speaking or communicating at all?'

'We see each other once a week when he comes to dinner or when he collects the kids, and at the moment he's staying in Mill Street whilst I'm here,' she said.

'Well, that's something!' her brother agreed, raising his eyes to heaven. 'You know, Martha, I still can't believe it, the things you're doing. Jack and Annie were telling me about all the people you've helped. That sure must feel good!'

'Sometimes. Other times it's not so good,' she said softly, telling him about Cass.

'God, if the old man were alive he'd have you running for Congress!'

'Oh hush, Brian!'

'How are you feeling?'

'I'm fine, not really tired at all. Believe it or not, my energy seems to go right up when I need it, when I'm healing.'

'I don't know how in the hell you're keeping this all together, what with the kids and Mike. I honestly don't.'

'I've got good people around me, old friends like Evie and Kathleen. I don't know what I'd do without them. Then there's Kim and Ruth and a whole bunch of other people that you mightn't know.'

Her brother topped up her glass with more wine, then sat on the couch. His dark curly hair was now receding, and he'd grown a beard since she last saw him.

'How's Mom doing?' he asked.

'She's fine. She and Bee play bridge one day a week and keep themselves occupied with all sorts of things.'

'How'd she take you and Mike splitting up?'

'I guess she was shocked at first, but she's just getting used to it. The fact we still see each other and speak makes her kind of hopeful that we'll get back together again!'

'And will you?'

Martha considered. 'No, I don't think so. Too much has changed between us and there's probably no going back at this stage.'

'I'm sorry, sis. I wish Mom would come visit. I know if she spent time with Lisa, and gave her a chance and got to know her, she'd realize what a great girl I married.'

'I know, Brian, but you know what she's like.'

Martha couldn't figure why her mother had taken Brian's remarriage so badly. Brian, her firstborn, had always been her favourite. When his marriage to Gail had broken up after only two short years, her mother had prayed and said novenas in the hope that they'd get back together. Maybe her brother's refusal to tell their mother of his wife's affair had insulated her from the true reasons for his divorce, but surely she couldn't expect someone as loving as her brother not to want to settle down again.

'Maybe Bee and Mom could fly out and stay with us. We'd love to have them! Please try and persuade her when you get back home. You know she listens to you.'

'I'll try, Brian, I'll try,' she promised.

Martha had a radio interview at 1 p.m. and a scheduled walk around the impressive modern university hall they were using for the healing session afterwards.

Leaving the TV studio she was amazed to bump into Dan Kendrick, recognizing his huge frame in a lightweight suit walking slowly along the corridor ahead of her. She didn't expect him to remember her and was just about to pass him when he stopped.

'Martha, don't tell me that you're about to walk by me!' he said accusingly.

'No, Dan, of course not!'

'Well, how's my favourite healer?' he joked, amused by her embarrassment.

'Fine.'

'I read about your visit in the papers. You're getting to be quite famous.'

She grimaced.

'Not something you enjoy, I gather?'

Martha shook her head.

'Would you like to join me for lunch and I can show you my good elbow again?'

She burst out laughing. 'I'm sorry, Dan, but I've an appointment that I'm already late for.'

He looked wounded. 'Well, what about tomorrow?' he suggested.

'No can do!' she apologized. 'I've a packed schedule and we'll be flying out this time tomorrow.'

'Dinner tonight?'

She shook her head again. 'I've got my session on.'

'Well, a quick bit of supper afterwards, then! I could pick you up about ten, and you can fill me in on how Bob and Gina are coping with parenthood.'

400

She didn't like to refuse him, and was in such a rush she agreed to see him later, without thinking.

Kathleen and Ruth were already in the circular hall checking the layout. There was enormous interest in Martha's work and a camera crew from the local TV station had asked if they could film during the event.

'No!' She was adamant. '*No.*'

Ruth and the guy from the events company were trying to persuade her otherwise.

'I will not have cameras used during the healing session,' she insisted.

'What about before or after, when the crowds are coming out?' suggested the events man. 'It would give you a lot more publicity!'

'The people that come tonight to meet me deserve their privacy. There can't be cameras at any stage, I'm sorry but that's it,' she said, digging her heels in, not wanting to break the trust between herself and those who came to see her.

That evening when she entered the hall Martha tried to hide her surprise when she saw a few members of the waiting crowd wearing T-shirts with the word MIRACLE on them. Who had made them or sold them? she wondered. Ruth just shrugged her shoulders and laughed when she pointed them out to her.

The hall grew hot, as the air conditioning worked haphazardly. Martha felt herself get warmer as she dealt with one person after another, sometimes barely having time to talk to them or find out their name or their particular problem. Ruth fetched her a jug of ice cold water and a fan. There were two couples with toddlers and she insisted on meeting them first, her heart going out to the young parents of sick children. As always she couldn't believe the huge range of problems that beset humankind and asked the Good Lord to help and guide her in his healing work.

Exhausted at the end, all she longed for was a cool shower and to fall into bed between fresh sheets. It was only as she walked out through the main entrance hall that she remembered agreeing to meet Dan Kendrick. Kathleen and Ruth were still inside dealing with things, wanting to go back straight to their hotel to put the money collected into the hotel safe until the morning.

'Oh, Dan, I'm sorry! I . . .'

'San Francisco is full of restaurants,' he began. 'So, tell me what kind of food you'd like! I've a favourite Cuban one, but that may not be to your taste.'

'Dan, I'm really sorry but if you took me to a restaurant now I'd probably just fall asleep at the table, so please don't waste your money.'

He stopped talking and looked down at her.

'You look beat. Did you get anything to eat earlier?' he asked.

'I'd a salad sandwich at about four o'clock.'

'Then you're hungry.'

'I suppose,' she agreed.

'What about a walk down on the pier and grab something there? Then I'll drop you straight back to your hotel.'

'I'm actually staying with my brother Brian in Mountainview,' she explained.

'Even better then – it's on my way home.'

The harbour area was lit up with strings of coloured lights that danced and reflected on the still water, Alcatraz out there in the far darkness. Gangs of tourists and couples hand in hand paraded by them. Martha appreciated the fresh air and the slap of the seawater against the pier as they strolled along the waterfront. They bought fresh fish and chips from a streetside vendor then walked along eating it out of paper containers. Dan treated them to two chilled pints of beer, served in plastic glasses.

'How's that husband of yours?' he enquired politely.

Martha was embarrassed as she told him briefly about the break-up of her marriage.

'I'm sorry to hear that,' he responded.

They wandered into one of the gift shops that opened late on the pier. Martha was unable to resist the music boxes. Dan helped her to choose one for Sarah, Gina and Bob's new baby; it was covered in bluebells and hidden fairies and she added one for each of her own girls, white unicorns for Mary Rose and mermaids for Alice. The night air was warm with a slight salt breeze; a lone seal was barking below in the distance as they strolled, Dan telling her about his tough Chicago childhood and Martha telling him of the rich Irish-American network that had sustained her family over the years. Dan eventually talked of his wife Teresa, who had died ten years earlier following a brain haemorrhage, and how lonely it had been since then. 'I still miss her,' he admitted.

Martha instinctively took a hold of his hand as they walked.

Later he drove her back to Brian's house. The fresh air and food had definitely revived her, as she felt more invigorated.

'That was the perfect dinner!' she teased, asking him to come in and meet her brother and his wife.

'No thanks, Martha, I'd best get home and anyways you have an early start tomorrow.'

They sat in the darkness, reluctant to end the night.

'You feel like any more midnight walks on the pier, let me know!'

'And you feel like any more cheap fish suppers you let me know,' she responded.

'Have a safe journey to Boston tomorrow, Martha,' he said quietly.

'And you take care of yourself, Mr Kendrick.'

Dan kissed her cheek politely before she got out of the car, Martha rushing inside like a guilty teenager.

Chapter Forty-five

Father Eugene Reagan returned angry from his visit to Bishop John Stevens's office in the city. The bishop had been adamant that the problem of Martha McGill, this so-called 'Miracle Woman', was to be sorted out.

'There's the Lucas boy, Sean Peterson, the man in the motorbike accident that was plastered all over the papers and a few others scattered throughout the country,' complained the bishop. 'Do you realize, Eugene, that in all the years since Our Blessed Lady first appeared to Bernadette in Lourdes, and with all the millions of pilgrims that have visited that sacred shrine ever since, there has only been a total of sixty-six documented authentic cures – or miracles, as some like to call them – and that is in one of the Church's holiest of places and yet we are to believe that one of your parishioners has been granted this sacred gift! The whole notion is preposterous, and I for one, Father, am waiting to see how you will put a stop to it!'

'I spoke to her already, Bishop Stevens, and put my concerns to her, but unfortunately she is not willing to listen.'

'Then you must *make* her listen, Father.'

Father Eugene sighed as he worked in the small study of his parish house. He did not appreciate being hauled over the coals by his superiors and admonished for the way he ran his business. He had two funerals booked into the church for the next morning and checked his message service in case any of the deceased's family members had been trying to contact him. There was a message on his machine from a newspaper journalist asking for a quote on 'the miracles', and 'What was the Church's and his position in relation to Martha McGill?'

Not having to debate the matter too long, he jotted down the number as he returned Lara Chadwick's call, knowing exactly what he wanted to say.

The *Boston Herald* carried the Church's denunciation of the Miracle Woman and those who believed in her, saying that people who attended her sessions or went for public healing were deluding themselves with false beliefs. The journalist quoted Father Eugene, her parish priest, and printed an official statement from the bishop.

Reading the report, Martha was dismayed. She felt that the priests were good men, men who had worked tirelessly for the Holy Roman Catholic Church for nearly all their lives and yet somehow along the way had lost their ability to believe in the healing power of the Lord God. Now they were condemning her because they knew no better and were afraid.

Chapter Forty-six

Sarah Regina Forrester's christening party was held that Christmas. Martha was honoured to have been asked to be her godmother.

'Who else could we have but you?' smiled Gina.

The baby, a tiny little thing, had had a rocky start but, after concerns for her first two months, had gradually picked up and was as bright and alert as any baby. Bob's other children had flown in to join them and were staying for the holiday period. Gina was thrilled to have the house for once filled with family.

A huge Christmas tree stood in the drawing room of Rockhall and Gina had arranged for a group of carol singers to come along and entertain her guests for an hour.

Martha smiled, renewing her acquaintance with Ted and Megan Harris, relieved that at least Mike hadn't been invited. Patrick had let slip to her that Mike had recently started dating one of the PAs in his office and Martha was still trying to get used to the idea.

She mingled and moved around the room, not knowing many of the guests, feeling a little out of place as she sipped her champagne and kept an eye on her new god-daughter. She could see one or two people getting ready to approach her with their problems when she spotted Dan Kendrick in the doorway, his coat covered in snow. It was nice to see him, she thought, and smiled in his direction. Dan waved to her before he disappeared in another direction with Bob and a few of the men.

The buffet meal was delicious and Martha realized as she ate that the champagne was going to her head: godmothers were not supposed to get tipsy and disgrace themselves! Gina, with the baby in her arms, came over to join her.

'She's so beautiful, Gina, and you and Bob are such good parents.'

'Why, thank you, Martha! That's a sweet thing to say.'

As Gina went and got some food for herself, Martha held little Sarah, glad of the opportunity to play with the baby. Dan Kendrick suddenly appeared and squeezed in beside her.

'Did she like her fairy music?' he joked.

'I'm sure she did. I think she might be a bit of a dancer, see how those little toes and feet keep moving.'

Ten minutes later Gina came over to reclaim her daughter and show her around.

'Have you had any more midnight walks?' Dan asked slowly.

Martha shook her head. 'And have you had any more cheap fish suppers?'

'Most definitely not!'

She flushed, feeling his eyes on her, suddenly awkward and shy in his company. As the party began to break up Dan offered to drive her home. Martha was relieved that she didn't have to try to order a cab as it was snowing heavily.

They drove home in silence, Martha watching the windscreen wipers of his Mercedes swish the falling snow backwards and forwards, Dan concentrating on the road.

'This is it!' she said as they pulled up in Mill Street. Dan turned as if he was about to say something to her.

'Would you like to come inside for a coffee or something?' She cringed, wondering how she had come out with such an inane sentence.

'Well actually, Martha, I might. This snowfall looks set for a while and there's no point in freezing my butt off out here in the car waiting for it to ease off.'

He locked the car and followed her up to the front door, Martha putting on the lights and thanking heaven she'd left the place reasonably tidy on her way out. She led the way into the kitchen and plugged in the kettle.

'Where are your kids?' he asked matter-of-factly.

'Mike's got them this weekend,' she said. 'Or maybe you'd like something to drink?' she offered, too late realizing there was probably nothing in the house.

'A scotch or a brandy would be nice.'

She opened a small cupboard. A half-bottle of crème de menthe, a liquorice-based liqueur and about two teaspoons of whiskey in the bottom of the bottle of Irish she normally kept for her mother. She'd lashed a full glass of it into the Christmas cake. 'I'm sorry, Dan. Since Mike left I just haven't got around to restocking it and I haven't got my Christmas wine or anything bought . . .'

'Sssh, it's OK!' he said, touching her lip.

'Though there's champagne!' she remembered, trying to think where in heaven's name she'd put the crate he'd sent her all that time ago.

They eventually found it alongside her dryer in the laundry room.

'Well, at least I don't have to worry about you being a raving alcoholic!' Dan teased. 'Why didn't you open it?'

'I guess I felt I had nothing to celebrate.'

He pulled a bottle out of the wooden packing case and began to open the wire. As the cork top popped and flew out across the kitchen,

Martha rushed to get two glasses. Champagne and coffee and hot chocolate, that's what they drank, Dan throwing a match onto the fire she'd left set.

'Tonight you've got to celebrate Christmas, your god-daughter's christening day and meeting me,' he declared.

'OK, I suppose some of those reasons are valid, but we've already met,' she reasoned.

'Yes, but meeting again this time is different!'

She looked at him, already seeing the twinkle in his eye.

'Because this time I'm going to do what I should have done in San Francisco,' he said, pulling her into his arms. Martha closed her eyes as he began to kiss her. His kiss was warm and strong and lovely, Martha thought as she responded.

Two glasses of champagne were her limit, Dan refusing to pour her more as she was excited and tipsy and curled up into his lap so he could just keep on kissing her. 'I think you should go to bed,' he suggested at about 3 a.m.

'Yes, please!' she said as she followed him upstairs.

She woke with a dry mouth and a pounding head, the comforter pulled over her. She was still wearing the knitted mauve suit she'd chosen for the christening party. Remembering the night before, she wondered if she'd disgraced herself. She found

Dan's note perched on her dressing table: 'Sleep well, princess, will collect you for dinner tonight at 7.30.' Martha thanked heaven that the kids were out of the house and hadn't witnessed Dan putting her to bed.

Chapter Forty-seven

Martha was nervous as hell about having dinner with Dan. She spent an age choosing just the right outfit, settling on a simple black cocktail dress that she had hardly worn.

She busied herself writing Christmas cards and letters, replying to many of the people with whom she had developed a correspondence, later wrapping the kids' presents, trying to find good places to hide them. It seemed strange to be having her first Christmas without Mike: though Alice and Patrick had begged and pleaded for her to invite him to join them for their Christmas Day meal, Martha was not so sure it was a good idea.

Dan collected her promptly, kissing her full on the lips before even getting into the car.

'I thought we might get another of those fish suppers we both like,' he said.

Martha was puzzled until she discovered they were eating in a tiny fish restaurant built on a jetty overlooking the harbour. The waiter led them to a table in the window and Martha's eyes widened when she saw the price on the menu. Dan burst out laughing at her reaction.

'Martha, you are some woman!' he teased. 'The only one I've ever met who doesn't want me to spend any money on her, which believe me is pretty rare.'

She smiled, telling him to hush up as she considered the menu. When the wine waiter came, Martha blushed from top to toe as Dan threatened to order a bottle of champagne. She stuck to a single glass of dry white wine.

The food was good and they both relaxed and chatted easily, Martha finding it easy to talk to him as she told him about her work and how important it was to her but how emotionally involved she tended to get.

'It must sure be something to be able to help your fellow man the way you do,' Dan said, praising her. 'You have a pretty amazing gift or ability, whatever you like to call it.'

'Since I discovered the healing gift, my life has totally changed. Mostly it's all right because I like to help people but other times it's almost unbearable.' She told him about Cass and the pain of losing her. 'No matter what I did there was no saving her.'

'She was the Lord's,' he said simply. 'So don't go blaming yourself.'

'That's a nice way of putting it, Dan,' she thanked him, realizing how kind he was.

'I think you are quite a sensitive being,' he said gently, 'and I'm a pretty lucky guy to be sitting here with you, holding your hand.'

She in turn asked him about his work and how it was going.

'You don't want to hear!' he joked. 'We dropped about ten million dollars in the past two months. Some people say the computer industry is up the Swanee, but I'm not one of them. OK, so we were all probably overvalued and our stock was in for a tumble and a bit of a downfall. As my mother, Lord rest her, would say: Danny, what good is paper money? Give me cash!'

He sounded so matter of fact about it that Martha respected him for it. 'That's a good way to think about it. Your mom was right,' she said.

'I know we're in for a rough ride for the next few months, maybe a year or two, but anyone who keeps their head down and doesn't bullshit should get through it.'

The evening passed far too quickly. Martha was enjoying herself more than she could have imagined as they laughed and shared disaster stories about their kids. Dan told her about his two grown-up sons who both worked in the business and lived in Silicon Valley too.

'I get to keep a good eye on them and make sure they behave!'

Martha sipped an Irish coffee as Dan settled the bill.

'Listen, Martha, I fly back to San Francisco

tomorrow, and probably won't be back to the East Coast till mid-January. I'm no young buck but I don't know how I'm going to last out that long without seeing you again. I don't know how you feel but I'm a straight talker and that's the way I feel!' he said.

Martha looked across at his broad face and hazel eyes, creased with laughter lines, his greying hair cut tight into his head, showing off his strong features, and knew it was a face she could love.

'I'll miss you,' she said simply.

Outside the house she asked him to kiss her, reaffirming her attraction to him.

'Do you want to come in?' she asked. 'The kids are still at their dad's, and I promise I'm fairly sober.'

Once inside she felt suddenly shy and nervous as Dan pulled her into his arms, asking herself was she ready to become involved with another man? Dan dispelled any such doubts as her body began to respond to his.

Chapter Forty-eight

Lara Chadwick turned in the bed, reaching for the phone. The night editor screamed down the line at her.

'Listen, Lara, I wouldn't normally do this to you but we got a tip-off that Glenn Harris, the investment millionaire guy, that his son Joshua committed suicide a few hours ago, and we need to get an official confirmation and file the story.'

'Jesus, Bill, it's Christmas Day! Can't it wait?'

'Sorry, but no. You're on to do relief so it's your shot!'

'Where was he found?' she asked.

'Hung himself off a fucking scaffold in one of his father's building developments!'

'What a Christmas present,' replied Lara, taking down the address. 'Anything else?'

'There were rumours about him being bounced out of college two years ago and mention of a habit, but maybe you can check them out.'

Lara sighed. She'd give it two hours, three max,

as she was cooking a turkey and had invited her parents and her sister to Christmas dinner.

Pulling on her clothes, she raced outside. The pavement was so icy she nearly slipped as she walked to her car, blasting the Harris kid for ruining her day.

Martha made the best of that first Christmas on their own, driving over on Christmas Eve with the kids to meet Evie and Frank at the midnight mass at St John's. The hymns and the simple crib moved her.

Paul and Sue Lucas had invited her and some neighbours for a festive drink on Christmas morning, young Timmy proudly displaying his new bike. Martha was amazed by the power of the human body and spirit to recover as she watched him cycle crazily on the snowy paths outside.

She put extra effort into decorating the house and cooking and felt glad when Mike accepted her invitation to join them for the Christmas meal. Alice, Mary Rose, Patrick and she did their utmost to pretend that nothing had changed, but it hurt when Mike made his excuses as soon as they'd finished eating about having to go and meet some friends. Martha tried to laugh it off and pretend to the children that it didn't matter, but she knew deep inside that it really did.

The next day Jack and Annie insisted she come

419

over to their place to join Sean and Carrie and her mother and all the cousins. When the news of Joshua Harris's suicide made the local evening news, Martha wept but felt comforted in having her own family around.

Chapter Forty-nine

The New Year brought heavy snows and freezing cold. Alice was sent home from school with influenza and Martha had to take the time out to stay home and mind her. Like dominoes it spread through their family, Mary Rose sick as a dog with it, shivering and shaking and running a sky-high temperature.

'Mom, if you're meant to be such a good healer then how come you can't cure us?' asked Alice through her stuffed-up nose.

Martha had no answer for such a simple, logical question! Patrick was floored with the flu and Martha was worn out running around after a house full of invalids, praying that they'd all get better.

Dan rang her every now and then, the two of them spending hours on the phone to each other. It was only when her own nose began to run and her bones ached that she realized she'd gone down with the flu too. She was lying in bed feeling absolutely awful when Alice gave her the sealed envelope that had just been delivered. Martha tore it open.

Stunned, she read it over and over again, not believing its contents.

Glenn Harris was initiating legal action against her for being involved in the death of his son. She was also being named in a similar suit by Beth and Tom Armstrong in respect of their daughter Cass.

Alice, seeing her reaction, ran and got her brother and sister. Martha tossed Patrick the letter to read.

'Mom, what are you going to do?' he asked, his young face like that of a ghost.

'I don't know, Patrick. I just don't know,' she replied, too sick and sorry to think.

She phoned Evie first in a panic, not knowing what to do.

'God, you sound crap, Martha! Maybe you need to get a good lawyer. You can't let people like that attack you and get away with it.'

Her brother Jack had told her to fax him a copy of the letter and he'd show it to a lawyer friend of his, promising her that they would find a loophole in the stupid charges and get them dropped.

She told Dan the next time he called. He took it seriously, telling her not to worry, he'd try to sort something out. Somehow Martha trusted him.

Lying in bed alone that night she gave in to her tears and anger thinking of the two young people she had tried to help, whose pain she had tried to ease, and how now it had all backfired and she was being held responsible.

She woke in the middle of the night, her temperature down, suddenly clear headed and feeling stronger. She had done nothing wrong and she would fight it!

Chapter Fifty

She still felt run down and tired when she returned to work and Ruth told her that the appointment list was running almost two years ahead.

'God, Ruth! There must be some way to fix it.'

'What do you want me to do? Write and tell all those good people to fuck off, is it! If you want me to start booking for four and five years' time I will, but you'd better book yourself in for the long stay, cos you'll be here till kingdom come, and you still won't have seen a quarter of them.'

'I don't believe it!'

'Believe!' insisted Evie, standing at the door. 'I brought up some more of your mail that was left in my shop by accident.' She dumped about thirty letters on the table. Martha looked up: Evie seemed peeved, annoyed.

'What is it, Evie?'

'Martha, I don't mean to complain but I just

never imagined so many people hanging around the shop all day. Some buy, but most don't and they're crowding out my own customers.'

Martha apologized, knowing how good her friend was to put up with the constant stream of traffic through her shop and up and down the stairs.

'Maybe upstairs here is too small. I don't know, maybe you need to get a bigger place, closer to the city,' said Evie.

'That's what I've been saying to her,' agreed Ruth.

Martha noticed the hurt on her friends' faces. Reluctantly she told them about Glenn Harris and what he intended. Evie backed her up, saying that they would just ride it out till good sense prevailed.

Dan had been to Boston twice in the past month and a half, taking the legal threat very seriously. He arranged to meet with herself and her brother Jack in his office.

'What can Glenn Harris do?' asked Jack. 'His son committed suicide! It's a tragedy, but Martha wasn't there. Wasn't near him at all. He hasn't a leg to stand on, as far as I can see.'

'Martha may not be guilty, but it could create a huge amount of bad publicity for your sister. The Armstrongs' joining suit is very damaging.'

'This is serious, Jack, I'm being charged with something I didn't do,' Martha protested.

'Listen, Martha,' advised Dan, 'I think you need to employ one of the best in the business. I've never met this Harris man but Bob Forrester told me last night that he's a tough cookie, used to getting his way. I hope you don't mind but I contacted one of the top law firms here in the city and the head partner James Coady has agreed to advise us.'

Martha felt shaky even thinking about getting involved in a legal challenge. 'What do you think I should do, Jack?' Her eyes flew to her brother.

'I think Dan's right and that you need to protect and defend yourself and your reputation. Those parents both sought you out, wanting you to help their kids. It's not your fault that either of them died.'

'Then we're agreed,' nodded Dan. 'I'm busy early tomorrow morning but I've already booked a provisional appointment with James for mid-day.'

Martha felt sick as she rode the glass elevator to the fortieth floor to the Coady Hill Bennet law firm. The secretary showed them straight in to James Coady's sunshine-filled office. Tall and rangy, Coady immediately shook hands with them all and Martha sat down. Dan passed him a copy of the original letter and outlined the situation. Putting on his reading glasses he studied it briefly as he listened.

'I've already spoken to the law firm concerned,' Coady said. 'And the partner there feels that Mr Harris, while wounded and distraught over the death of his son, is determined to seek out answers and apportion blame, if that's what you'd like to call it. I believe he is also suing the Rehabilitation Institute in New Haven, where Josh stayed up to his untimely death, and its director.'

'So he's like a sleeping bear who's just got stung by a wasp and wants to attack something or someone.'

'Yes, Dan, that's a good comparison, but a crazed bear can be a dangerous enemy,' warned Coady.

Martha spent over an hour telling her lawyer of how Glenn Harris had first approached her: how he had called and sent invitations and eventually pushed his way into her office.

'He loved his son very much,' she whispered. 'That's why he wanted me to work with him and try healing. He knew his son was in a very bad state.'

The so-called casual lunch meeting, the number of times she saw Josh, his failure to turn up for his appointments and his mother Wendy's plea for her to come visit Josh at home were all noted as James Coady meticulously recorded and checked everything she said.

'I want to be sure to have my facts straight.' He smiled, before asking her to tell him about the

Armstrongs and Cass. Martha recalled the first meeting, when Beth had approached her in the hospital canteen.

She was exhausted when she finished, hoping that she hadn't forgotten anything. James Coady thanked her, promising to be in touch once he checked a few details. Politely he escorted the three of them to the elevator. Dan had business meetings for the rest of the day but Jack insisted on driving her home. Martha refused his offer of lunch as she couldn't face eating with the thought of the accusations that were being made against her.

Nobody knew the how or the why of it but somehow the press had got hold of the story of the threatened legal action. Martha was shocked to find a journalist sitting on her doorstep when she got home. Jack dealt with him and phoned Evie and Dan to warn them.

The next few days were horrendous as Glenn Harris, the grieving father, gave copious interviews about the death of his son, claiming that Joshua had been let down by those who were supposed to help him and had been driven to take his own life. Beth Armstrong recounted the last few months of her daughter's life, blaming Martha for the fact that Cass was at home instead of in the hospital where she belonged.

Crucified by the media, Martha wanted to just curl up and die, the support of her family and her friends the only thing that kept her sane. Now the papers were implying there had been financial irregularities in the running of her 'Miracle Tour' and that she and her associates had amassed a small fortune along the way.

Chapter Fifty-one

Patrick, Mary Rose and Alice all surrounded Martha with their love as she battled to keep some control of her life, wondering over and over how her attempts to help and heal others had been so misunderstood. Mike had surprised her by offering to pay whatever legal costs were needed.

'I'm not having anyone attack the mother of my children like that,' he said firmly. 'You tell those bastards we'll see them in court!'

Martha sincerely hoped that it would never come to that as she did not know if she was capable of defending herself by attacking the grieving parents of two people she had cared for.

James Coady was collecting evidence and at yet another meeting in his office he assured her that in a court he would prove that Joshua's long-term drug addiction, fuelled by the vast amount of his father's money, was what really killed him.

'We can request copies of his bank account

statements which will prove it, Martha, and this is long before you ever knew him.'

'I don't want Joshua's name dragged through the mud,' she said firmly. 'He doesn't deserve it.'

'And the Armstrongs?' questioned Dan, who'd insisted on coming along to the meeting with her.

'There are full medical records that can be requested showing the child's congenital heart problem. We can call the anaesthetist who cancelled her surgery, the nurse who cared for her at home – even her father! We have a very strong case. Should we go to court, I think we can win and possibly ask the court for damages.'

'There you go,' said Dan.

'I don't want it to go to court,' insisted Martha. 'How can we stop it?'

James Coady pulled himself up to his full height, lifting his glasses off his long face. 'You're my client, Martha. Is that what you really want, even if you can win?' he asked.

'Yes.'

'Then I will talk to Steve Duncan, Mr Harris's lawyer, and see if we can sort this mess out.'

'I would like to be present, if that's all right with you, James,' said Dan. 'Glenn Harris is assuming that Martha has very little support – seeing you and I walk into a room together may change his opinion.'

*　　*　　*

Two days later both sides met at Coady Hill Bennet's office. Martha, too nervous to attend, agreed to meet them afterwards. She sat outside in the reception area on tenterhooks, praying silently and waiting. Acknowledging Glenn Harris when he walked out past her, she noted how much he'd aged since the death of his son.

'It's over, Martha honey!' called Dan, scooping her up in his arms. 'They've dropped all charges including those against the rehab place.'

'Thank God,' she said slowly.

James Coady made her sit back down as he explained it to her.

'I think that having Mr Kendrick on your side was a big asset, as Mr Harris could take it that costs would not be an issue.'

'How did you do it, James?'

'We just showed him our information, which would naturally be released to the press with time, and as you already pointed out, Martha, he's a man who loved his son, and was not about to let his boy's reputation be destroyed in open court.'

'Oh, thank God it's over,' she said, covering her face with her hands.

'The Armstrongs' suit is also being dropped,' he confirmed. 'Mr Kendrick here raised the matter of damages accruing to you as he feels you have been crucified by the press and media over this. Steve Duncan and I settled on an appropriate amount. Glenn Harris is prepared to pay two thousand dollars to you directly.'

'I don't want his money, James.'

'He is prepared to pay it.'

'Then take it, James, and donate it to that rehab clinic that Joshua was in. I don't want to see a dime of it.'

Martha was not a wealthy woman, dependent still on Mike to support herself and the kids, but she certainly didn't want any of Glenn Harris's money or to profit from his son's demise. She was so relieved that the threatened court action was finally over that she could only think of going home. 'I just can't wait to tell my kids and my mother the good news,' she smiled. 'Thank you, James, for looking after everything, I really appreciate it.'

'It was the very least I could do,' he said. Fumbling in his suit pocket, he drew out a leather wallet, passing her a photo of a pretty student.

'That's my daughter. Probably you don't remember her, we didn't want any media attention or fuss. She's had anorexia for years and we brought her along to meet you.'

'For a healing?'

'Yes. Whatever happened the night in the Tanner Radford hall last year I don't rightly know, cos she sure didn't want to be there or to co-operate but something you did started the healing process and let our daughter find herself again. If we'd had to go to court Melissa was prepared to stand up and let people see what you did for her!'

Martha was overwhelmed at James Coady's support and candour. Thanking him again, she and Dan left his offices, Martha feeling like a heavy constricting weight had finally been lifted from her shoulders.

Chapter Fifty-two

Martha thought long and hard about it, determined that this was a decision she alone had to make as she considered both herself and her children.

Patrick, Mary Rose and Alice all ached for a return to normal life, and to just having a mother who loved and cared for them alone – and in the aftermath of the legal accusations who could blame them!

Alice's sunny-natured openness was already changing, as she became suspicious of other children who asked about her home life or family, warned by her big brother and sister not to say anything.

The gift to heal had brought Martha great joy, the ability to help many people and alleviate much suffering. She had discovered strengths and a courage within herself that she had never expected. The journey of a healer was a long one and she still had much to learn, but the cost had been high, too high, and it had been borne by her husband and family and all those around her. She tormented herself thinking of Cass and now Joshua, and all the others she had failed. She had let herself become too emotionally involved, had grown too attached to them, which made losing them all the harder. Mike had been right: she was no saint! No Jesus come again! She was just an ordinary woman and she had sacrificed much to do the work of the Spirit. Too much.

She had invited them to come and sit at her table, good friends gathered together to eat. Mary Rose helped her to prepare and serve the large dish of lasagne and side salad. Martha passed the two bottles of red wine around and they all filled their glasses.

Tired and tense, she talked to them of her true feelings and her intention to stop healing and make a new life for herself and her children away from the public eye. Kim and Kathleen begged her not to give up her healing work.

'It's too important,' urged Kim. 'Look at all the people you've helped.'

'Think of all the people that I can't help,' she insisted. 'Those I disappoint and let down who are still sick, still lonesome, who cannot be healed and must accept their fate.'

'Martha, maybe you're making a mistake deciding so soon after all that legal crap,' suggested

Rianna. 'Why don't you take time out, think about it?'

'I've thought of little else for the past while,' she told them.

'What about the sessions we've organized and booked, the plans for next year, and the website?' demanded Ruth angrily.

'I guess we'll have to cancel them all. I'm sorry but I don't want to do any of it any more. I can't take the crowds! All the hundreds of faces. Often I can't remember their names or what's wrong with them. Sometimes when I touch them I feel nothing – absolutely nothing. It's not what I planned—'

'Don't go blaming us. We have all worked so hard, Martha, on your behalf! You can't just go and throw it all away and turn your back on what we've built. You can't!'

Ruth argued against her as Martha tried to be resolute. 'We have built a good organization around you. You can't just walk away from it! All the fucking hard work that Kim and I and Kathleen put in obviously means nothing to you now. We believed in you, supported you, and had such plans!'

'I'm sorry, Ruth, truly I am. I do appreciate everything you and everyone did, honest I do, but I'm not prepared to live my life like this any more. I'm sorry.'

She listened to their thoughts and concerns for her as she told them of the new life she had planned.

'I need to get away, to somewhere away from all that has happened, and just get back to being plain old me,' she confided.

'Where will you go?' asked Evie, concerned.

Martha slowly told them about going away and leaving them.

'We'll miss you,' murmured Kathleen.

'Sure will!' echoed Rianna, hugging her.

They were her good friends, loyal and true, who had been there from the start. How could she ever repay them for all they had done for her?

The kids had listened as she told them about the changes she planned, Patrick whooping with joy when she said that there would be no more tours, no interviews, no working in the upstairs room or people coming to the house any more. Alice's eyes widened with a look of sheer delight as she thought about it.

'But that means you're going to give up healing?' said Mary Rose softly.

'Yes, pet.'

Mary Rose squeezed her hand in sympathy.

They had seen it somewhat differently when she told them about the house she had arranged to rent for four months in Ireland.

'It's a load of crap!' complained Mary Rose. 'Why do we have to go there?'

'Your dad and I had always intended taking you guys on a trip to see Ireland once you were old enough and I guess with all that's going on right now this might be a real good time!' she explained, too scared to admit the truth. 'I'm going to rent the house and hire a car and we can just take it easy and relax and maybe get to see a bit of the countryside.'

'You're running away and trying to make us go with you,' argued Mary Rose. 'Why can't I stay here in Easton for the summer with Dad?'

'Because you're coming with me, that's why. Your dad will be working, and I'm not having you hang out all day on your own.'

'When are we going?' asked Patrick.

'As soon as possible, once I've made all the arrangements.'

'What about school?'

'I've cleared it with your teachers, Mary Rose. A few weeks discovering a new country is an education in itself.'

'But, Mom, I can't take time out of school, you know that!'

'I know, Patrick. You can finish off this semester in school and then come over to Ireland once you get your holidays. You can stay with your dad till then.'

Only Alice was excited about going away, talking about what she was going to take and what she was going to do over there.

Her mother came over for Sunday lunch and helped Martha to set the table and prepare the vegetables. Martha showed her the printout from the internet of the house in the Wicklow hills she was renting.

'That looks a nice place to spend the summer, pet. God knows you could do with a break after all you've been through this past few months!'

'It reminds me a bit of when we were kids,' Martha admitted. 'I guess even after a day or two I always felt I belonged there.'

'Your father felt the same,' declared Frances Kelly. 'He always intended ending his days back in Ireland, the two of us buying a retirement cottage in the old country and selling up here. That was his dream, you know.'

'Poor old Dad.'

'I'd thought of sending his ashes back to Cork when he died, but in truth I wanted to keep him here near me, near his family. Have a grave I could say the few prayers over. I'll really miss you,' her mother said.

'You've got Annie and Jack and Brian and Lisa and Sean and Carrie!' Martha reminded her gently.

'Aye, I know, but they're not you, dote. And how long are you going away for?'

'A few months, maybe more, I'm not quite sure yet, Mom,' she admitted.

'I could come visit.'

'Of course, Mom, that would be great and the kids would love it!'

'Bee's always saying she wants to go visit Ireland, take in the sights. It would be nice to have

440

someone travelling with me, show her the place I was born, come stay with you . . .'

Martha nodded.

'You sure you want to go away?'

'Yes, Mom, I'm sure.'

'I'm going to miss you and the kids,' sighed Frances, trying not to cry.

'And I'm going to really miss you too, Mom,' said Martha, holding her in her arms.

Chapter Fifty-three

Henry Madison rose early, showering and shaving quickly after his regular breakfast. The day was already overcast. He pulled on his clean white shirt, tweed jacket and fawn trousers. Moving slowly and stiffly, he cursed as he dropped his comb and was unable to bend to pick it up.

William was obviously tired; sleeping in like this was most unlike him but at least it gave Henry the opportunity to dress in peace.

His appointment at Mercy Hospital was for 10 a.m., and he had booked a cab from Jimmy Mulholland's local service, which would pick him up and drop him directly there. Celeste was due any minute and had promised to sit with William till he returned. There was no telling how long he'd be as probably he'd have to have an X-ray or one of those scan things and some blood tests done. The pain had eased for months following his visit to Martha, but of late it had begun to come back, dominating his waking and sleeping hours. Last night had been particularly bad.

Checking himself in the mirror he decided he'd better go in and wake William, and have him up and dressed at least. Celeste would give him a bowl of Cheerios or Lucky Charms and a slice of toast when he was gone.

'William! William! Come on, wake up,' he called, stepping into the room and reaching to open the curtains. His brother's huge frame was hunched up with the heavy comforter and sheet pulled almost up to his chin.

'Come on, William, get up! You have to get washed and dressed, come on now!'

There was no response. His brother didn't move, lying perfectly still.

'William!' he cajoled.

He was either fast asleep or being difficult, and Henry hoped it wasn't the latter. 'William!' he said sharply. 'Get up!'

Henry stood by the bedside and grabbed a hold of his shoulder, only then noticing how cold and stiff his brother lay. Apprehensively he reached forward to touch his face and realized at once that William was dead, a contented expression on his face. Just sleeping like when Henry had left him last night! There in the bed, he looked like the small boy he'd minded and cared for most of his life. Aware of the ringing of his doorbell, he went to open it and led Celeste to the bedroom where his brother lay. He heard her gasp, as she saw that

William was gone. His friend and neighbour put her plump arms around him and told him that everything was going to be all right, everything was going to be fine: both were grateful in their own way for William's ease of passing.

Chapter Fifty-four

Martha had driven up to West Hartford to say goodbye to Thea. She was surprised to see her using a walking frame, standing among a rich border of pinks and lavender.

'I can't do it for too long,' Thea joked, showing off, 'but at least I'm on my feet for a few minutes every day.'

She listened carefully as Martha told her about going to Ireland and not really knowing when she'd come back. 'Lord, I'm sure going to miss you,' she smiled.

'My kids think I'm running away,' admitted Martha. 'They don't see that I've got to make changes for all our sakes.'

'Are you happy about it?' asked Thea, the first person to enquire about her own happiness. Why, she had barely thought about it! Martha looked around the haven of peace that Thea had created for herself and her family, wishing for something similar.

'Yeah, I guess I am!' she smiled.

Martha went into the bedroom, helping Thea to lie down flat as for the last time she laid her hands on her. Martha could feel her fingers vibrate as she worked from chakra to chakra, and concentrated energy and light on the dark spots. Thea's life force was stronger even than on her last visit, and Martha could feel her body fighting back against the illness that had almost destroyed it.

Back outside they watched as Erik and the boys kicked a football down the bottom of the garden, the boys shouting and screaming at each other when anyone tried to score a goal.

'Thea, I'm sorry. I feel so guilty about going away and leaving you.'

'Martha, don't be! I should be dead by now by my doctor's reckoning, and yet because of you I'm here. Watching my sons play in the sunlight for another while. Each hour, each day, each week is precious to me and that's what you've given me.'

'I feel your body is trying to fight back against the cancer,' said Martha, 'but you need to take it easier so you don't tire and weaken yourself, and let the body gradually heal and renew itself. Promise!'

'I promise,' smiled Thea as they both said goodbye.

Martha had all the tickets and passports to hand, the bags packed and ready to go in the hall.

Alice's backpack was stuffed with such an assortment of teddies and toys that Martha hoped it wouldn't burst on the way.

Mary Rose was playing the drama queen, having loud conversations with her girlfriends, bitching about going away and how boring it was going to be.

Dan Kendrick had come to visit her the weekend before, the two of them doing nothing but talking and walking, grabbing a quick bite to eat before going back to his hotel room to make love.

'Martha, you know it's bad enough for me to have to fly halfway across the States just to see you, without you adding another six hours' flying time on to it!'

She was going to miss him so much it didn't bear thinking about. He'd made his position clear, telling her exactly how he felt about her and what he wanted from their relationship. Martha was the one needing time to think.

She'd said goodbye to Evie the night before, the two of them staying up till late, trying to make sense of all that had happened and wondering what the future might bring. Martha knew that the friendship between them would never change, no matter what, or no matter where they were in the world!

She checked the tickets one more time. Mike was driving them to the airport, and was minding the house while they were away. Arriving late he had to throw the bags in the back of the car and put this foot down to get them to Logan's busy departure terminal, then helped to carry their luggage and get the three of them checked in for their transatlantic flight. Alice clung to her dad like a little monkey as they said goodbye, with Mike and Patrick promising to behave and take care of each other as they walked them to the gateway.

Martha swallowed hard, hoping she was making the right choice as she boarded the Aer Lingus flight to Ireland, the familiar green shamrock painted on the side of the aircraft and the air hostesses in their green uniforms bringing back a rush of memories of her and her brothers, like a load of jack-in-the-boxes, going home to visit with their parents. Martha had to pretend to read the in-flight magazine as she tried to control her emotions.

Lara was in the office checking layouts when the phone rang. It was her sister, sounding hysterical. Lara tried to make some sense of what she was trying to tell her.

'Ben's in hospital!'

'What?'

'He was sick yesterday and when his room-mate went to wake him for college this morning he realized he was really bad. He's here in Mass General Hospital, Lara, and they say he's got some form of meningitis.'

Lara rapidly went through a mental list of what she knew of the disease, her mind numbed with a desperate sense of foreboding.

'He's unconscious!' sobbed her sister. 'They said they're doing everything but his kidney and liver are failing.'

Lara automatically switched off her computer and threw the files she was working on into the desk, grabbing her jacket off the chair, racing out through the newsroom and towards the elevator.

In the car, her brain began to function again and she flicked through her Filofax, pounding the number she wanted into her cellphone. Two, three times she called, but there was no response. Dread crawled through her veins as she drove, Boston's traffic moving at a snail's pace along the network of city streets as she cursed the roadworks and the excavations of the Big Dig. She remembered the small craft store in Easton, frantically trying to conjure up its name as she hit the button for directory enquiries, the operator putting her straight through.

'Hello, is Martha McGill there?' she enquired.

'Sorry, who's calling?'

'Is Martha there? Listen, we've met before and I really need to speak to her right now.'

'I'm sorry, Martha's not here.'

'When will she be back? I've left messages on her machine at home. It's urgent!'

'I'm sorry, but Martha doesn't work here any more. She's gone away.'

'Gone away! When will she be back?' she demanded.

'Who is that?'

'It's Lara Chadwick,' she said, embarrassed. 'I'm a journalist.'

'I know who you are,' said the voice on the other end of the line. 'Martha's left Boston, and has moved away for a few months, and to be honest, I've absolutely no idea when she intends coming back.'

'Do you have a number where I can reach her?'

'No!' replied Evie Hayes. 'Martha and her family are living overseas. I'm sorry, but I can't help you.'

Lara clenched the steering wheel, thinking of her nephew and his fight for life and how fate had decided she would be the one not only to meet the worker of miracles, his possible saviour, but also to drive her away.

Chapter Fifty-five

The house in Wicklow was everything she'd hoped it would be: an extended farm cottage on over two acres of land, close to the mountains with the sea and a beach of gold only a few minutes' drive away. The inside of the house was clad in stripped pine, with simple chairs and couches and a wood fire with a basket of turf and logs for if the evenings got cold.

Opening the back kitchen door she could see for miles, the view making her smile despite herself and lifting her spirit.

The kids each had a bedroom to themselves, Mary Rose's with a narrow gabled window that looked over their fields, Alice's sun filled and to the back where a silver lake glinted in the distance; the room overlooking the front path to the house was assigned to be Patrick's. Alice had made herself at home straight away, unpacking her toys and teddies and standing them in rows on top of the bed and the windowsill. Bored, the girls had complained at first about the archaic television in the corner, which only gave them four channels and which if the weather was misty barely seemed to work at all, but by the end of the first week she'd noticed they rarely bothered watching it.

Martha loved the peace of the place and felt totally at home in its almost familiar landscape.

Seamus O'Gorman the letting agent had also organized a car for her through Delahunt's, the local garage. The car was eight years old but seemed as if it would go for ever along the bumpy country roads. Seeing she was on her own with the children, the sixty-year-old grandfather had bent over backwards to advise her on the best places to go and where to shop, and what to do in case of emergencies.

The first few days she was so exhausted and jetlagged she had slept and slept and slept while the kids amused themselves and explored their new environment, the Irish weather fortunately clement and unusually dry and sunny. Then like a butterfly from a cocoon she had emerged, feeling much, much better, her thoughts clear, her body refreshed, ready to acquaint herself with her new surroundings.

Her nearest neighbours were the Clarkes who owned the two horses and a mare and a foal which had permission to graze on one of their fields. Alice nearly lost her mind when she first looked out the window and saw them.

'Mom, can I go out and see the horses?' she'd screamed with excitement. Martha had to get her to quiet down in case she spooked them.

The mare and foal trotted over immediately and Alice nervously patted them.

Mary Clarke had come over and introduced herself a few days later, a girl and boy about Alice's age accompanying her.

'This is Katie and this is Conor, they're eight and nine. They may as well have been twins as there's only eleven months between!' she laughed. Martha was delighted to have such a nice person living so close by and with kids just the right age for Alice to play with. While the two of them had a cup of tea and a chat she watched as Alice's shyness began to dissolve and she agreed to go out and play with the other two in front of the house.

Mary Clarke was Wicklow born and bred and filled her in about the neighbourhood and the places to take the kids and things they might all enjoy. If she was curious as to why someone like Martha was renting a house close by she disguised it, seeming to accept her at face value as an Irish American pleased to revisit the country of her forebears.

Martha and the kids spent much of the summer walking and exploring the countryside all around them, swimming in the freezing waters of Brittas Bay and Silver Strand and climbing the Sugarloaf mountain and driving up over the Dublin mountains through Sally Gap to the Featherbeds, watching young men cut out the turf and dry it in the sun in much the same way as she imagined their great-grandfathers had done before them.

Wet days, when the rain streamed along the window pane and pelted down, they drove to Dublin, visiting the busy crowded city and Trinity College and the Viking Centre and the ghostly Kilmainham Gaol where the 1916 leaders had been executed. Other times they explored the many towns further down along the Irish coast, visiting Waterford and its amazing crystal factory. There always seemed to be something to do, though most of the time they were just happy to stay put.

In Wicklow town the shopkeepers were beginning to know Martha, and she knew they had nicknamed her the Yank or the American. She came there to collect her purchases of meat and fish and eggs and bread every few days. The kids were already addicted to the creamy Irish ice-cream and chocolate.

Mary Rose had been sullen and uncooperative, and catching her trying to make an hour-long transatlantic call to her friend Cindy, Martha had banned her from using the phone without permission.

'It sucks, Mom!'

'When I can trust you, Mary Rose, then you can use the phone again, all right?'

There were a few days of silence between them and then she had signed the girls up for riding lessons at the local stables, which was only about half a mile up the road. Mary Rose yet again complained about being sent to do something she didn't want to do.

'Well, you can't sit in your room all day listening to your Walkman for the next few months,' argued Martha, 'or you'll drive yourself and everyone else in this house crazy!'

She'd gone off in a huff and Martha had pitied poor Alice having to put up with her.

The riding lessons had been a great success. After only a few, Mary Rose was insistent on joining the older age group.

Every morning Martha watched in disbelief as her older daughter pulled on a scruffy pair of jodhpurs and a T-shirt and sweater and after a quick breakfast set off for the stables where she would spend most of the rest of the day. Mucking out stables, grooming the horses, exercising them and riding, totally content with a load of other horse-mad like-minded teenagers.

Patrick had arrived over, mooching around a bit at first, feeling out of it, but after a night at the local disco with the oldest Clarke boy she reckoned he had begun to tag along with a crowd his own age. Mary told her the girls were all mad about his American accent and ways.

Martha loved the quiet and the solitude, the lack of rushing around and the time to sit and reflect, or just read a book or watch a lazy bee hover over the collection of wild daisies, montbretia and nasturtium that scrambled over the stone wall outside the house. She had no regrets about coming to Ireland and now knew that as far as the kids and herself were concerned she had made the right decision.

Content in herself, she kept in touch with her friends and family and loved to hear from them. Once or twice a week Mike phoned the kids to see how they were doing, surprised that they were busy and content.

Martha was pleased to see her kids relaxed and enjoying themselves without the pressure of summer camps and grind schools, happy to play silly games of cards or kick a football in the fields with the local kids till late into the night. She had discovered the local library and alone at night immersed herself in reading the great Irish novels, missing Dan more than she could ever have imagined; the sound of his voice was enough to make her smile, as he told her about what was going on back home. He'd mentioned he planned to take a nine- or ten-day vacation from work, and hadn't yet decided what he was going to do. Maybe play golf! Martha was unwilling to put any pressure on him, except to say there was a warm welcome if he wanted to come visit Ireland, but not expecting him to.

Chapter Fifty-six

Martha considered the August sky, clear and blue with only the slightest trace of clouds, hoping that the breeze would dry the huge pile of washing on the line. Later on she planned to take Alice into town with her, as she wanted to get some shopping for the weekend. The Clarkes had invited them over to a barbecue, Irish style, which meant if the rain came there'd be a mad run into the kitchen to finish off cooking the steaks and hamburgers. She wanted to buy them a good bottle of wine, and some strawberries and raspberries for the dessert.

Alice was outside playing with Conor and Katie and another child from a house down the way, the four of them racing around in their shorts and T-shirts trying to catch each other.

Martha smiled to herself. She'd just got off the phone from Dan, who had surprised her with the good news that he was due in Dublin the following week. His trip to Ireland was part business and part pleasure, he'd explained, and Martha's whoops of delight had no doubt confirmed to him which part she fulfilled. She couldn't wait to see that big lump of a man again and knew in her heart that Dan Kendrick had become far more than a friend or a casual romance to fill the gap left by her husband. He was someone she could trust and totally rely on and respect along with physically wanting him too, daydreaming like a besotted twenty-year-old about lying in his arms. Dan had told her of his feelings for her. Martha scarcely credited her own response, and the fact that she was finally ready to overcome all caution and admit she'd fallen in love again. Spending time with Dan would give them both the opportunity to see just how serious their relationship was.

Martha sat in the canvas deck chair out back and put her feet up, glancing at the rest of the post and the newspaper as she stretched out her limbs in the warm sunshine. Evie had forwarded on a bundle of mail from back home. Martha skimmed through it: she was saddened to hear from Henry Madison of his brother's death, but glad he'd had his surgery and was planning the trip of a lifetime to his beloved Italy with his friend Celeste.

Sitting there doing nothing she realized how she'd come to enjoy the pace of Irish country living, far removed from the frantic demands of her American existence. The peace was suddenly disturbed by the distant sound of the children shouting and screaming, and she jumped up wondering what in heaven's name they were fighting about. There was no sign of them around the cottage or in the field so she ran towards the gate, spotting the splash of their coloured T-shirts at the end of the lane. Alice ran frantically towards her screaming, 'Mom! Mom! Come quick! We need you!'

As fast as she could, Martha raced towards the group of children, alarmed to see a heavy farm tractor pulled into the ditch beside them, the driver hunched down over something. Filled with dread, she breathlessly ran towards them.

'Mommy, it's Conor and Katie's dog, he's hurt!'

Relieved that at least the children were safe, Martha immediately recognized the Clarkes' small white and black Jack Russell terrier lying on the rough ground.

'Tiny didn't see the tractor!' sobbed Katie. 'He was chasing a rabbit through the long grass!'

She bent down to examine the poor animal, shocked by its injuries. Blood was seeping from his stomach and nose where the tractor blow had caught him. Tiny whimpered wildly every few seconds, the sound of his pain filling the still air.

'Tiny, come on, Tiny, get up!' pleaded Conor, the small boy in shock kneeling beside his pet.

'Mom!' pleaded Alice. 'You can do it! You know you can. You can make him better.'

As the four children stared at her, Martha stood transfixed.

'My mom can heal him, Katie, she can,' Alice assured her, staring straight at Martha.

Innocence, trust and complete honesty in her child's eyes – how could she betray those ideals? The very things that as a parent she had taught her daughter every day of her life!

'She'll fix him, make him better! Just wait and see,' promised Alice. 'Mom's able to stop bleeding, and heal people, honest she is.'

Alice pushed her towards the animal. 'Please, Mom! Please!'

The tractor driver, eyes downcast, avoided the children's stares. 'Missus, do you think I could use the phone in your house to get the vet, maybe he could do something,' he offered. 'The poor thing's in a lot of pain and might need to be put down.'

'Oh, of course, the house just at the end of the lane, the back door is open and there's a phone in the kitchen near the dresser. I'll stay here with the children.'

They were looking at her, waiting, expecting her, the adult, to be able to do something to resolve the situation. Desperately she wanted to help the small dog, relieve his agony, and could see hope flicker in the children's eyes, the belief that she could restore their pet to the way he had been, back jumping and chasing across the Wicklow fields after rabbits.

The dog's eyes were glazing over, he was giving in to the pain, shudders racking his blood-matted body, tongue out, panting.

'Mom, please do it, don't let Tiny die,' begged Alice, pummelling her legs, hysterical almost. 'Please! You can cure him.'

The tractor driver had disappeared from view.

She couldn't do it. She just couldn't help the small creature! How could she, with so many witnesses? The children would talk! They were only children, after all. And the man if he came back! A pint after work down in the local pub and he might come out with it. She'd already lost so much, how could she go through it all again? The men, women and children of this new community would in their hour of need then call on her, and in fairness how could she possibly refuse them and turn her back on her calling once the word of her healing power got out?

The dog's eyes began to glaze, deep in shock, as instinctively she reached for him and made the decision.

'Good boy, Tiny! That's the good dog,' she urged softly as she laid her hands on his quivering body, gently feeling to see where he was bleeding from and trying to staunch the flow. 'It's all right, Tiny, I'm not going to hurt you,' she comforted as she tried to draw off the pressure and pain from his swollen abdomen.

The dog panted rapidly as if having trouble

breathing and Martha moved the position of her hands, feeling the energy flow through her fingers, hoping that the small dog would respond.

'Poor Tiny's in bad pain!' murmured the boy hunkered down beside her, gently petting his dog's paw with the tips of his fingers.

'He is, Conor pet, and I'm not sure if we can save him.'

Concentrating, Martha focused on the animal, hoping that the terrier would respond in some way to her touch and gain some alleviation of its pain. The four children were rapt with attention.

'Mom?' asked Alice.

'Ssshh, pet, let me work . . . Come on, boy! Come on, boy,' she pleaded, hoping that Tiny could still hear her and was responsive to the human voice.

'He moved! Look!' shouted the boy.

It was almost imperceptible but the dog had definitely tried to move.

'He's getting better,' murmured the little girl Maeve.

The animal gave a shudder and tried to stretch his paws, making an awkward effort to lift his head.

Martha, hardly daring to believe it, noticed that the blood seeping from the gash on his stomach had seemed to ease a little. Pulling off her waistcoat, she gently wrapped it around the small frame as she lifted the injured dog up into her arms.

'Come on, you lot. Tiny needs to be seen by a vet.'

'Is he going to get better, Martha?' begged Katie.

'I don't know, I can't promise anything. Tiny has had a real bad bang from the tractor and needs to get stitches and be checked over. He's bleeding inside and I think he's busted his leg. We'll just have to wait and see.'

The children began to follow her as she walked back towards the lane, Alice walking in step with her.

'I told you my mom could heal him and save him from dying! I told you!' A fierce pride was reflected in her youngest daughter's eyes.

Martha swallowed hard, knowing her secret was no longer safe. The children would bear witness to her healing power, whisper it among each other, tell their friends, tell their parents and like a ripple along the shore, she would no longer be able to hide the truth from those around her. Perhaps here in a place like this she could still live some kind of normal life. Have people accept her for who she was!

The dog whimpered in her arms.

'There, now. There now, good boy!' she soothed, holding him against her chest. In the distance she could see Mary Clarke coming towards her with the tractor driver, a look of utter surprise on his face.

Martha looked down at the dog and at Alice.

How could she have, even for a single moment, considered betraying her child's trust. She couldn't run away or hide, pretend to be someone different. There was no denying or escaping from what she was . . . she was a healer, and would no longer turn her back on the gift she'd been given.

THE END